GLENN TRUST
DARK WINTER

BOOKS

By Glenn Trust

Sole Justice

Sole Survivor

Road to Justice

Target Down

The Ghost

Dark Winter

Shadow Man

Vinci Books

vinci-books.com

Published by Vinci Books Ltd in 2025

1

Copyright © Glenn Trust 2022

The author has asserted their moral right to be identified as the author of this work in accordance with the Copyright, Designs and Patents Act 1988. This work is a work of fiction. Names, characters, places and incidents are the product of the author's imagination or are used fictitiously. Any resemblance to actual persons, living or dead, places and incidents is entirely coincidental.

All rights reserved. No part of this publication may be copied, reproduced, distributed, stored in any retrieval system, or transmitted in any form or by any means, including photocopying, recording, or other electronic or mechanical methods, nor used as a source for any form of machine learning including AI datasets, without the prior written permission of the publisher.

The publisher and the author have made every effort to obtain permissions for any third party material used in this book and to comply with copyright law. Any queries in this respect should be brought to the attention of the publisher and any omissions will be corrected in future editions.

A CIP catalogue record for this book is available from the British Library.

Paperback ISBN: 9781036704384

Printed and bound in Great Britain by Clays Ltd, Elcograf S.p.A.

ONE

No Choice

Don't stop. Keep moving. Eyes straight ahead, foot on the gas.

John Sole watched the rearview mirror, willing the car behind to follow him through the intersection. It was an older model sedan, stopped for the traffic signal. The driver hesitated too long. Several young men, some in their early teens, the oldest in their twenties, surrounded the sedan, street thugs looking for easy targets.

A few had been standing on the corner as Sole pulled up and stopped for the red light. They eyeballed him. He eyeballed them back. One standing on the curb lifted his shirt just enough to expose the butt of a pistol tucked in his waistband. He gave Sole his best narrow-eyed gang stare. Sole reached under the seat and pulled the Colt 1911, his go-to weapon. He held it up, then laid it on the seat beside him in easy reach. He locked eyes with gun-thug for a moment until he moved on to examine the car behind, looking for easier pickings, someone more vulnerable and less aware.

When the light changed to green and Sole moved forward into the intersection, more young men came from the alleys and shadows of the buildings. They surrounded the sedan behind him, pounding on the hood with their fists, kicking dents in the sides. The driver panicked and froze.

"Keep moving," Sole watched and muttered. "Put a foot on the gas. Run them over if you have to."

The driver didn't. He was older, staring wide-eyed, hands on the steering wheel in a white-knuckled death grip, his head swiveling from window to window as the mob moved around the car.

His wife beside him sobbed and whispered, "Oh God, no." She put a hand on the side window to cover the face of one of the gangbangers pressed against the glass, laughing wildly at her.

Two more emerged from a nearby alley and jumped up on the hood, using it as a trampoline. The old sedan's worn suspension bounced like a souped-up lowrider, tossing the occupants around inside.

Sole made it across the intersection, still watching the rearview mirror. *It's not your problem. You've got enough problems. Keep moving.*

They were trying to open the sedan's doors now, pulling at the handles and pounding on the glass, taunting and shrieking at the old couple inside. One grinned and leaned close to the driver's window. "Open the door, motherfucker, or you dead." His face was close enough to the window that drops of spit ran down the glass where he'd leaned in to shout.

Start driving. Get away from them. Sole tried to will the old couple forward. He looked up and down the street for signs of a police response. There was none.

The crowd around the sedan was growing. Traffic in the street swerved to miss it, cars and trucks sped up to get away and not be caught up in whatever happened next. What had started as a carjacking was growing into a small riot. Passersby went into self-preservation mode, avoiding the commotion in the street. No one was inclined to intervene and become the new target of the mob.

A heavyset young man, no more than sixteen years old, came around the back of the sedan with a baseball bat. He swung it over his head like an ax pounding on the trunk. Then he lifted it to his shoulder in a batter's stance, ready to swing for the stands.

"Shit," Sole growled. He spun the pickup's steering wheel and turned down a side street a block from the intersection. Pulling to the curb, he jumped out, holding the Colt down along the side of his leg, and ran the block back to the intersection.

The bat connected with the glass, and the side window exploded in a shower of glass. Two others pulled the door open and jerked the old man from the driver's seat onto the ground. They held him down while another pummeled him with his fists.

The teen with the bat moved to the passenger side. The old woman shrieked in terror, then the passenger window shattered in her face. Blood poured from lacerations where the glass fragments lodged in her paper-thin skin. She covered her face with her hands as more assailants reached in and dragged her onto the ground.

Fists raised high above her head, then froze. The Colt's thunder reverberated between the buildings. Sole had fired one round into the asphalt. He lifted his weapon and held it in a combat stance, ready to engage any threat that presented itself.

"Back away." Sole motioned with the pistol toward the curb. "Get away from them, and you might live through the next few seconds."

"Shit. You think you can take us all on, motherfucker?" Gun-thug put his hand on the pistol butt to pull it out.

Some of the mob backed away. Others moved toward their comrade to provide support. Several were armed, but they weren't professionals. They bunched together, providing easy targets if things went badly in the next few seconds.

"I said back away." Sole held the pistol on gun-thug who seemed to be the leader.

"Naw, man. We ain't backing away. We just about to …" Gun-thug jerked his pistol from his waistband. Before he could bring it up to bear on the stranger who had mixed himself up in their business, another roar thundered, and he dropped to the ground.

There was no Hollywood reaction to being shot. No dramatic stagger backward. No arms flung up in surprised agony. Gun-thug simply crumpled, his head smacking into the sidewalk with a thud and a forty-five-caliber hole punched through his sternum.

The round cut through his aorta and a pool of blood spread rapidly around him on the pavement. His partners in crime never saw it. They were running for the alleys as Sole swiveled to target the next attacker, but they were gone. Their leader gone, lying in a pool of blood, no one wanted to join him.

Sole went to the sedan. The old woman sat on the curb sobbing, incoherent, and unable to speak. It would take her a while to recover from the emotional trauma of the attack, but physically, she was in reasonably good shape … considering.

Her husband wasn't so lucky. Sole found him sprawled on the street by the driver's door. They had beaten him with something hard. Sole recognized the marks of brass knuckles in the contusions on the side of his face and wished he'd been able to put a round through the one who beat an old man senseless. Facial bones were fractured and the old man's right eye protruded from the orbital socket as if it might fall to the ground, hanging suspended from the optic nerve.

A man came from a store at the corner. Sole motioned him over. "Stay with him."

"Right." The man nodded excitedly. "I saw it all ... I mean, the way you took care of those assholes." He nodded at the old man on the ground. "You saved his life ... and the old woman's too." He shook his head. "I mean, that was some shit."

Sirens sounded a few blocks away, and the man added. "I called the cops. They'll be here in a minute. Don't worry, I'll be your witness."

Sole stood. "Stay with the old man. Don't move him until the paramedics get here unless he starts choking. If he does, roll him on his side and make sure nothing is blocking his airway."

"Airway?" The man from the store knelt by the old man.

"His throat. Make sure nothing is choking him."

"Oh, right." The man looked up, surprised to see Sole walking briskly away toward the intersection. "Where are you going? The cops will be here in a minute." He shouted at Sole's back. "You're gonna be a hero! I'll make sure of it. My wife got the whole thing on video."

Sole was trotting now, the Colt tucked in his waistband. He crossed the intersection and picked up speed, heading down the block to the side street. By the time he was in the pickup and pulling from the curb, the first police units were arriving at the intersection, followed by paramedics and a news crew that picked up the police call on their scanner.

People emerged from the surrounding buildings where they'd taken cover from the gang in the intersection. They milled around gun-thug's body until the police pushed them back to secure the crime scene.

Sole drove a dozen blocks along the side street, then turned onto a major highway that crossed through the city. A half-hour later, he made his way onto an interstate.

The city could have been any sprawling metropolis where the inner-city streets were largely controlled by gangs and street thugs. By sunset, he'd put a hundred miles between him and the intersection.

The man from the store said he'd saved the old couple's lives. Sole knew that was probably true, but something else the man said haunted him.

My wife got the whole thing on video.

When are you going to learn to walk away, John-boy? The voice inside was nagging again.

He shook his head. And do what? Let the gang terrorize, maybe kill, an old couple?

For once, the voice inside understood and shut up. He'd had no choice.

TWO

Balancing Accounts

"*Jefa*, excuse the interruption, but you should see this." Reynaldo Gutierrez stood in the office doorway in the hacienda high on a mountainside above the Mexican port of Lázaro Cárdenas. Beyond the plate-glass window, the distant swells of the Pacific reflected the sunlight into glittering points blinking in and out of existence with the movement of the ocean.

Juana Elizondo looked up from the cluster of papers scattered across the desk that had once been her father's. "Yes, Reynaldo. What is it?"

"This." Gutierrez entered and placed a tablet on the desk in front of her, touched the screen, and brought up a video. "It is a recording of a news report in the States."

"A news report? We have news reports here."

"This one is of special interest, *Jefa*."

Elizondo touched play on the video then stared at the screen for several minutes while an American reporter in a city two thousand miles away stood before the camera, microphone in hand interviewing witnesses interspersed with long shots of a heavily damaged older car and a blood-stained sheet covering a body sprawled on the sidewalk.

The reporter continued speaking off-camera while a series of low quality, but viewable videos taken by cell phone users appeared. One video, in particular, caught Elizondo's attention. Her eyes narrowed, and her body tensed, hands gripping the sides of the tablet as if she might crush it with her bare hands.

When the report concluded, she looked at Reynaldo. "Find him."

"*Si, Jefa*. I already have men searching now that we have a location."

"Keep me advised."

"*Si, Jefa.*" Gutierrez turned and left the office, leaving the tablet on the desk.

Elizondo played the video again, freezing the image that appeared during the segment taken from cell phones. She stared at the screen and the face frozen there. Finding that face had consumed her since her father's death in the Mexican desert.

Since that day, there had been no sign of the man who orchestrated the ambush that killed Bebé Elizondo, and his deputy, Alejandro Garza. Bebé might have headed up the deadliest cartel on the continent, but to her he was *Papi*, and Garza, her father's right hand and a merciless killer, was simply *Tio* Alejandro to the Elizondo family.

She had taken over the family business, running the *Los Salvajes* cartel's operations with ruthless efficiency, but never had she forgotten the man who took her father away. Others, including Reynaldo, suggested that the gringo must have died alone in the desert after the shooting ended. He may have been wounded, they said, or perhaps he ran out of water. Despite the cartel's efforts to find him, they were unable to recover a body, but there was no sign that he had escaped and his survival alone in the desert without transportation seemed unlikely. Others suggested that scavengers had eaten and disposed of the gringo's body. They laughed and joked that what was left of him was probably coyote shit scattered across the desert. It was only fitting that he should end that way, they said.

Juana never believed it. Somewhere the man who killed her father lived, and that was unacceptable. Before his death, she kept the accounts for her father, balancing debits and credits to perfection. She remembered his round, smiling face and the gentle pat on the head when she pleased him.

"Such a good little accountant," he would say. "Tell me, *mi estrellita*, my little star. Is everything in order?"

"Yes, *Papi*. The accounts balance perfectly."

But there was one account that had not balanced since her father's death, and she promised herself that she would find the man responsible. He would pay, and only then would the accounts be balanced.

In a motel room far from the intersection in the city, Sole watched the same news report, shook his head, and sighed. The reporter interviewed the witnesses standing nearby ... a crime scene the police were calling it.

When she asked a police captain with the homicide investigation unit why they were calling it a crime scene when the person who intervened saved the life of the old couple, he said, "We have a zero-tolerance policy for murder, regardless of who does it or why. A vigilante killing is still a murder and we intend to investigate and find the killer."

The reporter moved on to the witnesses who had kept their distance but saw what happened. Isaiah Selander and his wife Doreen stood beside her, recounting what they'd seen through the store window as the gang of young men terrorized the old couple in the sedan. The reporter had the studio play the video from Doreen's cell phone as they told their story.

"It was terrible what they were doing to those people. I mean, we called the police, but you know how long they take to get to this part of town these days, what with everything happening and all."

"It must have been terrifying," the reporter said, "seeing all of this transpire just outside your window." She held the microphone in front of Doreen to get the human-interest angle of the story. "A forgotten neighborhood where this kind of violence takes place." She shook her head sympathetically. "Tell me, how did it make you feel to know that such violence could occur here?"

"I was frightened. I admit it," Doreen said. "This used to be a quiet neighborhood, but not anymore."

"And you?" The reporter shifted to Isaiah. "I can't imagine the helplessness you must have felt."

"Well, we were helpless, I admit it. I mean, I don't have any experience dealing with this sort of thing, but ..." Isaiah leaned close to the microphone to make sure it picked up his words. "But he's a hero ... the one who took care of him." He nodded at the sheet-draped body on the sidewalk. "He's a hero."

"The police are calling him a vigilante ... a killer," the reporter said. "How do you feel about that?"

"If he's a vigilante, in my book he's a vigilante hero. He

did what had to be done, and if he hadn't, there's no telling what would have happened to the people in the car. I say he's a hero and I don't care what the police call it."

Sole turned off the television. He didn't feel like a hero. He had done what needed to be done at the exact moment it needed to be done. Gun-thug had the chance to make a different choice, to leave the couple alone and call things even. When he didn't, Sole did what he had to do. Nothing more.

He pulled up a map on his phone, looking for out-of-the-way places, the sort of places where people paid little attention to the news out of a big city back east. Tracing a route west, he made up his mind.

THREE

Dark Winter

"What are you doing?" She sat up in bed and looked across the room.

Her roommate sat on the edge of the bed against the opposite wall, dressed in sweats, tying on a pair of running shoes. She stood and pulled another hooded sweatshirt over her head. They were the warmest clothes she had. Reaching down, she pulled the blanket off the bed and draped it over her shoulders, and turned to face the other girl still in bed.

"Told you. I'm leaving tonight." She stared hard at the girl in bed. "You said you wanted out ... said you couldn't take it anymore, and you were coming with me. Well, tonight's the night. Was it just all talk or are you coming?"

The other girl turned in the bed to peer out the window. "It's dark."

"That's why we're going tonight. No moon. Nobody will be able to see us in case they're looking." She shrugged. "It's now or never, and I can't take never, so I'm leaving. You coming or not."

"Cold too," her roommate said. "Can we take the cold? We could wait until summer, Mila."

"No." Mila shook her head emphatically. "I won't last until summer. This is it for me. I'm leaving. You coming with me or not, Riley? If you are, get moving."

Riley looked out into the dark again, shivered, and repeated her assertion. "It's cold out there."

"It is," Mila said, nodding. "Double up on your sweats and take your blanket."

As a security measure, neither had winter coats. The winter temperatures and remoteness of their location provided all the security necessary to keep them in their prison.

Mila leaned over and peered out the window, pointing. "See those bright lights there. Can't be more than a mile or so ... twenty or thirty-minute walk at most. We bundle up and head for the lights. There'll be people there. We can get help ... call someone."

She stood up straight, holding the blanket over her shoulders, staring at Riley. They had shared this room for more than a year. "Weather report says there's a blizzard coming. If we don't leave now, we'll be stuck here for weeks, maybe until spring. Can you wait that long?" Miley shook her head again. "I can't."

"I guess not," Riley said softly. "I'd like to get back to my grandmother down in Missouri."

She stirred out of the bed and began dressing. A thought occurred to her and her brow wrinkled, concerned. "What about the money?"

"Write down your account number," Mila said. "You know your PIN. Just make sure you have your ID with you. When we get to a bank, we'll do a transfer to a new account."

"They'll take the money out, and we won't get any of it."

"You think they were ever going to let us have it?" Mila said scornfully. "Just because it's in an account with our name on it? It was just bait, something to keep us here and keep us quiet, and even if we got our hands on it, where would we spend it out here?"

In some ways, they were old beyond their years, tarnished and hardened by the life fate had dealt them. In others, they were young and naïve. The intricacies of handling large sums of money or bank accounts were far beyond the realm of their experience. The money deposited in their names in a bank they had never heard of in an island country they couldn't spell might as well have been on the moon.

Still, the money held the promise of a new life. Mila narrowed her eyes and said, "We earned that money, and we're going to get it out of those accounts and put it in a bank they can't get to. That's why we have to hurry. We need to get to a city and a bank before they see we're gone."

Mila would have left whether there was any money in an account with her name on it or not, but she used it to convince Riley to join her. It worked.

"Right." Riley nodded and finished dressing. She grabbed the blanket from the bed and wrapped it around her shoulders. "Alright. I guess I'm ready."

They left the bedroom, tiptoeing through the house. Most would not have called it a mere house. A dozen bedrooms with private baths, several large gathering rooms with fireplaces big enough to stand in, more smaller private rooms, library, movie theatre, a restaurant-style kitchen, and dining room. It awed them when they first arrived. In time, they learned that a prison is a prison, no matter how luxurious it might appear.

They walked through the main hall toward the front door. A small lamp on a side table under an ornate coatrack cast a yellow glow over the polished hardwood floors. They just reached the massive door when a voice spoke behind them.

"Where do you think you're going?" It was Loni, the longest resident of the house, having been there for nearly five years. She wore a nightgown and stood in the arched doorway that led to the dining hall and beyond that to the kitchen.

The girls froze in their tracks but said nothing. They turned wide-eyed to face her.

"Going for a walk?" Loni lifted a cup of decaf coffee laced with Irish cream, sipped, and smiled. "I needed a nightcap to help me sleep. Want some?"

The girls remained silent. Mila shook her head.

"It's cold ... freezing cold," Loni said. "You won't be able to go very far."

"We're not going far," Mila said without mentioning the building with the lights across the fields.

"Someone meeting you then?"

The girls remained silent. Loni had always been good to them, but she was part of whatever this place was ... part of what they were escaping.

"Alright." Loni sipped from the cup again, gazing at them over it, her eyes sad and weary. "I won't say anything."

She turned and walked down the hallway toward her room. She should have stopped them, but the girls were desperate. She understood desperation.

She heard them pull the door open and step out into the

night. Then the door closed behind them. A tear trickled down her cheek. She whispered, "I'm sorry."

Outside, the girls gasped as the cold hit them in the face and sucked their breath away. Mila pointed toward the horizon. "There's the light. That's where we go. Just keep walking until we get there. That's all we have to do."

They walked down the main drive toward the lights. When the drive took a bend, they continued straight, cutting across country, focused on the light, forcing themselves to take one plodding step after another toward it. The bitter cold of the night was a physical thing, clinging to them, creeping into their innards with icy fingers. They panted, struggling to breathe. At twenty below zero, the air temperatures began to freeze lung tissues and fill them with fluid.

They stumbled along, their arms around each other, both blankets wrapped around them, trying to stay as close as possible to preserve what little warmth remained in their bodies. They had gone a little over a mile, and still, the light seemed as distant as ever.

"I need to rest," Riley said.

"No, keep moving." Mila urged, panting. "Have to keep moving, or we'll freeze."

"Right." Riley nodded. "I don't want to freeze. Don't let me freeze, Mila." She trudged forward, clinging to Mila's arm, but a few minutes later, her numbed legs gave way and she sank to the ground, taking the blankets down with her.

Mila stood exposed for a moment, the cold attacking her with unseen hands, probing with icy fingers into every part of her body until she dropped shivering violently beside her companion, shaking her with both hands. Riley looked at her through dazed eyes and shook her head. "Just a minute. That's all. Let's rest for a minute. Come under the blankets with me and we'll get warm together. Then we'll start walking again."

Mila gave up and nodded, lying down and pulling the blankets tight around them both. They huddled together, pushing themselves together the way you would the dying coals of a fire to intensify the heat that remained.

"Just for a minute. That's all," Mila mumbled. "We'll just lay here for a minute and get warm, then we walk some more."

Riley nodded but said nothing and slipped into unconsciousness. Mila lay with her arms wrapped around her, trying to muster the strength to get them both up. Moving was life. Lying here was death.

Then the fire came. Wherever the icy hands found her and touched, they burned until her body felt as if she would explode into flame at any moment. She groaned under the onslaught, every nerve ending in her body crying out as they died, consumed by the frozen, burning fire.

Then the fire stopped, and the pain went away. She looked up at a million stars sparkling in the moonless sky. The stars faded away as her retina froze and the last nerve ending died. The dark winter descended over the two girls, claiming them as its own.

"How many?" To say the man on the other end of the call was not happy would have been an understatement.

"Two," Hubert 'Huey' Cooke said bluntly. There was no way to sugarcoat the news that two of their best had gone out and froze themselves to death during the night.

"Took a while to find them when they turned up missing. No one saw them leave." He sighed and shook his head. "They were wearing sweats and had a couple of blankets wrapped around them. Temperature hit fifteen below zero last night … wind chill around minus thirty." He sighed. "It was a stupid thing to do."

"What the hell were they thinking?" his boss growled. "Where did they think they were going?"

"They seemed to be headed in the direction of the grain elevator. Probably saw the lights and figured they could make it there."

"The damned elevator is ten stories tall."

"I know," Cooke said. "And ten miles away. They never had a chance."

"This is damned inconvenient."

"I know," Cooke said. "I'm making arrangements now."

"Alright. Get it done, Huey. This is important."

Orders given and received, the boss ended the call. Cooke punched a number into his phone.

A different man answered with a simple, "Yes."

"Need your help." Cooke explained and asked, "Can you do it?"

"I'll take care of it."

"Good. Give me a status report as soon as you have things set up."

"Will do."

Cooke ended the call and went from his heated office into the open main barn. Two men stood huddled over the bodies, waiting for instructions. They parted as Cooke came up.

The girls lay together, arms still frozen around each other. One had her head turned up, her hazel eyes open, frozen and crystallized like new ice over a pond.

The men were waiting for him to tell them what to do with the bodies. He thought and then decided with a nod.

"Ground's too hard to bury them, and we can't keep them around here until spring," he said. "For now, let's put them in the old grain bin. Storm coming in tonight. When the weather breaks, we'll take them out and dump them where they won't be found."

The grain bin was nothing more than a ten-by-twenty-foot storage building constructed from galvanized steel. Eighty years ago, it had been used to store forage for livestock during the winter. Now, it was the resting place for assorted used and worn-out equipment and tools. The men laid Mila and Riley beside a stack of sheet metal roofing salvaged one spring after a tornado had come through the county.

They left and sealed the girls inside. Outside, the winter wind rose and rattled the galvanized siding. The blizzard would be there in hours, dropping the temperatures even lower, but the girls were beyond caring.

FOUR

Not From Around Here

What the hell were you thinking? After everything else, this might just be the dumbest thing you've ever done.

The two-lane South Dakota highway stretched before him, a blanket of pure white. Behind him, the tracks of the pickup marking his path were quickly being filled in and blown away by the blizzard.

John Sole leaned forward over the wheel, peering through the partially covered windshield. The old defroster blew full blast, struggling to hold the encroaching ice at bay, but it continued to creep in from the edges of the glass, decreasing his field of vision as the miles passed. As it was, visibility was only a few feet. The headlights reflected blindingly off the snow, creating near whiteout conditions and forcing him to crawl along at a few miles an hour. Another hour or so and the glass would be completely covered, and he would have to stop.

What then, he wondered? Huddle down and wait for the storm to pass with the engine running, that's what. Air temperatures outside the truck were minus fifteen Fahrenheit and dropping. The windchill took that down to minus thirty. No way he was going to try and head out on foot.

And if the gas ran out, and the engine died and the heater ceased providing the already scant heat it blew in ragged puffs from the vents? What then?

That will not happen, he told himself. He gave the gas gauge a quick glance. Less than half a tank. That should last—but how long? He had no idea. A few hours at most, he reckoned, but think positive.

And the storm. How long would that last? He shook his head and asked himself the same question he'd been asking since the storm started. What in the hell were you thinking?

He'd left Sioux Falls that morning under a frosty but clear blue sky with a full tank of gas. He'd headed west across South Dakota for no particular reason, other than it was country he'd never explored before. The remnants of the last snowfall still covered the ground, but the roads were clear, and traffic around the city moved with no particular urgency.

Away from Sioux Falls, there was even less traffic and less urgency. He passed an occasional farm vehicle, trucks and harvesters, going to the barn for service or storage. They poked along at ten or twenty miles an hour for a few miles, then pulled off onto one of the section roads, dirt roads that ran for miles in straight lines. He'd seen them before, flying over in airplanes, the straight lines crisscrossing the land thirty thousand feet below, but he'd never driven them.

After dealing with the carjackers at the intersection and partly on a whim, he selected one from a road Atlas. On the map it looked like an easy drive west, running from one end of South Dakota to the other.

Relaxed and sitting back in the seat, he steered the

pickup one-handed, making no effort to pass the farm vehicles that pulled onto the two-lane road. Around him, the flat landscape stretched for miles to the horizon. He found the vast emptiness comforting.

Sometime after noon, clouds began building on the horizon. They didn't seem very threatening. Not at all like the thunderheads he was familiar with in Georgia. The clouds rolled over the land like a blanket, gradually filling the sky and turning the day gray. The horizon that had stood out sharp and crisp against the blue sky became a gray haze where the earth and sky seemed to melt into each other.

When the snow started in the late afternoon, he wasn't overly concerned, but he started looking for a place to stop. It had been a while since he'd seen a house or one of the little crossroads towns that dotted the countryside. Then the night fell, and it was as if someone had thrown a heavy blanket over the earth, obscuring everything except the road directly in front of the pickup. Nothing was visible beyond a few feet in any direction. He had no choice but to keep moving forward and hope that he found a suitable stopping place before the pickup's gas ran out and he froze.

The edges of the snow-covered road were barely discernible now. A slight depression on either side marked the roadside ditches. If he steered directly down the middle, between the depressions, he should stay on the road. That was his thinking, at least, and it worked pretty well.

At least it did until the pickup's front end sank violently, and came to a bone-jarring stop. A cloud of white powder cascaded into the air, blown away by the blizzard, only to be replaced by more falling snow.

Sole sat still for a few seconds, taking stock. He reached up to touch the lump on his forehead where he'd struck the steering wheel on impact. No blood, but sore as hell. He was leaning forward in the seat, the pickup angled steeply down in the front. The engine was still running. That was good. Don't turn it off.

It took some effort to push the door open in the deep snow and climb out only to sink waist-deep in the powder. He pushed through it to the front, trying to determine what damage the pickup suffered. With the hood buried down at a steep angle, it was hard to tell. He went to the rear, scrambling up the side of the ditch on all fours until he could grab the rear bumper and pull himself out of the ditch.

He zipped his jacket to his chin and crossed his arms over his chest to stave off the cold that was draining every bit of warmth from his body. The cold was more than biting. It was debilitating, mind-numbing, deadening to the senses. It was a cold he'd never experienced before and one, he knew now, he had not prepared for adequately.

Squinting into the blowing snow, he looked back along his path. The tire tracks were already covered, but the cause of the accident was clear. The road that he thought ran from east to west completely across South Dakota ended here in the middle of nowhere at a T-intersection. He'd driven across the intersection without seeing it and into the ditch along the intersecting road.

Do something, he thought, and then knew there was nothing he could do. The cold was sucking the life out of him as he stood in the road. He had to get back to the pickup and its feeble heater.

He slid down the bank to the bottom of the ditch, landing on his ass in slush and mud. The heat from the running engine had created a little pool of melted snow water. Dragging himself up by the door handle, he pulled it open and crawled back into his tiny engine-heated den.

"Done some stupid things in my life, but this might be the last one," he muttered through chattering teeth. Opening and closing the door brought the temperature inside the truck cab down drastically. Even without the windchill, the temperature had dropped below zero inside, and he wasn't sure the puny heater could bring the temperature up against the cold that seeped in and drained away every bit of warmth from everything it touched.

He checked his phone for a signal. There was none. The time showed seven-fifteen, but it had been dark for three hours, and he had not passed another vehicle or seen a light in two.

The gas gauge read a quarter now, but he didn't know how accurate that was with the truck sitting nose down in the ditch. The heater was on full blast, but the thin stream of air was barely warm by the time it made it through the ductwork to the vents.

An hour passed in shivering silence. Then another. Arms folded across his chest to conserve body heat, his head nodded and he drifted into a doze. There were no dreams, only the awareness that the terrible cold was seeping deeper into his bones with every passing minute, a monster that worked its way into his very core, seeking to devour what warmth remained.

Then, a metallic tap on the window and a light shining in his face forced his eyes open. Much as he hated to give the cold, creeping monster free passage into the truck, he rolled the window down a little and squinted into the light.

"Hey, fella. You need to come with me."

The man wore a heavy brown parka, fur-lined hat with earmuffs, and heavy gloves. A patch on the front of the parka read Deputy—*Sheriff's Department—Blanken County*. Sole stared at him vacantly.

The deputy pulled the door open, letting more of the terrible cold in. "Come on. We need to get you warmed up." He reached in, turned the ignition off, and took the keys.

"N-no... what are y-you d-doing?" Sole thought about trying to pull the door closed again, but the deputy's gloved hand had him by the bicep, tugging him from the pickup. He shook his head. "No ... cold..."

"Damn right it's cold. About minus twenty cold, and it'll be colder before morning." The deputy dragged him out and started pushing him up the ditch bank. "You're hypothermic, not thinking clear. We'll get you back in my car. Got the heater going full blast. You'll feel better in a few minutes."

Sole didn't argue, wasn't able to argue. The deputy pushed him up the bank until they were on the road, then led him around to the passenger door of his SUV. He gave Sole's jacket and beltline a quick rub down, checking for weapons, then pulled open the door and pushed Sole into the seat.

The blast of heat from the vents was almost too much after the numbing cold. Sole's body shivered even more and his teeth chattered uncontrollably for a minute as the warmth forced the cold out and his muscles came back to life, trembling reflexively to warm themselves.

The deputy pulled open the driver's door and dropped in behind the wheel. He looked at Sole. "You're not from around here."

"H-how'd y-you guess?" Sole managed a smile through his chattering teeth.

The deputy laughed. "Well, besides the Tennessee tag on your pickup and that five-and-dime, piece of shit jacket you're wearing, anybody from around here would be hunkered down by a fire on a night like this."

"Y-you're out," Sole chattered.

"And damn lucky for you that I am. I was making a last patrol before hunkering down myself to wait out the storm. Just barely saw the reflection of my headlights on your rear bumper sticking up out of the snowbank. If I hadn't …" He shook his head. "Well, we pull a couple out of the snowbanks every year. The lucky ones just lose some toes or fingers to frostbite. The others … we call them corpsesickles … frozen solid."

Sole nodded and leaned his head back on the seat rest. The shivering and teeth-chattering were subsiding. He loosened the jacket around his neck, letting the warm, luxurious, blessed blast of heated air from the vents penetrate into his core.

He turned his head. "Thank you, Deputy …"

"Bentz," the deputy said. "Lew Bentz."

"Thank you, Deputy Bentz."

"You betcha, but Lew is fine. No one around here adds the deputy. I grew up with these folks, dontcha know. They've called me a lot of things over the years, … Lewis, Lewie, little Lewie, some names you can't say in church … too much to expect them to add deputy to the name now." He spoke in an easy, friendly way, feeling no need to maintain the usual law enforcement emotional distance in public encounters. "You got a name?"

"Bill," Sole said, using the false identity he'd acquired years earlier. "Bill Myers." He started reaching for his wallet and ID in his back pocket.

Bentz lifted a gloved hand and shook his head. "Plenty of time for that later. Right now, let's get out of this storm."

He backed the SUV away from the ditch and turned north on the intersecting road.

"My truck and things ..." Sole began.

"No worries. We'll head into Alder tonight. Harry Langstrom's bar will be open, and he's got a cot in the back where you can sleep. Tomorrow, we'll get a tow truck and I'll take you back to pull your pickup out and get you on our way again."

Sole nodded and looked out at the blowing snow tapping and beating against the window, like a living thing trying to force its way inside and suck the life from the occupants. Deputy Lew Bentz was right. He was definitely not from around here.

FIVE

Decision
___

"You look cold."

He was young, thirtyish, probably. Malina Jenkins thought he had a nice smile, and his teeth were so white they seemed to shine at her from the dark of the van's interior. Still, she was new in town, alone, and wary. She nodded and pulled her thin jacket tighter around her, folding her arms over her chest, more for the sense of security it gave her than for extra warmth.

"It's a little chilly." She shrugged. "Not too bad."

"Lost?" he asked.

"No," Malina said, feeling a little more uncomfortable with the question.

"You look lost," he said, the smile widening. "I've seen lost kids before, and I know lost when I see it."

"I just got to Seattle, that's all so, I have to get my bearings."

"Really? Where from?" He leaned with both arms draped over the van's steering wheel in a casual way, smiling his white smile, talking in an easy manner that made it seem they had known each other for a while.

"Where from?" She was on edge now, smile or not. "Spokane …near there, anyway." Her eyes narrowed. "Look, I'm not one of those …" She nodded up Aurora Avenue, where three women stood near a corner.

"I'm sorry." He laughed now. "You must think I'm a real jerk. Out here on Aurora picking up girls." He shook his head, still laughing, took something from the dashboard, and handed it out the window. "Here. This will explain."

Malina hesitated, then reached up, keeping an arm's length distance, and plucked the business card from his fingertips. She read the card—*Seattle Youth Protective Association (SYPA), Rick Salver, Administrator.* There was a phone number with a Seattle area code and an address in the city's Central District.

"Seattle Youth Protective …" she started.

"We just call it SYPA to make it easy." He pronounced the acronym as *sippa*. "Look, you're doing the right thing. Be cautious. That's what we teach the kids we find on the streets here. Pay attention to your surroundings. Don't trust every stranger that comes along." He nodded and smiled again. "Especially don't trust strangers, but it's pretty easy to see that you're cold, don't have a place to stay, and probably haven't eaten for a while."

"I was looking for one of the shelters. I can get something to eat there, right? And a place to stay for the night."

"You're right" Rick nodded. "They'll feed you, but you missed dinner and the shelters are full by now. All the beds will be taken." He looked up the avenue toward the hookers and said, "Look, just be careful where you go. Okay?"

Malina stared at him without speaking. A tear started at

the corner of her eye, but she blinked and forced it away. She'd left her alcoholic mother and dope-peddling stepfather that morning after he accused her of stealing his cash and then choked her until she passed out. She didn't steal it, but looking back wished she had taken everything the son of a bitch had.

Her mother watched, blinking and doing nothing as her step-father's hands tightened around Malina's neck. When she came to, she left and spent the entire day hitching rides in truck stops to get to Seattle. She arrived after dark, and that was as far as her planning had taken her.

"Okay," she said, fighting back the trembling in her voice.

"Alright then." He nodded, speaking softly. "You just got to town, and it's understandable that you don't know how it all works. I'm not going to ask you to get into the van with me. That would violate everything we teach the youth who come to us. Look across the lake." He nodded toward Green Lake bordering Aurora Avenue.

She turned in the direction he was looking.

"See those campfires over there in the park."

She nodded.

"Way back in the corner off to the right is the biggest fire. That's our camp. Probably a dozen or so young people like yourself there. It's not much, but the fire is warm, there's food, and we have tents where you can bunk in for the night. Tomorrow you can decide what you want to do, but for tonight it's a warm, safe place to stay."

For several seconds, she stared at the glow of the homeless encampment that covered a good part of Green Lake Park, then turned back to Rick Salver in the van. She started to speak, but he held up his hand to cut her off.

"I'm making my rounds ... letting others, young

people like you, know how things work, where we are, how to get there. Then I'll be back at the camp. We don't take people off the street. You decide what you want to do, but if you decide to head to our camp, be sure and go around the side of the lake on the right and come in that way. Stay away from the main park. Some of the homeless there are ... let's just say, they aren't quite right in the head about things. Most are harmless but some ... well, they see a young girl walking alone, and ..." He shrugged. "You're not a child, so I don't have to paint a picture for you."

Malina nodded.

"Good." Rick put the van in gear and lifted his foot off the brake. "Hope to see you there."

"Thanks. I'll think about ..." she said, but the van was already rolling away, and Rick had rolled up the window.

She saw the van's brakes light up a few blocks down the avenue before it made a right turn, headed into the city. She walked for a minute toward the three hookers on the corner ahead, then stopped and leaned against a light pole and let the tears flow down her face.

It had all made sense that morning. Stuffing the eighty-nine dollars she'd managed to scrape together from her part-time job bussing tables, she walked away from home without looking back. Now, standing in the cold and dark, she asked herself what the hell she'd been thinking.

Her back stiffened, and she straightened up, wiping the tears from her eyes. You were thinking you didn't want that yellow-toothed bastard who smelled like piss and armpits to ever put his hands on you again or force his way into your bed one more night. That's what you were thinking. And you didn't want to look into the empty eyes of the woman who watched it all through a hazy, alcohol and drug induced stupor, no more a mother to you than the old picture of her hanging on the wall.

She peered through the evening mist that was building into a steady drizzle over the city. Across Aurora Avenue, the glow of campfires around Green Lake beckoned. On the farthest corner, the biggest of the fires flickered orange and warm. She made her decision.

SIX

Warm and Friendly

On a clear night, the drive from the crossroads into Alder would have taken fifteen minutes. Tonight, it took thirty.

Deputy Lew Bentz took his time, keeping both hands on the SUV's wheel and squinting through the white-out glare to keep the vehicle between the ditches that bordered both sides of the road. He steered as near as possible down the center, figuring correctly that no one else with good sense would be out in the storm, at least no one who knew anything about a South Dakota blizzard.

He looked at his passenger, leaning toward the heater vent, warming his hands. "Tennessee ... that's a long way from Blanken County, South Dakota."

Sole nodded, rubbing his hands together. "It is for a fact."

"Mind if I ask how you ended up out here in the middle of a blizzard?"

"Nope, I don't mind." Sole shook his head and leaned back in the seat. "Heard they're drilling for oil up in North

Dakota and figured I'd go that way and pick up some work if there's any to be had."

"There's work for sure in the oil fields." Bentz nodded. "You been working oil rigs somewhere else?"

"Nope. Just thought I'd give it a try." It wasn't just a cover story. He'd been thinking about where to go next. Oil rigs tended to be away from population centers—a good thing—and he'd never been afraid of physical labor. He just hadn't considered the uncertainty of a Dakota winter.

"Free spirit, huh … out for an adventure."

"Don't know about being a free spirit," Sole laughed. "But I keep on the move. Try not to stay tied down anywhere. I'm pretty handy, and I figured they could find something for me to do. I never mind starting at the bottom." He grinned and looked at Bentz. "Guess I didn't think things through as much as I should have before I set off."

Bentz laughed. "That's a fact. Might have been a better idea to wait until spring to give it a try."

"Might have," Sole agreed. "Except I need a job now."

"Tough times?"

"Just times." Sole shrugged. "No tougher than anyone else's I suppose."

"No family? Someone you can fall back on?"

"No." Sole shook his head. "Parents been gone for years. No brothers, sisters, wife, or kids. Just me."

"Alone in the world." Bentz said, a tone of sincere sadness in his voice. "That's hard."

"I don't know." Sole shrugged. "You get used to it … being alone." The memory of his wife and children threatened to boil to the surface. He pushed it down and forged ahead, changing the conversation's direction with a chuckle. "Unless you run your dumb ass off the road into a snowbank, in which case being alone definitely has its disadvantages."

"I expect it does," Bentz laughed.

It was just after ten PM when Bentz steered the SUV down the main street of Alder, South Dakota. Cars were parked along the side here and there, but the traffic was non-existent, and the few deep tracks made by passing vehicles were quickly filling.

Lights glowed from the windows of the small houses and shops that lined the short stretch of road that was the main street. Bentz stopped in front of a small building in the center of the town's single block of businesses. Several pickups, mostly older, were pulled in at a forty-five-degree angle to the curb. A sign over the door lit by a floodlight read simply—*Langstrom's*.

"Let's get warmed up," Bentz said, pushing the SUV door open and leading the way.

Sole stepped out and sank to his knees in the snow. He pushed through it to the sidewalk that someone had shoveled clear earlier, and that would soon have to be shoveled again. He followed Bentz inside.

Luscious, glorious, sensuous warmth surrounded him. Every muscle in his body relaxed and the nonstop shivering began to abate. A tingle went up his spine as his core warmed and he gave an involuntary but pleasant shudder. A dozen pairs of eyes stared at him, mostly curious and somewhat amused.

He nodded at them and beat his arms together to get the blood flowing as he examined the dimly lit interior. Most of the patrons and their curious eyes were seated on stools at a bar along one wall. A few others sat at the tables scattered around the room. A coatrack spanned the opposite wall, filled with heavy parkas, wool coats, and one insulated canvas-covered work coat. In the corner farthest from the door, a jukebox played an old country ballad.

A man standing behind the bar wearing an apron over a red plaid flannel shirt twisted his beefy face into a smile and said, "Lew, what the in hell you got there?"

"Found him adrift in a snowbank," Bentz said, pulling his gloves off as he walked to the bar. "Need to warm him up some, and then we'll answer all the questions you got."

Sole followed Bentz to the bar, nodding at the faces turned toward him. "Evening."

"Here. Got just the thing for you," the bartender said, pouring half a mug of coffee from a pot under the counter and filling the rest with bourbon. He placed it on the bar and said, "Make room for him to belly up, boys." He looked at Sole. "Step up, son. That'll burn the chill out of your bones."

Two men shuffled to the side and Sole stepped in between, grabbed the mug, took a swallow. Lips pursed together, he squinted and winced as the hot coffee and alcohol burned a path down the back of his throat.

"Good," he sputtered and took another gulp.

The men around him laughed. The bartender leaned forward and put out a hand. "Harry Langstrom, and you are?"

"Bill," Sole said. "Bill Myers."

"From Tennessee," Lew Bentz piped in.

"Well, it's plain to see he's not from around here," Langstrom said.

"What was your first clue?" Sole said, and the men gathered around laughed again.

"That little bitty jacket you're wearing, for one thing. No one around here would be out in this weather dressed like that unless they were planning on suicide." Langstrom grinned and leaned forward. "Not planning a suicide, are you, Bill?"

"Nope, not today." Sole took another sip from the mug.

"Good ... that's good," Langstrom said. "Ground's frozen hard as concrete now. Wouldn't be able to plant you until spring."

More laughter from the men and Sole joined them. The bourbon was taking effect and a mellow warmth started in his gut and spread upward.

An older man standing beside him nudged him with an elbow and said, "Lucky Lew Bentz found you out there. You'd be frozen hard as a popsicle in a couple more hours."

"More like frozen coyote shit," a gruff voice said from the end of the bar.

Sole looked around the shoulders of the men beside him down the bar to a burly man standing at the end. Dressed in insulated canvas pants that matched the work coat hanging on the rack, the man threw back a shot of brown whiskey and turned his head to stare at Sole.

"Don't worry about him," Harry Langstrom said, taking up position midway down the bar between the men, just in case trouble broke out and he had to reach for the bat under the counter. "That's Bob Shank. He doesn't much like anybody, which suits us 'cause we don't like him much either."

Laughter broke out along the bar, along with assorted comments.

"Got that right."

"Bob wins the asshole contest every year at the Blanken County fair."

"Son of a bitch wouldn't help his mama across the street unless she paid him."

"Go to hell," Shank snarled.

"Nope. So warm and friendly in here, I believe I'll stay here." Sole returned Shank's stare, lifted the mug in a mocking toast, downed the last of the coffee and bourbon concoction, and thumped the mug down on the bar top. He pulled a twenty out of his pocket and laid it beside the mug. "Harry, pour me another."

"You got it," Harry said, grinning. "You're gonna fit right in."

SEVEN

Safe

The evening had darkened. The drizzle was steady now, wetting her cheeks and soaking her hair so that it hung limp and dripping down her back. Hands shoved down in the pockets of her jacket, Malina trudged around the outer edge of Green Lake, trying to stay away from the homeless encampments in the main park while moving toward the glow of the Seattle Youth Protective Association's campfire.

Shadows moved in the trees surrounding the lake. She quickened her pace. The campfire was a beacon, a safe haven.

She turned her head at the sound of scurrying feet. Her body tensed, muscles taught, heart pounding. Two shadows crossed the path behind her and moved into the trees.

She heard voices. Whispers. Somewhere a low, deep laugh and then a high-pitched cackling giggle. She wanted to run but was afraid to take her eyes off the trail behind her, terrified that someone would creep up in the dark. She side-shuffled along the path, trying to watch her footing in front as she kept a lookout behind.

"Over here." The voice came from in front.

Her heart leaped in her chest, pounding against her ribcage. Her throat thickened and constricted until she could barely breathe. The scream that was trapped inside came out as a whimpering mew. Eyes wide, her head jerked around to face the source of the voice.

He stood in the path, directly in front of her, not fifteen feet distant, a dark, hulking silhouette lit from behind by the orange glow of the campfire. He took a step forward. She shrank backward, willing her feet to run, but her shaking knees nearly collapsed under her. She staggered and started to fall away from the silhouette.

He rushed forward now, hands outstretched, grabbing. They were strong hands, clamping hard around her arms. He jerked her up roughly until she stood on tiptoes, her hands pushing at his arms to free herself.

"Nooo," she whimpered, shaking her head, trying to turn away from the face that was leaning toward her.

"Calm down." The man clutching at her arms leaned closer until she could see his face. "You must be looking for us. You're safe now." Satisfied that she wasn't going to fall over, he released her and took a step back.

"Safe?" Malina stood breathing heavily and trembling, the drizzling rain mixing with the tears that ran down her cheeks.

"Safe." The man nodded. "I'm Tom Shaw, from the SYPA camp." He nodded at the campfire fifty yards away over his shoulder. "Just over there."

"The SYPA camp?" Her heart was beating slower now, the terror fading, leaving her limp, feeling as if she might fall over from relief now instead of panic.

"Yes." Shaw nodded. "I keep a lookout for people my

partner Rick might have sent our way. You must have met him ... Rick Salver."

"I ... yes, I met him," she mumbled.

"Good." Finch stepped closer and smiled. "I heard the voices out there behind you in the dark and figured someone was headed our way. It can be dangerous out here alone, so I thought I'd come check and make sure you were okay."

"I ... yes ... I ..." Malina leaned over, hands on knees, and dry heaved. "I thought you were ..."

Finch waited for the heaves to subside and for her to stand up again, then said, "I understand." He spoke in a soothing baritone, gentle and comforting. "It can be pretty frightening out here alone, not knowing anyone or who to trust. Follow me. I'll lead you to the camp. There are others there, and you know what they say. There's safety in numbers."

She stared at him without speaking for several seconds. He lifted his hands and stepped away. "I promise I won't touch you. Just follow me."

Several more seconds passed before she nodded and said, "Alright."

She plodded along behind Finch, her head turning alternately to watch behind and then back to him. He walked ahead without looking back at her, letting her follow or not as she chose. She began to feel more at ease.

They walked from the dark into the circle of light thrown off by the campfire. Tarps were strung up overhead on poles to provide shelter for a dozen or so others, young people like Malina, who huddled close to the fire.

Finch led the way forward. "Everyone, we have a new guest. This is ..." He turned to Malina. "Sorry, I didn't get your name."

She eyed the others sitting around the fire, their faces reflecting the orange flames, waiting expectantly for her to speak. "Malina," she said.

"Malina," Finch said with an affirming nod and smile. "Malina decided to come in out of the rain and join us tonight."

"Here." A bubbly young woman jumped up. "Come over here out of the rain." She took Malina by the arm and led her to an old aluminum lawn chair near the fire. "I'm Carlie. Been here a couple of weeks, but you can stay a night or as long as you like." Carlie looked at Finch. "Right, Tom?"

"That's right." Finch walked over to a camp table where a pot of coffee simmered on a Coleman stove and poured a cup. "Coffee, Malina?"

"No," she said softly, shaking her head and looking around at the faces, trying not to make eye contact, inexplicably embarrassed.

"It's alright. I know how it is. Hard to get used to people being nice, but you'll relax soon enough." Carlie patted her arm and sat in a chair beside her and waved a hand, motioning around the circle. "These folks here under this tarp are newbies like you. Those over there have been here a while like me."

The other newbies nodded without speaking then looked away, staring in to the fire. Carlie asked, "You hungry? Probably haven't eaten all day. I know how it is. Been on the run myself."

Without waiting for a response, Carlie was up and at the Coleman stove dipping something into a bowl from a pot simmering bedside the coffee. She came back and held out the bowl and a spoon toward Malina. "Eat this. It's just canned chili, but it's hot and thick and will warm you up some."

Malina stared without moving, her hand folded in her lap.

"Here." Carlie reached down and placed the bowl in Malina's hands and put the spoon in the bowl. "Now, eat. You'll feel better."

"Thanks," Malina mumbled. The bowl was warm in her hands. She lifted the spoon, took a bite, and nodded. "Good."

"Damn right it's good," Carlie said with a laugh. "Made it myself, opened the can and everything."

Soft laughter rippled around the campfire. The others went back to talking among themselves, tired voices and quiet conversations. Malina ate the chili until the bowl was empty.

Carlie watched and took the bowl from her. "Seconds?"

"No," Malina said and, for the first time, smiled. "I'm full."

"Good." Carlie took the bowl back to the table and stood there talking to Finch for a while.

Warmed by the fire and her belly full, Malina nodded in and out of a doze. Steam rose from her wet clothes as the fire dried them and the warmth finally penetrated to her flesh and deeper into her bones. Her body relaxed, like a spring when the tension is released.

She sagged in the lawn chair and listened to the muted talking around her. A thought forced its way into her mind. What now?

She shook it away. Think about that tomorrow. Carlie said she could stay as long as she wanted. Maybe she would stay, for a while at least.

For now, it was enough to be away from the hell of her mother's house. It was enough to be warm and dry. It was enough to be safe.

EIGHT

The Pheasant Hunters

"Trust me. You will not believe it." Senator William Kellin leaned back in a leather armchair in the VIP lounge of a Fixed Base Operator at a regional airport on the east coast.

It was the sort of airport and FBO that catered to the air travel plans of the rich and famous. Private jets owned by corporations and the very wealthy filled the hangars and lined the parking aprons. "I'm telling you, it is incredible." Kellin sipped a martini and spoke with an arm-waving, all-knowing expansiveness that his companions found annoying, but which they tolerated, partly because he was the organizer of the trip, but mostly because he chaired a powerful Senate committee and was not a person they could disrespect without expecting serious consequences.

"So, the hunting is that good?" Oliver Parson's brow furrowed, forcing himself to ignore Kellin's condescending tone. A glass with two fingers of scotch, neat, was clamped in his stubby fingers, resting on the arm of his chair.

"Exceptional!" Kellin waved his glass in front of them to emphasize how exceptional. "I've never seen anything like it

... pheasants everywhere. Bagged my limit the first day," Kellin said with a wink.

"And after that?" Parson asked. "Trip was over, right? Isn't there a ... uh, what's it called ..." Parson paused, thinking, choosing the right word, then nodded and said, "A bag limit, right?"

"Of course, there's a limit ... for some. But for our host, they make certain ... uhm ... arrangements, shall we say. Bagged my limit on day one, but stayed for the week, and trust me, I got my money's worth." Kellin's lips twisted into a sly grin. "More than my money's worth if you ask me ... all off the record, of course."

"You sound like the great white safari hunter out of a Hemingway story." Elizabeth Ranskill shook her head, a smirk on her face. "How many times have you been to the lodge? Once?"

"True enough," Kellin conceded with a condescending smile. "I've only been once, but the question is, how many times have you been?"

"Touché." Ranskill twisted the smirk into a wry smile, nodded, and sipped from a glass of cabernet.

"I don't have much experience at this sort of thing," Simon Taylor said. He was the fourth member of the group, and the least comfortable with the excursion Kellin had planned. "In fact, I've never done anything like this before."

"You mean going after pheasants?" Kellin said.

"Yes ... that and ... I guess everything about it." Taylor gave a half-embarrassed shrug. "I've never even fired a gun."

"Piece of cake," Kellin assured him. "The lodge will set you up on the practice range with some clay pigeons. Break a few of those and you'll be set to hit the fields."

"And then ..."

"And then you can relax, Simon. Stop worrying. You'll fall right into the swing of things." Kellin laughed, made a fist, and held up a stiffened forearm. "First time you pull the trigger, trust me ..." He shrugged, grinning. "All I can say is you're going to have the greatest hard-on you've ever had."

The others laughed. Taylor managed a small smile without looking anyone in the eyes.

"I have to admit," Ranskill said. "I am intrigued. I mean, getting a hard-on is physiologically impossible for me, but surely there will be some other manifestation for those of us with two X chromosomes."

"Out of my area of expertise," Kellin said, the grin spreading wider now. "Maybe a swelling of the labia? Or a distinct hardening of the nipples? When the time comes, I could check for you, Elizabeth."

"In your dreams," she snapped back.

The others laughed. It was a reasonably happy party, and the jibes were good-humored if sometimes cutting. They were not friends, not in the usual sense of the word, but they knew each other well because they orbited in the same social circles. The one thing they all possessed in common was power.

Each wielded their power differently and derived it from different sources. The desire to tap into that power had prompted their host to organize the excursion to the hunting preserve he maintained in a remote section of the South Dakota prairie. Those invited to the exclusive event were:

William Kellin—Senator and Chairman of the Senate Banking Committee.

Oliver Parson—Chief Investment Officer for a major financial services company.

Simon Taylor—Lawyer, well known academic and professor of law at a faith-based Texas university. He had testified before Congress on several occasions and even argued and won cases before the Supreme Court.

Elizabeth Ranskill—Hedge Fund Manager whose personal net worth approaching a billion dollars dwarfed the others, making her the most powerful member of the group, at least when issues boiled down to a matter of dollars, and most issues did eventually.

Kellin was the instigator and point of contact with their host and had approached the others with the idea of an exclusive week's pheasant hunt at a private South Dakota preserve. The invitation was framed as a respite from their respectively hectic schedules. None of them were deceived by this. They knew they had power and were accustomed to being approached by those who wanted them to use that power on their behalf.

The conversation and planning began in the summer, but the need to work around their differing schedules delayed the trip to early January. Normally, that would not have been a problem, but it was snowing in South Dakota. What was to have been their grand adventure was getting off to a slow start.

Hostesses from the jet that the hunt lodge had provided for their use tried to make them comfortable while they waited, serving them drinks and expensive catered hors d'oeuvres. They'd been sitting in the VIP lounge sipping and nibbling for half a day, and still, the snow in the upper plains showed no sign of letting up.

Parson nodded out the window. "Getting dark soon."

A light drizzle was falling, and the lights around the tarmac reflected off the wet pavement in little, shining points of light. "Weather doesn't seem so bad to keep us here," Taylor said.

"It's not the weather here that's the problem," Ranskill said with a shake of her head. "It's the weather in South Dakota."

"Oh." Taylor nodded, and the others exchanged amused looks the way they might have in a high school class when the really smart class nerd said something really dumb, demonstrating that brains do not necessarily equate to common sense.

The lounge's door slid open with an electric whir, and one of the pilots walked in. He smiled, nodded, and cleared his throat. They looked at each other, preparing for the bad news.

"Let's have it," Kellin said sharply.

"Yes, right." The pilot nodded and forced the smile wider. He was no novice at dealing with pampered clients accustomed to having their own way. Inconvenience was unacceptable, regardless of what the weather gods had in store for them. He plunged ahead. "So here it is. The weather is not going to break until tomorrow. The entire state of South Dakota, in fact, the entire upper Midwest is socked in until then."

The four would-be pheasant hunters exchanged looks. Kellin spoke. "And what does that mean exactly."

"It means we won't be flying to South Dakota today," the pilot said, bracing himself.

"And our time? Our inconvenience?" Kellin's condescension morphed into indignation. "We have wasted a day sitting here waiting for you to get things in order and get us in the air."

"Yes, well, we are ready to fly," the pilot said. "Unfortunately, the weather is not cooperating, and our job is to ensure you arrive there safely." He forced a smile and added quickly, "But the lodge has taken care of everything. A limousine will be here to take you into the city where they have booked five-star accommodations for you." The pilot was speaking rapidly now, trying to get it out before the objections started. "All meals and transportation will be provided at no expense to you, and in the morning, the limo will return you here. We should be airborne by nine AM."

"And what about the day we lost, sitting here on our asses, drinking cheap wine?" Ranskill said, her tone even sharper than Kellin's.

"Your host told me to pass on that you may extend your stay as long as you wish or reschedule for any time in the future, but he sincerely hopes you will fly out with us tomorrow."

The four exchanged satisfied nods. One of the hostesses came through the door and whispered in the pilot's ear. A look of relief flooded over his face. "The limousine is in front now."

"Thank God," Kellin said in disgust as he rose from the chair. "Can't stomach any more of this cheap booze. Let's get to the hotel, change clothes, and have a proper drink."

"I'm for that," Ranskill said.

The hostess led the group from the lounge to the limo outside. The pilot breathed a sigh of relief. When the sliding glass door whisked closed behind them, he muttered, "Fucking assholes."

NINE

Perfect

"Ladies and gentlemen, I give you this year's Falston Humanitarian of the Year, Mr. Avery Cromwell Demeron!" The banquet's master of ceremonies stepped to the side of the podium and extended an arm to stage right and added as if he and the guest of honor were long-time friends, "Come on out, A.C.!"

He was an aging actor, hired for the event because of his ability to project the proper aura of gravitas over the proceedings. Before his agent booked him for the event, he'd barely heard of the Falston Foundation charities, but then, few had.

The Falston Foundation was more a rich boy's and girl's club than anything else, a place for the wealthy to receive accolades and add the award to their list of accomplishments. The size of a candidate's contributions to the foundation determined where they ranked in the Falston annals of humanitarianism. This year, A.C. Demeron, South Dakota rancher, industrialist, financier, and now, humanitarian, had outbid all others for the award, offering up a cool million in U.S. dollars above the nearest award competitor.

Named after a Texas oil billionaire who departed the earth thirty years earlier, the Foundation did, in fact, support select charities around the globe. The exact amount of support was classified, ostensibly for security reasons, but the foundation provided frequent reports listing the recipients of their charitable work.

Naturally, there were also operating expenses. A significant portion of the foundation's receipts went to pay staff—mostly Falston family and heirs—but everyone understood that such a worthy endeavor had overhead costs.

This year's recipient, like those in previous years, was a man of considerable wealth whose donation, large as it might have been, had no impact on his lifestyle. Curiously, the bulk of the Foundation's donations came from people of more modest means, often watching the Foundation's commercials on late-night cable TV. It was a matter of record that no humanitarian award recipient had ever been one of the many retirees on pensions who gave up their last twenty dollars to support the foundation. The parable of the widow's mite was lost on the Falston Foundation's selection committee.

The lights over the stage dimmed. A spotlight threw a single bright circle of light on the polished wood planks. There was a lingering pause. Anticipation grew among the attendees. A.C. Demeron timed it perfectly. He always timed things perfectly.

At the precise moment when further delay might transform the anticipation into something else, he stepped into the spotlight to be greeted by a round of applause. There were no cheers, no cries of adoration. This wasn't that type of crowd. There was a certain decorum to be maintained.

Demeron stood before them, tall and patrician. He smiled, and his teeth shone sparkling white. His full head of silver hair brushed back from his forehead, glittered under the spotlight. Some of the women and a few men caught their breath at the perfectness of his appearance. He was an Adonis in perfectly pressed black silk and patent leather.

Another pause, and then he moved along the front of the stage, the spotlight following him. He smiled at those seated at the front tables and nodded at a few. Once or twice, he offered a friendly, acknowledging point of the forefinger to someone whose name and face he would never recall once he left the room.

He reached the podium. With a flourish, the master of ceremonies removed a velvet covering from a plaque and showed it to the attendees. The applause grew in volume. He handed the plaque to Demeron, shook his hand, and stepped back into the shadows.

Demeron stepped to the podium and waited. There was an unwritten protocol at play. He allowed the applause to continue for a few seconds longer than necessary, then raised a hand and it died away. He smiled beatifically, gazing around the room at the upturned faces. Then he spoke.

"Friends, I am humbled to stand here before you tonight. This ..." He held up the plaque for all to see. "This award belongs to all of us. Everyone here has contributed to the good works of the Falston Foundation. I accept it on behalf of you all."

The applause began again. He waited a few seconds before continuing.

"There are many people I should thank tonight." He looked down at the first table, front and center, where his wife smiled up at him. "First and foremost, I owe everything to my companion for these last twenty-seven years, my wife Lorraine." He blew her a kiss and a smattering of applause rippled through the room.

"I should thank my great grandfather, who took a quarter section of South Dakota prairie and turned it into the Demeron Ranch. My grandfather and his son, my father who grew the ranch into what it is today, preserving a way of life, and taking on the responsibility of protecting the land, a responsibility they passed on to me, and one which I hold sacred."

More applause.

"Finally, I thank you all, for I have watched and learned and benefited from knowing each of you over the years of our combined service with the Foundation."

Again applause.

"Thank you." He lifted the plaque, bowed his head humbly, and walked from the podium, the spotlight following him as he made his way back to the table to take his seat beside his wife.

It was perfect. The timing, the short and humble acceptance speech, the beautiful adoring wife seated at his side, giving him an affectionate pat on the arm now and then.

Wine was served with dessert. A paid comedian took the stage and poked fun at rich people. The rich people laughed and nodded at each other to show they were good sports. Then the evening ended.

A.C. Demeron departed with his wife on his arm. A limo waited outside to take them back to their downtown Houston hotel. The driver opened the rear door. Demeron waited for his wife to be seated, then slid in beside her. He gave a final wave from the window to others waiting for their limos to make their way to the curb.

When they had driven a block away into the city traffic, he tossed the plaque on the floor.

"Careful," Lorraine said. "You'll scuff it. We're going to have to hang that somewhere ... in your study, perhaps."

"Hang it wherever you choose." Demeron loosened his bowtie and leaned back in the seat, stretching his legs out.

"You were perfect tonight," Lorraine said.

"You think?" Demeron sat up straight, always ready to hear more about his perfection.

"I know." She nodded. "I was watching the faces. They loved you." She laughed softly. "Rose Carson looked like she might climax in her panties."

He laughed and closed his eyes, trying to remember which of the bejeweled women at the event was Rose Carson and what she looked like. "Is she the one that ..."

"Stop." Lorraine smirked and shook her head. "You're already fantasizing, aren't you? Wondering if Rose's panties are wet for you."

"You brought her up." He shrugged.

"I suppose I did." She reached over, lifted his hand, and placed it on her thigh. "You should be wondering if my panties are wet for you."

"Are they?"

"They could be." She moved his hand between her legs.

He took the cue. Her body tensed under his hand as he moved. She bit her lip to stifle a moan when she came.

After, she looked up at his perfect profile. It was perfect, she thought, and the son of a bitch knew it.

TEN

Sleep

He leaned toward her, nicotine-stained fingers reaching for her, a sweat-stained shirt hanging open, exposing his pale, bony chest. She shrank away, but he loosened his belt with one hand and grabbed her by the hair with the other.

"No ... no!" Malina shook her head, her hands raised, flailing in the air, trying to fend off the attack. Her voice rose. "Please ... nooo ..."

"Are you alright?" A voice spoke to her distantly from another place. A hand shook her shoulder, and when she didn't respond, shook harder. "Wake up!"

Her eyes moved, darting back and forth as if she could see through her closed lids, but all she saw was the man, the creature, panting and clawing at her, forcing her.

"What's wrong with her." It was a different voice, a man's voice. Malina cringed away from the new voice.

Carlie looked at Tom Finch and shrugged. "Bad dream I guess."

"Sure she's not tripping?" Finch leaned close, watching the rapid eye movement under her lids.

"No," Carlie shook her head.

"No, you're not sure, or no she's not tripping."

"She's not tripping," Carlie said, annoyed at being questioned. "Having a bad dream."

"Bad dream?" Finch stood up straight, staring down at Malina. "Helluva dream."

"Guess she's had it tough." Carlie jerked her head, motioning for him to step away. "Move off. I'll wake her up."

Finch walked back to the Coleman stove and poured himself a cup of coffee.

"Malina!" Carlie leaned close to her ear. "Wake up! You're alright. No one is going to hurt you."

The woman's voice again, pulling her out of her dream. Malina's eyelids fluttered and opened, blinking rapidly, then wider, confused and afraid.

"Calm down." Carlie was leaning close, speaking firmly to reassure her. "You're fine. Just a bad dream."

"Where …" Malina jerked herself up straight in the lawn chair, her head swiveling, taking in her surroundings. She nodded. "Oh."

"Just a bad dream. A really bad one from the sound of it. I won't ask what it was about." Carlie smiled and patted her arm. "You wait here, and I'll get you something to calm you down."

She stepped away to the group gathered on the other side of the fire by the Coleman stove and said something to Finch, who looked across at Malina and nodded. Carlie reached into a small plastic box by the stove and came back.

"This'll settle things down for you." She held up a joint, neatly rolled and ready to light up, placed it between her lips, lit it, and puffed it to life. She inhaled deeply, exhaled, and held it out. "Here. Take it."

"Grass?" Malina looked at the joint without reaching for it. "I'm not twenty-one. That legal?"

"Legal enough," Carlie said and shrugged. "How old are you?"

"Fifteen," Malina said and looked down, embarrassed, wondering if she should have said she was older.

"Well, Tom and Rick buy it. They're over twenty-one, so that's legal. As for smoking it, look around. You're with friends ... others just like you."

"Alright." Malina reached out, took the joint, and gave it a tentative puff, then drew more deeply on it and exhaled coughing."

"Don't smoke much weed?" Carlie grinned.

"Some ... not much," Malina conceded. "Expensive where I come from."

"Expensive everywhere since they legalized it." Carlie nodded at the joint. "That's good shit. Take it slow and let it go to work. You'll be feeling better soon. No more bad dreams, at least not for a while."

Carlie moved away, rejoining Finch and the other regulars by the stove. Malina looked around at those gathered under the newbie tarp with her. There were four, three girls and a boy. The boy looked even more dazed than Malina.

She settled back in the chair and pulled her jacket tighter around her. Carlie was right. The joint was beginning to ease things for her. "Fuck that son of a bitch," she muttered and chuckled.

"Say what?" The girl sitting in the nearest lawn chair looked at her.

"Fuck that son of a bitch," Malina repeated. "I hope his cock falls off."

"Wow." The girl laughed. "Whose cock."

"My motherfucking mother's fucking boyfriend, that's who." Malina took another hit off the joint.

"Oh." The girl gave an understanding nod and smiled. "I'm Sherry, by the way … Sherry Pettit."

"Malina Jenkins," Malina said and held out the joint. "Want a hit."

"Hell, yeah." Sherry took it, inhaled, and handed it back. "Thanks."

"What about us?" The speaker was clearly older than the other newbies who were all barely teenagers. There was a hardness about her, a weariness in her eyes and on her face that made her look to be in her thirties. In reality, she was barely twenty. She scowled and repeated more sharply, "Well? What about us?"

Sherry jerked her head in her direction and said, "That's Bobbi … no last name, she told us … just Bobbi." She motioned to the other two newbies sitting with them under the tarp. "This here is Cindy. She came in about the time I did. Got here in time for lunch."

"Hi," Cindy said. Unlike Bobbi, her cherubic face and blond curls made her look younger than her fourteen years.

"That guy over there …" Sherry nodded at the lone boy sitting in a chair removed from the others. "That's Brad."

Brad said nothing, his eyes focused on the fire.

Carlie shrugged. "Brad doesn't say much."

"Well," Bobbi insisted, staring at the joint in Malina's fingers. "You gonna pass it or just let it burn to ashes?"

"Here," Malina handed it over. "Pass it around."

Everyone took a hit except Brad. By the time Bobbi took a second, it was nearly gone. She handed the butt back to Malina without a thanks.

They sat by the fire without speaking after that. The

drizzle faded into a clinging mist that covered everything with fine drops of water, even under the tarp.

A van pulled up nearby, cut the headlights, and Rick Salver got out. He joined Carlie and Finch by the stove. They spoke softly among themselves. The other regulars began to disappear singly or in pairs into nearby tents. Carlie came over to the newbies, with five bottles of beer, expertly carrying the necks of three between the fingers of one hand and two in the other.

"Here." She held out the beers. "A nightcap, then I'll show you where your tent is. Not much, but it's warm and dry. Tomorrow you can decide what you want to do."

They all took the beers from her, except Brad. He sat huddled in the chair with his feet in the seat, knees up, and his chin resting on top. He shook his head.

"You don't drink?" Carlie asked, a surprised smile on her face.

"Sometimes," Brad said. "Don't feel like it tonight."

"Alright." She leaned over and put the bottle on the ground beside his chair. "I'll leave it here in case you change your mind."

"Whatever."

Carlie walked away. The other newbies sipped their beers. The fire burned low, the embers glowing hot in the mist, sending up little wisps of steam as the water evaporated away into the night.

Malina found herself drifting into a luxurious, sensuous, engulfing sleep. The foul, sweating man was nowhere around to disturb her.

She sank deeper and deeper away from the world. She wanted to sleep for a very long time. Nothing seemed as wonderful as the thought of sleeping ... forever. Then the world went black.

ELEVEN

Fact of Life

White light burst into the room, so bright it seemed it might pierce through his closed eyelids. Sole clenched his eyes shut tighter and remained motionless on the cot in Langstrom's back storeroom. Harry Langstrom had offered him the bed before closing the bar the night before and assured him no one would disturb him there.

Someone was disturbing him now, turning on the lights and rummaging through the stack of boxes and crates in the center of the room, unaware of the sleeper tucked away in the cot on the far wall. It was a woman. Sole could tell because she mumbled to herself as she inspected the boxes, pulling out an item here and there, moving around the stack.

Then she spoke. "Who the hell are you?"

Sole cracked open his eyelids and squinted into the astonishingly, painfully, blindingly white glaring LED lights lining the ceiling. The woman had worked her way around the stack of boxes and crates to stand over the cot. She held a 1.75 liter bottle of booze in each hand, the one in her right hand raised like a club.

"Harry said I could sleep on the cot," Sole said, pushing himself up, still squinting and wishing she would move so that he wasn't staring up at the lights.

"I didn't ask you that," she barked down at him, the bottle raised a little higher. "Pay attention. Who the hell are you?"

"Oh." Sole yawned and nodded. "Name's Bill Myers. You must be Alva. Harry told me you'd come around in the morning to open up. Said he'd let you know I was staying in the back."

"Humph. Sounds like something my husband would say," Alva growled, but lowered the bottle. "He forgets to tell me everything." She eyed the clothes piled at the foot of the cot where Sole dropped them the night before and nodded to the restroom door in the corner. "You can take care of your morning business and wash up in there. Then get dressed and come out front."

"Alright." Sole shrugged, pulled the covers off, and stood, wearing nothing but a tee-shirt, boxers, and a grin.

Alva eyed him up and down and gave a final, disapproving, "Humph," before turning and striding through the door into the bar.

Like her husband, Alva Langstrom was in her sixties, a large woman, but not fat. Sturdy might have been the best word to describe her physical attributes. Her long, gray hair was rolled up in a tight bun, and she walked away with the broad-shouldered, rolling gait of a linebacker. Sole figured he would not have wanted her to take a swing at him with the bottle clutched in her fist.

He went into the restroom and did as she instructed. A few minutes later, he walked through the door into the main bar. Several customers lined the counter. He glanced at the clock on the wall. Just after seven AM. Apparently, they started drinking early in South Dakota, he thought, then noticed Alva standing at a stove at the far end of the bar against the wall. She was breaking eggs into a pan with one hand and plopping bread into a toaster with the other.

She looked over her shoulder, saw him, and jerked her head toward the door he had come through. "Make yourself useful, Bill Myers. Go back in there and bring me eggs, milk, cheese, and butter from the cooler."

She turned back to her cooking without a second thought that he might ignore her directive. Sole had the impression that it was inconceivable to her, and the customers watching the interaction, that he might not comply with her instructions. It seemed few men defied Alva Langstrom, and certainly not any present at Langstrom's that morning ... including Sole.

He went back into the backroom, found the cooler in the rear wall, and retrieved the items as directed. Arms full, he went back into the bar and deposited them on the counter beside the stove.

"Good." Alva nodded. "There's a sink over there and dirty dishes on the bar top."

She gave no further instructions. None were needed. Sole nodded and went to the sink and began washing up dishes.

The customers at the bar glanced up but said nothing. He recognized a couple from the night before and nodded. "Morning, boys. How's the coffee?"

They nodded, muttering quickly, "Good. Just fine," as if anyone would dare criticize Alva Langstrom's coffee within her hearing.

Sole almost laughed out loud but thought better of it.

Dark Winter

He glanced at Alva standing wide-legged, hands on her hips, staring down at the toaster, willing it to pop up the toast. He decided it was best to follow the lead of the locals, so he focused on the dishes. When he had cleaned and wiped dry all that weren't currently being used, he stepped away from the sink, wiping his hands with a dishtowel.

"There." Alva didn't miss a beat and nodded at the coffeemaker on the counter. "Know how to use that?"

It was a large, industrial-style machine. Sole looked at it doubtfully, but said, "I suppose I can figure it out."

"Get a fresh pot going. Another crowd coming in at eight."

"Right," he said and turned to study the machine.

"Coffee under there in that cabinet," one of the men hunched over a plate of eggs and sausage said in a voice low enough that Alva couldn't overhear. Sole recognized him from the night before, one of the last to leave when Harry Langstrom closed up at two AM.

"Thanks," Sole said, got the coffee out, and turned to stare at the contraption that had to be fifty years old if it was a day.

"Goes in that basket at the top. Just open the lid, then turn that little valve on the side attached to the water line. Don't let it overfill, though. Turn the valve back when it gets to the fill line inside. Then hit the red button and stand back. If I told you right, it'll start gurgling and brewing. If not, ..." He shrugged and grinned. "Stand back before she blows."

"Who?" Sole said, returning the grin. "The coffee or Alva."

That got a round of laughter going until Alva turned her gaze on the men and they clamped their mouths shut.

Sole dared a whisper to the helpful customer. "Appreciate your help. I'm Bill Myers. Saw you here last night."

"Yep, I'm here most nights ... this time of year anyway," the customer said and extended a hand. "Roger Pedersen."

"Nice to meet you, Roger," Sole said and shook his hand.

Alva turned to scowl at them. Roger let out a laugh, not too loud, though. "Don't worry about Alva. Her bark's worse than her bite. Besides, she won't bother me ... not too much at least."

"Why's that."

"I'm the pastor at the Lutheran church here in Alder." Pedersen chuckled. "She wouldn't want to hurt her standing before the Lord by clanging me over the head with a frying pan."

"Pastor? Like the minister, you mean."

"Exactly like that." Pedersen smiled.

"Well, that's a hell of a thing," Sole said then added, "Sorry no offense intended."

"None taken, but what's hell got to do with it?" Pedersen asked, smiling.

"Back where I'm from, it's mostly Baptist, and you won't catch any Baptist preacher in a bar at two AM, or any other time for that matter."

"We're pretty open about sin around here," Pedersen said, and the other customers laughed. "And don't fool yourself. Just because those Baptists aren't sinning in public doesn't mean they don't take a nip now and then. Besides, the Good Lord drank wine ... even provided it for a wedding, if you recall. I don't suppose he'll look down on me too much for looking after his flock here at Langstrom's, even if I share a toddy with them on a cold evening."

Alva turned away from the stove, hands back on her hips, and barked, "That coffee going yet?"

"You better get it on, son," Pedersen said. "My position as a man of the cloth has its limitations. I might be reasonably safe, but I can't say the same for you."

There was more laughter along the bar now. Alva's scowl deepened. Sole got busy with the coffeemaker.

When the urn was full, he went along the bar with a pot refilling cups. By seven-thirty, most of the customers had wandered out into the gray morning, pushing their way through the snow that was still falling and piling along the street. As predicted, a second breakfast crowd wandered in around eight. Mingled in with these were a few nursing hangovers from the night before. A couple of them ordered bloody marys.

Alva looked at Sole. "You know how to pour?"

"Pour? You mean do I ..."

"I mean, can you make a drink? Put together a bloody mary? These boys need a little hair of the dog if you know what I mean."

"I know what you mean." Sole nodded. "That legal ... serving alcohol this early?"

"Bars open at seven AM in South Dakota ... state law. Sun may not be up yet, but it's legal. Spend a whole winter here and you'll know why. Now can you make a bloody mary or not?"

"I'll give it a try."

"Good. I'll get breakfast going for the others." She nodded at the sink. "There'll be more dishes and ..."

"I know," Sole said, and ventured a smile in her direction. "Wash the dishes and make coffee."

Sole scouted around the bar for the fixings and managed to put together a couple of reasonably decent drinks. What they lacked in aesthetics he made up for by adding an extra shot of vodka when Alva wasn't looking. The customers gave sincere nods of appreciation but kept their mouths shut and drank.

After the eight AM rush, things quieted down. Sole finished up the last of the dishes, wiped his hands on a towel, and looked around for something else to do before Alva ordered it.

She turned from the stove with a plate heaped with eggs, sausage, and toast and thumped it down on the bar top.

"Here, eat, and pour yourself some coffee."

"Thank you," Sole said, pulling a stool up to the bar. "I'll pay you."

Alva lifted a hand and said, "No need. I suppose you earned it this morning." She nodded at the coffee urn. "Pour me a cup too while you're at it."

They sat quietly sipping coffee, Sole eating his breakfast. When he finished, he poured more coffee for them and Alva said, "Let's hear it."

"What's that?"

"Your story. How'd a fella like you end up in Alder, South Dakota, in the middle of a damned blizzard?"

Sole gave her the story, the sanitized Bill Myers version. From Tennessee, drifting around looking for work, no family. He left out any references to the family he once had and his personal war with the Mexican cartel that took them from him.

When he finished, Alva nodded and sipped her coffee. "Sounds lonely."

"Not so bad." Sole shrugged. "You get used to it."

That was a lie. He never got used to it and had accepted that he never would.

"Why is it I get the feeling there's more," Alva said, looking into his eyes. "Some secret you won't tell."

Sole decided it was time to change the subject. "How about you? You got any secrets?"

"Secrets!" Alva snorted and slapped the bar top with her beefy palm. "More than I can remember. Little town like this is full of secrets, otherwise, everybody would be in everybody else's business, a sure recipe for trouble. Hell, Main Street would be lined with bodies inside a week, if it weren't for the secrets everybody keeps close."

"I expect that's true," Sole laughed.

Alva allowed herself a brief smile, the first real smile he'd seen on her face, then picked up her cup, leaned her elbows on the bar top, and nodded, reflecting on the mystery of secrets. "Me, I don't judge anyone for their secrets, because the hard truth is, if you've been born into this world, you've got secrets. That's a fact of life."

TWELVE

Tradeoffs

"I should be in South Dakota now." A.C. Demeron sat in a plushly cushioned wicker chair on the balcony of his penthouse suite in one of Houston's five-star hotels. "I have guests arriving."

"I know, but we don't control the weather." That was about six words more than most of Demeron's employees would have dared to venture. Charles 'Chuck' Goode had been Demeron's pilot for a decade, and their relationship was different. That may have been partly because you don't piss off the man who drives the plane at nearly six hundred miles an hour, thirty thousand feet above the ground. It was also because Goode, a former Navy pilot, was not easily intimidated, no matter how big a paycheck his boss could write.

"So, what's the plan, Chuck?" Demeron asked, dialing back his annoyance, and throwing in the familiar name to show what a good sport he was trying to be.

"We'll have you there before your guests arrive," Goode said. "The snow broke in Sioux Falls an hour ago. The runway will be cleared for incoming traffic by the time we get there."

"Sioux Falls? I need to be out at the ranch."

"The Blanken County airfield is still closed. Snow hasn't let up there yet, and when it does, it will take a while to get it plowed. Nothing we can do about that, but I've arranged for a helicopter to stand by in Sioux Falls and take you and Lorraine directly to the ranch once we land."

"I hate helicopters," Demeron groused.

Goode ignored it. "Your guests will arrive in Sioux Falls after you. The helicopter will drop you off and then return to Sioux Falls to pick them up. You'll be home, rested, and showered long before they arrive."

The insistence that he arrive at the ranch before his guests came tromping through the snow from the helicopter to his doorstep was typical A.C. Demeron. There was plenty of staff there to make them comfortable, but Demeron liked to play the magnanimous welcoming host, the founder of the feast, and great benefactor of all things good.

It was one of Demeron's defining personality traits, and Goode had learned to deal with it over the years. Dealing with it today meant inconvenience to his four guests so that their host could put on a proper show for them. They would fly out later than necessary to ensure that they arrived in Sioux Falls after Demeron. By the time they helicoptered them out to the ranch, Demeron would be standing on the broad, glassed-in porch, drink in hand, beaming and bidding them come in out of the cold and enjoy a toddy by the fire.

"Alright," Demeron sighed. "If there is nothing to be done about it ..."

"There is nothing to be done about it," Goode said

flatly before Demeron could muster up another objection. "A car will be downstairs to bring you to the airport within the hour. We'll be in the air in two. Is there anything else?" Goode was ready to get off the phone.

"No, that'll be all. Be ready when we get to the airport."

Goode would be ready. He was always ready, but Demeron had to end every conversation with some parting instruction, demonstrating that he was in charge, the boss of bosses, *el jefe*.

Goode ignored it without comment and ended the call.

"You don't look happy," Lorraine said, standing in the balcony doorway, a morning drink in her hand.

Demeron eyed the bloody mary, but said nothing. Lorraine was an alcoholic, a functioning one, but an alcoholic, always with a drink close at hand. They had argued about it for a time early in their relationship until Lorraine laid down an ultimatum. He could accept her drinking the way she accepted his foibles or she would divorce him, take a hefty settlement, and then proceed to tell the world what an abhorrent creature he was when the shades were drawn.

The prospect of having his perfect façade tarnished forced him to call a truce. She drank, and his foibles remained private.

"We have to take a helicopter out to the ranch." Demeron frowned. "I hate helicopters."

"I know you do," Lorraine said with false sympathy, sipping her drink. "Have a drink with me. It will ease your nerves."

A scowl flickered across his face, then vanished. She saw it, smiled, and sipped.

"No." He shook his head and rose from the wicker chair. "Are you packed? The car will be here soon."

"Packed and ready," she said.

"Good. I have to make some calls. If you don't mind, could you go inside and call for the bellman to come get our bags?"

"Don't mind at all, hon." Lorraine smiled demurely, took a last sip, drained the glass, and went inside.

He leaned against the balcony railing, looking out over the Houston skyline, breathing in the humidity-laden air. It was heavy, filled with city odors and exhaust fumes, difficult to breathe, and very different from the crystalline winter air in South Dakota. But then, the Houston temperature hovered in the seventies, while back home it sat anchored at fifteen below zero. It was a tradeoff. Muggy, pungent air in exchange for warm balmy temperatures, or crystal clear air for arctic-like freeze.

Everything was a tradeoff, he mused. He had accepted that particular aspect of life years ago and had become an expert trader. Lorraine's drinking for his privacy. Principles for profit. Morality for personal satisfaction. Lies for advantage. The tradeoffs in life had made him what he was, and he wouldn't have *traded* them for any other life. The play on words brought a smile to his face.

THIRTEEN

Agreeable

Harry Langstrom showed up around eleven AM. By that time, the breakfast rush was long over, and Alva was at the stove, getting things ready for the lunch crowd. A couple of early midday boozers sat at one of the tables sipping beers and staying out of Alva's way.

Sole sat at the bar, waiting for Alva to assign him another task as he flipped through a week-old copy of the Blanken County Sentinel. It was a thin read. Headlines on the front page above the fold reported on the sheriff's department search for the owners of three dogs found abandoned and freezing in a roadside ditch. Deputies were investigating and those responsible would be charged with animal cruelty and abandonment. The sheriff asked for anyone with information to come forward and provided a phone number where the report could be made anonymously.

It was all small-town news. Sole found it refreshing, and after his experience with the cold, Sole read it with keen interest, feeling more than a brief pang of concern for the dogs. He was relieved to read that, while they suffered from frostbite and malnutrition, the local veterinarian felt confident of their recovery.

After that, the paper mostly reported on the blizzard along with a brief mention of the county commission's decision to accept bids for plowing the snow off roads not covered by the state highway crews. That story appeared on page three.

Harry went behind the bar, poured himself a cup of coffee, then sat across from Sole. "Morning."

"Morning," Sole returned and laid the paper on the bar.

"Morning," Alva muttered by the stove. "The man shows up in the middle of the day and calls it morning."

Harry grinned and called out. "I love you too, dear."

Alva grunted a "Humph," took a plate from the warming oven over the stove, and placed it on the bar in front of Harry. "Here's your breakfast."

"Thank you, honey," Harry said, his tone all syrupy and playful, and patted her bottom, letting his hand rest there while she poured herself a cup of coffee.

She let out another "humph," but did not swat his hand away. Sole thought he detected a trace of a smile on her face, but she caught his eye and the stern look returned. She pulled up another stool and sat down beside her husband.

"So, what's your plan, Bill Myers." Elbows resting on the bar, coffee cup raised to his lips, Harry stared across the bar at him.

"Plan?" Sole shrugged and held his gaze. "Get my car towed out of the snow and make my way up to …"

"Lew Bentz told us … North Dakota and the oil rigs," Harry interrupted, nodded. "Is that something pressing … something or someone waiting for you to get up there?"

"Not especially." Sole shrugged. "Just something to do."

"Some sort of ramblin' man. That it?" Harry pressed but did it with a smile.

"Some sort," Sole said. There was nothing offensive in Harry's manner and Sole was familiar with small-town curiosity whenever strangers passed through, had grown up in a small town in the north Georgia mountains before heading off to the Marine Corps. He waited for Harry to get to the point.

"Used to be like you," Harry said.

Sole doubted that, but nodded and said, "You did?"

"Yep. Spent some years wandering … lost, you might say." Harry smiled and patted Alva's arm. "Until this woman here found me … or I found her … or we found each other."

Sole waited without speaking. He was dangerously close to being drawn into a conversation that might bring out memories he'd worked hard to bury.

"You see," Harry continued. "I had a wife once … before Alva, I mean … a baby too, a little girl, Annette. It was a happy time for me … for us. Built a little house on some land outside of Canistota. Figured we'd have some more kids, add on to the house over the years, and spend the rest of our lives there." He stared straight ahead, his voice emotionless as if the emotion had been drained out years ago.

"I was working at the grain elevator loading a train one afternoon." He spoke softly, his voice heavy with regret.

"It came out of nowhere. The elevator was too far from town for us to hear the warning sirens. The wind picked up quick like … sudden. We all knew what was happening. You live here all your life and you recognize tornado signs. Climbed up high as I could on the elevator stairs and saw it." He shook his head, working to keep the emotion from his voice. "I could see the damned thing, knew where the house was over the horizon and knew sure as hell it was headed for it, like the hand of God swiping across the land, slapping down everything in the way."

Harry took a deep breath to help push the rest out. "I got there quick as I could, but it wasn't any use. The house …" He stared down, seeing it all again in his mind, his voice not much more than a whisper now. "It was gone, nothing but splinters where it stood. Took three days to find my wife's body in a grove of trees a hundred yards away. The damned trees were still standing, but the house and my wife." He shook his head. "What was left of her was torn and mangled so bad … I made them show her to me, then wished I hadn't. We never found the baby's body." He finished and a single tear managed to escape the corner of his eye and roll down his red cheek.

Alva put an arm around his shoulder and looked at Sole. "Like I said, we all have secrets. This is Harry's."

Harry nodded and looked up. "Yes, it's my secret, and it's the reason I know that there's something more in you than just drifting from job to job for the hell of it."

"So what?" Sole shrugged, his tone sharper now, wanting to bring an end to this conversation. "So, there's more. Whatever it is, it's mine to carry and nobody else's business."

"Fair enough." Harry raised a palm in truce. "Not trying to pry into your business. I'll just say this and then I'll shut up." He leaned forward, looking into Sole's eyes. "I was lost, wandering … drifting like you until I met Alva. We settled down, bought the bar. In time, things got better. Guess you could say Alva … this place … living life … all of it healed me … made things better."

"That it?" Sole asked. "You think I should settle down here?"

"It's not such a bad place." Harry shrugged and laughed. "It stops snowing … now and then. It's a pretty good place to settle down and let things heal."

"I'll keep that in mind," Sole said and glanced out the window. "Still snowing now, though."

"You could stay," Alva said, her voice surprisingly gentle when she wasn't giving orders. "You'd be welcome."

"I see you made an impression on Alva. Not an easy thing to do." Harry laughed again. "She's right. You could stay, for a while at least, and then stay a bit longer if you want or just move on like you planned. Either way, it couldn't hurt to just give things a chance to heal."

"I'll think about it," Sole said, the finality in his tone ending the conversation.

"Fair enough." Harry grinned. "Anyway, snow's supposed to let up today."

As if on cue, the door opened and Lew Bentz bustled in, bringing a blast of frigid air with him. A large round man in a parka that made him seem even larger and rounder followed him inside. "Morning everyone," Lew called out. "How about a couple of cups of coffee, Alva?"

Alva nodded and turned to the coffee urn. Lew stepped up to the bar, rubbing his hands together for warmth. "How'd you sleep, Bill?"

"Pretty good," Sole said, glad to have someone else to talk to and something else to talk about. "Had an early wake-up though."

Lew laughed. "Alva does like to get an early start." He motioned to his companion. "Bill, this is Ernie Bullock … runs the garage and tow service here in the county. Figured we'd drink coffee here for a spell, and when the snow breaks, we'll head out to drag your pickup out of that snowbank, if that's agreeable to you."

"That is definitely agreeable," Sole said, relieved that the subject of conversation had changed. "Have a seat. The coffee's on me."

FOURTEEN

Here's to South Dakota

"There's a full bar in back ... everything you need for a bloody mary," the limo van driver said, loading luggage into the rear as his passengers took their seats. They were a slow-moving group this morning, some nursing hangovers, and he couldn't resist adding in his most innocently helpful tone, "If you'd like breakfast, I know a place on the way. Fix you up a plate to go ... anything you want. Eggs and bacon, sausage, biscuits and gravy ... anything. They make a great crab and shrimp omelet, or maybe you'd like something lighter. Lox and bagels loaded with cream cheese."

"Just get us to the airport," Senator Kellin growled.

"Yes, sir." The driver finished loading the luggage, suppressing a grin.

Once they were on the move, things were quiet, and no one had any interest in checking out the fully stocked bar.

After being deposited at their five-star hotel the night before, Senator William Kellin led them to the lobby bar, where they made full use of their host's offer to cover all expenses. The first round of drinks went down quickly. The second, nearly as quickly.

By the time the server brought the third round, their annoyance at being delayed by the blizzard in the Midwest had faded away. They ate in the bar and continued drinking, all the while Kellin expounding on his vast pheasant hunting experience gained from his single visit to A.C Demeron's hunting preserve. At one-thirty AM the server came around for last call orders.

"Last call?" Kellin boomed. "We're just getting started!"

"I'm sorry, Senator," the server said. "But our license requires us to close by two AM."

"Do you know who I am?" Kellin's eyes narrowed.

"Yes, sir, but we have to abide by the law. I'm sure you understand." She smiled and returned his gaze. Having served presidents in this hotel, she was not about to be intimidated by a mere senator.

A few seconds passed. She didn't flinch, and Kellin finally nodded. "I suppose we should call it a night, anyway. Long day tomorrow." He looked at the others. "Right?"

They finished their drinks, tipped the bartender and server, and made their way to the elevator on wobbly legs, except for Simon Taylor, who had nursed a single drink all evening, withdrawing quietly into himself as the alcohol-infused raucousness increased. In the morning, despite the wake-up calls they'd arranged, they made their way downstairs one at a time, Taylor first and Kellin the last to arrive.

"Glad you could join us," Elizabeth Ranskill said. "You look terrible, Bill."

Kellin ignored her and looked at the limo driver standing nearby, waiting with a smile on his face that seemed a bit too mocking. Kellin gave him a sharp look, and the smile evaporated.

The forty-five-minute drive from the city back to the regional airport passed in silence. Taylor read emails on his phone. Ranskill and Parson stared out the window. Kellin dozed, sparing them his usual bombast.

Arriving at the FBO, the driver was waved through a security gate and directed to the jet parked on the apron. One of the pilots waited at the foot of the passenger stairs, directing him to park parallel to the plane.

The van came to a stop and Kellin jerked his chin up off his chest, looked around, saw the plane, scowled at the driver, and said, "About time. Thought we'd never get here."

They piled out of the van and made their way up the stairs to be greeted by a flight attendant who got them seated and offered juice, coffee, tea, or something stronger. Everyone opted for coffee.

The limo driver unloaded baggage and then stowed it in the hold under the direction of the pilot. When he finished, he looked around. The passengers were all on board. No one offered him a tip. He shrugged, went back to the van, pulled out the trip order, and added a hefty tip to be paid by their host. The pilot looked it over without commenting on the tip and signed it.

Fifteen minutes later, they were airborne. None were strangers to flying on private jets. All had access to corporate jets, or in Kellin's case, to private aircraft provided by those seeking his political expertise, a polite word for influence.

They settled in quickly, munching the snacks the hostess

provided and chatting with the pilots, who took turns checking on their elite passengers. Taylor spent some time on the phone with his law office partners. Ranskill and Parson discussed investment opportunities. Kellin invited the hostess to sit with him and when she excused herself to see to her other duties, he followed her to the galley where he spent most of the flight talking to the back of her head as she tried to find a way to delicately tell him to buzz off.

By the time they reached Sioux Falls, they had mostly recovered from the prior night's revelry. Kellin, in particular, was ready to get his party on.

The smiling pilot met them at the bottom of the stairs. "We'll have your bags loaded on the helicopter when it's ready for departure."

"When it's ready?" Kellin's eyes narrowed. "What does that mean. We were told ... you told us ... that we'd be taken directly to the Demeron ranch."

"You will be." The pilot's smile widened. "The helicopter will land you at the ranch, but for the moment, it's being serviced from a previous flight. You can wait in the concourse, or there's a bar and grill where you can get something to eat if you'd like."

He omitted telling them that the delay was part of Demeron's plan to arrive first so that he could play the grand host when they flew in. The same helicopter had flown Demeron and his wife to the ranch earlier. Then the pilots took their time refueling and had lunch before returning to Sioux Falls.

"Fine." Kellin led the way through the door into the terminal. "I need a drink," he grumbled.

They walked as a group down the concourse. It wasn't a long walk. Sioux Falls is a regional airport with a total of seven gates. Compared to one of the big-city airport hubs,

Sioux falls is a backwater travel stop, and the locals like it that way.

Heads turned and eyebrows raised at the city-slickers decked out in their new hunting apparel, complete with designer field pants, new boots, and leather shooting patches on the shoulders of the shirts and jackets. The combined cost of their outfits was more than some of the onlookers earned in a month. More than a few chuckles followed them down the concourse, mostly from locals who did their pheasant hunting in blue jeans, sneakers, and jackets off the rack at Wal Mart.

The muted laughter was polite but not too polite.

"Would ya look at that."

"They sure are pretty."

"Looks like a damned safari."

"Yeah, what the hell they goin' after, lion?"

"Think I saw a price tag dangling from a sleeve."

More laughter, a little louder.

Not accustomed to being laughed at, Elizabeth Ranskill stiffened and muttered, "I suddenly feel overdressed."

"Just the locals having fun," Kellin replied, making an effort not to turn to a couple of the louder voices and lean into their face in righteous indignation—*Do you know who I am? A goddammed United States Senator, that's who!*

Wisely, he did not and kept his eyes forward, putting on his best politician smile as they walked past the gawkers. Parson and Taylor followed behind, their heads down, not making eye contact with anyone. "The pheasant hunting better be as good as Kellin says," Parson mumbled.

They made their way through the gauntlet of onlookers and found the bar and grill at the end of the concourse. Kellin led the way to the bar and ordered the first drink.

"I'll have a gin martini, dry, Bombay Sapphire, three olives."

"Sir?" The bartender raised his eyebrows and the confusion on his face was obvious. "A martini?"

"That's what I said," Kellin snapped.

"I ... uh ... Well, I don't know exactly how to do that, sir." The bartender was young, not more than twenty-one, inexperienced, and just barely legal to be working behind the bar. Ordinarily, that would not have been a problem, but today, Senator William Kellin and company had decided to pay him a visit.

"You're telling me you won't make me a simple martini?" Kellin's voice rose.

"Well, I would make it if I knew how, sir. It's just that ..."

"How did you end up behind the bar?" Kellin shook his head in disgust.

The young bartender's face reddened. He stammered, "Well, s-sir, I-I uh ... It's j-just that ..."

"Hey, pal!" A man seated at the bar had been listening to the exchange and had enough. He turned on his stool and stared hard into Kellin's eyes. "Leave the kid alone. You're in South Dakota. Order a damned beer and sit down!"

Kellin's mouth opened as if he might say something, then thought better of it and clamped it closed. He nodded, ordered a round of beers for the group, and they took them to a table near the door.

"Well, that was interesting." Elizabeth Ranskill raised the bottle of domestic beer between thumb and forefinger, gave it a disdainful look, and took a sip. Her face wrinkled, and she put the bottle on the table. "Here's to South Dakota."

FIFTEEN

On the Road

She became conscious of a cold steel surface pressed hard against her face. A jarring thump and Malina's eyes fluttered open, slits at first, then wider, confused and afraid.

One of the newbies, the boy, Brad, sat across from her, his back against a wall, his lip swollen, a lumpy bruise rising on the side of his face. She tried to sit up and found her hands secured together with handcuffs. She looked at Brad. "Are we arrested?"

Brad said nothing but nodded to a man sitting against one wall of the steel-lined cubicle. A handgun in his hand rested on his knee. She recognized the man, one of those who had been talking to Tom Finch by the stove at the SYPA camp.

"Are you a cop?" she asked. "Are we under arrest for something?" She remembered smoking weed. Was that it?

"Not a cop," the man said, shaking his head, a wry grin on his face. "And you're not arrested."

"What then?" Malina pushed herself up to lean back against the wall. "Where are we?"

"On a trip," the man said.

Things were confused. Remembering was like looking through a dirty window, everything fuzzy and distorted. She became aware of movement. They were in a vehicle, the back of a truck of some sort, moving along a highway. Her eyes darted around the confined space. The other newbies, Sherry and Cindy, lay on the floor on either side of her. Bobbi sprawled face down at the far end of the space.

"A trip to where?" None of this was making any sense.

"Home," the man said.

"No!" Malina's eyes opened wide, her head shaking side to side. "Not home. I can't go back there."

"Your new home," the man said with a grin.

Sherry, and then Cindy, stirred. Slowly at first, then opening their eyes as Malina had, staring at their surroundings in confusion, seeing Brad's bruised face, the man with the gun, Malina already sitting up, Bobbi still passed out.

"What the hell?" Sherry pushed herself up. Like Malina and the others, her hands were cuffed in front. "What the hell's going on?" She looked at Malina. "Did they arrest us?"

"He says no." Malina nodded at the man holding the gun.

"So why are we here?" Sherry pushed herself back against the wall as far from the gun as possible. She wobbled side to side and put a hand on the floor to steady herself. Her head turned, eyes wide and as confused as Malina's, taking in their surroundings.

"He says we're going to some kind of new home." Malina shook her head. "He's being an asshole."

Gun-man laughed, watching and listening to everything they said.

Still lying on her back on the floor, Cindy groaned. "I

don't feel so good." She put a hand to her mouth. "Think I'm gonna puke."

"Don't do that in here," Sherry said quickly. "Here, let's sit her up."

Gun-man watched, amused. They lifted Cindy by the shoulders and propped her up against the wall.

"Better?" Malina asked.

"Better." Cindy nodded, then shook her head. "I need to get out of here and breathe some air."

"Can't we stop for a minute?" Malina looked at Gun-man.

"Soon," he said and motioned with the pistol toward Bobbi, face down by the truck's back door. "Check on your friend."

Malina and Sherry crawled on their knees, using their cuffed hands for support. They reached Bobbi and rolled her onto her back. "Is she breathing?" Sherry asked.

Malina leaned close, her nose wrinkling at the foul breath Bobbi exhaled in her face, a combination of beer and vomit. She backed away and nodded. "She's breathing."

"What happened to her?" Sherry turned, scowling at Gun-man. "What did you do to her?"

"She got a double dose," he said.

"Double dose?" Malina's eyes narrowed.

The fog slowly cleared from their brains. She remembered sitting by the fire under the newbie tarp, passing a joint around. Then Carlie brought them beers, and then … nothing.

"You drugged us," she said. "Something in the beer."

"Chloral hydrate … knockout drops." He shrugged and laughed. "You drugged yourself, actually. No one forced you to drink the beer. Your friend decided not to drink." He nodded at Brad, sitting alone across from them, staring at the floor, looking as if he was wandering somewhere in a world far away from the back of the truck.

"What happened to him?" Malina's eyes narrowed, noticing for the first time that Brad's feet were also shackled and his hands cuffed behind his back and not in front.

"He didn't want to come on the trip." Gun-man shrugged. "Should have drunk his beer."

"What kind of fucking trip is this?" Sherry shouted. "I want out! Now!"

She tried to stand, stumbled, and fell back on her backside. The man laughed. "Soon enough," he said.

Another hour passed. The fog lifted from their brains. The girls' eyes darted back and forth, taking in everything, except there wasn't much to take in. The box truck's interior measured about ten by fourteen feet. The walls were covered in steel-gray sheet metal, and they could see the rivets that fastened the metal to the truck body. Malina figured it was some sort of delivery truck or maybe a rental truck like the one she had helped load once when they moved from Portland to Spokane to be with her mother's new boyfriend.

There was plenty of room inside for the five newbies and the man with the gun, but he was the only one seated on a chair. It looked like one of the lawn chairs they'd sat in around the campfire. Everyone else sat on the cold steel floor.

From the truck's movements and relatively smooth ride, they could tell they were traveling on a well-maintained highway. There was little road noise and just an occasional sway as the truck rounded a bend.

Through it all, Brad remained silent, his eyes fixed on a

single spot on the floor. The lump on his face took on a dark, purplish hue.

After an hour or so, Bobbi stirred. She moaned, rolled on her side, and drooled a mixture of saliva and stale vomit out on the floor, then tried to push herself up, but fell face down again. Her legs and arms moved spasmodically as if she were trying to swim across the floor. She managed to raise her head, saw the two girls, snarled incoherently, and then fixed her eyes on Gun-man gun.

"What the fuck?" she croaked.

He chuckled, reached to the side, and opened a door that led into the front truck cab. "They're waking up."

"Right," the man seated in the passenger seat said.

The driver nodded and a few minutes later, turned from the well-maintained highway onto a gravel road. With the door to the cab open, Malina had a narrow view out the front windshield. Traffic was nonexistent, and there were no signs they might be near any populated areas. They moved through rolling hills, bumping along the gravel road toward some distant, snow-covered mountains.

Malina figured they'd gone a couple of miles by the time the truck rolled to a stop in the middle of the gravel road. The men in the cab got out and opened the back door. Dim gray light filtered into the dimmer truck interior. The sky outside was overcast, threatening snow.

"Out," one of the men by the door said.

Malina and Sherry helped Cindy up and went to the door. Sherry climbed down first and helped Cindy down. Malina turned back and took a step toward Brad to help him.

"Get out," Gun-man said. "I'll take care of him."

Malina nodded at Bobbi. "What about her?"

"You just get your ass out."

Malina turned to the door, stepped on the bumper, and jumped down. The men from the truck cab handed out bottles of water and sandwiches in little plastic containers bought at some convenience store along the way. Bobbi eventually made her way out of the truck to stand swaying and leaning against its side for support. One of the men held out a sandwich for her. She gagged, turned away, bent double, and dribbled puke down her chin and onto the ground. The men laughed.

Gun-man stood in the door, stepped down, and then reached up to help Brad hop down to the ground. He nodded at the bumper and said, "Sit down."

Brad sat, and Gun-man removed the shackles from his ankles, then said, "Turn around."

Brad stood and turned around to face the truck, and the man released his handcuffs. Brad's arms fell straight by his side, and before he could raise them again, Gun-man spun him around and cuffed him in front like the others. He leaned close and said, "Don't cause any trouble now, and I'll leave you like this." He motioned at the surrounding countryside and said, "There's no place to run, and if you try …" He shook his head and spoke almost gently, lifting the pistol in front of Brad's eyes. "Well, don't try. We don't want to hurt you. Long as you do what we say, you'll be fine."

He stepped away to talk to the men from the truck cab. Brad stood alone, staring at the distant mountains.

When Gun-man moved away, Malina walked up, holding out a bottle of water. "Here." Brad looked at her without speaking and without taking the water.

"Take it." She lifted his arm and pushed the bottle into his hand. He took it but held it hanging without drinking. "Did they hurt you bad?" she asked.

For a second, she thought he would ignore her and was

about to rejoin Sherry and Cindy when his head turned and his blank stare focused on her face. "What?"

"Did they hurt you?" Malina repeated. "Bad I mean."

He shook his head. "Not too bad."

"Good." She nodded, smiled, and looked out at the horizon. "Wonder where we are."

He followed her gaze. "East of the Cascade Mountains … somewhere in eastern Washington." He nodded at the mountain range off to the west, then shrugged. "Looks like to me, at least."

"Any idea why we're here?" she asked, not expecting an answer.

"They sold us," Brad whispered, not looking at her.

"What?" Malina's head snapped around to face him.

"Heard them talking last night while you all were knocked out. Sold us and they're delivering us to whoever paid."

"That can't be true." Malina shook her head. Rape, robbery, kidnapping, ransom. These were all possibilities she had considered, but being sold … that added a frightening dimension to what was happening. Somehow, the idea of being sold as a piece of property seemed more terrifying than all the other possible motives. She shook her head. "That can't be right."

Brad shrugged and kept his eyes focused on the horizon.

"Want to come over and eat with us?" Malina changed the subject and smiled at him.

"I'm fine."

"Alright." Malina walked away to eat the stale sandwiches with Sherry and Cindy but decided not to mention what he'd said about being sold.

Bobbi sat on the rear bumper, alone and glaring at the others. She sipped water, avoided the food, and muttered under her breath. Once she looked up and shouted at Gun-man and his companions, "What the fuck, dudes! Look at me! You got me puking on myself!" She shook her head ending with a whimper, "Not cool, man ... just not cool."

They laughed at her and continued talking among themselves, standing a few feet away from the others, eating the same sandwiches as their passengers, seemingly unconcerned that they might try to escape. There was nowhere to escape to. The empty horizon yielded no clues as to their whereabouts, and there was no sign of habitation.

They spoke with the jovial abandon of young men out on a great adventure as if kidnapping and transporting slaves would be a great story to tell over beers. Malina was able to pick up their names as they joked and grab-assed with each other.

Gun-man, Riggs—they never called him by any other name—was the oldest and apparent leader of the group. He gave the orders, when there were any to give and did most of the interacting with the captives.

Hank spent most of his time in the passenger seat, occasionally giving the driver a break for an hour or two, then going back to the passenger side. Hank was bigger than the others, burly and muscular and carried a perpetual scowl on his face except when making fun of the driver.

Jimmy, the driver, was the youngest. Skinny and angular with a head that bobbed up and down on a pencil neck, agreeing with everything Hank said to him, he spent most of the time hunched over the steering wheel, hands positioned at two and ten, just like in the driver's manual.

When everyone had eaten and then relieved themselves behind nearby bushes, the men herded them back to the truck. Riggs climbed into the back first, sat in the lawn chair beside the door to the cab, and waited for his companions to check the handcuffs and load the passengers. When they were seated again, he spoke, holding the pistol in a relaxed way, waving the muzzle before their eyes as he spoke.

"I'll keep this simple. We've got a two-day drive ahead. Where we're taking you is a really nice place, probably the nicest place any of you have ever lived. You are valuable to us and we have no intentions of hurting you." He paused and looked into each apprehensive face. "But we will hurt you if you force us to, so don't force us. Do what we say, don't cause trouble and everything will work out."

He spoke calmly, reassuringly, trying to calm them and convince them they were not in danger, that things would be better, as long as they behaved. But these were not innocent school children. They'd been fed lies all of their lives. Trust was not an inherent quality in their psyches. What held their attention was the gun barrel waving back and forth. The gun was real, solid, threatening, and they paid attention to it.

Riggs finished his speech and pointed to a stack of padded, quilted blankets in a corner, the type movers use to cover furniture when they load it. They were dusty and torn where rats had chewed them.

"Each of you, grab a blanket. It's cold where we're going. This truck has insulated walls, and we'll keep the door to the cab open so the heat can circulate back here, but it will get cold anyway, so wrap up and huddle together for warmth if you have to." He allowed himself a wry smile. "Wouldn't want any of you to get sick."

Sherry was closest to the blankets and tossed them to the others. When they were distributed, the man nodded. "Good. Any questions?"

"Are you going to rape us?" Cindy, the youngest of the group, asked wide-eyed.

"No, I'm not going to rape you." He turned and looked through the door at his companions in the cab. "How about you guys?"

Hank and Jimmy grinned but shook their heads. He turned back to Cindy. "Nope, we're not going to rape you."

Relieved, she nodded and leaned back against the wall, pulling the furniture blanket up to her chin.

"Any more questions?" he asked.

Malina and Sherry stared silently at him. Brad lowered his head and focused on the spot on the floor. Bobbi slumped against the wall, took a deep breath to calm her stomach, and said, "For God's sake, just get us wherever you're taking us."

"Fair enough," Riggs said. "Alright, boys, let's get on the road again."

SIXTEEN

Guess I'm Staying

"So, you make up your mind about it?" Lew Bentz took his eyes off the road to glance at Sole.

"About what?"

Sole raised a puzzled eyebrow, shot him a quick glance, and then turned a cautious eye back to the windshield and the snow-covered road. If it weren't for the path that Ernie Bullock was cutting through the snow with the blade on the front of his tow truck, Sole would have said there wasn't any road at all for miles around, just a uniform blanket of white.

"About staying ... you know, here in Alder," Bentz said, turning the wheel a little to stay on the plowed path.

"You know about that?" Sole said, surprised enough to pull his eyes off the road.

"Harry mentioned it to me last night. Said he was going to throw the idea out for you."

"Is that a fact?" Sole shot him a hard look and straightened in the seat, lips pursed together as he considered the question, uncomfortable that someone else was prying into his business. Prying into other people's business seemed to be a thing in Alder.

He looked to the side at the expanse of white stretching to the horizon. His encounter with the South Dakota cold the night before was a vivid memory. This was not a place he would have selected as home.

"Don't be upset," Bentz threw out when Sole didn't respond. "Harry and Alva didn't mean anything by asking you to stay. Just the way they are ... good people, but they do tend to get involved, if you know what I mean."

"I know what you mean," Sole muttered.

"Probably a shock to you to have people you just met take an interest in your plans." Bentz shrugged. "Around here, it's not so unusual. People know pretty much everything about everyone. Takes some getting used to, I admit."

"Yes, it does," Sole said and turned back to Bentz. "To tell you the truth, I haven't decided yet. To be honest, South Dakota is not a place I had planned to stay."

"You were headed to North Dakota." Bentz smiled. "Seems about the same, except it's colder there."

"I appreciate what you and the Langstroms have done for me." Sole resisted the urge to tell him to butt out of his business, although Bentz would probably just smile and say he understood.

"Nothing we wouldn't have done for anyone else. This kind of country ... the weather and all ... people look out for each other."

"Even so, I'm grateful, but like I said, I haven't decided on staying yet."

"Fair enough." Bentz nodded and said nothing more on the subject, figuring he'd stretched the bubble of cordiality to its limits.

They drove in silence after that. Bentz rested his arms

on the steering wheel a little more casually than Sole thought safe, given the road conditions.

As the arctic storm front pushed through to the lower plains states, the gray overcast gave way to a lighter shade of gray. In places, he even spied an occasional patch of pale blue, but that didn't seem to mean much. The temperature display on Bentz's dashboard showed minus ten degrees Fahrenheit. A warming trend, Sole thought wryly, feeling more certain that neither South Dakota nor North Dakota were places he could call home.

Ahead, the tow truck plowed through the powder, sending plumes of frozen white dust to the side of the road. The tire chains on both vehicles made a metallic whirring noise, muffled by the snow but discernible. Bentz followed close enough behind that he had to run the wipers to brush the snow off the windshield.

The tow truck's brake lights flashed. Bullock let it roll slowly to a stop. Bentz followed suit, leaving room behind the tow truck for Bullock to maneuver, then pushed the door open and jumped out into thigh-deep snow. Sole followed him and was struck in the face by the cold. Even wearing a wool cap and parka borrowed from Harry Langstrom, he shivered. He followed Bentz through the snow to where Bullock stood, hands on hips, eyeing the white surface before him that seemed to Sole, uniformly nondescript.

"Don't go any farther," Bullock warned and grinned. "Wouldn't want you to sink out of sight. You're standing at the edge of the ditch."

"Really?" Sole looked down. If there was a ditch there, it was indistinguishable from the surrounding landscape.

"That it?" Bullock asked Bentz, without turning his head.

"That's it," Bentz replied.

"That's what?" Sole said.

The three men stood lined up in the snow beside the tow truck staring at what looked like to Sole ... more snow.

"Your pickup," Bentz said.

"Where?"

"That little hump there in the snow. That's where the snow drifted up over the tailgate."

"You're kidding," Sole turned three hundred sixty degrees, scanning the uniform blanket of white that covered everything. "Are you sure?"

"Pretty sure," Bentz said.

"One way to find out." Bullock pushed through the snow to the tow truck bed. "Let's get to work."

He pulled out shovels and handed them around. Fifteen minutes of digging convinced Sole that his truck did lie concealed in the snow. It took another hour of shoveling to expose the rear end and carve out a path to the door so that he could get behind the wheel.

Bullock got into the tow truck, reversed, and backed it up, careful not to get too close to the edge of the ditch. Without speaking, he went about his work, and Sole recognized that this wasn't the first vehicle he'd pulled from a ditch.

Running the steel cable out from the winch, Bullock held the heavy hook in two gloved hands and dropped to his knees. With an agility that seemed incongruous for a man of his bulk, he rolled onto his back in the snow, using his feet to push himself down under the pickup's rear end. He worked for a few minutes, moving snow out of the way with his gloved hands until he could secure the chain and hook to the truck frame. Then he scrambled out from under the pickup, his face red, but seemingly oblivious to the cold that had Sole shivering.

"Alright," Bullock said. "You climb behind the wheel. Make sure the transmission, all four wheels, are in neutral and keep the steering wheel straight. I'll do the rest."

Sole slid down into the ditch and made his way to the driver's door, holding the side of the truck for support. Once inside and ready, he gave a wave out the window. Bullock nodded and headed toward the tow truck's cab.

It was slow going at first. The steel cable tightened. Sole felt the pickup shudder as the tow truck moved slowly forward. He began to think that Bullock might not be able to pull him out, when the pickup lurched backward, then stopped as Bullock inched the tow truck forward, taking up the slack in the cable until it was taut again. Another lurch and Sole was sitting with his chest against the steering wheel, the pickup angled nose down at forty-five degrees. Another lurch backward and up and it leveled on the roadway. Bullock pulled away from the ditch, stopped, got out, and crawled under the pickup to retrieve the tow cable.

Bentz came over to the pickup grinning. "Old Ernie knows his stuff."

"He does that." Sole pushed the door open and climbed out.

Bullock was walking around Sole's pickup, checking the frame.

"I suppose you'll be wanting to leave now that we got you squared away."

Not this again, Sole thought, but smiled and said, "Well, not right this minute. I'll probably wait for the roads to clear some ... maybe stay a day or two with the Langstroms if they'll have me. But yeah, after that, I'll probably head out." He grinned. "Think I've changed my mind about North

Dakota, though. I hear they have oil fields down in Oklahoma ... and it's a helluva lot warmer."

Bentz laughed and nodded. "That it is!"

"Heard what you was saying." Ernie Bullock came over to stand with them. "Got some bad news for you."

"What's that?" Sole asked, shaking his head. A little good news would have been a nice change of pace.

"You got a busted tie rod ... maybe from when you hit the ditch ... maybe from jerking you out just now. Temperatures like these, metal gets brittle, breaks easier." Bullock shrugged. "Anyways, it's busted."

"Damn." Sole shook his head. "Don't suppose you know anyone who can fix it, do you?"

"Sure." Bullock nodded. "Me."

"Great. When can you do it?"

"I'll get right on it," Bullock said, nodding. "Soon as I get the parts."

"Oh." Sole let out a sigh. "How long for that?"

"Not long." Bullock thought for a second. "Roads the way they are right now ... a week, maybe two I guess."

Sole nodded. "Alright tow her in and order the parts, I'll come around and pay you."

"No hurry. We can settle up when she's done and you're ready to leave." Bullock went to the controls on the tow lift, preparing to lift the pickup's rear end.

Sole looked at Bentz. "I guess I'm staying ... for a while."

"A while is good enough," Bentz said, grinning. "Come on. I'll call ahead and have Alva fix us up a bowl of her hot stew."

SEVENTEEN

Never Shop Too Close to Home

"Where are they?"

The voice boomed through the van over the phone's speaker. Rick Salver shot a look at Tom Finch, who nodded, scowled, and thumbed down the volume on his phone. They'd been expecting this call, and neither was in the mood to listen to the caller's bullshit.

"Getting closer," Finch said.

"What the hell does that mean? Closer where?"

"Still a day out … maybe two." Finch laid the phone on the console so that Salver could hear the conversation as he drove.

"A day or two!" The caller's voice boomed again, louder. "That's unacceptable. We have an agreement."

"Yes, we do," Finch said, even-toned and calm. "But we don't control the weather. They're making the best time they can, given the road conditions."

"That's not my problem. You promised delivery."

"Not our problem either," Finch replied calmly. "You'll have your delivery."

"I need it today, damn it!"

"That's not gonna happen," Finch said and smiled, imagining the look on the caller's face at that moment.

"Not gonna happen ...you ...but!" the caller sputtered, his ire increasing exponentially at Finch's matter-of-fact reply.

"Look," Finch said, in a half-hearted attempt to calm him down. "The delivery will get there. We'll let them know they need to expedite things, but like I said, the weather is out of our control, and safety, protecting the inventory is the most important thing."

"I don't give a shit about protecting the inventory. I need delivery today."

"Already told you, that's impossible. The delivery will arrive as quickly as we can get it to you." Finch was growing tired with the call. "Anything else you want to discuss?"

"Yeah," the caller snapped back. "How about I deduct ten percent from your fee for every day the delivery is late."

"You don't want to do that." Finch's tone hardened. "You know who we work for."

The caller knew he was right and remained silent. He definitely couldn't do that ... wouldn't dare.

Finch broke the silence. "That's settled then. Tell you what. I'll give you a number so you can call and speak directly to the delivery team. They can keep you updated, and you'll know when to expect them."

He gave him the number and let the caller know the conversation was over, saying, "That's it, then."

He ended the call and looked at Salver, grinning. "Huey's having a bad day."

"Yeah," Salver nodded and grinned, steering the van around a long, swooping curve on the Pacific Coast Highway.

To the left, the Santa Lucia Mountains rose steeply away from the road. To the right, the ground gave way precipitously to the ocean swells below. An avid hiker, Salver would have loved to take a side trip to Big Sur and stretch his legs, but this was a business trip.

He and Finch were partners, the founders of *SYPA*—the Seattle Youth Protective Association. It was the perfect cover for their real business. Young people, girls in particular, who had the misfortune to trust them almost always vanished into the human trafficking network they supplied. The few who did not were marketed to domestic customers like the one on the phone.

Murmurs rose from the back of the van. Salver looked in the rearview mirror. "What's going on?"

"Couple of them have to take a leak," One of the two guards said. They were both young, early twenties, and thankful for the chance to make what they called *some real fucking money*. The payday for this trip would be more than either of them had earned in the last six months.

"Pass the shit can around," Finch turned in the passenger seat, "And keep them quiet."

"Right." The guard nodded. The other told the complainers to shut up, pass the bucket, and do what they had to do.

Besides the guards, there were six passengers, all young girls between the ages of fourteen and sixteen, the ideal age for the *SYPA* customers. A couple had been reported missing by their families. The others were runaways that no one was looking for them, or if they were, had long ago given up the search.

Salver and Finch opted for the scenic Pacific Coast Highway on this trip south, mostly because the PCH was less patrolled by law enforcement than the interstates. They had plenty of time to make it to the exchange, which wasn't scheduled until the next day.

There would be others there, part of the network of suppliers from around the country. They would meet the buyers at the appointed time, deliver their cargo, receive their payment, and leave without looking back.

If they felt any pang of conscience for the fate of the girls, the cash in their pockets soothed it. Some, like Salver and Finch, reasoned that the girls were better off with their new owners, or at least no worse off. Most had left home for a reason, and if life was hard in captivity, it was likely no worse than the one they had escaped. So, they reasoned anyway.

Of course, that rationale overlooked the fact that they were now slaves. There was no other word for it. Owned by others, their lives controlled in every detail by others, forced to labor, use their bodies, sexually satisfy others against their will. Slavery was the only word that applied, but that was a dirty word. So, they employed euphemisms like *inventory, delivery, product*.

Salver and Finch had developed a market niche for their employer and primary buyer, focusing on young girls and occasionally boys as the market demanded. A few in the ring of traffickers considered pedophilia beneath them. Forcing women and men into prostitution was one thing, but children were out of bounds. After all, even human traffickers had little sisters. Some even had children of their own.

Salver and Finch had neither and felt no qualms about preying on the youngest and most vulnerable. It was a far safer method of acquiring their inventory. The young were easier to control, and they rarely had to resort to force to snatch anyone from the street. Despite the hardness of their lives, the runaways tended to retain the naiveté of youth. It was fairly easy for the smiling, good-natured duo to convince their young victims to come with them—for their own good.

Huey Cooke sat at his desk, staring at the phone. He was, indeed, having a bad day. The boss was going to have questions—a lot of them—and Huey had no good answers.

How did the two girls, Mila and Riley, manage to get away undetected and then freeze their dumb asses to death? Yeah, that would be the first question, he figured.

Where are the replacements? That would be the second.

Third. Why aren't they here, bathed, groomed, and ready?

Fourth. Why didn't you find another way of filling the empty beds the girls left behind?

Because Finch and Salver had never let him down before. He knew they had other customers, bigger ones, including the one they called their employer. Providing girls for Huey's boss was a sideline, a little extra cash in their pockets, but hardly their primary source of revenue. That meant he had to take what they gave him, when they gave it to him. Usually, that wasn't a problem, but losing the last two girls just before the boss' big event had put him in a bind.

Huey had thought about taking a couple of the hands into Sioux Falls, or Mitchell, or maybe over to Rapid City and seeing what they could find in the way of replacements, but snatching up fresh blood was beyond his level of expertise.

Besides, the rule they lived by, the rule that had protected them over the years, the rule the boss himself had established, was simple. Never shop too close to home.

EIGHTEEN

A Message

"Where are they?" A.C. Demeron asked, his breath turning to icy fog as he pulled the parka hood tight over his head. After a week in Houston's balmy temperatures, the frigid air hit his face like an icy fist.

"Grain bin," Huey Cooke said from beneath his fur-lined trapper hat, the ear flaps raised so he could hear what the boss had to say.

"Let's see."

They trudged bent over under the helicopter rotor wash, kicking the snow up into a man-made blizzard. The swirling white powder stung their faces and forced them to squint their eyes until they were well clear of it. They'd gone nearly a hundred yards before they could straighten up as they walked. Cooke cast an apprehensive glance at his boss' face. It was inscrutable as if frozen by the cold, but Cooke knew it wasn't the cold that had the boss in an icy mood.

In the fifteen years Cooke managed Demeron's hunting preserve, he had only disappointed him once, and he did not want to repeat the experience. It happened in the preserve's first year of operation. A parasitic infection—coccidiosis—spread through the pheasant flocks he managed. He noticed the problem one morning while inspecting the netted pens and nests. Blood-streaked droppings were the first indicator. Then the birds started dying by the hundreds, killing chicks and adults alike. The preserve's hunting season was canceled. Demeron's rage was historic.

Denying him the opportunity to impress his friends, whose favors he required, was an almost unforgivable sin. It *would have been* unforgivable had there not been history between the two families.

Hubert Cooke's great-great-grandfather and Demeron's had been two of the first permanent settlers in the area to make a go of things. Banding together for mutual defense, they fought off assorted outlaws, rustlers, and the occasional Lakota Sioux who claimed the land as theirs, which it had been before the settlers came. Before the Lakota, other tribes—Arapaho, Kiowa, Arikara, Omaha, and tribes with names no one remembered—had claimed the land until a stronger tribe forced them out. The Demeron-Cooke alliance made them the newest and strongest force in the area.

Bound together for mutual defense, the families worked their ranch holdings independently. It turned out the Demerons were better ranchers and better businessmen. When creditors forced old-man Cooke to sell out to settle his debts, A.C.'s grandfather swallowed up his ranch, paying pennies on the dollar. Cooke agreed to the deal with a caveat. The Demerons were to provide employment and an income to Cooke's male descendants in perpetuity since he was leaving them without an inheritance. It was done on a handshake. A.C.'s grandfather and father had honored the arrangement, but in perpetuity seemed a long time to A.C. Demeron. Even so, he half-heartedly promised his father that young Huey Cooke, the last of the Cooke line, would have a job.

Cooke began working around the Demeron ranch, doing odd jobs. As it turned out, he was a worse rancher than his grandfather.

Meanwhile, under A.C.'s management, the ranch doubled again in size, but more importantly, he diversified. Armed with a Harvard MBA and more money than Midas, at least by South Dakota standards, he went on a buying spree.

A small regional investment bank that hovered on the brink of failure because of management ineptitude, but with sound financials. A microtechnology manufacturing operation that he purchased, brought to Sioux Falls, and turned into a major component provider for Detroit automakers. A chain of convenience stores throughout the Midwest. Controlling shares in an oil-drilling operation and the same in a trucking company.

One successful acquisition fueled the next until the Demeron empire spanned the continent. Some said A.C. Demeron had a golden touch. He hated the expression, found it insulting, as if his success was a matter of luck rather than skill, but when someone said it within his hearing he would nod, give a humble smile and say that he just recognized a good deal when he saw one.

As the Demeron empire and wealth expanded, he and his wife Lorraine rubbed shoulders with presidents, tycoons, and even an occasional bit of royalty. In those settings, he continued to play the humble South Dakota rancher from modest beginnings, but Demeron was anything but humble.

Driven by a need to be the center of attention, he fed on the approbation from business associates, and even more on the adoring gazes and soft, familiar touches from women at the black-tie events he attended with Lorraine. A newspaper story praising his philanthropy warmed his heart far more than it did those of the recipients of his charity. And the more recognition he received, the more he wanted.

Then Demeron hit on the hunting preserve idea. He took Huey away from the ranch where he was useless and put him over the preserve. Cooke had a lot to learn there, and Demeron saw that his preserve manager received the best training available.

Pheasant hunting is big business in South Dakota, and A.C. bought the best stock from the finest pheasant farms. In time, the preserve became a showpiece of his good works. While he brought friends and special guests in for exclusive pheasants hunts, guaranteeing they would bag their limit, he also made it known that he was using the preserve to protect South Dakota's native pheasant stock. With a little PR from some well-positioned South Dakota politicians and a couple of newspaper editors, all of whom had enjoyed time at the preserve as Demeron's personal guests, he became known as a conservationist, the pheasant-man, protector of one of South Dakota's most important natural resources. Along with the recognition came the awards and acclaim his ego craved.

While Demeron's world expanded and wealth grew exponentially, Huey Cooke learned how to manage his little corner of the Demeron empire, the hunting preserve. He never repeated the disaster of that first year. The Demeron preserve's flocks grew and were recognized as among the finest in the world.

After several years, Demeron informed Cooke that his hunting tastes were evolving. Without raising an eyebrow, Cooke took on the additional responsibility of managing what Demeron euphemistically called his special pheasants. He was to keep them housed, fed, happy, and ready to service Demeron and his guests. That most of the young women in his charge over the years were no more than children seemed not to concern him at all. What did concern him was pleasing the man who controlled his destiny.

As for Demeron, his new appetite grew slowly at first. A business trip to Thailand. Dinner and drinks with a wealthy Thai financier who provided a night with young girls fresh off the streets of Bangkok, cleaned up and perfumed for the event, and paid handsomely for their services.

On the flight back to South Dakota, Demeron couldn't stop thinking about it, wanted more of it. He planned everything down to the last detail. The expansive lodge he would construct on the preserve. Ways to entice and keep girls ready and available for service when required. How to identify those who might have similar tastes and how to introduce the topic of the *'special hunts'* to them.

He began by situating this special hunting preserve on land twenty miles from the main ranch. The location's remoteness provided privacy for his guests and made escape nearly impossible for the girls Huey Cooke procured for him. They might as well have been on a desert island. The closest sign of civilization was the grain elevator ten miles distant adjacent to railroad tracks.

It was possible to walk out when the weather permitted, but until now, no one had tried. Usually, the girls stayed for a time, several months to a year, or until Demeron or his guests tired of them. Then they were returned to the supplier to be trafficked elsewhere and replacements brought in.

Demeron wasted no time worrying about what happened to them after that. The bank accounts he used to entice them to stay at the preserve were closed; the funds were transferred to new accounts in the names of the new girls until they too were discarded and returned to the traffickers.

After a few years, the entire process operated with the same efficiency that Demeron brought to his business endeavors. The well-oiled machine was left in the care of Huey Cooke, who finally found something he was good at.

Cooke pulled open the corrugated steel door to the grain bin, stepped through, and hit the light switch mounted to the doorpost. Demeron followed him in, peering into the gloom at the far end.

"Over here," Cooke said and led the way, twenty feet to the far wall. The two girls lay curled in fetal positions, frozen, just as he had described. There was nothing to be done except dispose of the bodies and replace them as quickly as possible, and Cooke already had that in motion.

Demeron stared at the bodies for a few seconds, then shifted his gaze to Cooke. "This can never happen again."

Huey nodded rapidly, trying to explain. "I know. I should have paid closer attention. I thought they were secure here … out in the middle of nowhere … the weather and the …" He lowered his eyes away from Demeron's hard stare and muttered, "I understand."

"Do you?" Demeron's eyes narrowed. "Another fuck-up

like this and my grandfather's promises to yours won't count anymore. He can roll over in his grave for all I care."

"Yes, boss." Cooke nodded. "I just never expected them to try and run when it was twenty below outside."

"You should have," Demeron snapped. "That's what I pay you for."

"Yes, boss."

"When will the replacements be here?"

"Tomorrow," Cooke said, praying that it was true.

Demeron whirled, saying nothing else, and walked out. Cooke pulled the door closed behind them, settled himself deeper into his parka, and followed at a respectful distance. Demeron climbed back into the helicopter without speaking another word to him. Cooke watched him take a seat beside Lorraine. She exchanged a glance with him through the window, but said nothing and made no gesture. Huey might be in trouble again, but she had her own worries.

The pilots throttled up the turbine engines, and the spinning rotor overhead picked up speed. Cooke hunched over in the downwash. When the helicopter lifted up and away, he raised his head. Acid churned in his gut as he watched it disappear over the horizon toward the main ranch.

Demeron may have stopped by to bust his balls as usual, but he'd also sent a message. The arrangement between their grandfathers was officially terminated. Cooke had to get his shit together and keep it together, or he'd be out, and the thought of being out was more terrifying than any other.

He knew too much, had been involved in too much. His existence posed a risk to A.C. Demeron, and the boss had a way of making risks disappear.

NINETEEN

I'll Think About It

Ernie Bullock's garage hunkered down in the snow at a country crossroads a couple of miles out of Alder. Lew Bentz followed the tow truck and pulled to the side of the lot while Bullock lowered the tow lift and left Sole's pickup in front of one of the bay doors.

Sole watched, standing beside Bentz's SUV and feeling like he should do something useful. Bullock didn't seem to need any help. He moved his parka-encased bulk with an almost graceful efficiency around the vehicles, unfastening the tie-down straps and lowering the lift bar. Sole figured he'd be more in the way than helpful if he offered to lend a hand.

Bullock finished up and pulled the tow truck around the side of the garage. Four-foot piles of snow circled the lot, a sign that he'd already been at work with his tractor pushing the white stuff out of the way, but a fresh layer, six inches deep, had fallen since then. He came around the side of the garage, his heavy boots plowing a path through the new snow.

"Appreciate the help," Sole said. "What do I owe you?"

"Told you. We'll settle up when I get the job done," Bullock said from deep inside his hood, a white fog of breath hiding his face.

"Not even some money for the parts?" Sole offered.

"Nope. We're good." Bullock shook his head. "Wouldn't know how much to charge you for parts right now, anyways."

"Relax," Lew Bentz said, coming up from behind. "He knows you're not going anywhere." He chuckled and waved an arm. "Look around. Wouldn't get far in this on foot."

"True enough," Sole said.

The crossroads sat amid what seemed an endless expanse of frozen white. In the distance, across a mile or more of open land, a small grove of trees marked a homestead. The summer foliage had long blown away and the distant trees looked like tiny, gray skeletal fingers erupting out of graves to point at the white overcast.

Smoke curled from the chimney of a small frame house beside the garage. A thin woman came out on the porch, pulling a heavy wool sweater three sizes too large tight around her. She put a hand to her mouth and called out, "Ernie, you bring Lew and his friend inside out of the cold. Got some hot coffee on."

Bentz looked at Sole. "How about it? Addie Bullock makes a good cup of coffee."

"She's right," Bullock rumbled. "Let's get inside by the fire."

"Fine by me." Sole pulled his eyes away from the eerie emptiness of the landscape that was also somehow hypnotically comforting.

They followed Bullock up and over the snow piled around the garage lot and onto the shoveled path that led to the house's front door. Stomping the snow from their feet, they hung their heavy outerwear on hooks inside on the wall by the door.

"This is my wife, Adele," Bullock said and gave the thin woman by the door a peck on the forehead.

"Addie," she said immediately. "No one calls me Adele, except Ernie when he's putting on airs."

"Uh-huh," Bullock grunted and plopped down in a chair near the wood stove in a corner of the small living room. "You'll notice Adele has a bit of a mouth on her. Takes some getting used to, but after a while, she grows on you."

"What takes getting used to is living with a grumpy old bear like you," she shot back.

Bullock lowered his head to conceal the smile on his face and chuckled. Addie patted his cheek, smiled, and turned to Sole, hand extended. You must be the new fella in town I've been hearing about."

"Hearing about?" Sole reached out and shook Addie's firm, strong hand.

"Yah." Addie nodded. "News travels fast out here."

"You mean gossip," Bullock grumbled from his chair. "Snooping into others' business is a regular pastime around here."

"Not snooping," Addie said, turning back to Sole. "Just curious."

Sole smiled at the interaction between the two. "I suppose I am the new fella you've been hearing about ... Bill Myers."

"Pleased to meet you, Bill Myers." Addie nodded at the sofa. "Have a seat. I'll bring the coffee."

Lew Bentz sat on the sofa beside Sole. Addie disappeared through an arched doorway into the kitchen and returned a minute later with a tray loaded down with four china coffee cups, a pot of coffee, four small dessert plates, and some sort of confection that looked like a cross between a pie and a cake.

"Pour the coffee, Ernie," she ordered.

Bullock sighed, leaned forward in the chair, and poured coffee into the cups.

"Have some *kuchen*, Bill," Addie said, pronouncing it *koo-ken* and handed him a plate with a slice of the cake-pie stuff. It was an order, not a request.

"*Kuchen*?" Sole said, taking the plate.

"German for cake," Addie said, cutting a slice for Lew Bentz. "My people were German. An old family recipe handed down from my great grandmother."

When the coffee was poured and everyone had a plate loaded with *kuchen*, she sat, picked up her plate, and smiled. "Well, what's new?"

For the next hour, they sat in the Bullock living room chatting, sipping coffee, and eating *kuchen* filled with apples and topped with rich custard made from eggs and cream. Despite Addie Bullock's curiosity about him, he felt surprisingly at ease. The harshness of the weather outside made the hospitality inside even warmer.

There was no judgment here. The Langstroms, the Bullocks, Lew Bentz, the others he'd met in Alder. They lived simply in a world of quiet contentment, curious about new things and strangers, but not in a critical way.

Sole fended off Addie's questions with the well-rehearsed history of his false identity. The conversation shifted to other topics. It started with the weather, always a primary consideration Sole was learning. The talk shifted to the status of Bentz's wife and children, moved to a similar report on the Bullock grandchildren who lived in what seemed an impossibly faraway town in Arizona with the Bullock's daughter and her husband who were doing very well and who promised to visit soon in the spring when things warmed up a bit, then made a full circle back to a discussion of the weather.

At that point, Bentz placed his coffee cup on the table and stood. "I suppose we should get back to Alder. I have to be on duty in an hour."

Ernie Bullock pulled himself from his chair with a grunt and shook hands. Addie gave Sole a hug. "It's nice to have you here, Bill Myers. Hope you'll think about staying on."

"I'll think about it," Sole promised.

On the way back to Alder, Sole did think about it. It was not a place he would have ever considered as a settling down spot. Far removed from Georgia, from anything he'd ever known, he found the empty horizons, drawing him in. A place for forgetting things, where he could lose memories in the vast emptiness.

TWENTY

Speed It Up

A.C. Demeron stood with his wife Lorraine in the glass-enclosed front porch of the family ranch house, watching the helicopter's slow descent on the other side of the front yard. The space could have served as a playing field for three simultaneous football games. Ranch hands had cleared the snow away from a patch of grass, then drove tractors back and forth to tamp down the surrounding area to reduce the blowback from the rotor wash. It did little good. The passengers remained in their seats while the blades spun down to a stop, and the swirling white blizzard dissipated.

Once the snow settled back to the ground, Senator William Kellin was the first down the steps. At the bottom, he turned toward the cockpit and gave a snappy salute.

"What the fuck?" The pilots exchanged a bemused look. The one in the left seat shook his head and said, "This guy thinks he's the president coming off Air Force One."

"Practicing for the future, maybe," the right seat laughed.

"Not with my vote," left seat replied and threw up a sloppy half salute, half wave. Right seat chuckled and started going over the preflight checklist for the trip back to Sioux Falls.

Behind Kellin, Elizabeth Ranskill and the others heard the pilots laughing, saw the mocking salute from the left seat, and suppressed their own chuckles. Ranskill started down the steps, threw a look over her shoulder at her companions, and said, "Prepare yourselves, boys. Our leader has gone into full pompous ass mode."

Three ranch hands roared up in enclosed, four-seater ATVs. Kellin and Ranskill sat in the rear of the first, Parson and Taylor in the second. When the baggage was loaded in the third, they roared across the snowscape to the ranch house.

The ranch house was a rambling affair, expanded by each successive Demeron generation. A massive great room with a stone fireplace that filled an entire wall, added by Demeron's grandfather. A dining room with a thirty-foot table, added by his father. A.C.'s contribution was an entire wing to house his special guests.

As the ATVs rumbled to a stop, Demeron left the warmth of the enclosed porch and descended to greet his guests. A handshake and friendly pat on the shoulder and he sent them up the steps where Lorraine waited to give each a hug and pull them in out of the cold. Demeron followed the last, Simon Taylor, up the steps while the ranch hands trailed behind with the luggage.

Hot toddies were waiting for them in the great room. An oversized fire burned in the massive fireplace. Within a few minutes, warmed by sweetened whiskey, lulled by the firelight flickering off the walls, sitting deep in plush chairs, the trials of the trip were forgotten and any ill-humor they may have had about the inconveniences they'd endured faded away.

Lorraine saw that they were comfortable and then excused herself to see about dinner. She allowed Demeron a half-hour to play the beneficent host before returning to announce with a smile, "Soup's on. Hope you're hungry. Follow me to the dining room."

She led them down a wide hallway to the dining room, where one end of the long table had been set for them. The fine china and crystal glassware were Lorraine's contributions to the ranch's ambiance, a reminder to the guests that despite the rugged conditions outside, here, their world was protected and filled with the familiar elegance and comforts to which they were accustomed.

"How's the pheasant hunting?" Kellin looked up from his plate, a sly grin on his face. "I've been telling our friends here that they will have an experience to remember. I hope you won't let me down."

"The hunting is excellent," Demeron beamed. "Tomorrow we'll load up and take you out to the preserve. Tonight, let's relax. You've had a long trip. Dinner and drinks and a good night's sleep and tomorrow we'll be on the pheasants."

After dinner, the party moved to a den, smaller than the great room, and more intimate. More drinks and cigars for those who wanted one. Kellin and Ranskill were the only smokers, but everyone poured themselves a drink from the wood-paneled bar recessed into a wall.

When they were all settled, Demeron excused himself. "Have to go check on arrangements for tomorrow. Be right back."

He didn't go far. An alcove off the main hall held a computer, printer, and desk for the use of guests. Demeron sat at the desk, pulled out his phone, and punched in a number. Huey Cooke answered.

"Are we set for tomorrow?" Demeron asked tersely.

"Working on it, boss."

"Not good enough!" Demeron's voice rose. He looked over his shoulder to make sure no one heard and then leaned forward, elbows on the desk, speaking more quietly in a threatening tone that sent chills up Huey Cooke's soft spine. "Those girls didn't make it in the cold on foot. Maybe you will."

Most people would have taken the threat to send him packing on foot in the middle of winter with a grain of salt, hyperbole, just the emotion talking. Huey Cooke took it seriously. He'd seen Demeron's temper explode before if he didn't get what he wanted, when he wanted it.

"It's taken care of," Cooke said, swallowing hard. "They'll be here."

"They better be!" Demeron hissed and punched the end-call button on his phone.

Cooke sat at the desk in his barn office for a minute trying to calm his fluttering heart, then he looked at the notepad where he had jotted down the number Finch gave him earlier in the day. He thumbed the numbers into his phone. It rang four times, five times, six ... he worried no one would answer. Then a voice came on the line.

"Who is this?"

"I'm ..." Cooke hesitated. Even *he* knew that using names over the phone was a bad idea. "This is your customer."

"Customer?" There was a pause. Hank in the box truck looked at Jimmy and shrugged.

In the back, Riggs said, "Who is it? Finch?"

"No. Says he's our customer."

"Give me the phone." Riggs held his hand out through the door opening. Hank passed the phone to him. He held it to his ear and said, "Who gave you this number?"

"Not supposed to use names, but it was the people who sent you." Cooke paused. How could he prove to them who he was? Then he started speaking rapidly, "Look, I'm your customer. How else would I get the number? It's a burner, right? But I have the number, so you have to know where I got it."

Riggs thought that through for a second and nodded. "Alright. What do you want?"

"I need you here by morning."

Riggs laughed. "That's not gonna happen. You know what the weather's been like."

"It's getting better here, clearing up," Cooke said. "I need you to get here quick by morning."

"Dude, are you not listening? The weather is shit here. The roads are shit. We'll get there when we can. That's the best I can say."

"What if I make you a deal?" Cooke threw out.

"What kind of deal." Riggs looked at the others and shrugged. Then he was quiet while Cooke spoke. After a minute, he nodded again and said, "Alright. We have a deal."

He ended the call and looked at the men up front. "Let's speed it up."

"Really?" Jimmy said, glancing in the rearview mirror. "Just because he says to?"

"Nope. Not because he says to." Riggs smiled. "Because there's an extra thousand apiece in it for us, off the record, cash money."

"Seriously?" Hank turned to look through the door.

"Seriously." Riggs nodded.

"Works for me." Jimmy wrapped his hands tighter around the wheel and hit the accelerator.

Behind them, Malina and Sherry felt the truck jolt forward, the rear end fishtailing on the slick road before straightening out. They braced themselves against the wall and glared at Riggs.

Cindy let out a whimpering sob, her lip trembling.

Bobbi muttered, "Motherfuckers."

Brad sat with his forehead resting on his knees, eyes closed, pushing himself deeper into the world inside his mind, looking for some escape there.

Riggs rested the pistol on his knee and smiled. "Won't be much longer now."

TWENTY-ONE

Not Very Happy

A mile out of Alder on the way back from Addie and Ernie Bullock's place, the radio in Lew Bentz's SUV crackled to life. "Dispatch to unit four, Lew, are you on duty yet?"

"Can be, Lori. What's up?"

"Got some sort of dispute over repairs. Johnny Walts called it in."

"I'll handle it. What's the location?"

"122 Farm Road 280 at the section line."

"Shit," Bentz muttered, then keyed the mic. "10-4. I'm enroute."

"Problem?" Sole asked from the passenger seat.

"That's Bob Shank's place. Nothing good ever comes from dealing with that asshole." He pulled the SUV over and spun the wheel, reversing course. "Sorry for the delay. I'll get you back to Alder as soon as I take care of this."

"No hurry. I got nowhere to go," Sole said with a shrug. "Nice to be out and about, anyway."

"Nicer if I didn't have to deal with Bob Shank right off

the bat. Son of a bitch would pick a fight with his shadow on a cloudy day."

Bentz turned down a gravel road where the snow had been packed down by farm vehicles. A mile farther, he made another turn down another gravel road. Two more miles and he pulled into a long dirt drive lined on both sides by five strands of barbed wire.

The drive ended in a wide lot that would have been bare dirt if not for the snowpack. A hundred-year-old farmhouse sat on one side of the lot. A three-level barn stood a hundred yards away on the other side, its bottom level excavated into the side of a small hill as a place to keep livestock during the harsh South Dakota winters.

With a little upkeep, it would have all made a picturesque scene. As it was, the house needed paint, its bare plank siding warped and pulling away in places. The main entry door to the barn lay where it had fallen on the ground during a spring storm.

"There he is," Bentz said and steered toward the side of the house and a pickup parked beside a small six-by-six building. "That's the well-house."

The magnetic sign on the pickup's door read *Walts Plumbing*. Bentz pulled alongside and a gaunt man got out of the pickup in a billowing cloud of cigarette smoke. He pushed his hand down into the pocket of his canvass work jacket and retrieved a pack of cigarettes, took the butt from his mouth, tossed it into the snow, and lit another.

Gaunt was the best word to describe Johnny Walts. He stood waiting on spindly legs that made his heavy work boots look like oversized clown shoes. High cheekbones, sunken cheeks, eyes staring out from deep within their sockets, everything about him was skeletal. He looked like you might hear his bones click and rattle if he fell over.

Bentz got out and walked over. "What's the problem, Johnny?"

"Son of a bitch won't pay me," Walts said, lighting the cigarette and inhaling deeply.

"Explain. Gotta have more information than that."

"Alright," Walts said, taking the cigarette from between his lips. "Called me out here to fix his well. Pipes froze and busted. Dumbass didn't check to make sure the heat lamp inside the well-house was working" Walts nodded at the well-house. "Spent the whole day freezing my ass off, cleaning up the mess, fixing the pipes, putting in a new thermostat-controlled heat lamp, and now he says he ain't paying me."

"Why?"

"Because he's an asshole. That's why. We had a deal and now he won't pay. I want you to lock him up."

"Need more than that," Bentz said, stifling a smile. Shank did stand at the head of the line when it came to assholes, but no one had ever written a law to make assholery illegal. "Why's he saying he won't pay?"

"Because I installed the old heat lamp a couple of years ago, the last time his pipes broke So now, he let me do all the work today and then says he don't owe a dime because it's my responsibility the heat lamp burned out." Walts pointed a skinny finger at the house and spat into the snow, raising his voice so that Shank would have to hear it inside. "That's bullshit, and he knows it. Lamps burn out. That's what they do. It's his job to check them out now and again and put a new one in if it ain't lighting up. That's just regular common sense." Walts turned back to Bentz. "Ain't it Lew? Homeowner is responsible for taking care of things ... maintenance and stuff like that once I do the installation. Right?"

"Seems reasonable," Bentz said. "I'll go talk with him and get his side."

"You already heard my side. He told it to you." Bob Shank came trudging around the side of the house. "I heard what he said, and I meant what I said. It's his responsibility, so I'm not paying. Now get the fuck off my property."

Bentz turned to face him and stepped forward until they were less than a yard apart, their frosty breath mingling in the air. "I'm here investigating a report of a crime, so I think I'll stay."

"Bullshit! There's no crime." Shank bowed up and pointed a thick finger in Walts' face. "I'm not paying the little weasel for work that shoulda been done right the first time."

"It was done right, you sorry sack of …" Walts began, but Bentz held up a hand to silence him.

"I know Johnny's work, and it's always been good, so here's the way it is, Shank." Bentz leaned closer. "You called him out to fix your well. He did that, from what I can tell. Now you owe him …" Bentz looked at Walts "How much?"

Walts reached inside his jacket and pulled out a folded sheet of paper. "Says right here. Four hundred-twenty-two dollars … time, labor and parts."

Bentz nodded. "You heard him. Four hundred-twenty-two dollars."

"There is no fucking way I'm paying that!" Shank shouted. "And nothing you can do will make me pay it!"

"Then I suppose I'll have to place you under arrest for theft of services, and since the amount is over four hundred dollars, that makes the charge a class one petty theft." Bentz smiled. "That'll get you a two thousand dollar fine and a year in jail unless the judge cuts you some slack, and with your personality, Shank, I doubt that's going to happen."

"Arrest me?" Shank stepped closer still. "You think you're man enough to do it?"

Sole had watched the encounter from inside the SUV. Now he stepped out, walked to the front of the SUV, and leaned against the fender.

"What do you think you're doing?" Shank growled. "You want your ass beat too?"

"Nope," Sole said. "Just making room in the car for when Deputy Bentz cuffs you and drags your ass off to jail."

"Is that a fact?" Shank blustered, but his eyes darted from Bentz to Sole and back.

"That's a fact." Sole nodded.

"So, you gonna give him a hand," Shank smirked. "That it?"

"I don't figure he's going to need any help from me, handling a blowhard like you."

Shank's face reddened even in the cold, but he said nothing, looking from one face to the other—Bentz's hard as flint, Sole's amused, Walts' wide-eyed at the drama playing out before him.

Bentz ended the silence. "What's it gonna be, Shank?"

"Not right, what you're doing here," Shank grumbled. "His work was shoddy."

"I doubt it," Bentz said. "But you can always take Johnny to court and sue him over a heat lamp bulb you should have been smart enough to replace. I don't think you'll have much luck there either, but today, you're going to pay up or go to jail."

"This isn't over." Shank leaned toward Bentz. "We're gonna settle this some time. Come on a man's property, threaten him …" The red in Shank's cheeks turned deep crimson and he shook his head, speaking through his teeth. "It ain't over."

"Let's get your checkbook and settle up," Bentz replied calmly. He looked at Walts. "Johnny, let me have that invoice you wrote up."

Shank turned toward the house without speaking. Bentz followed.

"Lew, you goin' in there with him ... just like that?" Walts called after him, concerned. Standing outside arguing was one thing, but following the bear into his den seemed unnecessarily risky.

"I'll be fine. You stay here with Bill until I get back with your money."

Sole watched them go around the side of the house, and the cop inside him told him to follow. He listened for trouble —a shout, a struggle, something that might let him know what was happening inside. There was nothing, only the sound of the wind skittering across the top of the snow.

He knew Bentz was handling things correctly. Keep the civilians out of harm's way. He reminded himself that was exactly what he was now ... a civilian.

Several minutes passed. Walts whispered, "What's taking them so long?"

Civilian or not, Sole was about to head to the house and check on things when Bentz came around the side. He handed a check to Walts. "He's paid up. Now let's get the hell out of the cold."

"Thanks, Lew." Walts took the check and nodded. I was getting nervous some about how long it was taking."

"Just Shank being Shank. Had to pretend he couldn't find his checkbook, then a pen to write with." Bentz shrugged. "Just his way of dragging things out and saving face a little, and it didn't hurt anything to let him do it."

Sole realized Bentz was a good cop. He might come across as an easygoing country boy, but he knew when to stand his ground and how to let things simmer down after he'd won the battle. A lot of cops never learned when to let up, played the hardass all the time, and ended up getting themselves or someone else hurt.

They got into the SUV and followed Johnny Walts' pickup past the house and down the drive. Bob Shank came out on the porch, raised a fist, and shouted, "This ain't over! You motherfuckers, get off my property!"

"He's not very happy," Sole said, smiling. "And I don't think he likes you."

"Nope." Bentz shrugged. "It's okay. I don't like him very much either."

TWENTY-TWO

Creepy
___

"Well, aren't you lovely." It was a statement, not a question. Senator William Kellin emerged from relieving himself in the powder room off the main hallway and stopped, his eyes devouring the young woman standing in the foyer by the front door.

She stomped the snow off her calfskin boots. Kellin's eyes followed the tight-fitting designer jeans from the top of the boots up her legs and thighs to where they disappeared under the hem of her quilted jacket. She pulled a knit cap from her head, shook out her hair, auburn tresses falling over the jacket collar in a seductive, fashion-magazine way, and smiled radiantly, curious but not surprised to find a stranger in the house.

Eyes fixed on her like a man watching a girl work the pole in the front row of a strip club, Kellin strode down the hallway and extended a hand, damp with excitement and arousal. He introduced himself. "Bill Kellin, and who might you be?"

He took her hand in his and cupped the other over the

top in an uncomfortable, overly intimate way. She gave his palm a quick squeeze and tried to pull away, but he held on. Trapped, all she could say was, "Uh, hello. I'm Tessa."

"You are extraordinary, Tessa." Kellin held on in his two-handed grip as if the vision before him might vanish.

"Umm ... thank you." Tessa pulled again to free her hand from his grasp, and again he held firm, gazing into her eyes.

Kellin stepped closer. "Will you be here all week?"

"Well, yes ... I mean ..."

"Senator Kellin!" A.C. Demeron's voice boomed down the corridor. "I see you've met ... my daughter, Tessa."

Her hand might have been a hot coal fresh out of the fireplace. Kellin almost threw it down and away and turned red-faced toward Demeron. "Yes, I was ... just that I ..."

Tessa folded her arms across her chest, tucking her hands safely out of the way. Demeron stepped between them, leaned over, and gave his daughter a peck on the cheek.

"Tessa, Senator Kellin will be spending the night here. Tomorrow we're heading out to the lodge at the preserve for a pheasant hunt." Demeron smiled, ignoring the awkward moment between the senator and his daughter with an ease that made Kellin relax while his daughter raised a confused eyebrow. "Why don't you let your mother know you're home. She's been holding your supper for you."

"Alright." Tessa threw a glance at Kellin, mumbled, "Nice to meet you," and hurried down the hallway.

When she was out of earshot, Kellin began stammering. "Demeron, I had no idea ... I mean, she is such a lovely creature."

Demeron's face twitched. *Lovely creature* was not a term customarily used by older men to describe his daughter—

not to his face, at least. He took a breath before responding. He needed Kellin, and after all, no harm was done.

"I understand the mistake," he said in a nobly forgiving tone. "I should have warned you that Tessa was coming home from school for the weekend, but you understand that our business here will not include her in any fashion."

"Of course not," Kellin sputtered. "I understand completely, and please accept my apologies."

Message sent that his daughter was strictly off-limits, Demeron smiled and nodded. "No apology necessary. It was an honest mistake, Bill." He patted the senator on the shoulder and smiled. "Let's go back to the others. I want to discuss some business before we go off to the hunt tomorrow." He ended with a chuckle. "Things may be a bit too distracting to focus later."

"No doubt." Kellin nodded emphatically, relieved to change the subject.

Demeron led the way back to the den. Tessa went to see her mother, relieved to be away from the strange man and his damp, clinging hands. A student at Augustana University in Sioux Falls, she often came home on weekends, maintaining her independence by refusing the limo service her father offered and driving the H3 Hummer her parents had given her as a high school graduation gift.

"Who are those people with Dad?" she asked, sitting at the island bar in the kitchen, picking at the plate her mother brought out of the warming oven.

"Just some people your father wants to join him in a business venture." Excused by her husband from the business portion of the evening, Lorraine Demeron sat across the granite, scrolling through her phone while her daughter ate.

"Business?" Tessa looked up from her plate. "I met that

Senator Kellin. He's going into business with Dad? Is that legal ... a senator making business deals while he's in office?"

"I suppose it's legal. Depends on the business deal, I imagine." Lorraine shrugged and looked at her daughter. "When did you meet the senator?"

"Just now, coming in. He met me in the foyer."

"He met you?" Lorraine put down her phone. "What happened?"

"Not much. It was uncomfortable, though ... too familiar for a stranger." Tessa shook her head and made a sour face. "I thought he was going to hit on me, right here in my own house."

"What happened?" Lorraine's eyes narrowed, a sudden tension in her voice.

"Nothing, really. Dad came down the hall, introduced us, then whisked him away from me."

"Alright." Lorraine nodded. "He'll be gone tomorrow. Dad's taking him and the others out to the preserve for a pheasant hunt. You won't have to see him again."

"Good. Senator or not, he's creepy in a dirty-old-man sort of way." Tessa nodded and loaded her fork, then paused. "What kind of business does Dad have with a man like that?"

"Enough questions. You know I don't involve myself in your father's business. He's always working on something. I'm sure the senator is here in an advisory capacity, perfectly legal." Lorraine smiled and changed the subject. "How's your dinner?"

TWENTY-THREE

Change For A Twenty

"I'll take another, Bill ... before Alva comes back out."

"You got it." Sole grabbed the glass from the bar top, tossed in a couple of ice cubes, added equal amounts of Jack and Coke, and slid it across to a skinny ranch hand.

He'd learned that the ranch hand, Arnold Cowley, was a regular. Always grinning, and a non-stop talker, he stopped by each day at opening time for breakfast and again in the evening for dinner and a nightcap. He sipped and smiled. "You pour a damned good drink, Bill."

Sole ran a bar rag over the counter. "Glad you like it."

"I do ... I do." Cowley lifted the glass and took another long gulp and set it down. "How about another."

He turned to Johnny Walts, seated to one side. "Don't Bill Myers pour a fine drink?"

"He does, for a fact," Walts said, lifting his glass and staring into the amber liquid appreciatively.

"I see what you're doing there, Bill Myers." Alva Langstrom stepped from the back room with a stack of bar napkins. "No wonder my customers have taken a liking to you … pouring away my whiskey and my profits like that."

"What are you complaining about, Alva?" Harry Langstrom turned from the grill where he was browning up some burgers. "Look around. Damn place is fuller than it's been in months and they keep drinking. Whatever he pours away, we'll make back in volume."

Alva gazed up and down the bar. Thirsty ranch hands and farmers sat at every stool, and there wasn't an empty chair at any of the tables. A few customers at the end of the bar stood holding beers and waiting for a seat. Their prospects didn't look good, as everyone seemed to have settled in for the long haul, but they showed no sign of caring, drinking their beers standing, and swapping stories.

Alva let out a "Humph," giving grudging acknowledgment to her husband's reasoning, then added, "Just the same, Bill Myers. You give them an honest pour and not a drop more."

"As you wish, Alva," Sole said, and as Alva turned away, sloshed an extra half shot of scotch over the rocks in a glass.

The customers nearby laughed. Alva whirled, staring. The laughter ceased, and the drinkers stared at their glasses. Sole ran a bar rag over the surface, humming innocently, which prompted more laughter.

Alva gave a final, "Humph," turned, walked over to Harry, and gave him a peck on the cheek. "I'll see you at the house."

"Okay, dear." He returned the peck and went back to the burgers on the grill.

She gave a final warning to the crowd that parted like the Red Sea as she made her way to the door. "I don't suppose you boys'll be laughing when you drink us out of business."

Then she was out the door, and the bar erupted in laughter again. A dozen conversations sprang up, crossing over, mixing one with another. A snippet here got a response from someone over there, which required a remark from another corner.

Lew Bentz came in, stomping snow from his boots. He walked to the bar, and Johnny Walts jumped up. "Here, Lew, take my seat. I owe you for what you did today."

"Sit back down. You don't owe me, Johnny. Just doing the job. Besides, I just came in to warm up a bit."

"What'll you have, Lew?" Sole asked from behind the bar.

"Just coffee, black and hot. I'm on duty."

"Right." Sole reached for the pot, filled a cup, and handed it to him.

"What'd Lew do for you?" Cowley asked, sensing a good story. "Why'd you say you owe him?"

"Took care of that asshole Bob Shank, that's what," Walts said, sipping his drink.

"No shit. Let's hear it." Cowley leaned close so as not to miss a word. The rumble of voices ceased and everyone else did the same.

Walts swiveled around on the stool, drink in hand, and held forth on what an asshole Bob Shank was. He described in great detail the intricate repairs he made to the well, a day of honest toil at the end of which he expected a fair settlement. When he got to Shank's refusal to pay, the room filled with a chorus of invective.

"That asshole."

"What a son of a bitch."

"Cheap ass motherfucker."

Walts held up his hand and waited for the comments to die away, then wrapped things up. "But Lew, here, came and put the son of a bitch in his place. Told him he'd put him in jail if he didn't pay up."

Bentz listened, sipping coffee and wishing Walts would let it go. He shook his head and said, "Told you, Johnny, just doing the job. We don't need to be stirring things up about anyone around here," He smiled. "I like it nice and peaceful. Don't you?"

"Why sure I do," Walts said, grinning. "That's me, peaceful all the way. You know that. It's just that …"

The door opened and Walts clamped his mouth shut. Bob Shank stood hulking in the doorway, staring at the crowd for a few seconds, as if suspecting what they'd been talking about. Walts swiveled back around on his stool. Everyone else went back to their conversations, more muted than before.

Shank pushed his way to the bar. He leaned over, thrust his beefy arm between two patrons, put a twenty on the bar top. "Bourbon and Coke."

Sole nodded, poured the drink, and set it down. Shank reached in again to retrieve it and, without saying a word, the two men on the stools in front stood up and moved away to stand with another group in the corner. Shank took one stool. No one sat on the other.

Sole picked up the twenty to make change.

"Leave it," Shank said. "If I drink it up, I'll put down more."

Sole looked at Harry Langstrom. "That work for you?"

"I said, leave it," Shank snapped.

"Harry?" Sole kept the twenty in his hand.

"Goddamn, you. Put that bill back on the bar." Shank half rose from the stool.

"It's alright." Langstrom nodded. "Bob, usually lets his money lay until he's ready to go."

"Alright." Sole turned and put the twenty in front of Shank.

"Who the hell you think you are?" Shank glared at him.

"Tonight, I'm the bartender." Sole smiled and stared into Shank's eyes.

"Look like a fucking pussy to me," Shank sneered. "Ought to be wearing an apron."

Their eyes locked, the calm smile on Sole's face contrasted with the snarl on Shank's.

"That's enough." Lew Bentz put his coffee cup on the bar top and stepped up beside Shank. "Haven't you had enough trouble for the day, Bob?"

"Only trouble I've had is you meddling in my affairs. And here you are again, right in the middle of things." Shank's eyes narrowed. "That's a dangerous place to be. You might keep that in mind."

"Threatening a law enforcement officer? That's a violation of the law and …" Bentz said. "You might want *to keep that* in mind."

"Goddamnit. I told you before, this ain't over." Shank stood and reached for his money.

Sole picked up the twenty.

"What the fuck you think you're doing!" Shank shouted.

"I'll get your change," Sole said.

"Change hell! I didn't drink it! "

"I poured it. You'll pay."

"The fuck I will." Shank leaned forward over the bar. "You best hand over that twenty."

"I'll get your change." Sole smiled.

"You son of a bitch!" Shank's face contorted in frustrated rage, but he stood there powerless in the face of Sole's indifference. Others in the room were not so unconcerned. The general consensus was that at any moment, they would be picking what was left of Bill Myers up off the floor. Even Lew Bentz took a step closer, concerned that he might have to intervene.

He didn't. Shank glared red-faced and impotent at Sole, but he did nothing. Sole made the change for the drink and laid it on the bar top.

"Goddamn you," Shank sputtered. He scooped up the money and whirled, glaring at Bentz and then at everyone in the bar. "Goddamn, all of you."

He stormed out into the night. A sort of awkward silence descended over the room. Sole ran the rag over the bar nonchalantly and said mildly, "Well, that was interesting."

Laughter echoed around the room once more. The conversations picked up again, mostly about what an asshole Bob Shank was and how Bill Myers put him in his place by making change for a twenty.

TWENTY-FOUR

I'm In

The party was still in progress in a sedate sort of way. Ranskill was speaking to no one in particular about hedge fund investment strategies, short selling, and leveraged buyouts.

Parson half-listened to her for a while, nodding occasionally, then opened the humidor and took out a cigar, going through the process of clipping the end and lighting up as a way to politely ignore Ranskill's lecture. After a few puffs, his face wrinkled, and he placed it in an ashtray, but as Ranskill continued speaking without stopping, he picked it up again, twirling it between his fingers as a distraction.

Taylor remained aloof, as always. He sat in a corner, sipping a glass of cabernet, scrolling through his phone, and doing his best to ignore everything around him.

Demeron and Kellin sat in a corner of the room speaking quietly. A clock on the fireplace mantle chimed eleven times. The guests were well-lubricated, and relaxed. Timing was everything. Demeron nodded and Kellin cleared his throat loudly.

Parson breathed a sigh of relief and stretched as if he might stand and head off to bed. Taylor looked up from his phone and adjusted his eyeglasses. Ranskill's lecture ended as if she'd been speaking merely to fill the silence. With Kellin back in the conversation, there was no need for that.

"Alright, heads up. Our host wants to get down to business," Kellin called out like a head coach hustling the team together for a locker room pep talk, completely recovered from any embarrassment he might have felt over hitting on their host's daughter.

"It's a little late for business," Parson said.

"Yes," Ranskill added. "Can't this wait until tomorrow?"

"Trust me." Kellin smiled. "You'll be much too busy for business tomorrow." He stepped aside for Demeron. "They're all yours, A.C."

Ranskill and Parson exchanged an amused *can-you-believe-this-guy* look. Kellin was as much a pompous windbag in private as he was on the campaign stump. Taylor, oblivious to the humor and generally quiet in social settings, sat up straight and tucked his phone in a pocket.

Demeron ignored Kellin's bombast and began, "First, let me assure you that tomorrow starts the real hunt, and while the delays have been unavoidable ..." He gave a theatrical aside and shrug. "My extensive influence does not extend to the weather gods ... I assure you, the hunt will not disappoint you."

He paused for effect before continuing, signaling that it was time to get serious. "I want to make a proposal."

"We know that," Ranskill interrupted. "That's why we're here, so get to it."

"Very good." Demeron nodded, the smile unflinching. "Let's get down to business. I have a proposal that will make us all very rich."

"We're already rich," Simon Taylor said, his eyes narrowing. Quiet and even backward in social situations, he was the lawyer and academic in the group. Demeron knew Taylor would be the one asking the tough questions.

"True enough." Demeron nodded. "But what I am about to propose has enough potential that ..." He gave a wink and said, "That we might all be as rich as Liz Ranskill."

Ranskill smiled. "In your dreams."

Kellin and Parson chuckled. Taylor pulled out his phone again, opened a notepad screen. "Get to it then, Demeron. This is why we're here, no doubt ... pheasant hunting aside."

They all knew that the pheasant hunt was not an aside. It was the quid pro quo, the reason they were willing to listen to him at all. He nodded. "Alright, here it is."

Demeron took a breath like a swimmer on the starting block and dove in, outlining his plan.

He would fund the startup of a new cryptocurrency. Each of them would have a role to play in its success.

Ranskill and Parson would establish it as a desirable investment. Making it part of their various fund portfolios would increase demand for the new crypto in the marketplace.

Federal regulators were increasing oversight of cryptocurrencies. As chairman of the Senate Banking Committee, Kellin would use his influence to breeze through committee approvals and oversight.

Taylor would be the scholarly voice of reason, testifying before the committee when necessary. He would also serve as the cryptocurrency's Chief Legal Officer, adding an air of legitimacy to the venture.

As the discussion wound down, Taylor sat back. The

others remained silent while he scanned his notes. When he looked up, he made the obvious comment. "Seems risky."

"Of course, there is some risk." Demeron nodded. "You know the adage. No risk, no gain. Great risk, great gain. The risk is the reason I gathered you all here. Together we can mitigate the risk, reduce it as close to zero as possible."

"I have to admit to not knowing a great deal about cryptocurrencies," Taylor said. "But as I understand it, there is nothing backing them … not real money … no gold or silver … no product of any kind … nothing fungible. Their value is based on …" He shook his head. "Nothing."

"Not exactly nothing. The value of cryptocurrency is based on demand … what people will spend to acquire it."

"And when there is no demand?" Taylor asked, eyes narrowed. "Then there's nothing behind it."

"That's our job," Demeron said, nodding. "We create the demand … make them want to buy our new cryptocurrency. That's the point and the beauty of it. The fact that it doesn't represent anything except a number in a database somewhere works to our benefit. We don't have to amass any great quantity of any product to establish it as valid. No one can come to us and demand x-number of widgets, or gold, or cheese doodles in exchange for the like-value of the crypto coins they've purchased. We only have to market it … make people want it and mine it or buy it, and the more they want it and buy it, the higher the value goes."

Taylor's head was shaking back and forth again. "It seems very unreal … ethereal … like buying and selling air."

"You've got it!" Demeron pointed a finger at Taylor and smiled. "If people thought air was in limited supply or that others were going to get it all … breathe it all before they could or hoard it … store it away somewhere …" Demeron nodded. "The value of air would go through the roof, and those who ran the air bank would be ..." He paused and looked at the others. "Well, what would you pay for your next breath of air if you thought there wasn't anymore?"

"But there is more," Taylor threw back. "All around us. We don't have to pay for it ... just breathe it in. This cryptocurrency, as you explain it, would be numbers in a computer somewhere. Anyone can make up their own numbers. Like air, there is an unlimited supply of numbers."

"Except in this case, we control the supply of numbers ... of our crypto. Using your air analogy, we control the air supply."

"But why would they want our ... your ... crypto over any others?" Taylor shook his head doubtfully.

Unphased, Demeron pushed on, "That's where Liz and Oliver come in. We market it, make people think they have to get in on it, because their investment funds are buying it. Their role is to give our cryptocurrency substance ... value ... not because it represents anything, but because everyone else wants it."

Taylor sat quietly for a minute while the others waited and watched the wheels turning in his head. Demeron had chosen him carefully for his standing in the legal and academic worlds. His presence before Senate Banking Committee would lend an air of legitimacy to the project.

Taylor said nothing for a few seconds, then asked, "And what happens when there are no more buyers? We're left with a lot of meaningless numbers and nothing else."

"That's why I called you all here. This is a team effort. Look around." Demeron nodded at Ranskill and Parson. "The investment portfolios Liz and Oliver manage will invest ... buy the new crypto. Not too much at first, just enough to generate interest. Then, when the rush to buy is on, they'll keep us ahead of the game, and when the value drops, when demand decreases, they let us know and we sell our crypto holdings ahead of the plunge. We're left with the gains and …"

"And everyone else loses," Taylor said, his eyes narrowed.

"They would lose anyway," Ranskill interjected. "Crypto investors are speculators in the truest sense of the word. That the object of their speculation has no intrinsic value and could drop to zero overnight has not slowed them one bit. So, we capitalize on their demand for crypto, take our earnings … winnings really … then sell out before the market goes bust. It's the ultimate investment speculation."

"And you're alright with that?" Taylor looked at her over his glasses.

"Investors have been speculating on worthless investments for hundreds of years … Florida swampland, worthless gold mines, crappy art by famous, or infamous, people. The list of worthless investments is lengthy. The difference here is that we will control the market. We drive it up, and if it starts to go bust, we cash in." She nodded at Demeron. "I'm in."

"Me too," Parson said.

Kellin smiled and nodded. He'd been in all along, had bought into the idea when Demeron approached him two months earlier, had arranged the pheasant hunting trip for the group.

The scheme was a new take on an old fraud … insider trading, and it could land them in deep shit with the SEC. That's why they needed Kellin and especially Taylor to lend legitimacy to the project and make sure the Feds' prying eyes were focused elsewhere.

"We need you, Simon," Demeron said. "The Senate Banking Committee has taken a keen interest in the cryptocurrency market. Your participation ... your opinions ... will ease their concerns."

Taylor was silent again for a minute, thinking, then looked at Ranskill and asked, "What kind of return can we expect?"

Ranskill smiled. "I know of a crypto that grew twelve thousand percent over two months."

"Twelve thous ..." Taylor blinked and shook his head. "Did I hear correctly? You said ..."

"Twelve thousand percent." Ranskill nodded. "But that would be the exception. A more conservative estimate would be an annual increase of a hundred to two hundred percent if marketed correctly, and Oliver and I would see to that."

She failed to mention the thousands of cryptocurrencies that had tanked and were now worth exactly zero, their owners left with nothing because the crypto they'd bought was nothing more than a digit in a computer somewhere.

Taylor looked at Ranskill. "a hundred or two hundred percent ... annually?"

"That's right."

Taylor had asked all of his questions. He nodded. "I'm in."

TWENTY-FIVE

Pit Stop

"Slow it down," Riggs called through the door to the truck cab. "You're going to roll us into a ditch."

"You said speed it up," Jimmy replied over his shoulder, then leaned forward over the wheel to peer ahead, squinting into the glare of the truck's headlights reflected off the snow. Beyond the glare, there was nothing but black. He added, "I want that bonus money."

"You get us killed, there won't be any bonus money. We're getting close, slow it a little, and let's make sure we get there in one piece."

"I got things under control," Jimmy said.

"Do what he says," Hank snapped from the passenger seat.

Right." Jimmy nodded and eased up on the accelerator.

There was a perceptible shifting of the passengers in the back as the truck's momentum decreased. Everyone eased a bit from bracing themselves against the walls without having to worry about being thrown around by a sudden swerve or bump. Other than that, they were still miserable.

Huddled in their padded furniture blankets, their muscles cramped and aching from sitting on the hard steel floor for two days. They hadn't eaten in hours, which was just as well. With the truck's high-speed and swaying motion, using the slop bucket risked turning the interior cargo space into a cesspool. Riggs allowed them to take turns when the truck stopped for brief breaks, but there was never enough time for all five captives to use it before they were back on the road.

Malina had to go. She squeezed her legs shut, grimacing in discomfort. It was only a matter of time before she had an accident that would turn the rest of the trip into a soggy, piss-smelling hell.

"I have to go," she said to Riggs.

"Next time we stop." He leaned back in the lawn chair, relaxed, snug in his parka, the pistol resting as always on his knee.

"I can't wait," she said. "I didn't get a turn the last two times we stopped."

"We'll be there soon." Riggs shook his head. "Take care of it then. You'll be first."

"I'm telling you, I can't wait."

"For fuck's sake." Bobbi lifted her head from resting on her knees, glaring at Riggs. "Let her go before she pisses herself!"

"I really do have to go," Malina said softly, pleading. "I'm not lying."

Riggs shifted his scowl from Bobbi to Malina, then sighed and nodded. He called through the door into the cab, "Pull it over where you find a spot. They need a pit stop."

"Right." Jimmy took his foot off the accelerator and

scanned ahead. "Not much of anyplace to stop. Can't see far in the dark ... just snow to the horizon looks like."

"Just stop where you can. We'll make it quick," Riggs said, then looked at Malina and emphasized, "Make it quick."

"I will, I promise."

Jimmy let the truck roll to a stop. Malina forced her cramped legs to stand and shuffle to the five-gallon bucket they used as a toilet. She pulled the lid off, and her face wrinkled in disgust. They emptied the bucket into a roadside ditch after every stop, but the inside reeked with the residue of five people emptying their bowels and bladders into it for two days.

She dropped her pants and squatted over the bucket. As a matter of unspoken protocol, everyone averted their eyes. When she finished, she cleaned herself as best she could with a bit of paper towel from the roll they kept by the bucket and pulled up her pants.

"Anyone else?" Riggs said, looking around the interior. "Let's get this done and get back on the road. It won't be much longer and you can all get out."

"Oh hell," Bobbi said and stood. "I'll take a shit if you want me to. Get a good look while I do it, you fucking pervert."

Riggs grinned and looked at the others. "Anyone else. Last chance. After this, we're driving straight through."

No one spoke. As the hours passed, Sherry and Cindy had sunk into the same lost desperation that seemed to be Brad's permanent state. Sitting side by side, they stared at the floor without speaking or interacting with the others.

"We got company," Jimmy said from the front.

"Who?" Riggs craned his neck to see out the side mirror.

"Just headlights coming up behind us, but I'm stopped mostly in the road. Too much snow to get off on the side."

"Can they pass?"

"Maybe, but I'm not sure."

"Alright, just ease forward and get up to speed." Riggs looked at Bobbi. "Hurry it up."

"I'm hurrying, dammit," she said and steadied herself as the truck swayed and accelerated. "Can't even take a shit in peace."

TWENTY-SIX

Things Will Get Ugly

"What the hell are they doing out here?" Lew Bentz muttered and reached for the mic on the dashboard. "Lori, I'll be out on a possible stranded vehicle, ten miles north of the Alder crossroads on County Road 87. Vehicle is a box truck, about twenty feet. License plate is frosted over with snow, but appears to be out of state, Washington, maybe ... last two digits are seven B – seven bravo."

"10-4, Lew. Stay warm."

"Do my best," Bentz responded, and hung the mic on the dashboard.

A hundred yards ahead, the box truck started to move forward, the right wheels partially on the shoulder, spinning in the snow. The driver hit the accelerator. The tires spun faster, finally caught, and the truck lurched forward.

Problem solved, Bentz thought, but a box truck on a backcountry road after midnight in minus ten-degree weather was not an ordinary occurrence. He punched a console button and turned on the SUV's emergency lights.

The truck continued rolling slowly forward another hundred yards before the brake lights lit up and it slowed.

"Son of a bitch!" Bobbi reached out to steady herself against the interior wall, shaking her leg violently. The truck's sudden movement had slopped the bucket's contents over the side, drenching her shoe and leg. "You covered me in shit, you son of a bitch!"

"Shut up and sit down," Riggs said, pointing the pistol at her. He looked through the door into the cab. "Talk to me."

"The headlights were from some kind of cop car," Jimmy said. "He's got his blue lights on. Should I stop?"

"Hell, yes stop," Riggs snapped back. "You planning to outrun him in this?"

"No, not that. It's just …" Jimmy was frightened. Suddenly, the grand adventure and promise of cash became less important than saving his ass. "I'm on probation back in Seattle … drug charges. Some cop runs me here and I'm liable to do real time for violating probation."

"Well, fuck." Riggs's voice rose. "That would have been good to know before we put you behind the wheel."

"Maybe let Hank drive. He could climb over behind the wheel."

"No, that's your deal, man." Hank shook his head. "You fucked up, got stopped, now you handle it."

"If that cop starts asking questions and hauls me off, what do you think happens when he sees what's in the back?"

"Don't let that happen," Hank said through his teeth, the muscles in his jaw working. "Things will get ugly."

"There's no time, anyway," Riggs called through the

door. "He'll be up here in a second. Just be cool and remember the cover story." He paused and turned to look at Jimmy. "You remember the cover story, right?"

"I remember." Jimmy nodded.

"Then stick to it," Riggs ordered. "And for fuck's sake, calm down … be cool. Nervous as you are, that cop'll think you're Ted Bundy's long-lost brother."

"I'm trying," Jimmy muttered, and took a deep breath. "I'm fucking trying, okay?" He looked at Hank. "You sure you don't think it would be better if …"

"You handle it," Hank cut him off and waved his pistol, then lowered it out of sight between the door and the seat. "Or I will."

"Right." Jimmy's face blanched nearly as white as the snow outside. He pressed the brake pedal for a few seconds and then let the truck roll to a stop.

Bentz slowed and pulled slightly to the left behind the truck to give him a better angle on the driver-side door if trouble broke loose. The headlights shining in the truck's side mirror lit up the driver's face—young, white male, early twenties, and no one he'd seen around Blanken County before.

His left hand holding the flashlight up at eleven o'clock, his right hand on the butt of his service weapon, Bentz walked forward, scanning the truck's rear and side as he approached the driver. Hands held at ten and two on the wheel, Jimmy watched the deputy approach in the mirror, a dark form backlit and silhouetted by the headlights behind.

"Evening," Bentz said as he reached the driver's door and shined the flashlight beam over the interior, and saw for the first time there was a passenger.

Jimmy nodded and swallowed.

"You having some kind of problem out here?" Bentz asked.

"No, sir." Jimmy shook his head solemnly.

"Nothing?" Bentz said, immediately suspicious. Beads of sweat clung to the driver's ashen face. "It looked like you were stopped on the side when I came up. Thought maybe you were having some trouble with this old truck. The cold will do that."

"No, sir. We just wanted to stretch our legs a little."

"Stretch your legs? Out here ... in minus ten-degree weather?"

"Well, we just ..." Jimmy stopped, mouth open, struggling for something to say.

"Had to take a leak," Hank said from the passenger seat. He smiled. "I couldn't wait, so I told my partner here to pull over and let me piss."

"Uh-huh." Bentz let the flashlight beam play over the cab's interior as he spoke, taking in every detail. There was no sign of weapons or contraband, but the red flags were fluttering and alarm bells ringing in his brain. He looked at the passenger and motioned with the flashlight, at the same time his right hand taking a tighter grip on the butt of his pistol. "If you don't mind, put your hand up where I can see it."

"Sure." Hank lifted his hand from the side of the seat by the door, rested it on his knee, and smiled. "I guess you can't be too careful out here, right Deputy?"

Bentz ignored the invitation to engage in conversation. He focused on the business at hand, moving the flashlight beam to the driver's face. "License and registration, please."

"Right." Jimmy nodded and reached into his back

pocket for his wallet. He pulled it out. "Here you go, officer. Registration is in the glove box."

"Get it." Bentz nodded and watched as he opened the compartment and pulled out the truck's Washington state registration.

Jimmy handed over the registration. Bentz scanned it and the license briefly and asked, "So, what are you doing out here?"

"Just ... we were only ... I mean, we ..." Jimmy stammered.

Hank leaned forward and interrupted, "Have we broken any laws?" He spoke across Jimmy, letting the smile widen across his face.

"Not that I know of." Bentz's eyes narrowed. "Which is why you shouldn't mind telling me why you're driving around in a box truck, on a remote farm road in the middle of the night."

"Sorry," Hank said and nodded. "You're right about that, for sure. Just been a long day, and we wanted to make our delivery and get some rest."

"Where are you making this delivery? What is it?"

"Some sort of equipment and parts for the Demeron Ranch," Hank said. "I couldn't tell you what. I don't know the first thing about farming or ranching. We got delayed by the storm, and they called today and said it was critical to get the parts here ... said there'd be a bonus in it for us. We drove straight through. That's why I had to stop and take a piss. Been holding it since this afternoon."

"Uh-huh ... how about opening up the back and let me see what you have there," Bentz said.

"Well, that shipment belongs to the Demeron ranch," Hank said, reasoning. "I don't know how they'd feel about us opening up their load for inspection … just parts and equipment, after all."

"I know the Demerons," Bentz said. "They won't mind."

"Don't you need a warrant for that?" Hank smiled. "You know, fourth amendment and all that."

"You're right." Bentz nodded and smiled. "If you don't want to show me what's inside, I suppose I have enough probable cause to get a magistrate to sign a warrant for me. I'll just keep you here, call it in, and we can hang out. Shouldn't take more than two or three hours … if the judge hasn't been out drinking tonight."

Hank chuckled. "Well, if you put it like that."

"I do," Bentz said, his eyes narrowed. "Open it."

"Okay, sure if you say so. After all, you're the law." Hank nodded and smiled, pushed the door open, and started to step out on the passenger side.

"You get back in the truck and stay there," Bentz said.

"Whatever you say." Hank closed the door.

Bentz tucked the license and registration in his shirt pocket inside the parka and looked at the driver. "You come with me."

"Yes, sir," Jimmy said.

Bentz followed Jimmy along the side of the truck. "Open it up."

"Sure, no problem." Jimmy swallowed and raised the rear door.

Riggs and the captives heard the interaction with the deputy through the walls of the truck. It became clear that the deputy was going to inspect the truck, and Riggs knew their hands were tied. He muttered, "Son of a bitch."

He raised the pistol as the rear door started to roll up. Bobbi, still seated by the slop bucket at the rear door, jumped up and helped throw it all the way up.

"Help us!" she shouted but said nothing else.

Four shots cracked with ear-splitting sharpness through the air and echoed off the truck's interior. Bobbi fell from the back of the truck as two bullets from Riggs's gun slammed into her side. Her face smacked into the icy ground.

Lew Bentz had just started to draw his pistol when two rounds struck him. One hit him in the chest, penetrating the heavy parka, but stopped by the ballistic vest underneath. The impact staggered him without causing serious injury, but before he could recover and raise his gun, a second round caught him under the right eye and exited the back of his skull. As he moved out of Riggs's line of fire, Hank had come unseen around the side of the truck and killed him.

Lew Bentz fell in a heap beside Bobbi. The roar of the gunshots faded, replaced by Cindy's shrieks from inside the truck. Malina and Sherry huddled together, arms around each other, sobbing. Brad, immobilized, mouth half-open, stared wide-eyed at the door opening.

"Fuck!" Normally calm and controlled, Riggs roared.

Hank reached down and retrieved the deputy's pistol, but said nothing. White-faced Jimmy lifted himself from the ground where he dove to take cover when the gunfire started. He stared at the two bodies for a few seconds, then turned and vomited in the road.

More seconds passed while Riggs considered their options. There weren't many. Finally, he nodded at Bobbi and said, "Throw her body in the back of the truck and put the cop in his car in the passenger seat. We'll take him someplace where they won't find him for a while. Hank, you drive the cop car."

"We could leave him here," Hank suggested and nodded at Bobbi's body. "Both of them".

"No." Riggs shook his head. "They'll be looking for him soon as he doesn't answer the radio, and they'll start right here. We take him and his car somewhere where they'll have to search for it a while before they look for us. That'll give us a head start."

"Then leave her with him. We take her and she'll make a mess of the truck."

"Can't do that. A cop killed on a traffic stop happens sometimes. Somebody with warrants shoots it out. Even out here, that happens. But a girl dead with the cop and they'll figure there's more going on ... get more eyes looking at what happened. Next thing you know, the Feds will be joining in and our bosses won't like that." Riggs shook his head. "No, we take her with us."

"Okay." Hank shrugged. "Whatever you say." He reached down and took hold of one of Bobbi's arms and a leg and looked at Jimmy. "Get over here and help me clean up the mess. Time to earn that bonus you were so hot for."

Jimmy paled and retched again, but leaned over to help lift Bobbi's body from the ice. They tossed her in the back of the truck, then dragged the deputy over and folded him into the SUV's passenger seat. Hank climbed behind the wheel.

"You lead out. Find one of these farm roads and pull off. Get as far down it and stash the SUV. Use the four-wheel-drive if you have to. We'll follow as far as we can in the truck and wait for you to walk back out."

"Alright." Hank frowned. "Wasn't planning on hiking tonight. Fucking cold out."

"Move fast and you'll be alright," Riggs said. "We're not leaving without you."

"Better not," Hank said. "Or you'll have bigger problems than the cops looking for you."

He put the SUV in gear and pulled around the truck. Riggs climbed into the truck, pulled the door down behind him, stepped around Bobbi's body, and waved the pistol at the others. "We didn't want this to happen! If she'd stayed cool, it wouldn't have happened." He shouted through the cab door to Jimmy. "Get it in gear and follow Hank."

The truck lurched forward. Section line roads crossed the county road every mile. Hank passed the first two, and at the third made a right turn onto a gravel road. Farm vehicles that used it to traverse the fields had packed the snow down, and the gravel beneath offered decent traction.

Five minutes passed before the radio inside crackled to life. "Lew, everything 10-4?" Lori the dispatcher waited a minute and repeated. "Lew, come in. Dispatch to Unit 4 … is everything 10-4? Advise your situation."

Hank glanced over at the dead deputy, his body slumped toward him, head bouncing off the console. "They'll be looking for you soon." He spotted a turnout a hundred yards ahead. "That's gonna have to do," he muttered.

Behind him, Jimmy stopped the truck at the entrance to the section line road. Without four-wheel-drive, they didn't dare chance it. He saw the SUV's taillights veer off to the right and disappear. He called to Riggs in the back, "Looks like he found a spot, couple hundred yards down this side road."

"Good," Riggs said and nodded at the others in the back. "Won't be long now."

The turnout led into a stubbled cornfield. Hank accelerated through the deeper snow until the SUV was half buried in a drift. Then he pushed the door open and made his way through thigh-deep drifts to the section line road. Five minutes later, he was climbing in the truck's passenger door, slamming it shut behind him.

"Shit! Turn the damned heat on." He pushed the temperature control as high as it would go.

Jimmy had the truck moving again. Behind them, the radio in the SUV crackled, muted by the drifted snow piled around the car.

"Lew, this is Lori. Come in!" A pause and then, "Damnit, Lew. Report in!"

TWENTY-SEVEN

More Bad News

"It's about time." Huey Cooke, followed by Arnold Cowley and Delbert Ottley, walked out and met Riggs as he stepped down from the back of the truck.

"Came as fast as we could ... considering," Riggs said, hopping to the ground from the bumper.

"Considering?" Cooke shook his head, annoyed. "What's that supposed to mean? I could have used you here hours ago, and I told you there was a bonus in it for you if you'd hurry things along. Not so sure about that now."

"We did hurry," Riggs shot back and his eyes narrowed. "And we intend to collect that bonus."

Hank and Jimmy came around from the cab and looked from Riggs to Cooke and back. "Problem?" Hank said

"No problem," Riggs said and looked at Cooke. "Right?"

"Just said I could have used you here earlier, is all," Cooke said, conscious of Hank's hard stare boring through him. "We have a lot to do to get them ready." He nodded toward the dark opening of the truck door.

"Well, we would have been here a little sooner, but we had to deal with some unexpected business."

"What kind of business you got out here besides making our delivery?" Cooke frowned. "You're not using the blizzard as an excuse, are you? Hasn't snowed all day."

"No, not weather issues," Riggs said.

"Then what?"

Riggs pulled a flashlight from his pocket, thumbed it on, and turned the beam over the truck's interior."

"Holy Shit!" Cooke stood for several seconds, mouth agape, staring into Bobbi's lifeless eyes and the blood pooling around her just inside the truck's back door. "What the fuck happened?"

"She got in the way."

"In the way of what?" Cooke leaned in to peer at the body, then pulled back, shaking his head. "Who did it?"

"I did," Riggs said. "It was an accident."

"An accident! How the hell did you accidentally shoot one of our girls?"

"Like I said, she got in the way. Some nosey law came snooping around and we had to take care of him, but she jumped up … was hollering for him to help … stood up, right as I squeezed off a couple of rounds."

"Wait." Cooke held up a hand and ran the other through his hair, shaking his head and trying hard not to believe what he'd just heard. "You're telling me that you killed a deputy … is that what you're saying?"

"Deputy, cop …" Riggs shrugged. "Some kind of law. Anyway, we had no choice."

"No choice!" Huey Cooke's mind was whirling. His already tenuous position as Demeron's hunting preserve manager was going up in smoke and this asshole—this glorified delivery driver turned cop killer—was holding the blow torch. Cooke's words came out in a sputtering, jumbled, spittle-spewing rage. "Are you insane? Do you have any idea what you've done? We're fucked…you hear! Fucked, that's what we are! It's … it's … fucked! All of us are fucked!"

"Calm down," Riggs said. "We took care of it. No one will tie us to the dead cop."

Cooke stared at him, panting as if he'd just run a marathon. He took a ragged, deep breath. "Alright, I'm calm. How the fuck do you take care of killing a cop?"

"Not too hard." Riggs shrugged. "We stashed his car with him in it in a snowdrift off a farm road. By the time anybody finds him, we'll be long gone and there won't be any way to tie us to him."

"Snowdrift? Farm road?" Cooke's eyes widened with the sudden realization that things were even worse than he thought. "Where exactly did this happen?"

"About ten or fifteen miles from here."

"Ten or fifteen miles! Might as well have been in our backyard." He shook his head in disbelief. "That means it was here in Blanken County. Only two deputies work the overnight shift. Dean Weber works the east side of the county and Lew Bentz works …" Cooke's mouth hung open. "My God, you killed Lew Bentz."

Riggs shrugged. "Didn't get his name, but he didn't give us a choice. Started snooping around, wanted to see in the truck." He leaned into Cooke's face, raising his voice. "I don't suppose you'd have liked that too much. You said to get here in a hurry and there'd be another thousand for us each. We got here, so you pay up."

"No, no, no…" Cooke moaned. "Lew Bentz was everybody's friend."

"Before you go nuts on us, keep in mind that if you

didn't tell us you needed the delivery right away, they …" Riggs jerked a thumb toward the passengers huddled in the back of the truck. "Wouldn't have been desperate to take a piss, and we wouldn't have stopped out on that road in the middle of the night. We could have followed our regular schedule, and showed up with everyone rested and in good condition."

"Yes, but you killed Lew Bentz!" Cooke's voice rose in frustration. "Everybody in the county … in the state … will be out gunning for who killed him."

"All the more reason to give us the money you owe," Riggs said, his tone hardening. "You don't want to fuck with the people we work for. Pays us off and we'll climb back in that truck and be on our way."

"I'm gonna pay. Did I ever say I wasn't?"

"Actually, you said you weren't sure anymore." A thin, threatening smile flickered across Riggs's face. "You better get sure."

"You don't have to threaten me. Just hang on a minute. I gotta think."

Cooke shook his head back and forth, trying to make the truth go away, but it wouldn't. Here was the truck. There was the dead girl with bullet holes in her. Here were the men waiting for their money.

After a minute, he looked up. "You can't leave in that truck."

The thin smile on Riggs's face became a smirk. "You think you can stop us?" Hank stepped in closer, his hand on the pistol tucked in his waistband.

"Hang on … just hang on," Cooke said, raising a hand like a traffic cop trying to slow things down. "Let's talk this through."

"Alright." Riggs put a hand on Hank's arm to slow him

down and looked at Cooke. "Start talking. Why can't we leave in the truck?"

"Plain as day," Cooke said. "When Lew turned on his blue lights, he must have called it in to Lori the dispatcher, and told her about the truck. When he turns up missing, every fucking cop in the state will be looking for it. You'll get stopped somewhere, and when that happens, how long do you think it will be before they put the pieces together, figure out you killed Lew Bentz? Sooner or later, they'll figure out what you were hauling around in that truck … maybe make you some kind of deal and you tell them what we're up to out here. We can't let that happen."

"You saying you think we'll talk?" Riggs said, the threat in his tone plain.

"Not you." Cooke shook his head, but his eyes flickered over to Jimmy, standing to one side, pale, staring at Bobbi's corpse in the truck and looking like he had to puke.

Riggs nodded. "Alright. What's your plan?"

"We'll give you a ranch pickup. We got plenty of spares around, and they fit in around here. You can drive out of Blanken County and no one will bother you. When you get to a city somewhere, you rent a car and leave the truck in some parking lot. Call me and we'll come pick it up, and you be on your way."

"That should work," Riggs admitted. "What'll you do about the truck?"

"We'll take care of it … hide it around the ranch somewhere. Plenty of space and no one will come searching A.C. Demeron's place."

"Got me an idea about that," Arnold Cowley piped up.

Along with Delbert Ottley, he stood in the background, listening to the interaction between Cooke and Riggs. Older than most ranch hands, he and Ottley worked for Cooke at the hunting preserve as caretakers. Well-paid and sworn to secrecy, they had been there to drag the frozen girls into the grain bin a few nights earlier. Tonight, as they left Langstrom's in Alder, Cooke had called them to come out to the preserve to help with the delivery.

"Don't bother me now, Cowley. I'm trying to work things out." Cooke snapped.

"But I got an idea for a fact, and it's a good one," Cowley said.

"Alright, let's hear it." Cooke sighed, looked at the three men from the truck, and shook his head. "This ought to be good."

Cowley explained his idea. When he finished, he grinned. "See. It's a good one, ain't it?"

"Not bad," Cooke admitted. "Alright, get those others out of the truck and inside the house. Have Loni get them cleaned up and locked down. Then drag that dead one over to the grain bin. I'll be along after a while."

"Yes, sir," Cowley said and grinned at Ottley. "See, Delbert. I had me a good idea."

"First fucking time that's happened," Ottley replied.

Cooke turned to Riggs. "Come on. Let's get you paid and out of here before you spring some more bad news on me tonight."

TWENTY-EIGHT

Calls in the Night

The third time Blanken County Dispatcher, Lori Dahlquist, called for a situation report from Lew Bentz over the radio without response, Deputy Dean Weber's voice crackled over the radio. "What was his last location, Lori? I'll check on him."

"Pulled out on a truck, possible stranded vehicle, County Road 87 ten miles north of Alder."

"10-4. Description of the truck and tag number?"

"Twenty-foot box truck. Tag was unreadable, possibly a Washington state plate."

"10-4. I'll advise."

Weber was a fifteen-year veteran of the Blanken County Sheriff's Department. He cruised through Alder and out County Road 87. Ten miles out of town, he picked up the radio mic. "Lori, you said ten miles north of Alder, right?"

"10-4, Dean." Lori diligently checked her log, though it wasn't necessary, and said, "Ten miles … that's what Lew said."

"Okay. Not seeing him, but I'll drive on a bit."

"Alright, Dean."

Their voices over the radio sounded crisp and clear, but there was an underlying tinge of concern. Lew Bentz was no rookie. He would not have forgotten to update his status or advise Lori if he was changing positions.

The next time Weber keyed the microphone, the concern was more than a tinge. "Lori, I've passed the county line and still no sign of him. You better advise the sheriff and get hold of the on-call deputies. I'm going to need some help locating Lew."

"10-4." Lori punched the landline button on her console that rang the sheriff's cell phone.

Sheriff Willard Bedford answered on the third ring. "Yes, Lori. What is it?" He yawned and blinked at the alarm clock on the nightstand. "Why are you calling me in the middle of the night?"

"Sorry, Sheriff. I know it's late, but we have a problem."

Lori explained. Bedford sat up straight in the bed. When she finished her report, he said, "I'm on my way in."

"Remember to call when you park it." Huey Cooke stood outside the barn at the hunting preserve, hands jammed down in his pockets, his frosted breath wafting away in the dark.

Riggs nodded from behind the wheel of one of the Demeron ranch pickups. "I'll call. You just get rid of the truck."

Tires crunching over the snow and gravel drive, the pickup's headlights bounced away into the night, casting intermittent light and shadows over the surrounding fields and fences. Hank rode shotgun in the passenger seat. Jimmy sat in the rear crew cab staring out the window, clutching a brown envelope with ten one-hundred-dollar bills paper-clipped together inside.

When the pickup was out of sight around the bend, Cooke returned to his office and pulled off his parka. The door to the safe beside his desk stood ajar. He'd opened it to take out the petty cash to pay for the delivery and the promised bonus. He pushed the door closed and spun the dial. "Getting careless," he muttered.

Cooke sank into his chair and stared at the phone on his desk. There was another call to make, and he would have preferred taking a beating than making it. He'd made too many of these calls lately.

But he had no choice. He reached for the phone, muttering again. "Just get it done."

Demeron answered, sounding groggy. Up late drinking with his guests, Cooke realized.

"Uhmm … there's been another … well, a sort of incident."

"Stop yammering, Huey!" Demeron was waking up fast now. He pushed himself up and stumbled from the bedroom, his cell phone at his ear. "What happened? The delivery? Did it arrive?"

"Yes, sir. It got here."

"Then what's the problem?"

"Like I said, there was a sort of incident on the way, and …" Cooke hesitated.

"Just spit it out!" Demeron said.

Huey Cooke spat it out. "They killed Lew Bentz."

"What!" Demeron shouted and then immediately lowered his voice, standing in the darkened hallway outside his bedroom. The guest rooms were in the other wing, but someone might be up wandering around the house. "Start talking."

It took Cooke several tortured minutes to wind his way through the series of events that led up to the murder of a Blanken County deputy. Demeron listened, dumbfounded at first, then angrier as the narration continued.

"And so," Cooke said, taking a breath to wrap things up. "I think we're alright now."

"Alright!" Demeron reminded himself to keep his voice down. "Three cop killers are driving around in one of my pickup trucks. A deputy is dead and buried in a snowdrift somewhere not too far away. Not just any deputy, mind you, but Lew Bentz, everybody's friend and probably would have been the sheriff in another election cycle or two. Oh, and I almost forgot, now there are three bodies instead of two in my fucking grain bin!"

"Yes, but ... I mean, we're taking care of everything ... and we have a plan."

"A plan? What fucked up plan did you concoct?"

"Not me so much," Cooke modified. "Arnold Cowley came up with it. You see, we just ..." He ran through the details in a few words before Demeron could cut him off, then added, "So you see. This can all work out, boss."

"Unbelievable," Demeron seethed. He leaned against the wall, wanting to crawl back into bed and knowing he couldn't. "Alright. You stay there by the phone. Don't do anything else until you hear from me.

"Right, boss," Cooke said. "Sorry about the ..."

Demeron never heard him. He ended the call and punched up another. Surprisingly, it was answered on the first ring.

"I can't talk right now."

"Understood, but this is important," Demeron said.

"Tell me … briefly."

Demeron gave a summary of events.

"Alright. Meet me at your hunting lodge. It may take a while, but I'll get there as soon as I can."

The call ended and Demeron went back into the bedroom, sat on the edge of the bed, and put his head in his hands.

"Problem?" Lorraine asked from her side.

"I'm going to need your help today." He turned to look at her, lying on her back in the dark. "I have to take care of some things, and you'll have to …"

"What is it?" A.C. Demeron, the perfect one, always in control, suddenly seemed very unsure of himself. Lorraine sat up. "Just tell me what you need me to do."

A coyote trotted across the frozen landscape, a silhouette moving low in the dark, nose to the ground, to pick up the scent of a rabbit that had crossed the field earlier. It stopped beside a six-foot drift at the edge of the field. The wind had scoured the snow from the rise in the center of the field and piled it up here along the edge.

The coyote's ears came up, twitching. Its head lifted and turned. For a moment, it stood motionless, the only movement the vapor of its breath drifting away in the night breeze.

The sound. What was it? He knew the voices of humans, had learned since its birth to avoid them, but here it was. The sound, a voice, but not quite, out here where there should be no voices.

Seconds ticked by. The coyote waited, ears twitching, alert for some signal of danger. None came and finally, satisfied in some still-wild canine way that there was no immediate threat, it trotted away, nose to the ground, zigzagging across the field following the rabbit's scent.

Inside the SUV buried in the snowdrift, the radio spoke its last words, "Unit four, come in. Lew, can you ..." With a last static squelch, the battery died, and the radio faded away.

TWENTY-NINE

The Lies Began

It was a pajama party, not that these girls had ever experienced anything like that before, but that's what it was, and it was Lorraine Demeron's brainchild. She'd instituted it a few years earlier to help acclimate the new arrivals at her husband's hunting lodge. Hostesses they were called. That was the euphemism they used to ease the girls into their new roles, telling them their duties were to assist guests. They would soon learn the nature of that assistance.

The goal was to help the girls adapt to their new circumstances, to accept the abnormal as normal. Lorraine was no expert in mind control, but she instinctively knew that, given the right stimuli, people can adapt to almost any situation. She'd been doing it all her life.

She also knew that a lie told repeatedly eventually becomes truth to the hearer.

You're free, not a slave. This life we provide makes you free. See how good life is here—the best food, money, drugs, clothes, and a lifestyle you could have only dreamed of in the past. See how free you are. Free of your terrible past and those who want to hurt you. You will never want for anything ever again. You would never be so free anywhere else.

Lorraine knew the power of lies. She'd been accepting them and living them throughout her marriage to Demeron. So, she helped her husband with the biggest lie of all.

Brainwashing, mind control, a type of Stockholm Syndrome—she didn't bother herself with trying to put a name to her methods, but Lorraine did bring her special touches to the process. In explaining things to her husband, she compared it to the difference between hard-breaking and soft-breaking a saddle horse. Hard-breaking may work, but the horse would always resent the breaker. Soft-breaking made the horse your friend.

Malina, Sherry, and Cindy huddled on a king size bed in a room nicer than any of them had seen before. They eyed each other and their surroundings without speaking. Cindy's face was wet from crying.

Plush carpeting covered the floors and the furnishings would have been in place in the finest five-star hotel. Sconces along the walls threw soft ambient lighting toward the ceiling. The refraction through the crystal globes gave the smooth walls a textured, undulating appearance.

Beside the bed, a cushioned chair sat before a table fitted with a mirror. Toiletry kits—sparkling, rhinestone-covered zipper pouched bags—sat on the table along with an assortment of cosmetics, facial creams, eye shadows, blush, lipstick, perfumes. All of it came from an exclusive designer store in Minneapolis.

Showered and shampooed, they had been given expensive silk bedroom attire. No flannel pajamas here. The woman who greeted them called the clothes loungewear, although they were not comfortable lounging in it. The clothes were intimately revealing, and they sat with their knees up to their chins, bent over to conceal as much of their bodies as they could.

It was a very subdued pajama party. There was no teenage chatter, no teasing about boys, no playfully innocent pillow fight. These girls were old beyond their years. Youth and all its innocence had abandoned them long ago. Such homes as they had experienced in their short lives had been little more than places to sleep, to scrap for their share of food, and to avoid a swinging fist … or worse.

The door opened and two women walked in. One was Loni, the woman who met them as they arrived, took charge of them and away from the men that had surrounded them.

She'd been dressed in blue jeans, a cashmere sweater, and calf-high boots then. Now she was barefoot and dressed in loungewear similar to that worn by the girls. She loosened a silky, shimmering aqua and silver robe and let it fall, revealing a matching camisole and tap short outfit. She knelt and sat cross-legged on the carpet.

The second woman was older, her flowing blond hair tinged with silver. She wore a long, flowing silk robe in royal blue. The robe was open, revealing a matching nightgown beneath. She sat beside Loni on the floor, taking a somewhat more dignified posture, her knees tucked gracefully to the side.

Lorraine Demeron had promised her husband she would have the girls ready despite their late arrival. Complicit in everything he was doing at the lodge, she would see that things went smoothly, as she always had.

"My name is Lorraine." She patted the carpet beside her and smiled. "Come join me here. It's comfy, and we need to chat."

The girls looked at each other without moving.

"Really," Lorraine said. "I know you have questions, and I'll explain everything. I think ..." She paused, letting the smile widen until each girl lifted her head and met her gaze. "I think you are going to want to hear what I have to say. Your life has changed and some wonderful things are about to happen."

Malina frowned but moved to the edge of the bed and onto the floor. She looked at the others. "I suppose we should hear what they have to say."

Sherry nodded, slid off the bed, and looked at Cindy. "Come on."

Cindy joined them, and the three girls sat on the floor forming a circle with Lorraine and Loni.

"Good." Lorraine's smile flashed white at them. "We want to thank you for ..."

"Where's Brad?" Malina asked, interrupting.

Lorraine's smile never wavered. "He's fine. In a room just down the hall, relaxing."

"I want to see him," Malina said.

"Yeah," Sherry echoed. "We want to see him."

"You will. First, though, Loni and I wanted a little time with you." The smile widened. "Just us girls."

Before Malina could interrupt again, she continued, "As I was saying, we want to thank you for joining us."

The girls turned their heads, mouths open, looking at each other, a mixture of confusion and disbelief on their faces.

"Thank us?" Malina said. "They drugged us and threw us in a truck."

"What?" Lorraine's eyes opened wide in surprise. She shook her head. "That's not how it's supposed to happen. They are supposed to pick some young people like you ...

girls who can use our help … girls with nowhere else to turn for help. They invite them to come to our ranch, tell them what we can do for them. They come here and we help them. Give them a second chance in life … show them that life can be good to them."

"Well, that's not what happened," Malina insisted. "They drugged us, threw us in the truck, and drove us here."

"I am so sorry." Shock and disbelief played across Lorraine's face. It was an act, but she had long since perfected it. She shook her head sadly. "I can't understand it. That should never have happened. Our mission is to help young people like you. We don't kidnap them. I will speak to my husband about this, and he will deal with the men who treated you that way. There must have been some misunderstanding, but I promise you, we will make sure that never happens again."

"They killed Bobbi." Malina was not giving up.

"My God!" Lorraine's eyes opened wide in mock horror at the news. "They killed someone?"

"Another girl. She was in the truck with us."

"I promise you," Lorraine said solemnly, "We will report this to the authorities and see that those men are brought to justice." She allowed the horror to fade and replaced it with a gentle smile. "But I am so glad you all made it here safely, and I promise you are going to have a life you never dreamed possible. That's what we do here. We share our blessings with young people who could use some help and make the impossible come true for them."

And so, the lies began.

THIRTY

I'll Take Care of My End

"Here he comes." Huey Cooke stood at the window of his office in the barn.

Demeron had taken over the desk. He looked up and nodded. "Go get him and bring him in here. We don't need him inside the lodge with the girls right now."

"Right, boss." Cooke went out into the barn, opened the exterior door, and waved at Sheriff Willard Bedford, who'd already started walking from his county SUV to the lodge. "Over here, Sheriff."

Bedford turned, frowned, and changed course toward the barn. Cooke held the walk-through door open for him, then snugged it shut once he was inside. "In the office, Sheriff."

Bedford strode across the cavernous space, past an assortment of ATVs and tractors, and into the office. Demeron looked up from Cooke's desk and nodded. "I'd hoped you'd get here sooner."

"Where's my deputy, A.C.?" Sheriff Bedford leaned

over and planted his fists in the center of the desk, his face inches from Demeron's. "You've got some explaining to do."

"I explained on the phone, and as I said, it would have been helpful to have you here earlier."

"I got here as soon as I could!" Bedford stood up straight. "You killed one of my deputies! That's not something I can just brush off and come running because you called."

"I didn't kill him," Demeron replied calmly.

"Well, he's dead. At least that's what you told me. Nothing's changed, has it? Resurrected maybe?"

"No." Demeron shook his head. "Nothing has changed, as far as we know."

"As far as you know! What the hell does that mean?"

"Stop shouting, Willard." Demeron nodded at a chair across from the desk. "Sit down and we'll go over everything with you."

"I don't want to sit! I want to know where my goddammed deputy is!"

"Tell him." Demeron nodded at Cooke, standing in the door and not inclined to come any farther into his office.

"Yessir." Cooke took a breath and stepped forward. "You see Sheriff, we don't exactly know where Lew ... uh, Deputy Bentz is ... not exactly anyhow."

"What the fuck does that mean?" Bedford whirled and took a step toward Cooke, who took a step backward again. "You said he was dead ... killed. I've got every deputy from three counties out looking for him, so where the fuck is he?"

"Well, you see, the ones who did it ... well, they weren't from around here, so they didn't exactly know where it was they put him." Cooke saw the anger flare in the sheriff's face and quickly added, "But he's close by. I know that ... not too far at all. I'm sure of it."

"And just how do you know that?"

"Well, they said that to give them some time to get out of the area, they drove his car into a snowdrift with him in it ... hid it so to speak down a farm road." Cooke gave a satisfied nod as if he'd just cleared up a great mystery. "So, you see. It has to be close by because when they were done with him, they came directly here with our delivery."

"This is on you, A.C." Bedford sagged down into the chair across from the desk, ran a hand through his thinning hair, and looked at Demeron. "We had an arrangement, but this ..." Bedford shook his head. "This throws everything out the window."

"Really?" Demeron gave a wry smile. "Everything? Including the little nest egg we've put together for you." He shook his head. "I don't think so. Just consider this a minor glitch, the cost of doing business. We'll get past it and back to normal."

"A glitch!" Bedford's face reddened. "You killed one of my deputies!"

"Like I said. We didn't kill anyone. What happened was unfortunate and not intended." Demeron shrugged. "What matters is, no one will know why he was killed. Right now, all anyone knows is he just stopped to check on the wrong truck. Things like that happen in law enforcement, don't they? We will remember Bentz as a deputy who died in the line of duty ... have a nice ceremony for him ... raise money for his family. Things will settle a bit and then we'll get back to business as usual."

"Your business, not mine!"

"I beg to differ." Demeron snapped back, his patience wearing. "You made it your business the first time you accepted one of my tokens of appreciation."

"Tokens of appreciation," Bedford smirked. "That's what you call it?"

"Alright." Demeron shrugged. "Bribe … is that more to your liking?"

Bedford's face twitched and tightened, but he said nothing.

"You didn't mind those deposits I set up for you offshore. The way I see it, you've done pretty well for yourself through our arrangement."

"Look, I didn't mind turning a blind eye to your little … fetish … and the high-powered creeps you fly in for your parties, but killing a deputy …" Bedford shook his head. "That's going too far."

"As I said, it is unfortunate, but nothing changes." Demeron sighed. "I understand being upset about the death of a deputy. Everyone liked Lew Bentz. Hell, I liked him, but it was an unintended consequence."

"He was doing his job … the job I paid him to do," Bedford said.

"A crisis of conscience. How touching." Demeron nodded in false sympathy. "It's a little late for that, don't you think? Still, I do understand, of course, and I promise … I will make this right for you."

Bedford's eyes narrowed and he was silent for several seconds before he said, "How right?"

"Right enough that you won't have to worry about running for sheriff again … unless you want to. You'll be able to retire to that ranch in Montana I've heard you speak of … or anywhere else you choose."

Bedford said nothing, but Demeron knew he'd struck a nerve. It was time to close the deal.

"Circumstances combined to put Lew Bentz and our delivery truck on the same road at the exact same moment in time ... fate, you might say ... but nothing more." Demeron leaned forward across the desk, forcing Bedford to look directly into his eyes. "Now it's time to consider our fates. They are tied inextricably together. There is no way around it. We are bound by the arrangement we made and doing anything to end that will have disastrous consequences for both of us."

"Is that a threat?" Bedford asked lamely, his voice subdued by the harsh reality that everything Demeron said was true.

"No, merely an assessment of the facts." Demeron sat back again, confident that he'd made his point. "Now let's get down to business. We have a plan."

"A plan?" Bedford seemed surprised and relieved at the same time.

"Explain." Demeron looked at Cooke, standing in the doorway as far away from the conversation as possible.

The Boss had spoken. Surprised that he was called into the mix, Huey Cooke had no choice but to do as instructed. He took a breath and explained.

When he finished, Sheriff Bedford sat silent for a minute, thinking through the details. After he'd spun it in his mind every way he could think of, he asked, "Where's the truck?"

"Out behind the grain bin," Cooke said.

"Show me."

They bundled up and walked from the barn's back door to the grain bin, using the same path over which they had dragged the bodies of three girls. Bedford went over the truck from top to bottom, examining it as he might a crime scene. Discarded fast-food wrappers, scraps of notes the occupants had made, an old road atlas. He collected all loose items that were not part of the truck itself into a pile.

Then he nodded at the pile and said, "Burn it."

"Me?" Hands in his pockets, Cooke stared at the pile of junk Bedford collected as if it might be infectious.

"Yes, you. Burn all of it." Bedford turned and walked to the back of the truck. "Open it up."

Cooke pulled the door up and stepped away. Even in the frigid air, the stench from the slop bucket watered their eyes and brought the bile up in their throats.

Bedford didn't climb inside. He scanned the interior from the door. Besides the slop bucket, the only items left behind were the furniture blankets the occupants had used for warmth and the old lawn chair Riggs had used during the trip.

"Alright." Bedford nodded. "Burn the blankets, empty the bucket, and get rid of it and the chair."

"Right," Cooke said. "And then?"

"It's your plan. You know what to do next." Bedford looked at Demeron, who had followed them out to the truck and watched while they made the inspection. "Call me when it's done. I'll take care of my end."

THIRTY-ONE

Listening

"It's my fault," Lori Dahlquist sobbed and lowered her head into her hands.

She sat at a corner table at Langstrom's with Lew Bentz's wife Celia and Alva Langstrom. All three were subdued, speaking in low tones. Alva, in her usual way, projected a confidence that would not abide the possibility of any negative outcome. Celia kept up a positive hopefulness about her husband's situation. Lori was in utter despair.

"Don't be ridiculous," Alva said. "Whatever happened to Lew ... wherever he is ... it's none of your doing."

"Alva's right. It's not your fault." Celia Bentz fought back her own tears. "And we don't even know that there's anything wrong. Lew knows how to take care of himself." She shook her head, denying the possibility that anything had happened to her husband.

"You don't understand. I should have checked back on him sooner ... got him some help ... it was my job to ..." Lori broke down sobbing again.

She'd been a Blanken County dispatcher for twelve years. It was a job that supplemented the family income while her husband Gerald handled their small farm, growing corn and soybeans and running a few cattle.

It was a quiet job, too. Blanken had always been a quiet county, until now.

Gerald stood behind her now and put a large, calloused hand on her shoulder, struggling for something to say to comfort his wife. He gave up, sighed, and looked at Alva, his eyes pleading for her to say the words he couldn't find.

"Now you stop blaming yourself," Alva ordered, and reached out to pat Lori's arm. "The sheriff's got half the state out looking for Lew. For all we know, he's holed up somewhere or broke down in the snow and his radio quit working on him." She nodded defiantly, daring fate or anyone present to disagree.

"No … no" Lori shook her head. "Lew was never careless. He would have let me know what was happening. He was always very careful about …" Her mouth hung open, the words unfinished, realizing that speaking about him in the past tense was as good as admitting that something terrible had happened. More tears welled up in her eyes and streamed down her face.

As the word spread that Lew Bentz was missing, the usual morning crowd lingered at Langstrom's, augmented by late risers stopping in for their breakfast, only to become part of the drama. The numbers built throughout the day. By afternoon, it was standing room only inside the small establishment.

Harry Langstrom manned the grill. Sole tended bar. Breakfast gave way to lunch. Lunch gave way to beers and shots and still, there was no word.

Conversations were muted, out of respect for Celia and

Lori, and the mood was somber. No one truly believed that Lew Bentz would just disappear unless he was a victim of some sort of foul play.

"Maybe he has a girlfriend on the side and shacked up for the day."

Eyes turned to stare at the speaker, who whispered the comment.

"Shut up. Celia might hear you. Besides, there's no way Lew would do that to Celia and his daughters."

"Just sayin' it ain't like Lew to just up and disappear, either."

"Yeah, well, it ain't like him to have a piece on the side, and you know it."

The speaker nodded and sipped his beer without making further comments.

Another said, *"Lori said there was some kinda truck he was stopped behind. What you reckon was in it?"*

"Who knows?"

"Drugs maybe?"

"Seems like an out-of-the-way sort of place for a load of drugs, dontcha think?"

"Yah ... I suppose that's true."

Sole listened and said little, trying to unravel the undercurrents of local relationships, things these people knew instinctively from living in Alder all their lives. He knew that the most insignificant piece of information could open up a case ... might solve the mystery of Bentz's disappearance.

An alcohol-fueled comment. A word muttered under the breath. A hard look at the mention of a name.

Cases had been solved on less, and he was glad now that he hadn't left town the day before. Lew Bentz was a good man and in the space of a couple of days, had become a sort of friend.

But the more he listened, the more he realized that

Bentz was what they all said—everyone's friend. In the short time Sole had been in Alder, he'd seen Bentz have a problem with only one person. He thought about that as he listened and served beers.

Arnold Cowley steered the box truck down a frozen gravel road. Delbert Ottley led the way in one of Demeron's ranch pickups, fitted with a blade to the front to push the deep snow to the side and scrape a reasonably passable path for the truck.

They got to a turnoff that was nothing more than a two-tire track across a field. Ottley led the way toward a grove of trees on the far side. He spent a few minutes working the truck and blade back and forth across the space, piling the snow up beside the remains of the stacked rock foundation of a house that had once stood protected from the north winds by the grove.

When he backed out of the way, Cowley drove up under the trees and between the piles of snow beside the rock foundation. The box truck's wheels spun in the muddy slush Ottley had created with the blade. Cowley jerked the gearshift into park and climbed out, wading through the snow to the pickup.

"Let's get the fuck out of here."

Ottley already had the pickup moving. The sun was lowering by the time they made it back to the gravel road.

"Wanna go get a beer at Langstrom's?" Ottley asked, leaning over the wheel as he drove.

"That's the plan." Cowley smiled. "Things should be getting interesting."

It was the dinner hour, but no one was eating. Men and women in work clothes crowded the bar, trying to keep a respectful distance away from the corner table where the three women had waited out the day.

In the afternoon, Celia had called her sister and asked her to go to the house so someone would be there when her children got off the school bus. The sobbing and tears had dried up now. She and Lori sat holding hands, staring dazedly at the walls, waiting.

When Dean Weber walked in with Sheriff Bedford, everyone in the room drew a collective breath. The murmurs faded away. Eyes followed them as they made their way to the corner table.

Bedford nodded at Celia. "We found him."

The explanation was brief. It had taken most of the day to find the county SUV partially covered in a snowbank. Lew Bentz was inside … murdered.

Gerald Dahlquist reached out to grab Lori as she fell from her chair. Celia Bentz leaned over, her face against the hard table surface, shoulders heaving, all hope gone, she wept inconsolably.

Alva sat stoically, a hand on each woman's shoulder as they grieved. John Sole watched from behind the bar, still listening.

When Arnold Cowley and Delbert Ottley walked in, they saw the sheriff and heard the women crying. Cowley pushed his way to the bar. "Jack and Coke, Bill."

"Alright," Sole nodded and grabbed a glass.

"Me too," Ottley said coming up behind Cowley.

Sole put the drinks on the bar and stepped away to get another beer for a customer.

"Sheriff's here," Ottley muttered into his glass.

"I see him." Cowley sipped his drink.

"Should we do it now?"

"Finish your drink." Cowley looked in the mirror behind the bar and watched the reflection of the sheriff and Dean Weber with the three women at the corner table. "Make it look natural."

"Right," Ottley said and tipped his glass back.

Cowley gulped down the rest of his drink and slid the glass across the bar. "Take another, Bill."

"Me too," Cowley said.

"Sure thing." Sole smiled and refilled the glasses.

When they finished their second drink, Cowley stood and walked to the corner table. Ottley followed.

"Sheriff, we got something to say, you might not have heard yet."

Bedford turned and nodded. "Say your piece, Arnold."

Cowley said his piece. Ottley backed him up. And Sole was listening.

THIRTY-TWO

No Worries

The regional airport in Rapid City was a small affair as airports go, but it had the two things they needed—a parking lot and rental cars. Riggs pulled Demeron's ranch pickup into the long-term parking lot while Hank went to the rental desk.

They'd briefly considered flying back to Seattle, but all the available flights required connections in Denver or Minneapolis-Saint Paul, and hanging around airports, in general, seemed like a bad idea. After all, they'd just killed a cop the day before. They may not have been the most experienced outlaws on the run, but they were smart enough to figure out that buying tickets, showing identification, and strutting through security checkpoints under video surveillance might be pushing their luck. They would have avoided the airport altogether if they hadn't needed a car to get the hell away from South Dakota.

Riggs left the parking ticket in the pickup's console and walked back to the terminal. Hank and Jimmy met him outside. Jimmy wore a ball cap purchased in the terminal gift shop. A patch on the front read—Black Hills—along with an embroidered image of a buffalo. He held out matching caps for Riggs and Hank.

"You went inside the terminal?" Riggs shook his head. "I told you to stay away from the video cameras."

"Well … I mean Hank was at the rental desk, so I figured it'd be alright to run into the gift shop," Jimmy said. "I was only in there for a minute."

"We need a car." Riggs glared at the cap on Jimmy's head. "We don't need souvenirs."

"I thought we could use them to cover our faces … you know while we're traveling and all."

Riggs shook his head in disgust.

"Come on. Let's get out of here." Hank turned and led the way to the rental car lot.

"What'd you get?" Riggs asked.

"Little piece of shit rice burner," Hank said. "All they had left on the lot."

"As long as it drives." Riggs lowered his head as they passed under a light pole with a security camera mounted high up. "We need to get out of South Dakota."

"Don't you guys want the hats?" Jimmy asked following behind.

"Shut up," Riggs snapped. They found the rental car on the lot, and he nodded at Jimmy. "You drive."

"Me?"

"Yeah, you."

"Alright, if you think I should, but I mean …"

"You fucking mean what?" Hank growled.

"Well, I mean my driver's license … that cop …"

He didn't have to say more. Riggs and Hank exchanged a look that might have seemed ominous to Jimmy, had he been doing anything except trying to avoid their angry stares.

"The damn cop took it, put it in his pocket," Riggs muttered. He looked at Hank. "You didn't think to ..."

"No." Hank cut him off. "I didn't. I was a little busy trying to hide the car and not freeze to death walking back to the truck."

"Right." Riggs nodded. "You drive."

"Fine." Hank climbed behind the wheel.

"You think it's a problem ... the cop having my license and all?" Jimmy asked. "I mean I think it'll be okay ... as long as I lay low. Don't you?"

"Get in," Riggs ordered.

Hank showed the rental agreement to the gate attendant, and set a course for the closest point out of the state. Forty-five minutes later they passed Mount Rushmore on their way through the Black Hills. An hour after that they entered the city limits of Newcastle, Wyoming.

"Stop somewhere," Riggs said. "I need to make a couple of calls and don't want to lose the signal."

"Right." Hank pulled into a convenience store and stopped at the gas pump. He looked at Jimmy. "I'll gas up. You go inside and grab some road food ... sandwiches, snacks, drinks. I don't plan on stopping if we don't have to."

"Okay." Jimmy got out of the back and headed across the parking lot.

"Be sure and keep that cap pulled down," Hank called after him.

Jimmy waved and tugged at the cap brim.

"Dumb shit," Hank muttered. "Wouldn't be in this mess if he'd just stayed cool. You know what we got to do."

"Yeah, I know." Riggs shook his head, "We can't cut

him loose. If he got picked up, it wouldn't take long before he spilled his guts about us?"

"Yeah." Hank nodded and smirked. "About thirty seconds I figure."

"Exactly. He's a liability," Riggs said, "They have his driver's license. If he gets spotted and we're with him we go down too."

"I'm not gonna let that happen.," Hank shot back.

"Me neither," Riggs agreed, nodding. "We'll deal with him, but not here. For now, we keep him close and put distance between us and the dead cop."

"Sooner the better, if you ask me." Hank got out and went into the store to pay for gas with cash.

Inside, Jimmy was browsing through the cooler, picking out sandwiches and drinks. Hank ignored him and went back to the car to fill the tank.

Riggs pulled out his phone and punched up the first number, Huey Cooke answered. The conversation was brief.

"Yes?"

"Airport ... Rapid City ... long-term lot." Riggs gave the location of the Demeron pickup and disconnected the call before Cooke could ask questions or start talking about the plan they were executing to cover their tracks. It was irrelevant. If it worked—and Riggs was less than optimistic that it would—but if it did, all the better. Meanwhile, they were proceeding as if the cops were on their trail, and talking about plans over a phone was another unnecessary risk.

The second call was more difficult. He took a deep breath and punched in the number.

"Where the hell have you been?" Tom Finch was annoyed.

"We had a little problem," Riggs said. "But we're back on track now."

"What kind of problem?" Finch's voice rumbled low like the warning growl of a dog that does not want to be disturbed.

"We had to deal with a nosy cop," Riggs said and prepared himself for what was coming.

"What do you mean, deal with?" Finch's growl became a snarl.

"We got stopped. The cop started nosing around … wanted to see our load … we had no choice but to …"

"To what?" Finch was shouting now.

"Well …" Riggs took a deep breath. "We had to get rid of him."

"To kill him!" Finch exploded. "You fucking killed a cop! When?"

"Last night," Riggs said and got ready for the next explosion. "A little after midnight."

"Last night! What the hell were you doing out on a South Dakota back road in the middle of the night in that damned truck. We had a plan, a cover story, parts and equipment to the Demeron ranch. It didn't occur to you that making the delivery in the middle of the night might look a little suspicious, even to some country cop?"

"Sorry, Tom. It's just that the weather has been shit and we were running behind schedule." He didn't mention the promise of a thousand-dollar bonus to expedite the delivery.

"Sorry, doesn't cut it." Finch took a breath. "Where are you now?"

Riggs hesitated, then lied, "Nebraska, making our way down to I-80. We figure on taking the interstate west and circle back to Seattle ... you know, take the long way to sort of cover our tracks."

Hank had filled the tank and was back behind the wheel, listening. He raised an eyebrow when Riggs gave the false location, then nodded, understanding. How Finch and Salver were going to react to the news of a dead cop was anybody's guess, but Riggs was right. It was better and safer to lay low and out of sight than pin a target on their backs.

"Get your asses back to Seattle!" Finch shouted. "Meet us there!"

"Will do," Riggs said. "Anything else?"

"I think you've done enough." Finch ended the call.

"How'd it go?" Hank asked, knowing the answer.

"About as expected," Riggs said. "He said to get our asses back to Seattle."

"So, what do we do?"

Riggs looked at Hank and shook his head. "I'm not going to Seattle."

Hank nodded. "Me neither."

Jimmy pulled the door open and climbed in the back with a bag of sandwiches, snacks, and canned soft drinks. "You make the call?"

"Yep." Riggs nodded.

"So, what are we doing?" Jimmy handed plastic-wrapped sandwiches and drink cans over the seat.

"Headed back to Seattle," Hank said smiling.

"Alright then. You sure seem in a good mood." Jimmy grinned like a teenager back on the grand adventure. "Let's do it."

In a remote corner of the Arizona desert, five miles from the Mexico border, Tom Finch tossed his phone on the seat of the truck and turned to Rick Salver. "We have a problem."

"I heard. You weren't too quiet about things." Salver nodded to their cartel contact, standing a few feet away. "So did he."

Luis Ibarra leaned against the fender of the refrigerated produce truck he had driven across the border that was now loaded with the girls Finch and Salver brought down from Seattle. He took a long drag off a joint he held between two fingers then looked up.

He was a middle man, a cartel runner, not at the top of the organization, but trusted to handle affairs with their North American contacts. He'd listened to Finch's conversation with Riggs, understood that some sort of police officer was killed. Killing police officers in Mexico was one thing. Killing them across the border was something else. The *Norteamericanos* took such things very seriously. He offered up a word of warning.

"You know, *amigo*, this thing you're doing can be very dangerous for you."

Finch and Salver exchanged a glance but said nothing.

"I know the temptation to make more money is very strong. That's how I paid for this." Ibarra patted the fender he leaned against and smiled. "And, of course, it is your business, but you understand that if your separate business interferes with our business ... if the police start looking at what we do here because of something you are doing somewhere else ..." He shrugged and took another hit off the joint. "The people I work for, they will respond very harshly."

"We understand," Salver said.

"Good." Ibarra smiled. "To be honest, I have grown fond of you two and our arrangements. The cartel pays me well to bring back the passengers you provide. We all profit, I think but ..." He shook his head and the smile faded. "But if they think that you have become a liability, things will be out of my hands. Is this the right word ... liability?"

"It's the right word, and I said we understand," Salver replied and both nodded. They understood very well what it meant to be a liability to the cartel.

"Good." Ibarra's smile was back. "Then I trust you to take care of this and make sure there are no connections between your little problem and our business."

"You can trust us," Salver said.

"Excellent! Then I can tell my bosses there are no worries. Right?"

"No worries," Salver and Finch said in unison.

THIRTY-THREE

Loni

Loni Shaw was an anomaly. While most residents only stayed at the Demeron hunting lodge for a few months to a couple of years at most, she had managed to stay there for almost five years. Flowing red hair and striking green eyes made her stand out and may have given her an advantage over some of the other girls, but A.C. Demeron had particular tastes when it came to the *hostesses* he brought in, and it took more than looks to remain in residence as long as she had.

In residence—that was the euphemism they used to describe imprisonment of the girls, and the occasional boy, who serviced Demeron's guests. Like the newest arrivals, they were supplied by the human traffickers Huey Cooke had connected with over the years. That's how Loni ended up at the hunting lodge.

As A.C. Demeron's appetite grew, he had given Cooke the assignment to find a source of young girls. Cooke smiled and said, "Yes, sir." With no idea how to accomplish the task, but frantic to please his boss, he scrambled to figure out how to carry out the assignment. After puzzling over it for a while, he did what most people would do. He turned to the internet.

It didn't take long for him to discover an online source who was willing to speak to him about the lodge's special needs. It was amazingly easy, but he was also amazingly lucky.

He managed to avoid the scrutiny of law enforcement agencies monitoring internet traffic and the traps they laid to catch pedophiles and human traffickers, mostly because of the clumsy nature of his searches rather than skill. Unfamiliar with the language of human traffickers, he never used the specialized code words and phrases that would have immediately triggered an investigation.

Kiddie stroll – prostitution involving minors

CU46 – See you for sex

5sX – Sex

WTGP – Want to go private

LMIRL – Let's meet in real life

Daddy – Pimp

Date – Exchange money for sex

These phrases and others, along with the coded series of emojis used by traffickers on social media, would have been enough for law enforcement to take a deeper look into his intentions. As it was, when he got on a general forum and asked a simple question, he was largely ignored.

Can anyone tell me how to find a girl?

If investigators noticed the post, they probably thought he was a desperate loner looking for love on a dating site. It took a couple of days, but one person finally responded.

I can relate. It's hard to meet the right person.

The ensuing series of messages back and forth seemed innocuous enough, just two lonely people commiserating.

Cooke was becoming frustrated, getting nowhere, and about to move on when the person on the other end of the messages wrote:

Can we meet sometime?

Cooke wasn't looking for a girlfriend and almost ignored the message, but because he was desperate to find a link into the human trafficking underworld, he responded.

Sure, I guess

The response came immediately.

Can you text me?

Cooke texted the number. Things moved quickly after that. A series of messages to several different phones used by the person on the other end of the conversation resulted in a meeting in Salt Lake City. That's how Cooke came into contact with Rick Salver.

Salver thought he was working a John, someone looking for sex, and as part of their trafficking operation, he was going to pimp one or more of his girls. It turned out to be much more than that.

Cooke was too inexperienced, or too dumb, to realize that Salver could have been an undercover investigator. Salver picked up on that immediately and saw the possibilities for a side business with the Demeron ranch.

That's where Loni Shaw came in. She was one of the first sent by Salver and Finch to the hunting lodge. It wasn't long before she became one of A.C. Demeron's favorites. For a while, she remained that way, but as her experience with Demeron and the other men who visited the lodge grew and she matured from adolescence into young adulthood, her special appeal faded.

She knew it was only a matter of time before they sent her on her way. Enticed at first by the money and drugs promised to her, she became accustomed to her lifestyle at the lodge. Sex was sex, a commodity of exchange for her since puberty. Offering it to Demeron and his associates was the price of living in a way she could only have dreamed about in the past.

But the inevitable process of maturing took place. She transformed from a barely pubescent child into a young adult, and Demeron lost interest in her.

Loni became desperate. She'd seen others disappear from the lodge, sent back to the streets or to Salver's and Finch's stable of young flesh to be trafficked again or sold to the cartels where they would disappear for good.

Somehow, she had to find a way to be useful, needed by Demeron, if not for sex, then for something else. Returning to the empty desperation of her previous life was unthinkable. So, she curried favor with Huey Cooke and especially Lorraine Demeron, and when the chance came to assist Lorraine in acclimating some new arrivals, she jumped on it.

She said the words they told her to say. Made the promises. Lied when it was necessary. Reassured the new arrivals that life there would be a wondrous experience with opportunities they would never have anywhere else. Sure, the men who used their bodies for pleasure were older, but they were kind—or at least, not too rough usually—and most were generous in showing their gratitude to the girls. Besides, many of the girls had been using their bodies to survive for years. For them, sex for money was not an unfamiliar experience.

Those who were new to prostitution required special handling. That was Loni's job. She talked with them late into the night, when necessary, cultivated a one-girl-to-another comradery, took them on walks, hosted private little parties when there were no guests to entertain. Created a sorority-like atmosphere that won them over, most of them at least. Salver and Finch replaced the few who couldn't adapt, but Loni was persuasive and most stayed, at least for a while.

The years passed. Girls came, stayed, then disappeared back into the trafficking underworld to be replaced by others. Loni did what she had to do, but with the passing years, a wearing fatigue descended over her. Eventually, the faces coming and going pierced through a conscience calloused by her life. She felt guilty.

When she discovered Mila and Riley making their escape in the middle of the night, she didn't have the heart to call Huey Cooke and stop them. She watched them go, knowing they could never get away, but unable to crush the hope she saw in their eyes. Let them have their hope. Whatever fate awaited them could be no worse than what would happen if they remained at the lodge. She watched from the window when their frozen bodies were brought back and taken to the grain bin. Tears rolled down her face, but she never said a word.

Then the replacements arrived.

"You're going to like it here." Loni smiled, sitting cross-legged on the floor beside Lorraine Demeron.

"Why are you doing this?" Malina said. "Why are you part of this?"

"Doing what?" Loni forced the smile wider.

"Pretending that everything is fine ... that all of this ..." Malina waved an arm around the room. "All of this is normal and right." She shook her head. "It's not and you know it."

"It's a good life here," Loni said, ignoring the questions. "Good food, money in the special bank accounts Mr.

Demeron set up for you. You'll have things you never had before."

"How long have you been here?" Malina asked.

"Almost five years." Loni nodded. "I like it here."

"Really? When was the last time you left?"

"Well …" Loni had to think for a moment. "I Went down to Mitchell with Mr. Cooke last month. He had to check on some equipment for the hunting preserve." She smiled. "He took me to lunch."

"That's it? You went to a place called Mitchell … no city I've ever heard of … and had lunch … last month?" Malina frowned and shook her head. "Sounds like prison to me."

"Like I said, life is good here." Loni leaned forward and patted Malina's hand.

She watched Lorraine's face from the corner of her eye. Was she being convincing enough? Sincere enough? Was there something she should say, or not say, to ensure that she wasn't locked in the next delivery truck, headed back to the streets.

Lorraine maintained her dignified, elegant posture, her face calm and composed. There was no sign of irritation, no twitch of a muscle or tic of the eye that might indicate her displeasure. Loni breathed easier.

"It's great here. Why would I want to leave?" Loni said.

THIRTY-FOUR

Sonofabitch Never Learns

"What the hell." Bob Shank came out on his porch and stood, arms folded, glaring at the procession of headlights that skirted his house, went through a pasture gate, and headed across a field. "Sonsabitches," he grumbled and hurried inside to retrieve his truck keys.

By the time he was back outside, the vehicles had disappeared over a rise, but he could make out an eerie headlight glow through the tops of an old grove of trees on the far side of his property. He gunned the engine and roared across the frozen ground, then slid to a stop as he topped the rise and found the vehicles circled up in the grove.

He jumped from the pickup and charged across the clearing. Most of the vehicles bore the Blanken County Sheriff's Department insignia on the door. Sheriff Bedford stood to one side, watching two deputies record images of a box truck backed in under the trees by the old house foundation. One took still images while the other moved through the grove, making a video recording of the proceedings.

When Shank came running up, the deputy with the video recorder followed him.

"Get the fuck off my property!" Shank came to a stop within inches of the sheriff, leaning toward his face.

"I don't think so." Bedford stood calmly watching his deputies work.

"You got no cause to be here. Now get off my property!"

"This your truck?" Bedford asked.

Shank stopped and examined the box truck for the first time. "Hell no! Never seen it before. Now get off my property and tow that truck along with you." He nodded at Ernie Bullock's tow truck parked at the edge of the grove outside the circle of department vehicles. "I see you came ready to do it."

"Soon enough." Bedford nodded, then said, "I understand you threatened Lew Bentz last night."

"That's bullshit!" Shank glared at the circle of deputies and spotted Arnold Cowley and Delbert Ottley standing beside one of the SUVs. "You did this, you little weasels! You sonsabitches are trying to set me up."

"Set you up for what?" Bedford asked.

"Don't play possum with me, Bedford. Everyone knows Bentz got himself killed last night. Doesn't take much brainpower to figure out this has something to do with that."

"Did you threaten Deputy Bentz?" Bedford asked, carrying on the pretense of an investigation.

"I had some words with him ... for him." Conscious of the circle of deputies glaring at him, Shank took a breath and lowered his voice. "Look, he came around here about me paying a bill he said I owed ... said he would lock me up if I didn't pay, so yeah ..." He nodded. "I said some things. I was angry. He didn't have any right to threaten me about going to jail, but that don't mean I killed him. I was just blowing off steam."

"Right." Bedford nodded and looked at the deputy with the video recorder. "Are you getting all this?"

"Yes, sir." The deputy nodded, and the camera joggled for a second before straightening out again. He looked at Dean Weber standing nearby. "Make sure you record in your notes the date and time of all of Mr. Shank's spontaneous statements ... that he admits to threatening Deputy Bentz and says he was just blowing off steam ... an indication that he was angry."

Weber nodded and scrawled in his notepad.

"I told you!" Shank's voice rose again. "I was just blowing off steam. It wasn't any kind of real threat."

"Sheriff, over here." The deputy taking pictures of the truck had rolled up the rear door. He stepped back and nodded as Bedford approached. "There, Sheriff. Looks like blood to me."

Bedford peered into the rear of the truck, then stepped back nodding. "That's blood, all pooled up and frozen, but it's blood. Get a sample of it." He turned to Dean Weber. "Did you check the tag?"

"Yes, sir." Weber nodded. "Last two characters match the partial tag Lew ... I mean, Deputy Bentz ... gave to dispatch." He looked at his notes. "Seven bravo ... seven B."

"That's enough," Bedford said, turning to Shank and nodding to Weber and the deputy with the video recorder. "Charge him ... homicide ... murder in the first degree."

"You motherfuckers!" Shank shouted. "That's bullshit and you know it!"

Weber stepped forward and spun Shank so that he faced

one of the county SUVs, then he pushed him forward. "Put your hands on the car."

"Fuck you! Get your hands off me!"

Weber gave a satisfied smile, happy to have the chance to put his hands on Shank. Reaching out to take Shank by the back of the neck, he bent him over and forward as he put one foot between Shank's legs and kicked his feet apart side to side until he stood leaning against the car in an awkward spread-legged stance, forced to support himself on his fingertips.

Weber searched him for weapons, then pulled Shank's right hand from the car, ratcheted a handcuff over his wrist, then did the same with the left hand. He spun Shank around and, with the video recording a few feet away, said, "Robert Shank, you are under arrest for the murder of Lew Bentz. You have the right to remain silent. Anything you say can and will be used against you in a court of law. You have the right to an attorney. If you cannot afford an attorney, one will be provided for you. Do you understand the rights I have just read to you? With these rights in mind, do you wish to speak to me?"

"Yeah, you motherfuckers! I'll say something to you! This is all bullshit, and you know it!" He glared at Bedford and tried unsuccessfully to pull away from Weber's grasp. "This ain't over! You'll pay for this!"

"Make a note that Mr. Shank continued making threats as he was placed under arrest ... threats similar to those made to Deputy Bentz," Bedford said and nodded at Weber. "Take him away."

Weber dragged Shank, stumbling across the frozen ground, to his SUV and shoved him in the back seat. Standing at the far edge of the circle of deputies, as far away from Shank as possible, Arnold Cowley smiled and called out, "Hey, Sheriff! You need us for anything else?"

Bedford turned to face the two ranch-hands-turned-informants. "Not now, Arnold. You and Delbert stay handy in case the district attorney has questions."

"Will, do." Arnold grinned at Ottley. "Come on, let's go let Cooke know how things went down.

"Right," Ottley said with his usual sparsity of conversation.

Weber drove by them, and Shank's voice thundered from the back seat. "You motherfuckers! This ain't over. You'll pay for this!"

"Sonofabitch never learns, does he?" Cowley said with a chuckle.

Delbert Ottley shook his head. "Nope."

THIRTY-FIVE

Questions

"Did you hear?" Johnny Walts rushed through the Langstrom's door and skidded to a stop in front of the bar, catching his breath.

"Hear what?" Alva turned from the grill.

"The son of a bitch did it!" Walts shook his head and leaned on the bar, breathing heavily. "I was down the street at my shop and Dean Weber came in. Said he was doing some follow-up investigation." Walts stopped and took a deep breath. "I can't believe it … I mean I can, but then no …" He shook his head and wrinkled his brow. "Then I can't believe it. I mean, who'd a thought it?"

"Johnny Walts!" Alva snapped. "Slow down and talk plain. Who did what?"

"Bob Shank! He's the one who murdered Lew Bentz."

"The hell you say." Alva clanged a spatula onto the grill and wiped her hands on a towel dangling from her waistband. "That big tub of hot air wouldn't have the nerve."

"Wouldn't have believed it myself, but it's true. Weber said he was investigating it."

"What did he say?" Harry Langstrom came from the back storeroom carrying a case of beer under each arm.

"Said he was investigating Bob Shank for the murder of Lew Bentz," Walts said and added, "Alva won't believe me."

"Neither do I," Harry said.

"Shit, Harry! You heard him the other night. He as much as said what he was gonna do."

"Yeah, he was in here making threats." Harry Langstrom leaned across the bar, put a beer in front of Walts, and shook his head. "But that doesn't mean shit. Shank's a blowhard, and everybody knows it, including the sheriff. Hell, he's threatened me like that when I cut him off for being drunk. Probably threatened every adult in Alder one time or another and half the children."

Langstrom looked at Sole, washing glasses at the sink, listening to the conversation. "What do you say, Bill?"

"I don't know Shank as well as you," Sole said, and nodded as he rinsed a glass. "But it seems unlikely that he would have anything to do with Lew being killed. Lots of people make threats. That doesn't make them murderers. You called him a blowhard. I took him as a bully and, in my experience, bullies tend to be on the cautious side when it comes to taking chances. They want a sure thing without a lot of risk. That's why they pick on someone weaker. There's less risk." Sole turned away from the sink, wiping his hands on a towel. "Everyone heard him make the threats against Lew. A man would be pretty foolish to do that and then go out and commit the murder. Too risky. He'd know he was the prime suspect ... too much chance of getting caught."

"Sounds about right to me," Harry said and looked at Walts. "Like Bill says, killing Lew after threatening him in front of everyone in town would be risky. Shank is a bully, but I don't take him for a fool."

"Well, they arrested him for it just the same," Walts said and thumped the empty beer bottle down on the bar. "And it wasn't just because of the threats."

Langstrom put another beer down in front of him. "What else then?"

"They found that truck Lew stopped to check on. It was out at Shank's place, on the back quarter section where the old homestead used to sit." Walts looked up from the beer and gave a satisfied nod. "Bully or not, I'd say that sort of ties up the case against Shank."

Langstrom frowned and tugged at his lower lip a moment, then looked at Sole. "What do you think, Bill?"

"I suppose the sheriff has his reasons." Sole shrugged. "Can I borrow your pickup for a little while?"

"Sure," Langstrom said and nodded at the keys hanging from a hook by the door to the backroom. "Got errands to run?"

"No, just feeling a little cooped up, I guess. They call it cabin fever around here, don't they?"

"They do for a fact." Langstrom laughed. "Where you going?"

"Just want to take a ride around." Sole smiled. "Everyone keeps telling me I ought to settle here. Thought I'd have a real look around and get familiar with the lay of the land. I'll be back to help out before the evening rush."

Five minutes later, he was headed out of town on County Road 87, thinking about the news of Shank's arrest, trying to put the pieces together in his mind. He'd heard Shank's threats. He'd also looked into the bully's eyes when they exchanged stares, and the caution behind the glare convinced him more than anything else that Shank was an unlikely murder suspect.

But there was more than that. He picked up on Sheriff Bedford's barely perceptible reaction when Arnold Cowley and Delbert Ottley showed up at Langstrom's after Bentz's body was found, and listened while they dutifully recounted Shank's interaction with Bentz, saw the faint conspiratorial smiles on the two ranch hands, the look of warning in the sheriff's eyes. He could read deception when he saw it, and he knew a lie when he heard it.

Then there were all the unanswered questions. In his detective days, he would have wanted those questions answered before he filed murder charges, if only to make sure the charges would stick and the defense attorney wouldn't find some loophole to free his client.

About ten miles out of town, he slowed and pulled over behind a Blanken County deputy's SUV. Dean Weber was walking slowly along the shoulder, staring down at the still-snow-covered road. He turned as Sole came up behind him.

"Don't mean to intrude," Sole said. "But it looks like maybe you have some questions about things."

"What of it?" Weber looked up from the road.

"I've got questions too," Sole said.

"Is that a fact?" Weber's eyes narrowed. "You some kind of law?"

"Not anymore," Sole said. "Long time ago, in another life."

Weber was not so easily satisfied. "Where? When?"

"Doesn't matter."

"Might matter to me," Weber said. "The way you say it makes it sound suspicious."

"Just memories I try to avoid." Sole sighed. "Let's just say I have some experience in this sort of thing, and if it makes you feel better, I'm not wanted by the law for anything." Sole failed to mention the cartel that would have paid dearly to have his head in a bag.

"Fair enough." Cops had memories. Some not so good. Some they didn't want to talk about. Weber nodded. "Yeah, I have questions."

"I hear you've arrested Bob Shank for Lew's murder."

"Sheriff's orders," Weber said. He shrugged. "Felt good when I did it. My friend was dead, so I put the cuffs on him and threw him in the car, but that was in the heat of the moment. Now …"

"Now, you still have questions," Sole nodded. "So do I."

"Alright, what questions do you have?" Weber looked into Sole's eyes, still not sure about trusting him, but thankful to be able to share his doubts with someone.

"Okay," Sole began. "Let's start with this. Lew was about here when he stopped a box truck. That right?"

"Somewhere hereabouts." Weber nodded.

"But he was found in his car down a gravel road a couple of miles away."

"Three and four-tenths miles, to be exact," Weber said.

"Right. So, first question—was someone working with Shank?"

Weber shook his head and gave a wry smile. Sole had hit on the reason he was out here walking along County Road 87. "Not that we know of."

"Then the second question—if the box truck is somehow part of the murder and it was stopped here, how did Lew's car end up in a snowbank three and four-tenths miles from here?"

"Damned if I know?" Weber nodded. "Any other questions?"

"Yep." Sole nodded. "Assuming Shank worked alone,

could he have killed Lew and driven his car to the snowbank and made his way back here on foot in the cold without being discovered, or freezing to death?" Sole shook his head. "That seems like a stretch, even for someone from South Dakota and familiar with the winters."

"Especially for someone from here," Weber agreed with a nod.

"So, maybe Shank lured Lew to the snowbank and killed him there. Did Lew say anything to the dispatcher about changing locations?"

"No." Weber shook his head. "Not a word."

"Would that have been typical of Lew … not to stay in touch with the dispatcher?"

"No. Lew was a by-the-book deputy. He had a family. He could be tough, but he didn't take unnecessary chances."

Sole nodded. "And the truck? Is it the one that Lew was checking?"

"Maybe." Weber shrugged "I suppose so. At least no reason to think that it wasn't."

"Anyone ever see him driving it?" Sole asked.

Weber bit his lower lip and shook his head. "No."

"What about registration? Is it registered to Shank?"

"No." Weber frowned and shook his head. "Washington state plates, but they don't belong on that truck. Off another vehicle but not reported stolen and the VIN registration isn't tied to Shank any way that I can find."

"State of Washington?" Sole's forehead wrinkled. "What did Bedford say about that?"

"Not much," Weber said, his eyes narrowed. "In fact, nothing at all. Hasn't followed up on the truck registration that I know of."

"Doesn't that seem strange to you?"

"It does." Weber nodded, then shrugged. "Still, we've never had a deputy killed out here, so maybe the sheriff just wants to put Shank away as quick as he can and get past this. Sort of put everyone's mind at ease."

"And you believe that," Sole said wryly. "That's why you're out here trudging along the side of the road in minus ten-degree weather."

"Yeah, I guess." Weber smiled. "Sounds pretty lame, I suppose."

"Nope." Sole shook his head. "Sounds like good police work." He nodded at the road. "I'll tag along if you don't mind."

"I don't mind. You seem to know the ropes."

They walked, staring down along the side of the road for almost half a mile before Weber stopped and pointed to the snow. Pink and red blood-soaked ice crystals sparkled, reflecting the afternoon sun.

"Could be an animal," Weber suggested. "Quite a bit of blood, and it's scattered around."

"No sign of a carcass," Sole said, scanning the area.

"Coyote might have dragged it off," Weber said, but reached for his phone and took several images, making sure the date and time stamp was activated.

"Have an evidence bag?" Sole asked.

Weber nodded and pulled several plastic envelopes from an inside pocket. Kneeling beside the blood spot, he took the blade of a pocket knife, scooped up some of the pink-red snow, and placed it in the bag, then sealed and initialed it. He jotted the date, time, and location in his notepad.

He opened three more bags, gathering samples from different points in the snow. Taking photos of the place where he took each sample, he repeated the process of sealing and recording the evidence envelopes, then stood and faced Sole.

"You going to have problems getting it analyzed?" Sole asked and used Weber's words, "Since the sheriff wants to *get past this quick*."

"Friend at the state crime lab will do it for me," Weber said. "I'll run it over to Pierre after my shift and ask her to expedite it."

"Without the sheriff knowing?" Sole sounded doubtful.

"Doesn't take the sheriff's approval to submit evidence to the crime lab." He held up the plastic bag. "Just have to maintain the chain of custody. I'll start a file using the same case number. If it's rabbit blood, then nothing comes of it."

"Sheriff finds out he's liable to be pissed."

"I'm pissed. Someone killed my friend. I want to know who did it. If it was Shank, so be it." Weber shrugged, but then his eyes narrowed. "If it wasn't him, I'm going to by-God find who pulled the trigger."

"Fair enough." Sole's respect for Weber increased, out here acting alone, possibly putting his job on the line by defying the sheriff. "Mind if I have your cell number, and you can have mine. Might come in handy later."

"I don't mind." Weber pulled out his personal phone.

They exchanged numbers and Sole said, "If you need anything, if I can help, you know where to find me."

"I know where to find you." Weber nodded.

THIRTY-SIX

The Hunt

"Welcome to the Demeron Preserve," Huey Cooke beamed.

"What's the hunting like, Huey?" Senator William Kellin led the pheasant hunters out of the plush Mercedes passenger van.

"You know how that is, Senator." Cooke smiled broadly. "The Demeron Preserve always promises you'll get your limit ... and then some."

"You've never failed me yet." Kellin grinned and turned to the others, following him out of the van. "This is Huey Cooke. He runs the preserve and lodge for A.C."

Elizabeth Ranskill came down behind Kellin and pulled her parka tighter around her. "We hunt in this cold?"

"Oh, this is a warm day," Cooke said with a grin.

Taylor came from the van, followed by Parson. They stood gazing across the snow-covered fields to the trees on the horizon. "One might call this the middle of nowhere," Parson observed.

Taylor nodded his agreement without speaking. He eyed

the barren whiteness, a sort of tentative suspicion in his eyes that said, is this all there is?

"Trust me," Cooke said, smiling even wider as if to convince them. "We're going to keep you out of the cold, and once you have a few pheasants in the bag, you'll feel toasty warm." He nodded to a nearby tent erected in the lodge yard. "In fact, let's get started. I've got just the thing to warm you up."

Cooke's duties as the preserve's manager included welcoming and seeing to the comfort of Demeron's guests when the boss wasn't around. He nodded to Arnold Cowley, the van driver, and Delbert Ottley standing nearby. "Take the bags inside. Loni will show you the room assignments."

Cowley and Ottley nodded and went to the rear of the van. Cooke turned to the guests. "This way."

The tent was the type used for large outdoor parties and receptions. To accommodate South Dakota's cold, heavy insulated drapes were hung around the interior walls, and electric space heaters took the chill from the air.

The guests followed Cooke inside, smiled, and opened up their parkas. Kellin headed for the bar along the far wall. A youngish man wearing a white jacket and black string tie stood behind the bar. Drinks were laid out and waiting, hot toddies garnished with lemon slices and cinnamon sticks.

"Come on, everyone," Kellin called and, as usual, led the way. When he came up to the bar, the young man smiled. "Good to see you again, Jolly." Kellin turned to the others. "Everyone, meet Jolly, the chef and bartender, who will be taking care of us while we're here."

Jolly smiled and nodded. "Good to see you again, Senator."

"And you." Kellin picked up a glass and sipped. "Ah, good. Just the thing to start off a cold day."

The others joined him, sipping their drinks, speaking in low tones, and agreeing that A.C. Demeron did things up right. First-class all the way.

Ranskill looked at the bartender. "Jolly ... that's an unusual name."

"I've heard that before." Jolly smiled and leaned over the bar, speaking softly as if he didn't want the others to hear. "At least you didn't follow up with the usual question."

"Let me guess," Ranskill said. "Are you jolly, a happy person?"

He laughed and nodded. "That's it."

"Well, are you?" Ranskill put a hand out and rested it on his arm.

Jolly made no effort to pull away and said, "I try to be."

"That's good," she said without moving her hand from his arm. "Do you have a first name?"

"Ted," Jolly said and leaned a little farther over the bar top.

Taylor sipped his drink and nodded at the pair, speaking in soft, almost intimate voices. "Looks like Elizabeth is ahead of us."

"Don't worry," Kellin said. "You'll catch up soon enough."

"Kind of a comical pair, don't you think?" Parson said and reached for another toddy. "She must have twenty years on him."

"More like thirty. You'll find that age differences don't matter much here," Kellin said and shot a knowing look at the others. "That's why we're here, isn't it?"

"It is indeed." Parson nodded and sipped his drink, his eyes fixed on Ranskill, chatting intimately with Jolly, the bartender/chef. "Does he actually cook?

"Absolutely ... an excellent cook," Kellin said. "In the kitchen and elsewhere."

That got a chuckle from the others. They were all working on their second round of drinks when A.C. Demeron made his appearance, coming through the tent's opening and pulling off his parka.

"Excellent!" Demeron smiled. "I see everyone made it."

"I was wondering if you were going to join us," Kellin said as Demeron came up to the bar.

"Had some business to attend to."

He'd had a rough night. Between dealing with the delayed and botched delivery of girls, one of them killed in the process, a dead deputy, a pissed-off sheriff, and a plan to keep them all out of prison, he never made it back to bed.

"Nothing to interfere with our affairs, I trust," Kellin said, eyes narrowing.

"No, no. Not at all. Just some ranch business." Demeron forced a smile. "Cows don't pay attention to clocks."

He looked around at the gathering. "So, are we ready for the day?"

"Ready and willing," Kellin piped in immediately.

Parson and Taylor nodded. "We're ready," Parson said

"Alright then. Let's load up the van and head out to the fields." Demeron noticed Ranskill, leaning over the bar, speaking with Jolly. "Come along, Elizabeth. Jolly will be here this evening when we return." He grinned. "He might even cook up a pheasant just for you."

Ranskill gave Jolly's arm a pat, then turned to follow the others out. "Alright, let's get this hunting thing done."

Hunting was a generous word. The shooting of pheasants at the Demeron preserve was more accurately an execution. There was no sport involved, no sense of fair play.

Shooting a duck on the water is generally considered to be unsportsmanlike. It's not hard to understand why. A bird floating on a pond is a much easier target than one winging away at fifty miles per hour. Over time, the expression *sitting duck* came to mean someone or something exposed, vulnerable, and subject to imminent destruction.

Such was the plight of the pheasants at the Demeron preserve, except they were far worse off than any sitting ducks. They were condemned and marked for extinction. It was just a matter of when, by whom, and how messy their deaths would be.

Demeron's guests tended to be far from experienced hunters. Cooke's hunt assistants herded pheasants by the hundreds out into an area fifty yards by fifty yards. From heated blinds, relaxed, and seated on cushioned stools, the hunters took turns shooting their brand-new shotguns at the unfortunate birds.

At the first recoil of his Purdey, side-by-side, twelve-gauge shotgun, purchased especially for the occasion, Simon Taylor yelped in pain. It was his first experience shooting a firearm of any type.

Ranskill and Parson were likewise inexperienced but managed not to cry out in pain when they pulled the trigger. Senator Kellin had the advantage of having been to the Demeron preserve before, but that only meant that he managed not to react to the recoil and could snicker at the others with a sense of superiority. Otherwise, his aim was just as poor.

The hunt was a slaughter. Many of the birds were maimed rather than killed outright, and the hunt assistants had to end their misery, picking them up by the feet, twirling them violently until their necks snapped, and tossing them in a pile of rejects, the flesh too badly mangled to be used by Jolly in preparing the evening meal.

Feathers and gore exploded from the birds hit at too close a range. When the birds avoided the killing area around the blind, Cooke's men herded them back, forcing them to cross in front of the hunters. Once a sufficient number of pheasants had been sacrificed to appease the egos of his guests, Demeron's hunt ended.

After a few hours of sporting fun—interrupted only by a break for a lunch that included sandwiches, cheeses, wine, and beer packed and sent along by Ted Jolly—the smoke cleared and the last gunshots faded away. Huey Cooke coaxed everyone out of the blind and into the cold for a trophy photograph.

The hunt assistants went through the pile of dead birds, picking out the least mangled of the carcasses, and handed one or more to each of the guests. Ranskill stood straight and resolute, holding a dead bird in each hand out in front of her, a look of grim determination on her face. Parson's hands dangled from his sides, a couple of birds in each, almost touching the ground and giving his arms an overly long ape-like appearance. Taylor held one bird in his left hand as far away from his body as possible, his face white with disgust and his lips pursed together into a thin line above his narrow chin.

Only Kellin got into the spirit of the trophy pictures. He grabbed three birds in each hand, holding them up high by the necks, a wide grin plastered across his face.

Cooke snapped digital photos of each guest with their *trophy* birds, then a group photo in front of the blind. When he finished, Demeron stepped away from the group and turned to face them, like the leader of a safari.

"I hope you enjoyed your hunt today." He smiled. "We have more in store for you … much more."

"Well, let's get to it," Kellin said, rubbing his palms together like a child excited to open his Christmas presents.

THIRTY-SEVEN

Somewhere Out There

It wasn't much. In fact, it was pretty damned little, considering the Blanken County Sheriff's Department was investigating the murder of one of its own. Sole watched Dean Weber drive away with the samples of suspected blood in plastic evidence bags and a few images on his camera.

That was that. Sole knew it wasn't enough. That there wasn't more was a giant red flag.

Someone killed a deputy. The sheriff should have his investigators out swarming over the countryside, looking for more evidence to make certain that the suspected killer was convicted and received the maximum penalty. Did South Dakota execute murderers, Sole wondered, then shook off the thought. It didn't matter.

Justice mattered. A sure conviction in court with no chance to overturn on appeal mattered. The sheriff should be demanding more evidence from his deputies, scouring the county for anything and everything that would strengthen the case, but he wasn't. Why?

He had a suspect in custody, and it ended there, but it wasn't enough to arrest a suspect. It had to be the killer, with no possibility that a defense attorney could plant reasonable doubt in a juror's mind. That's all it would take, one doubtful juror and the case would be over in a mistrial. The prosecution could try again, but there were no guarantees in court.

So, what did he have? Some witnesses heard Shank threaten Lew Bentz. Threats from a bully with a history of threatening anyone who pissed him off did not make him a killer.

In court, it would go something like this:

Ace Defense Attorney: You testified that you heard Mr. Shank threaten Deputy Bentz, correct?

Witness: Damned right I heard it.

Ace Defense Attorney: Have you ever heard Mr. Shank threaten anyone else?

Witness: Well, yes ... on occasion.

Ace Defense Attorney: And on these other occasions, did Mr. Shank actually kill the person he threatened?

Witness: Well ... not that I know of.

Ace Defense Attorney: Let's get to a case closer to home, one that you must know of. Did Mr. Shank actually threaten you on such-and-such a date, as reported by several others?

Witness: Uh ... yes, I suppose he did.

Ace Defense Attorney: And he did not kill you, did he? I mean, you're sitting here with us today, so despite Mr. Shank's threats to kill you ... the threats of a man known to make threats against many people when he was angry ... despite those threats, you are still alive and well ... (attorney turns to the judge, smiling) Your Honor, if the court pleases, I could have a physician brought in to verify that the witness is, indeed, alive.

Judge: (Hiding smile, then putting on a stern face) Continue your examination, Counselor. The witness seems alive enough for our purposes.

Ace Defense Attorney: Very well, Your Honor. (Then turning back to witness) So, despite the threats you heard Mr. Shank make in this case and in many other instances, you don't know of anyone he has actually killed.

Witness: Well ... Deputy Bentz.

Ace Defense Attorney: Did you see Mr. Shank kill Deputy Bentz?

Witness: Well, no I didn't see him, but I heard ...

Ace Defense Attorney: So, you didn't see him kill anyone, including Deputy Bentz, despite the threats you heard him make, the sort of threats he has made to many people in the past ... that he even made against you ... all without killing anyone. Is that right?

Witness: I suppose so.

Ace Defense Attorney: (Turning to judge) Your Honor, the defense moves that any testimony regarding threats, without specific knowledge of the murder of Deputy Bentz, should be excluded from the record, and the jury should be instructed not to base their deliberations on testimony that the defendant threatened Deputy Bentz as the record shows that, while threats may part of his personality, he has never actually harmed anyone. In short, Mr. Shank may not be a nice man ... he may even be a bully, and a loudmouthed one at that, but threats do not make him a killer. In fact, his many threats in the past have never led to any serious crime, and there is no reason to believe they did in this instance.

Judge: (Sighing deeply) I've heard your argument, but I will not exclude the testimony regarding threats. (Turning to the jury box) I will, however, instruct the jury that you must not convict the defendant solely on the fact that he made threats. You may consider them along with the other evidence the prosecution presents, but threats alone do not make a person a murderer.

Sole let it play out in his mind. Maybe the defense attorney would be a dud instead of an *Ace*. Or maybe the jury would ignore the judge's instructions. After all, it would be a hometown jury. Bentz was one of their own, well-liked and respected. They would be in the mood to convict. That happened ... a lot.

On the other hand, maybe the seed of doubt would be planted in the minds of one or two jurors. That's all it would take for a hung jury, and maybe a new trial would be ordered, and it would all be repeated. Or, maybe the jury would take the judge's instructions to heart and look for that other evidence the prosecution was supposed to present, except Sheriff Bedford seemed uninterested in finding it.

There was another *maybe*. Maybe Shank was innocent, and the sheriff had the wrong man. It was too early to know, but Sole's gut told him there was more to uncover before making a decision.

Other than the threats, what evidence did they have? The truck found on Shank's property? A truck with no registration connecting him to it. A truck that no one had seen him drive before. A truck with an out of state license plate. What was it doing there? Who put it there?

A real investigation into Bentz's murder would seek answers to those questions. A real investigation would provide a jury with enough evidence to override any reasonable doubt the defense tried to plant in the jury.

Sheriff Bedford's investigation was not that. The rush to pin it all on Bob Shank and push aside a deeper look at the facts didn't smell right. Sole knew it, and so did Dean Weber.

Alright, you seemed determined to dig deeper, John-boy. Where do you start?

He looked down at the blood-stained snow. If it's

possible the box truck wasn't Shank's, then whose was it? What was it doing out here in the middle of the night? Where was it going?

He raised his head and stared up the road, then got back into Harry Langstrom's pickup and headed north on County Road 87. The answer to those questions lay somewhere out there.

THIRTY-EIGHT

A Knot

"You've done this before." Loni sat on a chair beside the bed and smiled.

Brad sat on the bed in his usual position, knees up, arms dangling over them, chin resting on top. He turned his head toward her without speaking, sullen and glaring.

"Fine." Loni ignored the glare, shrugged, and continued. "You've done it before for money, so, let me remind you how this works."

This was no pajama party. Brad was not one of the newbie girls. He'd been turning tricks on the streets of cities up and down the Pacific coast for years. Seattle, Portland, San Francisco, Los Angeles, he knew them all and the places in each for a young, attractive boy-man to hook up with other men in exchange for money. It was a specialized niche in the sex-for-money industry, and if you knew where to look, where to market yourself, there were enough buyers to provide a steady income. Brad knew where to look.

He'd even worked for Salver and Finch a couple of times and been to the Demeron lodge when business was slow. Business was not slow now, though, and when Finch approached him about handling a special assignment for Demeron, Brad refused.

As it turned out, refusal was not an option. Finch and Salver were under pressure to procure the girls, along with someone proficient in Brad's specialized niche. He resisted. They insisted, using force. He resisted more, and they used more force until they tossed him in the back of the truck with the girls, banged up but not seriously injured.

"You'll be paid your usual fee for your time," Loni continued, "plus a ten percent bonus for your trouble."

Brad spoke his first words since arriving at the lodge. "And after?"

"Good. You can talk." Loni smiled. "It's time to get down to business and stop sulking."

"Answer the question." Brad stared at her.

"After, you will be returned to Seattle, or wherever you choose to go."

"In the back of another truck?"

"No." Loni's eyes narrowed, and she leaned toward him, speaking sharply. "Not in the back of a truck, unless that's what it takes. If you had cooperated, they would have flown you out here. You'd be rested and fed, on a sort of vacation before things got started, but as I understand it, you weren't cooperative, so ..." She shrugged. "So, you're here anyway. My advice ... make the best of it. Take your money and the bonus and the next time they ask you to come along ... come along."

Brad asked another question. "What about the girls who came in the truck with me?"

"What about them?" Loni gave another indifferent shrug. "They'll probably stay for a while. One day they'll go back."

"How?" Brad lifted his chin off his knees.

"I don't know. Bus ticket to Seattle," Loni lied, knowing they'd be thrown in the back of another truck making a return run To the SYPA camp.

"You believe that?"

"Why all the questions?" Loni snapped back, annoyed. "Yes, I believe it. That's the way they always come through. They stay for a while and then get sent back. Finch and Salver take over then and do whatever they do."

"They witnessed two murders."

Loni opened her mouth to respond, then closed it, eyes narrowed, brow wrinkled. Murder. In the rush to make Lorraine Demeron happy, she'd pushed that thought aside, focusing on getting the girls oriented, comfortable, and compliant. But people had died. What did that mean for them ... for her?

"One was a cop," Brad continued and shook his head. "They saw it happen. So did I. Do you honestly believe they're going to just send us back? Witnesses to murders they committed?"

"I ..." Loni began, then stopped, her mouth open, eyes staring.

"Didn't think that through, did you?" Brad said, his lips twisting into a sour smile.

"I can't believe ..." Loni shook her head. "I mean, no one is ever hurt ... they've never hurt anyone."

"That you've seen," Brad said. "Once the girls leave here, you don't have any idea what happens to them, do you?"

"Well, I know ..."

"What?" Brad seethed. "What do you know? You stay here, safe in this house, doing whatever they want. You tell the lies for them, smile, and give hugs. When they leave and the new ones come in, you do it again."

"But you come back. You've been here before." Loni struggled to come up with a response. "It must be the same for the girls. They go back to whatever they were doing."

"I'm different ... a specialty market they only need now and then. Demeron has no interest in me, but some of his guests do. They know they may need me again, so they keep me around. The girls ..." he shook his head. "They leave here and I never see them back on the streets again. So, where do they go?"

"I ..." Once again, she started to speak, then stopped. She didn't know where they went but didn't want to say it.

Questions. The little shit was asking too many damned questions. The worst part was she didn't have any good answers. A thought occurred to her, and a knot twisted in her stomach.

"You saw something, didn't you?" Brad's eyebrows raised, suddenly curious.

"What do you think you are? Some kind of mind reader?" Loni shook her head brusquely. "Hell no, I didn't see anything."

"Yes, you did." Brad nodded. "I saw it on your face, just for a second, but it was there. You saw something and now you're worried too."

She had seen something. Standing in the lodge's front door, waiting for the girls to come inside from the truck, she saw it, a body, dragged from the back of the truck and across the yard until it disappeared behind the barn toward ... she took a deep breath. Toward the grain bin. There were three bodies in there now. Two might have been explainable, killed by the South Dakota winter, but the one she'd seen dragged was bloody, the girl they'd shot.

What did that mean for her? Was she a witness too? If fucking Brad was right about them not wanting witnesses, was she going to be … what?

Stop! She shook her head. She was Lorraine Demeron's right-hand assistant, the lodge's chief hostess. They needed her. Even so, the knot in her stomach tightened.

Brad watched the worry and emotion play out on her face. "Don't know what to do, do you?"

"Yes, I know what to do!" Loni's eyes focused on him, narrowed and angry at having her world disturbed by the worries this little shit was planting there. "Get yourself cleaned up. They'll be back from hunting soon." She peered at the marks on his face from the scuffle when they forced him to come along. "And what about that? Do something about that."

Brad touched the scrapes on his face. "Don't worry about this. I'll use it … make it work." He looked into her eyes. "But you should worry about yourself, even if you're not concerned about the others."

Loni rose from the chair and walked across the room to the door. She reached out to open it, then hesitated when he spoke.

"Think about it," Brad said. "We might get out of this if we work together."

Loni pulled the door open and slammed it behind her. The little shit was trying to cause trouble. Whatever concerns he and the new girls might have, they weren't hers.

After all, Lorraine Demeron needed her, she thought, reassuring herself. She grimaced and put a hand over her gut where the knot twisted again.

THIRTY-NINE

As Good a Place as Any

"That looks like as good a place as any." Riggs pointed at a dirt road ahead on the right, heading off into the Wyoming backcountry.

Hank was driving. He nodded, without comment, and steered for the turnoff.

"We stopping already?" Jimmy asked from the back seat.

"Yeah, I could use a stretch and a piss." Riggs turned in the seat, smiling. "You got any of those snacks left?"

"Yeah." Jimmy rummaged through the plastic bags on the seat beside him. "Got some little donuts, a couple bags of nuts, and a couple of Cokes."

"Just a couple?" Riggs said.

Jimmy looked up and added quickly, "They're for you guys. I already drank my two."

"Guess you go thirsty for a while then," Riggs said. "It'll be a while before we stop again. Next time you might want to go easy on the supplies and make them last."

"Right." Jimmy nodded. "Sorry. Guess I fucked up."

Hank shot a glance at him in the rearview mirror but said nothing. Jimmy shrugged and forced a smile. Hank's glares were becoming more frequent as the miles passed.

They bumped along a dirt road for a half mile before Hank braked to a stop at the side of a wash. Dust swirled around the rental. Jimmy pushed the rear door open before it settled back to the ground, and fine grit covered everything in seconds.

"Dammit," Riggs grumbled. "What the fuck are you doing?"

"Sorry," Jimmy said, "I wasn't thinking. I just wanted to …"

"Close the damned door!" Riggs cast a sidelong look at Hank. "Like I said, good a spot as any."

Jimmy stood outside, holding the plastic bags with the snacks and drinks, one in each hand. He avoided the two scowling faces inside the car. When the dust finally settled and Riggs pushed the door open, Jimmy smiled.

"Got your snacks and drinks here." Jimmy held the bags out as a peace offering.

"In a minute. Gotta take a piss first." Riggs walked to the edge of the wash, unzipped, and started peeing over the bank. The stream splashed in the rocks and sand ten feet below.

Hank came out from behind the wheel and went to join Riggs, standing on the edge of the wash. He took a breath, sighed in relief, and unzipped.

They were squeezing out the last few drops when Riggs called over his shoulder to Jimmy, watching from beside the car. "You better come take a piss."

"Don't really need to right now," Jimmy said.

"Try anyway. You said you had your drinks, and we

won't be stopping again for a while. I don't want you complaining you need to take a leak."

"Alright." Jimmy placed the bags in the dirt beside the car and walked over to the wash. He stood a few feet from the others, opened his pants, and stood there straining, trying to squeeze out a pee to make Riggs happy.

The others finished up and turned back to the car. A few drops finally trickled out and then a full stream splashed into the wash. He hadn't realized he needed a piss. Must be the tension, he thought, shriveling everything ... his balls, his asshole, his bladder. Jimmy shivered and sighed the way guys do during a good pee, relieved that he'd been able to do what Riggs wanted. He turned his head and grinned as the stream slowed, then focused on squeezing out a few more drops.

He was giving it a last shake when the shot cracked behind him, but he never heard it. A hundred and fifteen grains of copper-jacketed, nine-millimeter lead slammed through the back of his skull, exploding in a gush of blood and brain matter from his forehead. Jimmy toppled forward into the wash, landing in the puddle of piss he'd made, still holding himself like he might just keep on peeing.

Hank stood three feet away, his arm outstretched, the pistol pointed at the point where Jimmy's head had been a moment before. A second or two passed before he lowered his arm and turned to Riggs, a satisfied look on his face. "Shoulda done that before," he mumbled.

"The phones," Riggs said and pulled his phone from his pocket. He knelt beside the wash, looked around, and grabbed a large rock.

"Right." Hank nodded and followed his example.

They used rocks to crack open the phone cases. Then they removed the SIM cards and batteries and tossed the wrecked phones into the wash, where they splashed into the blood and piss beside Jimmy.

Hank pulled a drink from one of Jimmy's plastic bags and a bag of nuts from the other. "What now?" he asked, tossing a handful of nuts in his mouth.

"Now we disappear," Riggs said and pulled out the last Coke.

Eleven hundred miles to the south, Rick Salver was behind the wheel of the truck. Tom Finch was in the passenger seat. The two guards who'd accompanied them to watch over the cargo of young women on the way to the cartel transfer point had been paid off and sent on their way.

They weren't happy about that. One tried to argue.

"What the fuck is this?" he'd demanded, holding the wad of cash Salver handed him.

"Your pay."

"And you're just cutting us loose? That's bullshit!"

"No choice," Salver said. "Something came up, and we have to take care of it."

"You said we were on the team now … part of the operation … that there'd be more cash like this if we hung around."

"Like I said, something came up."

"You can't …" The young man's mouth shut and his eyes widened.

"We can." Finch's pistol was in his hand, pointed at a spot between his eyes. "Now take your money and get the fuck out of here."

"Right … Look, man, I didn't mean nothing by it. Just

that we thought we had some kind of arrangement … something permanent, so to speak. You know, a deal."

"The deal changed," Finch said.

They stood on the side of a county road in southern Arizona. The two young men looked up and down the road at the barren desert. One said, "You just leaving us here? We could die out here."

"There's a town about five miles out on this road." Salver nodded to the west. "You can make it in about an hour and a half … less if you hustle. You've got your money, and you can go anywhere you want … just not with us."

The young man started to open his mouth again, but Salver shook his head. "Get moving."

The two who'd had dreams of making some *real fucking money* on a long-term basis turned and shuffled along the shoulder of the road. Salver and Finch watched for a minute to make sure they didn't turn back, then got into the truck. Salver reversed, backed around, and headed in the opposite direction.

"Any ideas?" Finch asked after they'd driven several miles.

"Not a fucking one," Salver said.

"Well, you heard Ibarra. We have to clean up the loose ends … A dead cop is not good and if any heat comes down on our friends down south, that cop won't be the only one dead." He looked at Salver. "You think they're going to meet us in Seattle … Riggs and Hank?"

"Would you?" Salver looked to the side, a smirk on his face.

"Fuck no." Finch stared out the window. "So, where do we go?"

"I'm no cop, but seems like the last place we know they were at is a place to start."

"Makes sense," Finch agreed. "Long ways from here, though. Ditch the truck and hop a flight? We could be there in a few hours."

Salver thought for a few seconds and shook his head. "No, we need to be mobile, and we don't want to leave a trail at airline counters and car rental agencies. I say we drive the truck ... for now."

"Fair enough." Finch nodded. "Let's get on the road."

FORTY

More Questions

It wasn't exactly a dead end, but there was nowhere else to go. County Road 87 cut straight as an arrow for miles across the landscape, an asphalt gash in the pristine white expanse of snow.

The road builders a hundred years earlier may not have heard of Archimedes, but they understood this basic principle of geometry—the shortest distance between two points is a straight line. Flying over the midwestern United States provides the perfect visual demonstration. Roads stand out starkly, cut in perfectly straight lines east to west, or north to south.

County Road 87 was no exception. Sole followed it for a dozen miles. Eventually, the asphalt turned to gravel, and the road narrowed, but its course never altered. The snowbanks on either side closed in. He followed it until it ended abruptly at a blank wall of snow.

The sun was lowering but still hanging in the western sky, and visibility was good. Sole was grateful for that. He had no desire to spend another night trapped in a South Dakota snowbank.

He turned in the seat. A gravel drive cut off at ninety degrees through a gated fence to the left. It led off across the fields and disappeared over a rise. Someone had plowed the snow from it and it seemed to be reasonably well-maintained. Fair enough. He'd come too far to be stopped by a closed gate.

He pushed the pickup's door open through the fender high snow at the edge of the drive and trudged through it to pull open the gate. It swung easily. Someone was using it regularly, and the tire tracks in the snow showed that vehicles had passed over it recently.

Sole climbed back in the pickup, drove through the gate, got out and closed it again, then followed the drive. Lew Bentz stopped on County Road 87 to investigate the box truck, but whether it came this far before being stashed at Bob Shank's place was one of several unanswered questions. It seemed doubtful that Sheriff Bedford had taken the time to find out. Following this road was the next logical investigative step in any normal search for Bentz's killer and if Bedford wasn't going to do it, Sole would.

He took his time, scanning ahead and to the sides. He was on private property. There weren't any posted *No Trespassing* signs, but he had opened a closed gate and come in uninvited. Where he was from, that was enough cause for some people to pull out a shotgun to deal with the interloper.

He topped the rise and caught the sun's reflection off a windowpane. Squinting into the distance, he could make out a cluster of buildings a couple of miles distant across the fields. If he could see them, whoever was there could see him, he reasoned and shrugged. There didn't seem to be any point in trying to conceal his movements now. He steered for the buildings.

Five minutes later, he pulled through another gate—this one open—and into the yard surrounded by the buildings. Things were laid out neatly. An expansive residence of some sort to one side, a large barn across the way, and several smaller utility buildings.

A man came from the barn and hurried across the yard to the pickup. Sole got out and met him, smiling.

"Can I help you?" The man's tone was brisk, businesslike, and annoyed.

"Hi," Sole said, smiling and standing, hands on hips, swiveling to survey the surrounding yard and buildings like a curious tourist. "I was just out driving and followed the county road to here. Hell of a nice place you got."

"This is private property," Huey Cooke said. "You'll need to leave."

"Sorry about that. I didn't know," Sole said.

"There's a gate," Cooke said. "A closed gate."

"Oh, right." Sole nodded. "The gate." He smiled wider and shrugged. "I figured that was just to keep the livestock in. I closed it good behind me."

"You need to head back out through it," Cooke persisted.

"Will do," Sole said, without moving toward the pickup. "Just admiring your setup here. What is this place, anyway? Pretty fancy to be way out here in the middle of nowhere."

"I said, you need to …" Cooke's words were cut off.

"Bill?" Arnold Cowley came from the barn and called out. "What the hell are you doing out here?"

Sole turned and grinned at Cowley. "Well, everyone keeps inviting me to stay on in Alder, so I thought I'd get out a bit and learn the lay of the land." He nodded at the pickup. "Harry let me borrow his truck for the afternoon."

"Well, you sure came a long ways to nowhere," Cowley said and turned to Cooke. "This is Bill Myers. Got stuck in a snowbank in the middle of the night a few days ago. Coulda froze to death if it wasn't for Lew Bentz coming along, he woulda ..." Cowley shut his mouth abruptly and shot a nervous look in Cooke's direction.

Cooke's jaw pulsed, his teeth grinding together, but he said nothing.

Cowley recovered and finished the introductions. "Bill, this is Huey Cooke. He runs the Demeron Hunting Preserve."

"Nice to meet you, Huey." Sole pulled off a glove and put out his hand.

Cooke stared at it for a few seconds, threw a look at Cowley, then put his hand out and gave Sole's a brief shake before nodding at the pickup. "Like I said. This is private property. So, I have to ask you to leave."

"Right." Sole nodded and turned to the pickup, then paused, a curious look on his face. "What do you go for around here?"

"What?" Cooke stared at him.

"What do you go for ... what do you hunt? Big game? Deer? I hear you have mule deer around here. Back where I'm from, it's all whitetail ... no mule deer."

"Pheasants," Cooke said. "Now, you need to ..."

"Pheasants!" Sole said enthusiastically. "I've heard about South Dakota pheasant hunting. Never did any, though. Maybe I can come out someday and hunt with you."

"The preserve is closed to the public," Cooke said. "Hunts are by invitation only."

"Oh, well then ..." Sole gave a conspiratorial wink and

leaned forward. "Maybe you can arrange an invitation for a newcomer."

"Look, I said this is private property and you'll have to ..."

A Mercedes van pulled through the gate into the yard. Cooke sighed and his shoulders sagged. Several people climbed out of the van and moved toward the house where a woman and young man came out to greet them on the porch. One remained by the side of the van and motioned to Cooke.

He walked over, head down, like a dog about to be scolded.

"Who is that?" A.C. Demeron demanded.

"Just some newcomer out exploring in Harry Langstrom's truck. Got here a few minutes ago. Told him this is private property."

"Get rid of him."

"Yes, Boss," Cooke said.

"Now," Demeron emphasized, and turned to the house.

"Yes, Boss," Cooke said to his back then walked over to Sole watching from the pickup. "You have to leave."

"Right." Sole climbed behind the wheel and cranked the engine. "Boss is pissed off, huh? Sorry about that, Huey."

Cooke winced at hearing his name come from the stranger's mouth. Sole smiled and headed back out the gate and down the drive. He pulled out onto County Road 87 and closed the gate behind him.

The sun was below the horizon now, and night was coming on. Time to get back to familiar territory. He drove slowly toward Alder, mulling things over.

Question—The box truck Bentz stopped was on the road that ended at the Demeron hunting preserve, and they were sensitive about their privacy there. Why would a pheasant hunting preserve be sensitive about privacy?

Question—Arnold Cowley worked there, and he had been all too eager to fill Sheriff Bedford in about Shank's threats to Lew Bentz. Did Sheriff Bedford know Cowley worked at the preserve?

Question—Cowley mentioned that Lew Bentz rescued Sole from the snowbank, but then clamped his mouth shut nervously when Cooke shot him a look. Why?

Sole began the day with questions. Now he had more.

FORTY-ONE

All Ties Cut

Rick Salver woke with a start, sat up straight in the seat, stretched, and looked out the window. "Where are we?"

"Colorado ... somewhere." Tom Finch looked down at his phone on the truck's console, his map app open and showing the route to South Dakota. "Getting close to Pueblo ... another 11 hours or so to South Dakota."

"Shit." Salver shook his head. "Too long."

"I said we could fly," Finch snapped back. "You said no ... didn't want to leave a trail. So, here we are ... eleven hours away."

"I still say flying would have been a bad idea. We don't know how things are unraveling thanks to those two assholes. Not just the law we have to worry about. The cops are the least of our worries if we don't get things cleaned up."

Finch nodded. Salver was right. Any trail the cops could follow, the cartel could follow, and they were usually quicker to pick up the scent than the law. Billions of dollars gave them the power to buy any information they wanted without the inconvenience of obtaining warrants.

They drove in silence for a while. Greenhorn Mountain rose to the west. Ahead, clusters of buildings appeared on the outskirts of Pueblo. It took less than thirty minutes to pass through the city and its suburbs along I-25.

They emerged onto the high Colorado plains. The Rockies towered in the west. To the east, the land stretched for miles to the horizon.

Salver looked at Finch. "Give them a call?"

"Don't think it will do much good." Finch shrugged. "What the hell. Give it a shot."

Salver pulled his phone out of his pocket and punched in the number. "You never know. Maybe they're dumb enough to answer."

They weren't. The remains of their phones were rusting away in the wash beside Jimmy's body.

"Where do you think they are?" Hank asked.

"Somewhere out there looking for us," Riggs said. He was driving now.

"Yeah, but where?" Hank persisted. Usually, the hardboiled member of their little group, Hank was slowly realizing the depth of the shit pool they had fallen into.

Salver and Finch always paid them well, treated them like partners, gave them important runs in the box truck to deliver their human cargo. But they weren't true partners, and they knew it now. They were delivery men ... expendable delivery men.

The cartel they all worked for did not tolerate mistakes. Killing cops in Mexico was one thing. Not all police in

Mexico were on the take, but with monthly pay hovering at the poverty level, it was common for cops there to contract with one cartel or another to supplement their income. Payoffs and bribes were a way of life. Straying into the line of fire amid the constant turf wars was an occupational hazard.

Killing a cop north of the border was another matter. North American police took a particularly dim view of people taking shots at them, and when one was killed, police agencies unleashed their full investigative efforts to bring the perpetrator to justice. They would shine spotlights into every nook and cranny to find those responsible for the murder of a cop, and cartels were especially averse to having spotlights shined in their direction.

Riggs and Hank knew they were marked men unless they could disappear. They drove south on I-25, careful to stay within five miles an hour of the posted speed limit, and only stopped for gas or a quick snack and restroom break. They alternated driving, taking turns sleeping.

Now Hank was awake, scanning down the highway. "They could be out there," he said. "Looking for us, right there on this interstate."

"Definitely a possibility." Riggs nodded. "That's why we keep moving for a while ... south, then out to the east coast and figure the best way to get out of the country."

"That's gonna be hard," Hank said. "Neither of us is exactly rich." He felt the wad of bills in his pocket, the travel money Salver and Finch advanced them along with the thousand-dollar bonus Huey Cooke had paid them. "Shit!"

"What?" Riggs looked at him.

"We didn't get that asshole Jimmy's share ... the thousand bonus Cooke paid him."

"Shit," Riggs echoed. "Never even thought about it. Just wanted to get away as quick as we could."

"Yeah." Hank nodded, then shook his head. "I wouldn't have wanted to climb down in that wash in the piss and blood to go through his pockets, anyway."

They drove in silence for a few minutes, then Hank said, "So, where do we go?"

"I don't know." Riggs shook his head. "I was thinking maybe Miami or somewhere along the Gulf. Maybe find a job as a deck-boy or workaway on a freighter. They don't pay, but they give you passage on the ship in exchange for work. Maybe end up in Europe or the Mediterranean." He shrugged. "Somewhere … anywhere where they won't be able to track us down."

"Sounds like a lot of work," Hank mumbled.

"Then I guess you shouldn't have killed that cop!" Riggs's voice rose, annoyed.

"What the hell else was I supposed to do?" Hank snarled back.

"Take him hostage maybe," Riggs smirked. "You know … don't kill the guy with the badge … take him with us … let Salver and Finch know and see what they say to do."

"What they say to do?" Hank shook his head in disgust. "Are you serious? If we hadn't tried to get there in the middle of the night to collect that bonus, we wouldn't have ever met that cop."

"So, you're saying this is my fault? We put it to a vote. We all wanted the bonus … including you."

"I'm just saying that this isn't all my fault." Hank's tone was uncharacteristically subdued. He was the hard-core muscle of the team, but Riggs was the thinker and planner. "Alright, it's nobody's fault. Shit happens. So, tell me about this workaway thing on a freighter."

They talked for a while. Riggs explained as best he could. They needed passports and a vaccination card and would have to get them on the black market under false identities. Then they'd hang around a port somewhere and start asking around for ships that might need extra hands. Riggs had read about it before. You signed on as a workaway, going to wherever the ship was bound. Probably have to be a foreign ship as American flagged ships and the big cargo lines required maritime certification and references, but there were still freighters, smaller ones that hired on workers for passage.

The discussion of the freighters wound down. Riggs and Hank drove in silence, each knowing that if they survived—and that was still a very large if—they would spend the rest of their lives hiding in some foreign place under an assumed name with all ties cut to everything and everyone they had ever known.

They paid no attention to the box truck that passed northbound on the other side of the interstate with two men inside wondering if they should have flown to South Dakota.

FORTY-TWO

And They Did

The night of horrors began with a buffet-style banquet provided by Chef Jolly. Pheasant was the main course. Smoked, sauteed, fricasseed, simmered in garlic and wine sauce, roasted, the platters overflowed with Jolly's pheasant creations. The birds used in preparing the meal came from the preserve hatchery since most of those killed by the hunters were too badly mangled and full of No. 6 shotgun pellets to be much good for anything other than the trash bin.

Lorraine Demeron showed up during pre-dinner cocktails. Martini in hand, she mingled with the guests, Loni at her side. A mixture of subtle questions and flirtatious comments helped her begin to match the guests with their hosts for the evening. The process of selection was fairly simple but relied heavily on Lorraine's practiced eye and ability to read their guests. A few words, and veiled comments, a bawdy joke here and there helped. Like a sommelier pairing fine wines with a lavish dinner, she soon understood what each was looking for and gave instructions to Loni.

The hosts—the girls and Brad—stood clustered near the buffet table, each holding a drink in their young hands, watching Lorraine and Loni. Despite the Xanax they'd given them to calm their anxiety, they shifted nervously from foot to foot, except for Cindy. The most emotional of the group, she'd received two, and now stood bleary-eyed, leaning against the buffet table for support.

Lorraine spoke a final quiet word to Loni, who nodded and sauntered over. "Alright," she said, smiling. "This is where the fun begins."

Cindy's eyes opened wide. "Fun? You mean …"

Loni took her hand and held it between hers. "Trust me. You can do this and have a good time here with us, and remember …" She leaned closer. "This is just the beginning."

Malina exchanged a glance with Sherry, who shrugged. Brad said nothing.

While the guests were out hunting and after the day's briefing with Loni, each had returned to their room to find an envelope on their bed stuffed with ten one-hundred-dollar bills. The money went a considerable distance toward gaining their compliance with what was about to happen.

From poor and abusive backgrounds, a thousand dollars was more money than any of the girls had ever held in their hands at one time. In his years on the streets, Brad had made as much money at times … but then spent it the next day. For all of them, a thousand dollars sitting on the bed seemed the equivalent of the pot of gold at the end of the rainbow. Maybe things would not be so bad here after all.

A brief note inside the envelopes read:

This is just the beginning

Wide-eyed, holding the cash in their hands, that promise began to have substance. It did not make them forget the murders they'd witnessed, but it helped dull the memory. Lorraine said she would make sure the killers were prosecuted. They didn't know if it was true, but they didn't know it wasn't either.

Loni promised them a new life, a better one. They didn't know if that was true either, but the Xanax and the fact that there was nowhere to run resigned them to what was about to happen. After all, it couldn't be any worse than things that had happened to them in their homes, the places they should have been the safest.

Even Malina, the most rebellious of the group, decided she could do what she had to for tonight or several nights if necessary. Accumulate some cash ... a lot of cash ... and then hit the road and put distance between her and this place and her past.

Loni explained their assignments, then walked with them across the room, escorting each to their partner for the night.

Cindy approached Senator Kellin, her eyes downcast, a slight tremble in her hand as she looked up, bleary-eyed from the Xanax, and brushed her long hair out of her eyes.

"My Lord. What have we here?" Kellin almost drooled, staring at her like a hungry dog before a chunk of red meat. He put an arm around her shoulders and pulled her close so that their hips touched as he walked her to a quiet corner of the room.

Oliver Parson was more subdued when Sherry came to him. He looked up from a sofa and smiled, then patted the cushion beside him. "Sit with me so we can talk. I'd like to get to know you."

Brad went to Simon Taylor, and without a word sat

beside him on another sofa placed before a picture window overlooking the fields to a distant tree line. A minute passed, then another as they stared out at the setting sun, casting an orange glow over the snow. As it dipped below the trees, Taylor said, "I'm Simon." He put a hand on the sofa between them, waiting. When Brad put a hand out on top of his, Taylor sighed and nodded.

Elizabeth Ranskill spent her time chatting with Jolly by the bar. He served her drinks, and they chatted more until the leader of one of the largest hedge funds in the world was acting like a giggling school girl.

"I understand you're a fiery little thing," A.C Demeron said when Loni walked Malina over.

"Fiery?" Malina said, but she held eye contact with him and didn't flinch when he put a hand out and took hers, pulling her close. "I don't know about that."

"Well, my wife does. You've met my wife, Lorraine, haven't you?" Demeron's eyes narrowed as if he were studying a lab specimen under a microscope.

"I've met Lorraine," Malina said.

"Excellent! Well, I hope she's right! Nothing like riding a spirited horse."

Lorraine Demeron stood in a corner for a few minutes, watching the proceedings. Satisfied with her work, she turned and left. There were private quarters for her tucked away on the far side of the lodge, but she preferred the half-hour drive back to the family ranch. Her husband could do what he wanted to satisfy his needs, but open marriage or not, she drew the line at watching. Besides, her daughter was waiting. They could spend the evening together while Demeron and his new business partners lived out the fantasy his wife had arranged for them.

Guests and hosts served themselves from the buffet Jolly

had prepared, then sat at a massive table that might have come from an old movie set about castles and lords. A.C Demeron treated his guests like lords, although he retained the position of king of the realm. He surveyed the group gathered around the table and nodded. The evening's debauchery was off to a grand start.

Ted Jolly sat knee to knee with Ranskill. Now and again, her hand would drift under the table for a minute and Jolly would bite his lip, his eyes half-closed dreamily as she did whatever it was she did under the table. A while later, his hand would drift down and Ranskill's face would redden, her breaths coming in quick gasps that she tried to conceal by holding a hand over her mouth.

There was no need. No one was paying attention.

Senator Kellin sat with a vodka martini in one hand, an arm around Cindy, his other hand draped over her still developing breast. He jabbered in her ear as if she understood what he was saying. Cindy stared glassy-eyed at the tablecloth, alcohol amplifying the effects of the Xanax, and indifferent as the senator's hands roamed over and explored her body.

Oliver Parson leaned close to Sherry, asking her questions about her life. When she related to him some particularly unpleasant event out of her past, his eyebrows would raise and his hand dropped to his crotch. He stroked himself for a moment, then took her hand and placed it under his and continued stroking. "Poor baby. You've had such a hard life. Tell me more."

Simon Taylor was the least talkative of the guests. He sat quietly, holding Brad's hand for most of the evening. Once he blurted out, "I'm circumcised."

"What?" Brad looked at him, eyes opened wide at the confession.

"I'm circumcised. I hope that's alright."

"I've been with circumcised men before," Brad said. "It's better that way."

"Good." Taylor nodded.

"Come here." A.C. Demeron pushed his chair away from the table. He patted his lap. "Sit here."

Malina's eyes narrowed, and she remained where she was.

"Aha." Demeron grinned. "The spitfire comes out." He reached out an arm and jerked her from her chair, forcing her onto his lap. "There, that's better."

Malina wanted to struggle, but she was trapped. She thought of the money in the envelope in the dresser drawer where she'd hidden it and forced herself to relax, remembering the feel of the crisp bills, smelling like they'd just come off the press at the mint. She wanted more of those ... a lot more.

Demeron pulled her rump hard into his lap. He groaned, and she felt him throbbing beneath her.

At sixteen, Brad was the oldest of the so-called hosts. Malina was fifteen and the other girls fourteen. All were children.

Only twenty-one-year-old Ted Jolly would have qualified as an adult. His flirtations with Elizabeth Ranskill might be unseemly but were at least somewhat consensual. He was on the Demeron payroll and happy to do what the boss wanted for the bonus he was promised. If that meant getting it on with a woman who could have been his mother, so be it.

If Demeron and his hunter-guests were modern-day royalty. Accustomed to buying anything they desired, they intended to savor every minute of the night before them. They felt no pang of conscience. Isolated at the lodge, away from the outside world, fueled by alcohol and drugs, their power overwhelmed their victims. They could do whatever they wished, even to children.

And they did.

FORTY-THREE

Pieces of the Puzzle

"How was the drive?" Harry Langstrom turned from the burgers sizzling on the griddle.

Sole came through the door, stomping snow from his boots. "Good. Just getting the lay of the land."

"That so?" Harry eyed him and laughed. "It all lays pretty much the same. Snow to the horizon." He shrugged and turned back to the burgers.

A dozen customers were scattered around the room, most at the bar and a few at the tables. The dinner crowd was gathering to be followed by the evening barfly rush.

Alva came from the backroom as Sole hung his coat up on a hook near the bar. "About time you got back. Need a case of Miller Lite."

"I'm on it." Sole nodded and went behind the bar into the backroom.

He grabbed the case of beer from the cooler and turned to go back through the door, then stopped. Someone had tidied up the cot that served as his bed and made it up with clean sheets and a bigger pillow. The bag with his belongings, including the weapons he carried, was pushed far up under the cot against the wall.

He put the case of beer on the floor and knelt to examine the bag. Nothing was out of order. The weapons were as he left them, buried at the bottom under his clothes, loaded and the safety on. It was the best he could do given the circumstances of his arrival.

He lifted the Colt, ejected the round in the chamber, dropped the magazine, examined the loads, then replaced it and chambered a round. Someone had neatened things up, but it did not appear that they had tampered with anything.

Having a firearm in this part of the country was unlikely to raise any particular concerns. Everyone had guns. Not having one would have been more curious to the locals. Still, he imagined there would be questions if they had noticed the weight of the duffle and realized there was more than one firearm inside.

Sole picked up the case of beer and went back out to the bar.

"About time," Alva said. "Got thirsty customers here."

"Sorry." Sole started loading the beers in the well. "Looked like someone made up the cot."

"Humph," Alva grunted. "Man ought to have a decent place to lay his head after a day's work." She turned toward him, eyes narrowed, and added, "Long as he's working, that is."

"I'll keep that in mind." Sole smiled. "And thanks for tidying things up for me. That pillow looks nice and soft."

"Yours to use." Alva reached in the well, pulled out a bottle, and placed it in front of a customer. "As long as you earn it."

"Leave him be, Alva," Harry called out. "Bill's earning his keep."

"Never said he wasn't," she snapped back brusquely. "Just making a point,"

"Have to excuse her, Bill," Harry said, grinning. "That's Alva's way of saying thanks."

Alva shot a narrow-eyed stare at her husband and turned to go into the backroom. Harry laughed out loud and the customers at the bar dared a brief chuckle. The door opened and Alva came back into the bar, eyeing the customers. Abrupt silence settled over them.

Harry laughed louder. "Bill, take these burgers to that table in the corner."

"Will do." Sole took the platters loaded with burgers, fries, and two bottles of beer and walked them to the table. He collected the empty bottles and went back to the bar.

As the dinner rush slowed, Alva wiped her hands on a towel, walked over to the griddle and gave Harry a brief, stern peck on the cheek, then retrieved her coat from the back room. "I'll see you when you get home," she said and turned toward Sole, adding, "Breakfast crowd comes in early. Get some sleep."

With that, she was gone, out the front door and onto the sidewalk.

Led by Harry, the crowd inside called after her, "Gooood niiiight, Alva,"

It was a nightly ritual. She scowled at them through the window, pulled the coat collar up around her ears, and plodded off toward their house a block away. Laughter broke out for real.

Sole smiled. The familiarity among the people in the bar. Alva's good-natured grumpiness. The simplicity of life here. The invitation that everyone except Bob Shank had offered him to stay on and make Alder home. All of it was appealing.

But first, there were a few things to settle. Simple as life was here, it was not immune to tragedy. Lew Bentz's murder was testimony to that, and Lew Bentz, brief as their acquaintance had been, was a friend. Sole felt the old familiar pull to settle things, find the killer, and see that justice was done.

Therein lay the problem. The rush to arrest Bob Shank for the murder left him feeling that justice was not being done. And if not, why?

The evening crowd cleared out a little after one AM. Harry put two glasses on the bar and poured two fingers of top-shelf scotch in each, picked one up, and leaned his elbows on the bar as he sipped. "What's eating you, Bill?"

Sole had been waiting for the opportunity to speak in private. He picked up his glass, took a sip, and nodded. "Did some poking around while I was out riding."

"I figured as much. Stir anything up with your poking?"

"Questions," Sole said.

"Mind if I ask what kind?" Harry pulled a stool over and sat.

"Same one as before," Sole said. "And a few new ones."

"Such as?"

Sole thought about what to say for a few seconds. He had no right to talk about Dean Weber's concerns with the investigation. On the other hand, he figured his own observations were open to discussion.

"Alright," he began. "Why the rush to pin Lew's murder on Bob Shank? He wasn't going anywhere. I didn't see him as a flight risk."

"You're right about that," Langstrom agreed. "Bob wouldn't know what to do with himself if he went more than twenty miles over the county line."

"Yeah, I got that impression. Tough guy around here,

king of the roost, but anywhere else, he'd be just another chicken in the coop." He looked at Harry. "Mind if I ask you a question?"

"Shoot," Harry said and took another sip from the glass.

"What do you know about a fella named Demeron?"

"A.C. Demeron?" Harry's eyebrows raised. "About what everyone else knows, I guess ... not much, really." He put the glass down. "Big rancher around here. Family money that's been around for generations, but he went off and made more in business ... investments, I think, and companies he bought up. We don't see him much around Alder. Not really his type of place." Harry smiled. "He makes an appearance at the county's Fourth of July picnic, but mostly he keeps his affairs private. Moves in different circles, if you know what I mean."

"I know what you mean." Sole nodded. "Anything else besides just being a rich rancher? Hobbies, special interests, gossip about him?"

Langstrom thought for a few seconds and shook his head. "No, nothing I know about." Then he raised his head, remembering. "Oh yeah, he got an award ... from the state conservation group ... for pheasants."

"For pheasants?"

"Yep. They gave him an award for his efforts to protect the state bird ... the ring-necked pheasant. Some kind of breeding program he runs out on a preserve he has. Releases healthy birds and increases the numbers." Harry laughed. "Pheasant hunting is big business in South Dakota, so I'm sure that had something to do with the award."

"You ever been out there?"

"Where? His hunting preserve?" Harry shook his head and laughed louder. "Hell, no. Like I said, he moves in different circles. I hear he brings folks out there to hunt, but it's by invitation only ... high-rollers and politicians with influence. Keeps the workings there private, doesn't like people prying into his business. Arnold Cowley works out there for him, but even that blabbermouth never says a word about the preserve." Harry shrugged. "That's fine with us. He doesn't want our company, so we don't care for his. Kind of a mutually acceptable arrangement."

Harry's eyes narrowed. "Why the sudden interest in A.C. Demeron?"

Sole considered telling Harry about his ride out to the preserve and encounter with Huey Cooke, and the other questions flying around in his brain.

"Nothing in particular." He shook his head. "I'm just trying to sort out all the pieces of the puzzle."

FORTY-FOUR

Cracked the Case

"Yeah?" Detective Leonard Purdy drove, one hand on the wheel, one holding his personal phone to his ear.

"Something I need you to do. It needs to be quiet." The caller spoke with an accent, not heavy, but enough that it was obvious he didn't come from the streets in this city.

Purdy knew the caller, or knew whom he represented, but he had no ideas about his nationality. Somewhere south of the border, he figured. Columbia, Mexico, Cuba ... fucking Spain for all he knew. They were all the same to him. It didn't matter. What did matter was that he paid in dollars ... lots of dollars.

"It always needs to be quiet, doesn't it?" Purdy said. "Hang on while I pull over and take down what you need."

"Nothing written down," the caller said.

"Just so I don't forget any of the details," Purdy said and pulled to the curb on a downtown city block with the car's flashers activated.

"You won't forget." The caller said sharply. "I said nothing written. I mean it. *¿Comprendes?*"

"Yeah, yeah. I *comprendes.*" Purdy pulled out his notepad anyway. "Tell me what you need?"

The caller was right. He listened for a minute and shoved the notepad back in his pocket. After the caller explained what he wanted, Purdy said, "Understood."

"We want this quickly," the caller said.

"I'll do what I can." The wheels were spinning in Purdy's brain, trying to figure out how he was going to get what the caller wanted. "This won't be easy. There was already an investigation."

"Do it fast and there will be a bonus in it for you."

"A bonus? On top of the usual fee?" Purdy smiled. "How big a bonus."

"Listen, this comes from the top, and they want results. You deliver, and you'll be able to get out of that cheap car and shitty house you live in ... drive a Ferrari and find yourself a spot on some island somewhere ... if you deliver, *cabrón.*"

Purdy had picked up enough Spanish to know that the caller had just called him an asshole. He ignored it and said, "I'm on it."

Assigned to the police department's Major Felony Investigations Unit, the underworld types who paid him for inside information about police activities, investigations, and pending prosecutions considered Purdy a valuable asset. His fellow investigators and supervisors did not share that opinion.

He remained in the unit for one reason. His mother's brother was a deputy chief in the patrol division. At his sister's request, he pressured his counterpart in the investigative division to keep his nephew in the unit and off the streets. If not for that relationship, Lenny Purdy would have long ago been handed his pink slip and sent off to muddle his way through life on his own.

A bumbling, ineffective, petty, and occasionally heavy-handed man with a badge, the major felony unit seemed the best place for him. As a detective with no real duties, he would present less hazard to the public and patrol officers forced to work around him. In Major Felony, he was surrounded by ace investigators, and while the crimes were serious, the environment was calmer than street policing, where officers were forced to make split-second decisions, not Purdy's strong point. In Major Felony, they could monitor him closely and generally reduce the risk of having him in contact with the public.

That was the thinking, at least, and it suited Purdy to a tee. Mostly he was assigned busy-work. Running messages between investigators. Recording people who came and went from suspected drug houses without approaching them. Speaking to the occasional criminal informant and turning in a statement. Always, these assignments were accompanied by strict orders not to engage with the public and not to take law enforcement action without authorization and backup from other investigators.

This left him with lots of time on his hands to do nothing. Everyone was happy with the arrangement, including Purdy who found a profitable way to make use of his spare time.

It started small, taking a payoff to let a drug dealer know that there was a raid planned against his main distribution house. His contacts and business grew from there, along with his bank account.

The caller said this new assignment came from the top. That could only mean from the callers' bosses up the drug distribution chain, and the top link in that chain resided in Mexico ... the cartel supplying drugs to the city's dealers.

This was it! The big one! He didn't give a shit about Ferraris, but the caller said that the payoff could send him to live on that island he'd been dreaming about.

He began by returning to the office to sit in his solitary cubicle in a corner, going through an investigative file on the computer. No one paid him any attention. Lenny Purdy often sat in his cubicle, pretending to be doing investigative work while he napped in his chair.

After two hours of reviewing all the files, interviews, images, and recordings, he headed for a neighborhood in a low-rent part of the city. When he found the store on the corner, he parked along the curb without bothering to turn on his flashers. The blue sedan was clearly a police vehicle and bore a police department license tag because wasting limited department resources to provide Detective Purdy with a true undercover car was deemed unnecessary.

Inside, Purdy found Doreen Selander behind the cash register. Purdy put on his most official face and walked up, holding out his badge. "Afternoon, Ma'am. I'd like to ask you some questions about the shooting on the corner a few days ago."

Selander looked up, surprise in her eyes. Police officers were not regular visitors to the store, and having them return so soon was more than a little unusual. "Is there something wrong ..." she leaned over the counter, peering at the badge and ID card. "... Detective Purdy, is there something wrong? I mean, I told the others everything I knew ... even gave them the video I recorded on my phone."

"No, Ma'am, nothing's wrong. My captain just wants

me to make sure we got everything we can, you know, after someone getting shot and all."

"He was a bad man," Doreen said, shaking her head. "Very bad."

"Yes, Ma'am. Well, he gunned down someone right in front of your store."

"No, not him ... not the man who shot. I mean the man who got killed ... he was a very bad man. I didn't know his name, but he was always around the neighborhood, hurting people, roughing them up, robbing and stealing, and taking things from the store without paying. He would just look at me laughing, daring me to try to do anything about it."

"Right." Purdy nodded sympathetically. "I understand, but we can't have people shooting other people without doing something." He shrugged and smiled. "So, my captain wants me to do some follow-up before we file the investigation as a cold case."

"You know what I think." Doreen leaned across the counter, her voice sharp and to the point. "I think they should find him and give him a medal." She nodded emphatically. "Yep. A medal for shooting that bad man."

"Can I help you?" Isaiah Selander came from the backroom with a dolly loaded with cartons of canned goods.

"This is another detective, Isaiah," Doreen said. "He wants to know if we have anything else to say about the shooting and that man they're looking for."

"Ought to give him a damned medal is what you ought to do," Isaiah said.

"That's exactly what I said ... a dammed medal!" Doreen repeated.

"Well, before we give him a medal, we need to find him." Purdy smiled again, and the Selanders exchanged a skeptical glance. "Look, I read through your statements, and I just wondered if you could help me with one thing."

"What's that?" Isaiah said, the corner of his mouth raised in suspicion.

"Well, you say he ran off down the street after the shooting."

"Not right after," Isaiah said. "First, he told me to take care of the old man who was beat up real bad."

"Right, and then he ran down the street."

"If that's what I said, that's what he did."

"Well, did you see him go into any of the stores along the way?" Purdy knew that even in this neighborhood, most stores had cameras of some sort for security purposes. If he could turn up a video recording of the shooter, it might give him another lead.

"I already told the others. No, he didn't go into any of the stores."

"Oh." Purdy, the ace investigator that he wasn't, pursed his lips trying to think of another question but drew a blank.

"He turned down a side street, the next one a block up," Isaiah said.

Purdy's head snapped up. "Did you tell the other detectives?"

"Well, no." Isaiah scratched his chin, thinking. "No, they never asked. We were standing there talking, and the radios started squawking at them and they said they had two more shootings they had to go to. Big fella, they said was a captain, got them together, and they all left … all but one."

Despite his statement to the media about not tolerating killers, vigilante heroes or not, the truth was that Captain Dwayne Mallard and his team were overworked and understaffed. The shooting of a low-level street thug quickly dropped off the investigative radar amid the upward spiraling crime wave that had consumed the city for over a year.

"So only one detective stayed when the others left?" Purdy asked.

"That's right." Isaiah nodded. "That one stayed behind with the paramedics and got things cleaned up. Then he asked if the other detectives had taken our statements, and I said they did, so he left too. Only the news reporter lady stayed around to ask some questions. She had a fella running a camera for a while. Then they left."

"Show me," Purdy said. "The side street he turned down."

"I suppose I can do that." Isaiah looked at his wife. "Will you be alright here for a few minutes while I walk this fella down the block?"

"I'll be fine," she said. "If you think you have to."

"Let's go." Isaiah turned to the door. "I don't like to leave Doreen here alone here for long."

Outside, they crossed the intersection at the corner and continued for a block. Isaiah stopped and said, "Here. This is the street."

Purdy looked up and noted the name on the street sign on his notepad. The store at the corner was a bookstore. Based on the books displayed in the window, it specialized in porn.

The street ran for several blocks in a straight line. Purdy sighed.

"I'll be getting back to the store now," Isaiah said and walked back up the block.

Purdy went into the bookstore and started asking questions. The clerk remembered the day of the shooting and a pickup truck that parked suddenly in a no-parking loading zone on the curb at about the same time. The man in the truck ran back down the street and returned a few minutes later, still running.

"You didn't report this to the detectives?" Purdy asked the clerk.

They never came by to ask." The clerk shrugged. "Didn't think much about it then, except he was in the loading zone on my curb and I had a delivery coming. But he was back and gone in a few minutes, so I didn't say anything."

Purdy took a detailed description of the pickup and driver and repeated the process at every store on the block and then the next. He reached a liquor store on a corner with a traffic signal. Scanning the exterior of the building, he saw what he was looking for, and rushed inside.

For two hours, he sat in a dusty closet reviewing the video recording from the cameras outside the front door. It took a while to find the day of the shooting. When the pickup came into view, he banged his fist so hard on the table the screen almost toppled over. "Got you, you son of a bitch!"

The store clerk came in. "Everything alright back here? I heard a loud noise."

Purdy ignored him, pulling open drawers, searching.

"Hey," the clerk said. "Stop that! You can't …"

Purdy pulled a flash drive out of a drawer and held it up in triumph. "This'll do."

He put the flash drive in the computer's USB port and downloaded the video, then pulled it out and put it in his pocket.

"What are you doing? That's private property! You can't take that!" the clerk shouted at his back as Purdy almost ran from the store.

"Police business," Purdy shouted back over his shoulder.

By the time he got back to his car parked on the corner, it was getting dark. Inside the store, Isaiah was alone behind the cash register. His wife was nowhere in sight, probably gone home.

Purdy climbed in the car and left the curb, spinning the tires as if he were in a high-speed pursuit. Fifteen minutes later, sitting in his cubicle, he inserted the flash drive into his computer and slowly played back the images of the pickup at the intersection. Zooming in, he could even make out the profile of the shooter, sitting patiently waiting for the light to change to green. The image was grainy but discernible, the same man the news reports played from Doreen Selander's cell phone.

The light changed, and as the pickup moved away, and the angle improved, he froze the image. It wasn't crystal clear, but it was decipherable. The pickup bore a Tennessee tag. A quick check on the Tennessee motor vehicle database and Purdy had a name to go with the tag.

The story of the vigilante killer-hero had quickly faded away. While the department struggled with manpower shortages and budget cuts and the need to respond to an overwhelming number of police calls, only Detective Purdy found the time and motivation to dig deeper into the killing of the gun-toting thug nobody was going to miss and whose gang nearly beat an old man to death.

"What are you still doing here, Purdy?" Captain Mallard stood in the cubicle's entry regarding him with a curious look. "Not like you to be working late."

"Well, I was ..." Detective Leonard Purdy had finally cracked a case but there was no one at the police department he could tell, least of all that strait-laced son of a bitch, Mallard. "Just ... uh, looking through some travel sites on the computer. Was planning some vacation next month."

"Get the hell out of here, Purdy. I catch you using department resources for personal business again and no one, not even your uncle, is going to save your ass." Mallard stomped away.

Purdy took the flash drive from the computer and the registration printout from Tennessee, stuffed them in his pocket, and headed for the door. He had a call to make.

FORTY-FIVE

Night of Horrors

The night of horrors seemed unending. Any flame of decency burning in the hearts of Demeron and his guests flickered and went out like a candle in a hurricane. Inhibitions were unleashed, fantasies played out, secret desires fulfilled.

There were limits to what the alcohol and drugs could do to dull the senses of their victims. By the time they gathered for breakfast in the dining hall the next morning, each bore the scars—physical, emotional, or both—of the night's ordeal.

More experienced, and familiar with the lodge's working, Ted Jolly was in the best condition. He was merely exhausted. Elizabeth Ranskill was insatiable, and there were limits to what even a young, sexually adept partner could do to satisfy her.

She wanted it every way and from every position. Not that Jolly wasn't sufficiently skilled. He was a young, sexually active man, young enough to be Ranskill's son. But there were limits to what he could do and how often he could do it in the space of a few hours.

The next morning, Ranskill glided into breakfast, the flush still on her face, glowing and radiant. Jolly walked behind her, slowly, stiff-legged and wincing in discomfort as he moved around tending to his other duties, setting up the breakfast buffet.

Oliver Parson and Sherry came in, neatly groomed, shaved, scrubbed, and smelling of cologne and body wash. Arm around her waist, Parson guided her to the buffet and helped her fill her plate. He spoke softly, intimately, in her ear from time to time. Each time Sherry forced a resigned smile that didn't fool anyone watching, except Parson, who practically beamed at every weary nod of her young head. In short, he acted like a love-struck teenager, completely smitten by the prom queen. Except he was no teenager and Sherry would never be a prom queen.

Young as she was, Sherry was not a sexual novice, but her partners in the past were teenage boys of her approximate age. They'd screwed like rabbits the way teens do--in cars, in back rooms, once under a porch. Hormones surged through their bodies, and with the careless abandon of youth, hungry for the passion of the moment, they screwed. Then it was over.

But not with Parson. Fascinated by her girlish body, profoundly aroused by it, he treated her like an adult lover, speaking intimately as he might have to a more mature woman. But Sherry was not a mature woman. She was a child, and his adult attentions overpowered her, disgusted her, and frightened her.

Simon Taylor walked in stiffly beside Brad. His eyes darted around the room, nodding at Parson and Ranskill, a bit sheepishly, as if he'd been caught in some compromising situation, like the time his high school classmates found him masturbating in a restroom stall after leaving the boys' locker room shower in gym class.

He was new to the school, had transferred in from a predominantly Jewish area in the northeast, and the sight of so many uncircumcised penises mysteriously shrouded in foreskin had mesmerized him. Already predisposed to favor the intimacy of males, the fetish for uncircumcised companions dominated his sexual fantasies.

Brad's member had aroused him to the point that, after a couple of hours, Brad begged him to stop handling it. Taylor looked up from between Brad's legs and said like an attorney summarizing his case for the jury, "I paid for this. It is only fair. In fact, you have an obligation to submit." Then he went back to his fantasy.

The money. Think of the money. Brad lay spread eagle on the bed trying to think about the thousand dollars in the envelope and the dollars Loni and Lorraine promised for staying. By the time Taylor insisted they shower together and dress for breakfast, Brad had decided to hell with the money. Prostituting himself was one thing, but Taylor's freaky obsession with his penis was more than he could take.

Cindy walked in huddled under Senator Kellin's arm, his hand clutching her breast possessively. Bleary-eyed from drugs and alcohol. Tears streamed down her face.

She'd spent most of the night nearly comatose. Kellin was indifferent. In fact, he preferred that she was mostly unconscious, submissive, and compliant. With Cindy unable to respond or object, he was free to do what he did without the need to discuss it. Senator Kellin was not into small talk or explanations. He was into sex with children.

So, he forced himself on her, which is to say, he raped her. He raped her in every way imaginable, from every position he could force her inert body to assume. Once, Cindy awoke from a period of drug-induced somnolence to find his penis shoved in her mouth. She gagged, but Kellin would not release her head as he pumped. She was blacking out when he finally allowed her to gasp a breath of air before he began the assault once more.

By the morning, every orifice on her body was sore, tender, and swollen. When she went to the bathroom, she found she was bleeding from both ends. She began crying.

Kellin ignored her as he readied himself for the day, then threw her clothes at her. "Get ready. They'll be waiting for us."

Cindy avoided the looks of the others, allowed Kellin to push her into a chair at the table, then sat sobbing while he went and piled a plate with pancakes, eggs, and sausage for himself. He returned, sat next to her, and said, "Get something to eat." He grinned. "You need to keep up your strength."

Last, A.C. Demeron appeared in the doorway, surveying his kingdom, smiling benevolently. "Well, how was your night?" he called out. "Everything to your satisfaction, I trust."

He reached behind him and jerked Malina forward so that she stumbled into the room at his side. "Come in and join the party." Demeron pushed her toward the buffet table and ordered, "Get yourself something to eat."

Eyes blazing, she stared straight ahead, without looking

at the others. The purple bruise blossoming across her cheek was evidence of how her night had passed.

Parson averted his eyes and leaned close to Sherry, patting her hand.

Taylor sat stiffly beside Brad and looked at his plate.

Ranskill and Jolly ignored her, she stroking his groin under the table, and he trying not to wince in pain.

Malina glared at Demeron when she returned to the table. He reached out to touch her face, ran a fingernail over a split in her lower lip from one of the slaps she'd received, touched a finger to the bruise on her cheek, and tapped it hard. She jerked away in pain. He smiled. "I do like them fiery."

FORTY-SIX

Information

"Got some results for you." Tanya Lindt sat in her office cubicle at the state forensic lab in Pierre, South Dakota, leaning over and speaking in a voice just barely louder than a whisper. "But first I have a question."

Dean Weber had delivered the blood samples from County Road 87 to her personally, asked her to rush the testing through, and call as soon as she had something. That was yesterday. He'd been waiting for the call since then ... and the question.

"Go ahead." He put the phone on speaker as he cruised along a Blanken County back road.

"Am I going to lose my job for this?" Lindt raised her head to look around the cubicles. Most of the staff were at lunch, and none were within listening range.

"No," Weber said without hesitation. "I'll take the heat if there are questions."

"Then why all the secrecy?"

Tanya and Dean had been a thing back in high school ... for a while. It had never been a case of first-love-true-love. They were just kids who liked to make out under the stars on a summer night in the bed of Dean's old pickup. Sometimes they did more than make out, but they were always careful about it and made sure there were no ties beyond the pleasures of the moment. Graduation came. Tanya went off to an out-of-state university, and Dean headed to a community college in Sioux Falls. With no pre-planning on their parts, both ended up with degrees in related fields, Tanya with a BS in forensic science and Dean taking a two-year degree in criminal justice before heading back to Blanken County.

For a couple of years, Dean worked around as a hand for local ranches, then when he turned twenty-one, he signed on with the sheriff's department. About the same time, Tanya went to work for the state forensic lab.

They didn't really keep in touch over the years. Life moved on. Both married, had kids, and established themselves in their careers. Occasionally, they ran into one another around the county when Tanya came back for holidays or to visit her parents and siblings. Their high school relationship transformed into a casual and distant acquaintance. Beyond that, they never communicated, so when Dean called her and asked for a favor, below the radar, it was a stretch.

"Not exactly a secret," Weber answered her question but knew she expected more than that. "Just trying not to make waves." He grimaced, waiting, knowing that still wasn't a sufficient explanation.

"What the kind of waves? Speak plainly." Given the mystery around Weber's request for help, Lindt had a right to be cautious. "You sent me blood samples with a case number attached ... to my specific attention when any lab technician could have handled the analysis. Before I give you the results personally by telephone as you requested, instead of through normal official channels, I want to know what is going on."

"Fair enough." Weber took a breath and said, "You know from the case number this is about the Lew Bentz murder, right?"

"Yes," Lindt said quietly. "Terrible what happened. Sheriff Bedford made an arrest, though. Bob Shank, I heard."

"That's right. We arrested Shank, but …" Weber hesitated.

Lindt filled the blanks for him. "But what if Bedford got the wrong guy? Is that what you're saying?"

"I guess what I'm saying is, the sheriff rushed the entire investigation. Some of the evidence seems to point at Shank, but there are things we haven't looked at yet. Things that might lead us to another suspect."

"Like this blood sample," Lindt said.

"Like the blood sample." Weber agreed. "I sent it to you to examine, because the sheriff, and everyone else for that matter, is convinced that Shank killed Lew Bentz. I'm keeping a low profile on this until I know for certain one way or another, and for now, I'll bury the results, whatever they are, with the rest of the investigative paperwork. If there's nothing to it, then great. That means Shank is probably our man and everything is fine."

"But if there is something to it," Lindt finished for him. "Someone is trying to push this along, convict Shank without all the evidence, and the question is why."

"Exactly," Weber said.

"And what are you going to do if there is something to it?"

"I haven't figured that out," Weber sighed. "Tread carefully, I guess. I'd like to keep my job."

"You may need to worry about more than your job." Lindt shuffled through the report printout on her desk. "There *is* something to it."

"I was afraid of that," Weber said softly. "Give me the details."

"Determining the blood types from the samples you sent was routine. What is interesting is that they come from two different people."

Weber listened without speaking. This was the news he didn't want.

"One sample came back as type A-negative. I checked the state police academy personnel records and found Lew Bentz's file and a note from his physical evaluation that his blood type was A-negative. It's a relatively uncommon type, and we can be reasonably certain it came from Bentz. A DNA test would determine that conclusively."

"And the other sample?"

"O-positive," Lindt said. "The most common blood type. About thirty-five percent of the population carry around O-positive blood. DNA testing could identify whose blood it is but without a body, living or dead, to match it to, the blood type result is almost meaningless." She paused while Weber absorbed the information, then asked, "Do we have another body?"

"No," Weber said firmly, making his mind up about something. "We do not."

"Then what do we do next?"

"*We* don't do anything next. I told you, I'll take the heat if there is any problem." He thought for a second, making up his mind. "There is only one thing to do."

"Go to Sheriff Bedford and don't bury the report,"

Lindt said. "That's all you can do. You have to let him know that things aren't wrapped up as neatly as he thought."

"I'm not sure about Bedford," Weber said. "But I have to keep digging until I find a body and DNA that matches that second blood type … living or dead, as you pointed out."

"What do you mean, you're not sure about Bedford? Are you saying …" Lindt stopped mid-sentence. "You think Bedford is covering up something about the murder?"

"I don't know what I think," Weber said. "And that's the bottom line. I don't know, and until I do, I can't take the chance that …"

"Stop," Lindt ordered. "I know you said you'd take the heat and keep me out of it, but this is different. If you think there is more to Lew Bentz's murder, you don't have to protect me. You have to investigate it. I did my job, now, you do yours."

"I am going to investigate it … quietly, though," Weber said.

"On your own? Without department resources?"

"I'm not sure." He spoke slowly, trying to come up with a plan now that Lindt had confirmed his suspicions. "Can you email me the report, but sit on the official submission until I have a chance to look into things?"

"I can, but not for long. I used lab resources, chain of custody and all that. We have checks and balances, and my work will be reviewed by others and then forwarded with the corresponding case number to the investigating agency. That's the Blanken County Sheriff's office." She paused and added, "Besides, sitting on the report is exactly the *wrong* way to go about this."

"No. I told you, I'd take the heat. I don't want this to blow back on you if there are any repercussions."

"Look, if you're really concerned about me ... about us ... bucking the sheriff, maybe uncovering something dirty, then the best thing to do is to have it out in the open. We want more eyes on this, not fewer. Get it out there so Bedford will think twice about doing anything that could draw suspicion his way."

"You may be right." Weber thought it over and nodded. "You always were quicker on the uptake than me."

She laughed. "Just quicker to cover my ass. If my daddy had ever found us in the back of that pickup, neither one of us would be here to talk about it today."

She was right. "Fair enough," Weber said. "I'll go to Bedford with your forensic report and tell him I'm just following through. He won't be happy ... probably blow up at me for circumventing the chain of command, but I'll make sure others know about it. He might discipline me for insubordination, but I don't see how he could do more than that."

"Do you have someone you can work with? Someone you trust?"

"I think so."

"Good. Get that person in the loop before you go to Bedford. The more people who know what you're up to, the better."

"Right."

"And one more thing."

"Yes?"

"Take care of yourself, Dean."

"You do the same, Tanya." He disconnected and scrolled through the numbers on his phone, then punched the call icon. It was answered on the first ring. "Yes."

"I have some information," Weber said.

"Tell me."

FORTY-SEVEN

About As Expected

Weber reviewed the forensic report, blood test results, and conversation he had with Tanya Lindt. When he finished, he asked, "What do you think?"

"You sure you want me involved in this?" Sole asked.

"Yeah, I think so," Weber said. "I know you were some kind of cop, and right now it seems you're the only other person questioning the investigation into Lew's murder. I need someone to bounce things off, and unless you didn't mean what you said about helping, you're elected."

"I meant what I said."

"So, what do you think?"

"Your friend at the crime lab is right. You need to go to Bedford. If he's clean in this, he might blow up, but he can't fault you for doing your job. If he's dirty, the more people who know that you're looking into things, the safer you are."

"I'm heading back to the office to speak to him now."

"Good. Make sure someone else knows what you're doing ... another deputy ... or several deputies would be better. We want plenty of people aware that you're about to piss off the sheriff. The more eyes looking at him, waiting for him to react, the more likely he is to keep his head down ... if he's dirty."

"What do you think?" Weber asked quietly, trying to wrap his brain around what they were getting into. "You said you were in law enforcement once. Is it possible a sheriff could be involved in something like this ... covering up the murder of one of his deputies?"

"You mean, is he dirty? I don't know." Over the years, Sole had seen the best and worst in people, including cops. The vast majority were good people doing a tough job ... sometimes an impossible job ... but he knew they weren't all saints, either. He'd run across a few rotten apples, and he didn't imagine that South Dakota was immune to police corruption. "I can help you ask the questions, but that's one question you have to answer for yourself, Deputy Weber."

"Fair enough," Weber said. "And call me Dean. Looks like we're going to be partners for a while."

"Looks like it," Sole said and added, "I'm Bill."

"I know. Everyone around Alder knows how Lew got you out of that snowbank." He laughed. "Or you'd likely be a corpse-sickle about now."

"So, I've heard. Lew told me that himself and used that same expression the night he rescued my ass."

They were quiet for a few seconds at the mention of Lew's name, then Weber said, "Alright, I'm gonna go get my ass chewed out by the sheriff. After that, we should meet up."

"I'll be at Langstrom's. Some people we should talk to there."

"Got somebody in mind?"

"I do, and a couple of thoughts on how we move forward."

"Good. I'll meet you there when my shift ends."

Weber pulled his county vehicle into the public parking lot outside and walked through the front door of the sheriff's department headquarters. He stopped by the reception desk to stomp the snow off his boots on the rubber welcome mat, then looked up and smiled at the receptionist. "How you doing, Bev?"

"Just another day in heaven," Bev replied. She wore a sheriff's department uniform but with a name tag that read *Beverly Sands, Administration*, and without a badge. "You're in early."

"Just stopping by to brief the sheriff. I got some news from the state crime lab about Lew Bentz's murder. He should hear it."

"Really?"

"Yeah, it could be important."

"What kind of news?" A deputy wearing sergeant's stripes on his shoulder, seven service stripes on his sleeve, and a name tag that read *Sergeant J. Patterson* appeared on the other side of the half-wall behind the reception desk.

"Test results from some blood samples I took at the scene where Lew checked out the box truck."

"We already have plenty to put Shank away for the murder." Patterson shook his head and gave a wry smile. "You bucking for a promotion?"

"Nope." Weber returned the smile. "But the blood test results show that someone else was at the scene ... and bleeding."

"Bleeding?" Sergeant Patterson's brow furrowed. "So, what does that prove? Lew put up a fight. Maybe he drew some blood from Shank."

"If I remember right, Shank didn't have any injuries when we arrested him. At least, not any that would leave a blood trail on the ground."

"What's going on?" Another deputy, this one wearing captain's bars, came up behind Patterson.

"Weber here wants to stir up the shit with the sheriff. Says there might be somebody else involved in Lew Bent's murder."

"What the hell's your problem, Weber?" Captain Paul Trundle shook his head. "Making waves and rocking the boat? That your thing now?"

"Doing my job is my thing, Captain," Weber snapped back. "Is the sheriff around?"

"Sure, he's around." Trundle nodded to a short hallway at the far end of the office area. "It's your ass. Go for it."

"I will." Weber crossed the room. A couple of deputies working on reports looked up from their desks, exchanged glances, and shook their heads as he passed. He walked down the hall, reached Sheriff Bedford's office, took a deep breath, and rapped on the door.

"Enter!" Bedford called out from inside.

Weber pushed the door open, stepped through, and left it ajar behind him. Better to let everyone hear what he had to say.

"What is it, Weber?" Bedford said, sitting back in his chair as he removed his reading glasses.

"I've been following up on the murder investigation." He didn't have to explain which murder investigation. There was only one in Blanken County.

"Following up?" Bedford's eyes narrowed. "What the hell does that mean?"

"Just that I went out along County Road 87 to where Lew said he was checking the box truck."

"Bob Shank's box truck," Bedford interrupted.

"It's not registered to Shank," Weber shot back.

"Parked on his property. That's as good as being in his name in my book."

"More like hidden there … could have left been by anyone."

"Get to the point," Bedford ordered.

Weber took a deep breath and continued, "Anyway, I was out on the road and I found a blood trail frozen in the snow, right about where Lew said he was checking the truck."

"So, what does that prove?" Bedford leaned forward and rested his elbows on his desk. "Lew was shot. That would be the logical place to find blood."

"I had the samples tested by the crime lab."

"You did what?" Bedford's voice rose. "On whose authority?"

"On mine, I guess. Following up on the investigation, like I said."

"You had no right … no authority to do that. I told you. We made an arrest. The investigation is closed, and the DA is satisfied with our case."

"Our case could be stronger," Weber said and continued before the sheriff could interrupt again. "The test results came back with two different blood types. One was the same as Lew's, the other was different."

"The other was …" Bedford's face flushed and his eyes narrowed even more until he was squinting at Weber.

"Different," Weber finished for him. "That means …"

"Don't try to fucking tell me what it means!" Bedford was shouting now.

Heads turned out in the office area. Sergeant Patterson

and Captain Trundle exchanged glances and grinned. "Tried to warn him," Trundle mumbled.

"I'm just trying to get to the bottom of things, Sheriff." Weber spoke quietly, knowing that all he could do now was stand there and absorb Bedford's rage.

"I'll say this one last time, Weber. We have Lew Bentz's killer in jail. He will stand trial for murder. And you ..." Bedford raised a stubby finger, pointed it at Weber, then thumped it hard on his desk. "You are not to waste another minute of department time or resources on a case that is closed." He stood and leaned over his desk to look Weber in the eyes. "Do you understand me, Deputy?"

"I understand, Sheriff."

"Now get your ass out of here before I write you up and suspend you for insubordination!"

"Yes, Sheriff." Weber nodded, turned, and walked the gauntlet between the chuckling deputies, heading outside to his car. He climbed in, cranked the engine, pulled out his cell phone, and called Sole.

"How'd it go?" Sole asked as he answered

"About as expected."

FORTY-EIGHT

Down Payment

"I got what you wanted," Detective Leonard Purdy beamed over the phone, visions of the cartel's bonus for his rapid work dancing in his brain. Hell, fuck the Caribbean. If he played it right, that island he dreamed of might be in the south Pacific somewhere. He closed his eyes and could see scantily clad, brown-skinned beauties swaying their hips under palm trees while blue waters lapped against white sand.

"Not over the phone."

Purdy's cartel contact brought him back to reality. "Right. Where do you want to meet?"

"Come by the shop."

"The shop?" Shit, not the shop, he thought. "When?"

"Now." The cartel man disconnected.

Purdy knew him by his street name, *El Gordo*—the Big Man—a name that stemmed from his six-foot-four, two-hundred-fifty-pound stature plus the fact that he controlled the cartel's interests in the city. Purdy knew from Gordo's extensive criminal file that the name his mother had given him thirty-eight years earlier in Guadalajara was Jorge Rodriguez. But no one dared call him by his real name publicly, including detective Purdy.

"The shop," Purdy muttered after the call ended. "I hate meeting at the fucking shop?"

Why not the club where Gordo and his associates hung out? Why not the check cashing service the locals used to wire money back to their families south of the border? Why not someplace public with plenty of eyes around? Why not anywhere except the shop?

Purdy knew that was the reason. For this bit of cartel business, Gordo wanted no eyes around, no possibility of an overheard conversation. Purdy was on his own, and he had a decision to make—meet Gordo as instructed or call back and ask … beg … for an alternate location, one that would be safer for him if things didn't work out the way he planned.

Shit. He had no choice, and he knew it. Gordo said the shop and asking for a change would only piss him off and put the entire exchange of information for the promised bonus in danger of falling apart, and despite his reservations, Purdy was not about to give up his big payday.

Purdy steered his unmarked but plainly identifiable police sedan to a dark corner of the city. Garbage overflowed the tops of trash cans and littered the streets. Tattered scarecrows, barely recognizable as humans, slumped in doorways or lay sprawled on the sidewalks for others to step over. There was no way of telling if they were dead or alive without getting close enough to inhale the stench emanating from their unwashed bodies and rotting teeth, and Purdy was not about to do that.

He turned at a corner. Four men—Gordo's men—stood, two each, on opposite curbs, hands resting on the butts of pistols tucked in their designer jeans, ready to pour gunfire into any threat that might appear. Purdy lifted a hand from the steering wheel and nodded, trying to appear nonchalant and harmless. The cold-faced men gave no acknowledgment, watching as he drove slowly down the block and parked along the curb in front of an old storefront.

He got out and looked back at the corner. One of Gordo's men watched him, speaking into a cell phone to alert Gordo of his arrival. The others kept their eyes on the adjacent street, scanning up and down the blocks for anyone who might have followed the police detective.

Purdy wiped his damp hands on the sides of his trousers. Gordo's people had nicknamed him *El Suda*—the one who sweats—because of Purdy's unfortunate tendency to perspire heavily whenever in Gordo's immediate presence.

He stepped up on the curb. This section of the street was clear of trash and derelicts. He was about to knock on the glass door when it opened out, forcing him to step back. Another of Gordo's steely-eyed guards looked out to scan up and down the street and said something into his phone to the man on the corner. Purdy didn't speak Spanish, but he grimaced when he heard the words *El Suda* and saw the man grin as he stepped out of the way to allow Purdy to pass through the door, locking it behind them.

The old store's plate-glass windows and doors were draped in heavy black cloth, preventing light from entering or escaping. Thick, sound-proofing tiles covered the walls.

The guard led him to a back room where he found Gordo seated in a leather chair behind a large executive desk. Without preliminaries, Gordo looked up from the laptop on the desk and said, "Show me what you have."

"Sure ... sure ..." Purdy wiped at the sweat dripping over his eyebrows, threatening to blind him. "I mean, I thought we could talk about ... you know ... well, how much ..."

"How much!" Gordo roared. He glared at Purdy a second before his broad face split into wide-mouthed laughter. His shoulders heaved, and the chair creaked under his bulk. "You hear that? *El Suda wants to negotiate ... with me!*" Gordo shook his head, laughing harder now.

The guard still standing behind was laughing now too, his breath tickling the back of Purdy's neck and making the hairs stand up. Dripping now from head to foot, Purdy's clothes clung to his body. Perspiration ran from his armpits along the sides of his chest to his waist, tickling and sending an icy chill through him.

He shoved his hands inside his pockets to try and dry them. There seemed to be no limits to the amount of water flooding from every pore in his body, but he had a bigger problem now. Alone in the shop with Gordo and the guard and their mocking laughter, he felt defenseless, fragile, a bug about to be pinned to a board for their entertainment. His bladder threatened to empty, spilling its contents over Gordo's expensive carpet. No, he thought, desperate. Please, please, please. Purdy clenched his groin and shuffled from foot to foot.

Gordo picked up on his body language. The laughter ceased abruptly. He looked at the guard. "Take him to the bathroom before he pisses on my floor."

The guard escorted him out of the office and to a small room near the bolted back door. "Do what you gotta do."

It came out in a dribble at first, and then the floodgates opened. Purdy pissed and pissed some more, the guard standing outside the door, watching and shaking his head.

The hot stream splashed in the toilet and took some of his anxiety with it. When he finished, he sighed, zipped up, and let the guard direct him back to Gordo's office.

Gordo looked up. "So nervous that I might kill you that you almost pissed your pants." He shook his head in disgust. "You really are a stupid man."

Purdy's mouth opened and closed, gasping like a fish suddenly yanked from water. "I only meant …"

"Shut up. I know what you meant." Gordo leaned on the desk. "Do you really think I would do something to you here, with your cop car parked on the curb? Even in this neighborhood, people see … people talk. Even a sorry-ass cop like you would be missed and they would begin looking for you. Sooner or later, they would come here."

Purdy shook his head. "It's not that. It's only …"

"I said shut up." Gordo shook his head. "Unlike you, I am not stupid, so here is what we will do." He tapped the desk beside the laptop. "You will give me the information you bring. I will examine it … check things out … if it is good information, you will be paid, just as I promised. Do you understand?"

Purdy nodded.

"Good. Now let's have the information."

Purdy reached in a pocket, retrieved the USB flash drive, and placed it on the desk. "This is a video from surveillance cameras not too far from the corner you told me about. I have it edited down to the important part."

Gordo put the flash drive in the laptop's USB port and leaned forward. He began with an air of bored indifference, but as the video came to the images of the pickup stopped at the signal, the profile of the driver, and the closeup of the tag, he nodded and looked up. "And the license plate number?"

Purdy pulled out his notepad, ripped out a page, and laid it on the desk. "All there, a Tennessee tag registered to Bill Myers, with his last known address."

"Hmmm ... no doubt the address is a fake, as is the name."

"But ..." Purdy began.

"Relax," Gordo said. "This is good. The man in the image is the one we are looking for, and the information on the tag will be useful in tracking him down." He took the flash drive from the laptop and placed it on the desk. "You've done well, but there is more for you to do."

"More?" Purdy's shoulders sagged. "If the information is good, I thought ..."

"What?" Gordo interrupted. "You thought you'd go live on your island somewhere." He laughed. "In good time you will, but for now, we need more than what you've given me today."

Gordo opened a desk drawer and pulled out a strapped bundle of one-hundred-dollar bills. He laid the bundle beside the flash drive. "Consider this a down payment. Ten thousand dollars ... It's yours. A very nice day's work for you, but I'm afraid not enough to buy that island you dream of. Finish this for us ... with us ... and you will live like a king wherever you wish for the rest of your life."

Purdy's eyes focused on the money, then lifted to Gordo's smiling face, then back to the money. He reached out and lifted the bundle of hundreds and nodded. "What do I have to do?"

FORTY-NINE

Choices
———

"I've got one fucking question for you?" Malina stormed into the small suite of rooms that served as Loni's home at the lodge.

Seated in a chair beside a window with a view of the barn and grain bin behind, Loni looked up from the game of solitaire on her phone. "I don't know what …"

"Stop!" Malina shouted. "Don't even try to pretend you don't know what I mean." She stood over Loni, glaring. "I want to know how you live with yourself. You knew exactly what was going to happen! All your lies … a new life, money, freedom to go where we want after … it's all bullshit!"

"Calm down," Loni said and looked toward the door. "Someone might hear you."

"Let them!" Malina glared at her. "What fucking difference does it make? We're prisoners here. You set that up real nice, didn't you … you and that Lorraine bitch, smiling her smile like she was some kind of princess and this is some kind of tea party."

"Look, I'm sorry if things were harder than you thought they would be."

"Harder!" Malina touched the bruise on her cheek and winced.

"I know ... I know. Mr. Demeron can be a little rough sometimes, but he makes it up to you later. Trust me, you'll see. There'll be a bonus in your next envelope."

"Fuck the bonus!" Malina's fury was a raging torrent now. "Did you see what that son of a bitch Kellin did to Cindy! She's bleeding ... can barely walk and just sits in her room blubbering. She's terrified that she has to do it all over again tonight." Malina leaned toward Loni. "And she does, doesn't she? This wasn't some kind of one-night stand deal, was it?"

Loni opened her mouth to speak and then closed it. There was nothing to say. Malina was right. Their ordeal would continue tonight and the next until Demeron's guests departed and the next group came in, and then when he grew tired of them ... she'd seen too many sent back to the streets to be prostituted out, all the money they were promised taken from the accounts set up in their names.

Except this time, it was different. They had witnessed the murders.

Malina saw through Loni's silence, could see the wheels spinning in her head, at a loss for something to say, for some way to defend what was happening ... what she was part of. She wanted to spit on the floor in disgust.

She didn't. Instead, she continued her tirade. "And Sherry ... she doesn't say much. She actually thinks she's going to get the money you promised, but that creepy asshole you put with her could be her grandfather, hanging all over her like she was going to be some kind of lover and run off with her."

She leaned even closer, her face a mask of anger. "Who the fuck does that? What kind of place is this? A bunch of sick old men going around fucking ..." She took a breath, considering the word she was going to use, hesitant to use it to describe herself, then decided it applied and nodded, spitting the word at Loni. "Kids ... that's what they are ... what we are ... kids. Those assholes like to fuck kids."

She rose to her full height, staring down at Loni. "And you're part of it ... as sick as they are because you're part of it."

Loni's face twitched as if Malina had slapped her. "You don't understand," she began lamely, but Malina cut her off.

"No, *you don't understand*. We want out. You've been here the longest. There has to be a way out ... something we can do."

Loni's head turned toward the window, her eyes focused on the grain bin behind the barn. Three bodies lay frozen and stacked inside, waiting for a break in the weather and the ground to thaw so someone could bury them in a place where no one would ever find them. She'd watched two of those girls leave, hoping they would find a way, not strong enough to stop them ... and they died.

"There isn't anything I can do." Loni shook her head and looked at Malina. "It's been tried ... they didn't make it."

"They didn't ..." Malina's eyes narrowed. "What does that mean ... they didn't make it?"

"What the hell do you think it means?" Loni snapped back. "Look, you're not the first ones to come here and you won't be the last." She took a breath and spoke more softly. "I know from experience that you can't get away ... until they're ready for you to leave."

"Bullshit!" Malina shouted, then stopped, her eyes

opening wide. "You ... you were like us ... brought here in the back of a truck."

"Not exactly like you, but yes, I was brought here."

"And you stayed!"

"I stayed." Loni nodded. "I saw there was nothing else to do, so I made the most of it ... made myself useful and they let me stay without sending me back to ..." She shrugged. "Anyway, they didn't send me back."

Malina sagged down on the bed across from Loni, processing the desperateness of the situation Loni described. "So, you're a prisoner here ... like us?"

"Not exactly, like you." Loni shook her head. "It took a while, but they trust me now."

"Trust you?" Malina sneered. "You mean they use you to keep us in line." A thought occurred to Malina, and she raised her eyebrows, curious? "If they trust you, then you can leave ... right?"

"Why would I do that?" Loni gave a wry smile. "I have everything I want here. Good food, clothes, a nice place to live, and money to spend shopping when we go to Sioux Falls for supplies." She nodded. "I live better here than I ever have anywhere else ... than I ever could anywhere else. Why would I want to leave?"

Malina's shoulders sagged, deflated and defeated. "So, you'll just let it happen to us."

"I'm not letting anything happen," Loni said defensively. "It just is. I didn't do it to you."

Malina looked up. "You could help us get away."

"I told you, there's no ..."

Malina interrupted, "There are cars here. You said they trust you, so you could sneak one out and drive us away."

"And what about me?" Loni said, angry now. "What happens to me after you get away ... if you get away? What happens when they don't trust me anymore and they throw me out ... send me back to ..." She shook her head. "I can't go back to living like that."

Malina stood and shook her head, staring into Loni's eyes. "Then I guess you have a choice to make. Help us get away, or be like them." Malina stared at her.

"Don't you understand?" Loni said. "There are no choices."

"There is always a choice. You say they trust you," Malina sneered. "They killed one of us ... Bobbi ... and that cop. We saw it. You think they're ever going to trust any of us?"

"Think about that," Malina said then spun and disappeared down the hallway.

Loni stared out the window at the grain bin, huddled across the yard behind the barn. Inside, there were others who had made their choices, and paid the price for them.

FIFTY

Assisting

It was ten PM when Dean Weber stopped by Langstrom's. Sole looked up and nodded, motioning him to a table in a corner, then turned to Harry Langstrom. "Gonna take a break for a few."

"Take all the time you want. Pretty slow tonight." Langstrom pulled a bottle of beer from the well, opened it, and put it in front of Arnold Cowley, seated in his usual spot at the bar.

Sole walked to the corner table and noticed that Weber was out of uniform. "You not on the job tonight?"

Weber shook his head. "Called in sick."

"How's that going to go over with the sheriff?"

"At this point, I don't think that matters." Weber shrugged. "Anyway, you said meet here ... I'm here."

"Right." Sole went back to the bar, grabbed two beers from the well and returned. "Drink up. Might be here a while."

Weber nodded and lifted the bottle. "Thanks."

They sipped the beers for a few minutes before Weber

asked in a low voice, "The person you want to talk to is here, right?"

"Yep." Sole nodded at Arnold Cowley.

"Right." Weber took another sip from the bottle. "So, how do you want to do it?"

"Ever work a CI before?" Sole spoke in a low voice, but casually, as if they were discussing the weather.

"Criminal informant?" Weber shook his head. "Can't say as I have. Not much call for that around here." His eyes narrowed. "You thinking of having Cowley inform on someone? Who?"

"Best keep things quiet until we're alone. Drink some beer and I'll fill you in when we leave."

"Alright." Weber sipped his beer, more slowly now, trying not to fidget in his seat.

A half-hour passed before Cowley stood up, placed a twenty on the bar, and gave a wave to Langstrom. "See you next time, Harry."

"I figure that means tomorrow, Arnold," Langstrom grinned. "Unless the world stops turning between now and then."

"Yep." Cowley hitched his pants up and shuffled to the door.

A minute later, the headlights on his pickup lit up the plate-glass window, and he pulled away. "Let's go," Sole said and called out to the bar. "Be back in a while, Harry."

"Okay, Bill." Langstrom leaned back against the counter, watching the single television screen where the Milwaukee Bucks were battling it out in a close game with the Cleveland Cavaliers.

Outside, they climbed into Weber's SUV. Blanken County allowed deputies to take their assigned vehicles home, not an uncommon practice in smaller departments. Sole figured they could make good use of it tonight.

"So, what are we doing?" Weber asked as he cranked the engine.

"Follow Cowley."

"Right," Weber said and pulled away from Langstrom's, following Cowley's dwindling taillights. "Good thing there's no snow tonight, or we might have to get on his bumper to keep him in sight."

"Do you know where he lives?" Sole asked.

"I do." Weber nodded. "Little doublewide shack of a place over near the Demeron ranch."

"Good. I expect he'll be headed home, so we can back off and stay just out of sight ... give him time to get home and get comfortable."

"We want him comfortable? I would have thought just the opposite."

"Oh, we're going to make him plenty uncomfortable," Sole said, smiling. "But first we'll let him get nice and snug at home so he's not expecting anything but a good night's sleep."

"Okay." Weber nodded. "In the meantime, maybe you can fill me in. Why are we going after Cowley?"

"After we met out on the county road, I decided to see where it led ... followed it out to ..."

"A.C Demeron's hunting preserve," Weber interrupted. "Cowley works there."

"Yes, he does. Came out to greet me when I pulled in. His boss didn't seem too happy about that ... like Cowley might say something he shouldn't."

"So?"

"So, we're looking for a weak link. I got the feeling that Arnold Cowley might be their weak link."

"Weak link to what?"

"I don't know." Sole shrugged. "Maybe nothing … maybe I'm just chasing shadows, but someone drove that truck away from where you took those blood samples and that road leads directly to Demeron's place, not to Bob Shank's house."

Weber mulled it over. "Okay, how do we do this?"

The best leverage they had was Cowley's own doubts about what they already knew. Sole outlined the strategy. "If he protests, ignore it. If he asks questions, ignore them. Don't ask him direct questions. Questions will let him know we don't know much and will make him think he can say little or nothing to us, or just outright lie. Yes or no answers or an *I don't know* won't get us anywhere."

"If we aren't asking questions, then how do we get information out of him."

"Be assertive. Make open-ended statements. Let him think we know a lot more than we do. Put it out there so he fills in the blanks for us." Sole shrugged.

"Alright. I'll try." Weber sounded doubtful.

"Follow my lead. You'll see how it goes," Sole said with a lot more confidence than he actually felt. "Anything he tells us will be more than we have now."

They drove in silence after that. Cowley's taillights had disappeared. By the time Weber cut his headlights and pulled into the lot around Cowley's doublewide, one dim lightbulb lit up a window inside.

"Let's see what we can stir up," Sole said and pushed the SUV's door open.

He led the way through the unshoveled snow to the front porch, and before Weber could say anything, pounded on the door hard enough for the hinges to rattle. Footsteps thumped inside and the blinds on a side window moved enough for Cowley to peek outside. "Who the hell is that?" he shouted.

Sole nodded at Weber. "Get him to open up."

"It's Dean Weber! I need to talk to you."

"What the hell you need to talk to me about?" Cowley replied, without opening the door.

"Open up now, Arnold ... official business," Weber said, wondering what else he could say to coax Cowley to open the door. As it turned out, he didn't have to say anything.

Cowley jerked the door open. "What the hell you want with me this time of night? You got no cause to ..." His mouth closed mid-sentence. He eyed Sole standing to the side of the door.

"Hello, Arnold," Sole said, smiling. "We need to talk."

"Talk?" Arnold stood wide-eyed, looking from Sole to Weber and back. "About what?"

"About what happened out at the Demeron hunting preserve." Sole gave a nod. "I think you know what I mean."

It was a bluff. A smarter man or more seasoned criminal might have called the bluff. Cowley was neither and opened the door wider so they could enter.

Sole walked in ahead of Weber, looked around the shabby room, and nodded at a threadbare sofa. "Sit down, Arnold. We're going to have a talk."

"Can he do that?" Cowley's head spun toward Weber.

Weber ignored the question and simply said, "You should sit down, Arnold."

Cowley sat, his right knee bumping up and down nervously, fingers drumming on the sofa cushion beside him, his face taut with apprehension.

"We've got some things to talk over. If I catch you in a lie ..." Sole said and shook his head in warning. "Don't lie Arnold."

Cowley blinked and swallowed the lump threatening to choke him. "What kind of things do you want to talk over?"

"Let's start with the house." Sole stood over him, staring down.

"The house?" Cowley looked confused.

"The big house out at the hunting preserve ... the one where you work."

"Oh." Cowley nodded. "You mean the lodge."

"Alright, the lodge," Sole said patiently. "You know what I mean and you know what's going on there."

"No ... no, not really." Cowley swung his head back and forth. The wide-eyed stare, almost afraid to blink and lose sight of them for even a second, told Sole he'd struck a nerve.

"I warned you about lying," Sole said. "Tell the truth, and we'll do what we can to keep you out of trouble."

"I swear. I don't get involved in what goes on inside."

And with that answer—*what goes on inside*—Sole and Weber edged closer to the truth.

"We know you don't, or we wouldn't be here talking right now, and you'd already be in jail," Sole said, the hard tone replaced by one of understanding. "But we are going to move on the target, and when that happens ..." Sole let the words hang in the air where they swarmed like angry bees around Cowley's imagination.

"The target? Y-you mean the lodge." Cowley was sweating now. "Please, I swear I don't know anything about what Demeron and the people he brings do when they go inside."

Sole knew that was probably true. Arnold Cowley was

not someone a man of A.C. Demeron's stature would keep close at hand.

"The point is, right now ... before we make our move ... we're concerned about safety ... for everyone involved." Sole said, adding another layer to the bluff. "Things will happen quickly. We want to make sure everyone is out of the line of ... let's just leave it at we want everyone safe."

"Right ... keep everyone safe." Cowley nodded, by this point, wanting very much to be one of the safe ones

"To do that ... keep them safe," Sole continued. "We need to know how many and where they are inside."

Cowley could have stopped speaking at any time. He could have told them to get the fuck out of his house or to come back with a warrant. He could have said he didn't know what the hell they were talking about. He could have done any or all of that, but he didn't. Sole had chosen his man carefully.

"Okay," he said, taking a deep breath and exhaling to calm his pounding heart. "There's four with Mr. Demeron. Business types who came here to do some sort of deal with Mr. Demeron."

"Right, we know that." Sole said. They didn't know, but he nodded to Weber. "The ones we talked about."

"Right." Weber made a show of pulling out his notepad and jotting something down.

"The ones?" Arnold said. "You saw them, right? When you came out to the lodge and Huey got upset that you were there, and then Mr. Demeron came back?"

Sole ignored the question. "Inside there are a number of rooms, some set aside for the people he brings in. People can get hurt if we don't know exactly where they are inside."

"I don't know where they are exactly. Like I said I don't

get involved inside the lodge." Cowley's eyes were blinking fast now. "I do know they give them rooms over on the east wing away from the others."

"Good." Sole looked at Weber.

Weber made another note.

Cowley worked at swallowing the lump in his throat.

"And the others," Sole said, throwing out another bluff. "Besides the business types."

"Well, I mean … I don't really know much about that." Cowley's eyes darted from Weber's pen moving over the notepad to Sole's hard gaze. "I mean, I don't deal with that end of things." He spoke rapidly, his terrified brain cells trying to process what was happening.

"Arnold," Sole sighed. "You're doing good. Don't fuck it up and start lying now."

"It's not a lie," Arnold protested. "I don't deal with the girls. That's Huey's job."

Weber shot a look at Sole. Jackpot.

Sole remained focused on Cowley. He nodded and said, "It's important to keep the girls safe … to know their location inside."

"In rooms … different from the others … in a different part of the lodge. I don't get to go there so I don't really know much about that. I swear."

Weber made some more notes on the pad. Cowley's eyes darted to the pen in his hand and back to Sole.

"Please …" Cowley looked like he might puke. "Please … I don't want no trouble. I just work there … you know, handy work is all … fixing things, carrying things around for them. I don't have nothing to do with what they do with those kids. You got to believe me."

Weber looked up from the notepad, a dark look clouding his eyes. "The kids?" he said.

"Well, yeah. The girls ..." Cowley looked from one to the other. "You didn't know they're just kids, them and the boy." A light of hope flickered in his terrified eyes. "I mean that's good information ... right ... something you didn't know, right? Just so you know I didn't have nothing to do with those sorts of things."

"Those sorts of things?" Sole said

"You know ... the boy." Cowley shook his head and kept talking, the flood gates open now, unable to stop the torrent of words from spilling out. "I don't go that way, if you know what I mean." He shook his head. "But some of these business types must, because sometimes they bring in a boy to stay for a while."

"Alright so they're all kids. The girls and the boy." Sole looked hard in Cowley's eyes and said, "The truck ..."

"The truck?" Cowley's face paled. His mouth opened and closed like a man gasping for air.

It was not a question. It was a shot in the dark, but an aimed one, and Sole knew he'd struck another nerve. "The truck," he repeated and smiled. "You know, the one that ended up out at Bob Shank's place."

Cowley looked like he might fall over onto the floor. Hands shaking, he reached for a pack of cigarettes on the table beside the sofa, lit one up, and stared up at the men towering over him.

"You know about the truck?"

"We know," Sole said without adding that Cowley had just confirmed their suspicions.

"You have to believe me. I didn't have nothing to do with that."

"Convince me," Sole ordered.

"It's like this. The truck just shows up. I don't know the fellas driving it ... nothing to do with me." Cowley swallowed and shook his head. "They come from out west somewhere."

"Washington," Sole said, offering up the only piece of hard truth he could add to try and convince Cowley that he knew more than he did. It was shaky, but it worked.

"Right, right … Washington state. Anyway, they show up here now and again whenever Huey Cooke calls them. Then they drop their load off, get paid, and leave." He shook his head. "But I didn't have nothing to do with the dead girl. No, sir. She was already dead when they got to the lodge."

Sole's brain was whirring now, putting together the pieces. A dead girl … two blood types in the snow. Weber's pen was moving furiously over the notepad.

"You didn't have anything to do with the dead girl," Sole repeated his words back to him and the flood gates opened again.

Cowley looked up at Sole, his eyes pleading. In a voice not much more than a whisper, he said, "I swear I didn't have nothing to do with that." He shook his head rapidly. "I never killed no one. She was already dead when they opened up the back of the truck." Cowley stretched out a shaking hand, crushed the cigarette in an ashtray on the table, and dropped to his knees off the front of the sofa, begging to be believed, tears in his eyes. "I swear to you I didn't do nothing to that girl. They did it before they got out to the lodge."

"Where is she?" Sole asked the first real question they'd thrown at Cowley.

"You have to believe me. I didn't have nothing to do with it," Cowley begged.

"I believe you," Sole said mildly and put a hand on his shoulder. "Now tell me where she is."

"In the grain bin."

"*You* put her in the grain bin," Weber said, nodding.

Sole could see the anger in his eyes, but he seemed to have himself under control. He listened while Weber took over the questioning. Cowley was an egg cracked wide open. It was time to turn the heat up in the frying pan.

"And Huey Cooke ..." Weber said, prompting Cowley to go on.

"Huey's my boss. We did what he told us to do ... that's all." Cowley looked up, eyes pleading for understanding. "You got a boss. You get that. You gotta do what the boss says ... right?"

There were only a few people Huey Cooke could boss around. The preserve's hunt assistants and Arnold Cowley and Delbert Ottley. Weber added, "You and Ottley dragged the dead girl from the truck to the grain bin."

"That's right." Cowley lowered his head and nodded. "We did."

"Now tell us something we don't know," Weber said.

"What? I'm telling you everything." Cowley was on the verge of tears.

"What time did Demeron get there?"

"Huey called him ... woke him up. He probably got there an hour later." He shook his head. "I don't know the time exactly. Sometime in the middle of the night."

"Demeron was pissed off," Weber said.

"Pissed as hell." Cowley's head bobbed up and down. "Don't know when I've seen him so pissed. Me and Delbert watched it all from the barn where they thought we couldn't hear, but Demeron was shouting and we heard it all."

"Tell me about Demeron's call." Weber added another open-ended statement without knowing where it would lead or if Demeron had called anyone.

Cowley shot a look at Sole. "That's why you're here, isn't it? Some kind of undercover cop, right? They bring in undercover cops to find dirty cops, or something like that, right?"

"Something like that," Sole said, letting Cowley's imagination run free. "Finish what you were saying."

"Just that after Mr. Demeron, they had to let …" Cowley shrank away from Weber standing over him. "They had to let Bedford know."

Weber worked hard to control the emotions playing across his face. It was one thing to suspect the sheriff was dirty. It was another to hear from the mouth of Arnold Cowley.

Sole stepped in to take over the questioning. "You're doing good, Arnold. Just a few more details you can help us with." He smiled reassuringly and pulled Cowley from the floor and guided him back to the sofa. "The plan … the truck …"

"The plan." Cowley nodded and reached for the pack of cigarettes again. "I was afraid you knew about hiding the truck out at Bob Shank's place."

"Yes, we know," Sole said solemnly.

Cowley lit another cigarette, inhaled deeply and then exhaled, his body seeming to deflate with the long plume of smoke. He looked up. "I did it on Huey's orders. I mean, I was just doing what I was told."

"Alright," Weber said. "Get up. Put your shoes on, and grab your coat. You're coming with us."

"But you said if I helped, I wouldn't be in no trouble."

"We said we'd try to keep you out of trouble," Weber said bluntly, then forced a smile. "Right now, you are an accessory to murder, but you assist us in our investigation, and I promise you we'll talk to the prosecutors about a plea deal for you and a reduced sentence."

"Right ... a light sentence." Cowley's head bobbed up and down emphatically. "I swear to God I'll assist."

FIFTY-ONE

No Illusions

They arrived before dawn. In the lodge, another round of horrors for the young hosts was underway.

"We're there." Tom Finch was driving now. He killed the rental's headlights, letting the moon guide them past the lodge, around the barn, and onto a gravel drive that led to a house a quarter-mile away.

Rick Salver sat up in the seat and yawned. "What time is it?"

"A little after three AM."

"He's not gonna be happy to see us." Salver stretched, shook his head to clear the cobwebs, and leaned forward to peer out the window. "Haven't been here in a while, but doesn't look like much has changed."

Initially, Salver and Finch took on the job of making the deliveries. As their operation expanded and the cartel's human trafficking demands increased, they passed the Demeron runs on to others, Riggs, Hank, and Jimmy being the latest.

Finch slowed the car and let it roll to a stop in front of a tidy single-story brick home. The windows were dark. A dim bulb over a shed door fifty yards away, provided the only light as they navigated their way from the car to the front door.

Salver took out his phone and punched in a number, shaking his head as he waited through ten rings for it to be answered. Knocking on the door would have been simpler, but sound carried in the frigid air, and they did not want anyone snooping around to see who was making the racket.

"Yes," Huey Cooke mumbled over the speaker and squinted at the display, unable to read it without his glasses on.

"Open the door," Salver said bluntly.

"What?" Cooke sat up in his bed at the back of the house.

"We're outside. Open the door."

"You're here ... now?"

"Yes, damn it. Now open the fucking door."

"Right." Cooke rolled over and pushed himself out of the bed and shuffled through the house to the front door, cell phone still in hand. He pulled the door open and stared at the two men on his porch. "I didn't ..."

"What? Expect to see us here?" Finch pushed past him and entered, followed by Salver. "What did you think we were going to do after the cluster fuck you created?"

"Me?" Cooke shook his head, not yet fully awake. "But I didn't ..."

"Yeah, you did." Salver stopped him in midsentence. "You offered a bonus to our guys ... pushed the timetable forward so that they were out in the middle of the night on a road that led to nowhere but here. You figure it out. If you didn't rush things, the boys would have made the delivery and been long gone with no deputy snooping around."

"And no deputy dead," Finch added.

"It couldn't be helped," Cooke said. "I was under a deadline."

"Hell with your deadline," Finch snapped at him. "Thanks to you, we have the cartel on our asses to fix things."

"Fix things?"

"Yeah," Salver smirked. "You know what that means?"

"Well, I …" Cooke had a good idea what it meant and preferred not to think about it.

"I'll spell it out for you, Huey. They don't like the idea of our people killing cops and drawing heat from every other cop in the country right down on their asses." Salver glared at him. "So now we have to fix things, or they fix us."

"And we're not gonna let that happen." Finch shook his head. "That's why we're here."

"I don't see how you can fix it? They're gone." Cooke left the door open and shuffled backward a few steps, suddenly terrified.

"Knock it the fuck off, Huey. You know there is only one way to satisfy the cartel … prove to them there are no loose ends," Finch said. He closed the door and turned back to Cooke.

Eyes wide, shaking his head, Huey Cooke backed farther away from the two men crowding into the entryway. "But I didn't …"

"Calm down, Huey. We're not here for you … not yet, anyway. We need to find our people. Where are they?"

"But …" Cooke took a deep breath to calm his pounding heart. "I don't know where they are. I haven't heard from them since …"

"You helped them make a plan to get away," Salver said. "What was it?"

They were double-teaming him. Cooke's head bobbed back and forth like a man trying to fend off jabs as they fired questions at him.

"Look, all I know is they rented a car ... took one of our pickups and left it at the airport in Rapid City, then picked up the rental. After that ... you have to believe me ... after that, I never heard a word from them."

"They had to use a credit card to rent the car," Finch said. "We need to track that credit card and get a read on where they're headed."

"But, I don't ... I mean, I don't know anything about that sort of thing."

"No, but there is someone who does," Salver said. "And you're going to take us to him."

"He won't meet with you." Cooke shook his head. "There's no way."

"We're not giving him a choice." Finch's eyes could have bored a hole through Cooke. "Or you. Get dressed."

"Now?" Cooke looked at the display on his phone. "He's not even there yet."

"Now," Salver said. "We'll be there waiting for him."

Somewhere on I-10 in southern Louisiana, Riggs and Hank cruised along in their rental car averaging five miles an hour over the speed limit. They were careful not to drive so fast that a bored cop might stop them to write a ticket.

They'd tried to be careful about a lot of things since leaving South Dakota. The car rental agency at the airport had required a credit card to complete the transaction. That had them worried. Since then, they had avoided using credit cards, dipping into their cash for fuel and food, but they knew they were riding on borrowed time.

The longer they were on the road, the greater the chance that Salver and Finch would pick up their trail. Convinced that the only thing for them to do was disappear, get out of the country and start over somewhere, they were driving to the port at Jacksonville, Florida at the eastern end of I-10. After that, they'd do whatever was necessary to hop a ride on a freighter out of the country. They convinced themselves it was a good plan. Truth was, it was the only plan they could come up with. The cartel's reach and resources far exceeded their ability to hide.

"How much longer, do you think?" Hank asked.

"Another day," Riggs said. "We'll ditch the car somewhere in the city, then find out about fake IDs. After that …" He turned from the steering wheel to nod confidently at Hank. "We find a freighter to hire on for a ride."

"Where to, do you think?"

"Dunno." Riggs shrugged. "Doesn't matter, as long as it's away from here. Asia would be good, but hell, as long as it takes us away from the cartel, I'm not going to be picky."

"Yeah." Hank nodded.

They rode in silence after that. They had no illusions about what would happen to them if the cartel caught up to them—their headless bodies thrown in a ditch or hung from a bridge overpass with a note or just enough evidence left behind to show investigators that they were the ones who had killed the deputy in South Dakota.

The cartel would want to make sure law enforcement agencies understood there was no need to continue searching for the killers, and their deaths would serve as a warning to others—stupidity and carelessness have a price.

FIFTY-TWO

Desperate

"Where are we going?" Arnold Cowley sat behind the plexiglass screen in the back seat.

"Just keeping you safe," Weber said over his shoulder.

"Safe?" Cowley paled. The farther they went, the more he shook, his hands fidgeting non-stop in his lap, the muscles in his face twitching, sweat breaking out on his brow despite the minus twenty temperatures outside. "Safe from what?"

"What do you think?" Weber looked at him in the rearview mirror. "If what you're telling us is true…"

"It's true," Cowley interrupted. "It's all true."

"Then I don't suppose Demeron and Bedford will be happy about our conversation." Weber gave an indifferent shrug. "What do you suppose they'll do if they're not happy?"

"Do?" Cowley paled another couple of shades. "You said I could have a deal or something. That means you gotta keep them away from me, right?"

"Right." Weber nodded. "That's why we're taking you

where we can keep you under wraps until we check out your story and …"

"Check out my story? You mean you don't believe me?" Cowley desperately wanted to be believed and to have a plea deal. The prospect of prison as an accomplice to murder was terrifying, but more chilling was the thought that he might share a prison cell with A.C. Demeron or Sheriff Willard Bedford. They were not the sort of men who understood betrayal, even when it happened in the middle of the night, wakened from a deep sleep, and threatened with prison for just doing what the boss told him to do.

Sole looked over his shoulder from the passenger seat. "Verifying the details … routine police work."

"Routine? So, what happens to me while you do your routine?"

"For now, you stay with us," Weber said. He didn't add that if Cowley's story was accurate and Bedford and Demeron were involved, there weren't many safe places in Blanken County for them to take him. "So, sit back, relax, and stay quiet."

Cowley slumped back on the seat, but relaxation was out of the question. He fidgeted, his head swiveling back and forth between the two heads in the front seats to the windows and the blackness outside. His hands and fingers moved and twitched as if they had minds of their own. He felt sick to his stomach and swallowed it down, taking deep breaths.

They drove another twenty minutes before Weber pulled off the main road onto a snowy back lane. Someone had run a tractor blade down the middle, but it was lightly traveled and snow had continued to pile up. Weber shifted into four-wheel-drive to keep the SUV between the ditches.

He made another turn onto an even less traveled drive

and headed around the perimeter of a field. At the far side, he stopped under a grove of trees, their bare, snow-covered branches stretching up into the night sky.

Cowley roused from his sullen unease, put his nose to the window, squinted out, and recognized where they were. Then he shrieked, "No!"

"Shut up, Arnold," Weber ordered, then cut the engine and got out. Sole got out on the other side.

Cowley pushed himself away from the rear door, shaking his head. "No. I don't want to go up there."

"You're not," Weber said. "We are. You stay here."

"Here?" Cowley's head swiveled to look out the window and then back to Weber. "You're leaving me here? Without the engine running? I might freeze to death."

"You might," Weber agreed. "If what you're telling us isn't true, and we get delayed, you probably will."

"It's true. I swear to God it's true."

"Good," Weber said and went around to the rear hatch to retrieve two emergency blankets from the storage bay. He threw them in the back with Cowley. "Huddle under these until we get back. The doors won't open from the inside, and if I find out you've been kicking at the windows trying to get out, there'll be hell to pay when we get back."

"Try to get out?" Cowley frowned and pulled the blankets around him. "Where the hell would I go?"

Weber slammed the door shut and led the way into the trees. "Let's go."

He and Sole walked slowly, without flashlights, their boots crunching softly in the snow. Weber stopped once to listen to a rustling in the trees.

Something swooped through the black, near enough to feel the wind of its passing. A moment later, the crying scream of a rabbit in its death throes filled the night, followed by unseen wings beating heavily as the owl lifted from the ground, carrying its prey to a branch high in a nearby tree.

Weber moved forward again until they emerged from the woods. Three hundred yards away, Demeron's hunting lodge sat in a cleared patch of snow. Assorted vehicles were parked to one side.

Weber led the way along the edge of the trees to a point immediately across from the barn that also served as the Huey Cooke's office. Behind the barn and fifty yards closer to their position, an oval-shaped galvanized steel building squatted in the snow.

"The grain bin," Weber said and started across the snow toward it.

Sole nodded and followed. When they reached the bin, Weber stopped and leaned against the steel wall for a few seconds, listening, then moved around the side until he reached a door facing the rear of the barn.

"Alright," he whispered. "Let's see if Arnold's full of shit."

Weber pulled the door open a few inches. It swung stiffly on frozen hinges. A hollow metallic echo rumbled inside. Weber paused, then squeezed himself through the opening into the grain bin. Sole followed, pulling the door closed behind him.

They stood for a moment in the blackness, listening, then Weber took a flashlight from his pocket, pointed it at the floor, and thumbed it on. He kept the light aimed downward to prevent a stray beam from shooting out into the night through a seam in the metal walls.

Swinging the light back and forth across the floor, they circled the interior until Weber stopped. "Shit."

Sole came up beside him and nodded. "Yeah. Arnold

was telling the truth, but it looks like he left out a couple of details."

As Cowley had described, the body of the girl he and Delbert Ottley dragged from the box truck lay half on her side, her arms extending at grotesquely odd angles, her torso covered with frozen blood. He had failed to mention the bodies of two other girls, younger, curled beside each other as if they had snuggled up together for a nap.

Weber stood, almost as frozen in place as the girls on the floor. He was a good deputy, but patrolling rural Blanken County had not given him much experience in dealing with death, and certainly not three dead girls almost young enough to be his daughters.

Sole knelt beside the bodies, giving each a brief examination. The cause of death for one was obvious. The gunshot wound had bled profusely before hardening into a reddish-brown icy frosting on her clothes.

The other two showed no signs of trauma or injury by force. Their bodies were frozen solid. Sole looked up at Weber. "Take a medical examiner to say for certain, but looks like these two died of exposure."

"Froze to death." Weber nodded, his brow furrowed. "Why would they be outside dressed like that? How'd they get locked outside? That's not a mistake people make around here, not in the winter."

"Maybe not a mistake," Sole said. "They could have been trying to run, desperate to get away, but weren't prepared to deal with the cold."

He stood to face Weber. "You have yourself a serious investigation here. How are you going to handle it?"

"I'm going to need some help, I think." Weber stared at the bodies, then at Sole.

"I'm a civilian," Sole said, shaking his head. "I'll help where I can, but I have no legal authority to be involved."

"Right." Weber nodded and looked at the bodies doubtfully. "This is more than I've ever handled before."

"Break it down into steps. Take one at a time," Sole said. "You know you can't go to the sheriff. Everything points to Bedford's involvement at some level."

"I know." Weber nodded. "The Feds maybe?"

"I'd say that would be a good start," Sole said. "Murder of a deputy, and a girl, possibly involving a sheriff …" He nodded. "Throw in some sort of prostitution ring, potentially human trafficking and pedophilia …" He looked at the two frozen girls. "The Feds will chomp at the bit to get involved."

"I'm going to need you with me on this," Weber said. "You know what you're doing. I'm just a rookie at all this detective work."

"I'd say you're doing pretty well, but I'll stay involved … only in an advisory capacity," Sole said, and for once, the little voice inside was hushed by the girls lying on the cold concrete floor.

Weber cut the light and led the way out of the grain bin. They walked slowly through the woods. Somewhere nearby the owl hooted at their passing, then went back to its midnight meal.

They could have been out on a night like this, Sole thought. Two desperate girls walking, surrounded by the cold, dead silence, their feet crunching in the snow until they couldn't walk anymore.

FIFTY-THREE

Not His Strong Point

Sheriff Willard Bedford wheeled into his parking space in front of the sheriff's department, grabbed a briefcase off the passenger seat, got out of his car, and stopped in his tracks.

"Sheriff! Hold on!" Huey Cooke waved at him from a pickup parked in the lot and walked briskly toward him, flanked by two men.

Bedford glared at Cooke. "Are you out of your goddamn mind, bringing them here?"

"Sorry, I was just ... I mean, I didn't know what to do about ..."

"You stupid son of a bitch." Bedford lowered his head and nodded at the building. "Come inside. Keep your mouth shut until we're in my office."

He led the way through the front door.

"Morning, Sheriff." Beverly Sands looked up from her desk, smiled, and then furrowed her brow. "Morning Huey." She eyed the two men with him. "Everything alright?"

"Everything's fine," Bedford said. "Hold my calls."

"Will do." She watched them cross the office area and down the hall to Bedford's office. "You want me to bring you your coffee?" she called after him. The sheriff's office door banged closed. "Get it yourself then," she muttered.

Bedford strode around his desk and sat. He glared at Salver and Finch. "What the hell do you want?"

"You know who we are," Salver said.

"Don't pull your fucking drama bullshit on me. Yes, I fucking know who you are!" Bedford took a deep breath and lowered his voice. "I know who you are and I want you out of here … now."

"Soon." Salver said and nodded at the two chairs arrayed in front of Bedford's desk. "We need to talk. Mind if we sit down."

He didn't wait for an invitation and sat in one chair. Finch took the other. Cooke remained standing, doing his best to avoid Bedford's stare.

"I said I want you out …" Bedford began.

He clamped his mouth shut when Finch raised a hand, shook his head, and said, "If you know who we are, then you should keep in mind who we work for."

"What has that got to do with me?"

"We have a problem," Salver said. "A problem created by your people." He turned and nodded at Huey Cooke, standing with his back against the door, trying to make himself as small as possible.

"Not my people," Bedford snapped.

"Same thing," Salver smirked. "You both work for the same man. You may not be on Demeron's books, but I'm pretty sure you take home a nice chunk of change for turning a blind eye to what happens out at his so-called hunting lodge."

Bedford ground his teeth, the muscles in his jaws tensing nervously. "What do you want?"

"We need to find them," Salver said.

"Them?"

"Come on, Sheriff. Don't play dumb." Salver shook his head. "We don't have time for that." His eyes narrowed. "Neither do you."

"Me? What's all this got to do with ..."

"Cut the bullshit!" Finch snapped and Bedford's mouth closed in midsentence. "The people we work for don't like loose ends. They don't tolerate mistakes. That means we have to find the two assholes who killed your deputy and make them go away."

"We have to find them before they get picked up somewhere by real cops," Salver added with a smirk. "Cops who will prosecute them ... maybe offer them a deal for a reduced sentence or to go into witness protection after a short hitch in jail. If that happens, everything falls apart ... for Demeron ... for us ... for you ... and there will be consequences for everyone." Salver shook his head. "Like it or not, we're all in this together."

"I took care of everything," Bedford said. "Fixed it so no one will know. I made an arrest."

"Maybe, maybe not." Salver shook his head. "That bullshit arrest might not hold up."

"Besides, it doesn't matter," Finch said, staring hard at the sheriff. "Our people want us to take care of things and make sure. That's what we're going to do."

Bedford's eyes snapped back and forth between the two as they fired words and threats at him. He sank back in his chair. He'd wanted to believe he'd taken care of things, but here they were. The cartel would not walk away simply because he'd thrown a local bully into jail to cover their tracks. "Alright. What do I need to do?"

Salver and Finch exchanged a look of disbelief.

"What the fuck kind of cop are you?" Finch said.

"I'm ... I mean I have to ..." The truth was, Sheriff Bedford was more politician than a law enforcement officer these days. Appeasing voters and his off-the-record boss, A.C. Demeron, had been his top priorities for too many years for him to remember much about real police work. He shook his head. "I'm not sure what ... where ..."

"Look," Salver interrupted. "They rented a car. The rental agency won't release any information to us, but they will to a sheriff."

"Right." Bedford nodded and sat up straight, thankful for a starting point. "The rental agency. We can get a make and model on the car, put out a lookout for it, and try to get a lead on where they're headed, maybe have some other agency spot them and pick them up."

"No." Salver shook his head. "No one else gets their hands on them but us. That's the only way this gets handled."

"Then how ..." Bedford's face twisted in confusion.

"You're the sheriff. You get the rental company to give you the GPS tracking coordinates on the car."

"GPS tracking?" Bedford's eyes opened wide and it was clear they might as well have said use your crystal ball to find them, and it would have made as much sense.

"Look," Finch said, "We'll need a specific location to find them. It's a big country."

"I don't see how that can be done." Bedford shook his head.

"I'm sure you don't," Salver sighed, then explained, "Cars these days have GPS mapping systems, emergency systems to call for help, that sort of thing. Rental companies especially like to keep tabs on their cars. You're a cop. You get the rental agency to give you the GPS tracking data. That will tell us exactly where the car is. We find the car and we find our boys."

He waited for a glimmer of understanding to show up in Bedford's eyes. When it didn't, he snapped. "Do you understand?"

"Yes ... I mean, I think so," Bedford sputtered. "Get the GPS data from the rental agency." He nodded. "Yes, I understand that."

"Good," Salver said.

"Where will you be so I can tell you what I find out?"

"Not anywhere around here," Finch said. "Call Huey when you have the GPS data. He can relay it to us."

"Alright." Bedford nodded. "Which rental company do you think I should check with?"

"Son of a bitch!" Finch exclaimed. "How the fuck did you ever get to be a sheriff? Do some police work ... investigate!"

"Okay," Bedford said and decided not to ask any more questions.

The two men stood and left the office. Huey Cooke followed them and closed the door, careful to avoid Bedford's eyes.

The sheriff of Blanken County sat staring at his desk, wondering where to begin. Investigative work was not his strong point.

FIFTY-FOUR

So Much for Anonymity

The Federal Building in Pierre, South Dakota is a nondescript affair in a nondescript business district of town. Chain drug stores, budget motels, restaurants, banks, and hair salons occupy the adjacent streets. All in all, it's a very ordinary building in an extraordinarily ordinary city for a state capital.

Winter temperatures aside, Sole had discovered that the ordinary simplicity of life in South Dakota appealed to him. So much so that he had begun to consider seriously the good-natured suggestions by the Langstroms and others to stay on permanently. That was all about to change.

Dean Weber parked his county SUV in a visitor spot in the parking lot, and with Arnold Cowley uncuffed but wedged tightly between them, they walked through the front door to be met by Special Agent Derrick Weems.

Weems was only two years out of the FBI academy in Quantico, Virginia, and as the junior agent in the office, he handled what the other agents termed the shit calls. Mostly, they were baseless complaints or conspiracy theorists with a need to vent to someone in authority. That's how the call from Dean Weber was received, at first.

The administrative assistant handling incoming calls was more than a little skeptical. Every law enforcement officer in the state knew about the murder of Deputy Lew Bentz. They also knew that the sheriff in Blanken County had arrested a local man known to have made threats to Bentz. The case was closed.

"Tell me again why you want to speak to an agent?" the admin said.

"I have information about the murder and that the wrong man has been arrested," Weber replied.

"Who are you?" The admin sighed and started making a note on his message pad.

"I can't say right now. I can't take the chance that this gets back to Blanken County until I've spoken to someone who can do something about it."

"You want to speak to an agent, but you don't want to give me your name," the admin said. "It doesn't work that way."

"Look, everything has to be kept confidential until someone higher up the chain than me can get involved."

"Higher up the chain?" The admin rolled his eyes at the clerk seated across from him and they exchanged a smile. Just another nut case on the line. "Are you in law enforcement?"

Weber hesitated for a few seconds before saying, "I am."

"Where?" The admin sat up a little straighter, but not much. These rural deputies could be just as conspiracy crazy as the wackos staking out Area 51, hoping to get a glimpse of an alien.

"Like I said, this has to be confidential." Weber was becoming annoyed. "If word gets out, evidence might disappear. Lives are at stake."

"I am with the FBI. You can trust me to keep it confidential."

"Are you a special agent?" Weber shot back.

"I'm the person you talk to if you want to speak with a special agent," the admin said, getting huffy now.

"Oh, for God's sake," Weber growled.

Sole held out his hand. "Give me the phone."

Weber handed it over and took a deep breath to calm himself.

"This is Bill Myers," Sole said brusquely. "I'm working an undercover assignment for the Bureau. My clearance code is Alpha-Tango-7-3-Tango-Zulu." Sole raised his eyes and shot a grin at Weber. The stream of letters and numbers meant nothing, but a clerk in a local office was unlikely to know that ... not at first, at least.

"You can take the time to verify my code if you want," Sole continued. "It may take a while since I'm deployed out of D.C. and my work is classified, but keep in mind that, as my partner said, lives are at stake, and wasting valuable time could put those lives at risk. In the meantime, give me your name and put your supervising special agent on the phone."

"My name?" the admin said nervously.

"Your name, rating, and security clearance level," Sole snapped back.

"My name is, uh, Larry Connor ... my security clearance?"

"That's right. Let's see if you're even cleared to hear what we have to say."

"I'm sorry for the misunderstanding Agent ... Myers, was it?" The admin was talking fast now.

"That's right. Myers."

"I'm putting you through to Special Agent Weems right now."

Sole handed the phone back to Weber and waited.

"Special Agent Weems," a voice said over the phone.

"Is this line recorded?" Weber asked.

"Of course. You're speaking to the FBI, but all calls are confidential."

Weber shot a questioning glance at Sole, who nodded.

"Alright, I have information about the murder of Deputy Lew Bentz in Blanken County," Weber began, taking a breath. "Also, several other murders. It involves Sheriff Willard Bedford and Mr. A.C. Demeron."

The name of the sheriff in a backwater county meant nothing to Special Agent Weems, but when he heard the name of one of the most prominent citizens in the state, his ears perked up a bit. "How do I know your information is valid," Weems said, jotting notes on the pad in front of him.

"I have crime lab evidence," Weber said. "And an eyewitness."

"An eyewitness? Who?"

"Not over the phone."

"When can you be here?"

"It'll take us about three hours."

"Come directly here," Weems ordered. "Call when you're in the parking lot. I'll meet you in the lobby."

As promised, Special Agent Weems met them in the lobby of the Federal Building. He checked their IDs—Weber's county ID and badge, Sole's Tennessee driver's license, and Cowley's South Dakota license—then waited while they were processed through the security checkpoint.

"Alright, let's go upstairs and talk." Weems led the way to a bank of elevators and escorted them to a windowless interview room in the FBI suite of offices.

When they'd all taken seats around a conference table, Weems put a recorder in the center, turned it on, and said, "Interview concerning the murder of Blanken County Deputy Lewis Bentz with ..." He checked his notes. "Present are Deputy Dean Weber from Blanken County, South Dakota, William Myers from Tennessee, and Arnold Cowley, resident of Blanken County."

He looked up from the recorder, nodded at Weber and said, "So, you think they arrested the wrong person in the Bentz murder."

"I know they did," Weber said.

"Explain," Weems said, looked at the clock on the wall, and added, "As briefly as possible."

Weber explained, and the more he explained, the more questions Weems had. He began filling pages on his notepad.

When he got to the discovery of the bodies in the grain bin at Demeron's lodge, Weems stopped the interview and stood. "Stay here. I'll be right back."

He left the room and returned a minute later with two other agents in tow, both senior to him. They sat across the table beside Weems and the most senior said, "I'm Special Agent-in-Charge Robert Grimes. Start over and tell us everything."

"Alright," Weber said, "but like I said earlier, lives are at stake."

"Then speak fast," the Grimes said.

It took another thirty minutes to explain and then answer the questions they fired at him. When he finished, Grimes looked at Sole. "And why are you here?"

"As a witness," Sole said. "I saw the bodies in the grain bin ... the blood in the snow."

"Right. But you're not law enforcement ... correct?"

"No, I'm not."

"And yet, Deputy Weber here involved you in his off-the-record investigation, turned to you for advice."

Sole didn't like the direction the questioning was taking and remained silent.

"Are you some kind of law enforcement officer?" Grimes gave a wry smile. "And don't try that undercover agent bullshit on me you pulled with our admin. That supposed clearance code meant nothing to anyone, anywhere."

"We had to speak to someone." Sole shrugged. "Seemed the thing to do."

"So, you're a bullshitter ... a good one at that." Grimes nodded and his eyes narrowed. "Don't bullshit us again."

"I won't," Sole said.

Grimes turned to Cowley. "Arnold Cowley, you are under arrest as an accessory to murder and will remain in custody here."

"But they said I could have a deal."

"You probably will, but that will be up to the DA," Grimes said. "Right now, we have some work to do and you're going to remain in custody until we sort things out."

Grimes turned to Weems. "This is your case, your op. Get it set up, coordinate with the State Division of Criminal Investigation ... transportation, manpower. Move quick ... that means today."

"Yes, sir." Weems jumped up and rushed from the room.

Grimes looked down at the notes he'd made. "Murder, human trafficking, a ring of pedophiles, and a corrupt sheriff. All of it happening under our noses." He nodded at

Weber. "If it's all true, you did an outstanding job under difficult circumstances, Deputy."

It's true," Weber said. "I'd like to be there when you move on this, if that's possible."

"We'll make it happen," Grimes said. "You've earned it." He looked at Sole. "As for you …"

Here it comes, Sole thought. He returned Grimes's stare.

"You said you are not a law enforcement officer, although you attempted to impersonate a federal agent. I could charge you for that, you know." He frowned. "I probably should, but considering the assistance you provided Deputy Weber, I won't … as long as you tell me who you really are."

It was just a matter of time. It wouldn't take the Bureau long to figure out who he was. Facial recognition software and fingerprint files of police officers maintained by the FBI would make it fairly easy. Hell, they were probably checking him on some computer right now.

"The name is John Sole. I was a detective in Atlanta."

Dean Weber turned toward him. He'd had no doubts that Bill Myers, whoever he was, had been a cop. Still, hearing it now stated so matter-of-factly was surprising.

"Thank you," Grimes said. "I'll do some checking, and assuming you are telling me the truth this time, there won't be any charges for impersonating a law enforcement officer."

"It's true," Sole said.

"One more thing." Grimes leaned toward Sole. "Don't pull that shit again."

"I won't," Sole promised.

"Good. I suppose you'd like to be present as well when we move on this."

Every cop wants to see his case brought to a conclusion. Sole nodded. "I would."

"I'll see what I can do, but you'll be watching from the background. No active participation," Grimes said firmly then added, a touch of understanding in his tone, "I figure you have your reasons for wanting to see a cop-killer brought down."

"I do." Sole nodded. "Lew Bentz was my friend and a good deputy."

"Fair enough." Grimes stood and left the room.

The Pierre Field office of the FBI became a whirlwind of activity. Agents scurried about making preparations for the operation in Blanken County.

So much for anonymity, Sole thought. Any ideas he had about settling and starting over in South Dakota had just been blown away like powdered snow in a strong wind. When this was done, he would be moving on.

FIFTY-FIVE

Conscience

It was another fine day of orchestrated slaughter. The hunters sat cozy and warm in their heated blinds while Huey Cooke's hunt assistants herded pheasants into the killing zone. When the snow was stained and littered with blood and feathers, they took a break, sipped hot toddies, and waited while the hunt assistants cleaned things up a bit and rounded up more pheasants.

Then it started all over again. They pulled the triggers on their shotguns with the carefree abandon of children playing with toy guns. The banter between the hunters was light and easy as feathers blew away over the snow.

"How many is that?" Kellin asked.

"I'd say I got about a dozen," Parson replied.

"Seems like plenty," Kellin said. "Maybe we could call it a day and …" He grinned.

Parson gave a nod and a smile. Kellin was eager to get back to Cindy, thoughts of the night before and visions of using her young body in new ways dancing in his brain. He was not alone in his perversions.

Pulling the shotgun trigger with a ferocity rising out of his new passion for Sherry, Parson couldn't stop thinking about her. Hidden away at the preserve, his wife and children would never know about her, and when it was time to go ... he pushed that thought away. For now, he told himself, enjoy the moment, the secret fantasy. She was his secret lover. Never mind that she was a child. That's not your problem. Demeron would certainly take good care of her and the others.

"Got one!" Ranskill said excitedly. She turned to her hunting blind companion, Taylor. "Did you see that?"

"I saw," he said. "You seem very animated today." He gave a wry smile. "Gushing like a schoolgirl."

"Are my cheeks rosy and red?" Ranskill asked, laughing.

"Very."

"Yep." She lifted the shotgun to her shoulder and pointed it in the general direction of a cluster of four pheasants, thirty yards away. "Nothing like a good fucking to put a bounce in a girl's step and a blush on her face."

She pulled the trigger. Blood and feathers exploded from three of the birds. The fourth managed to escape, dragging an injured wing on the ground, until one of the hunt assistants grabbed it by the feet and spun it around, breaking its neck.

"How about you?" She turned to Taylor. "How was your evening?"

Reticent as always, Taylor replied simply, "It was fine."

"I'll bet it was." Ranskill grinned.

"Brad is a very nice boy."

"I'm sure he is nice ... and soft where it counts," she smirked. "Or do you prefer it hard?"

Taylor ignored the smirk, aimed the shotgun at nothing in particular, and pulled the trigger.

The hunt lasted for several hours, with a break for lunch. A.C. Demeron watched his guests closely, sensing that all would like to hurry back to the lodge and rejoin their young hosts.

Truth was, he was looking forward to another night with fiery Malina, but he knew the delay would whet their appetites. He was a master at that—whetting appetites, teasing and pleasing the senses. Keep them all on the hunt a while longer and by the time they returned to the lodge, they would barely be able to control the urge to continue their fantasies.

Those fantasies, the great secret of their time at the lodge would bind them together permanently, the way secrets always do. They would be his.

"We have to get out of here." Malina stood at the door to his room staring at Brad. "We can't just sit here. This is our chance. We have to do something."

"Like what? Loni's our only way out and I talked to her. She's not budging."

"You talked to her?" Malina's eyes widened in surprise. Brad hadn't said so much as ten words to any of them since arrival at the lodge.

"I talked to her. Like I said, she's not budging." He looked out the window at the bleak, snow-covered landscape beyond. "Besides, where are you going to go?"

Malina sighed. "I talked to Loni too."

"*You* talked to her?"

"Yes. The things you said to her ... things I said to her ..." Malina shrugged. "Maybe it was hearing it from a girl.

I don't know what exactly. I got the feeling she's got something on her conscience. Anyway, she's ready."

She moved farther in the room and lowered her voice. "Unless you just want to stay and let that sick old asshole put it in you any time he feels like it." An involuntary shiver ran through her. "Doesn't it make your skin crawl? I know it creeps me out every time Demeron looks my way, and I see the bulge in his pants." She almost gagged. "It's like being fucked by my grandfather."

"I don't know." Brad shrugged. "Taylor's not so bad, I guess."

"Not so bad?" Malina's face twisted in disgust. "He treats you like some kind of pet ... feeds you, strokes you, fucks you ... and you're okay with that?"

"I've seen worse ... been with worse."

"Well, we haven't," Malina said.

He changed the subject. "Have you talked to the others?"

"Not yet. I needed to make sure you're with us."

"Why?" He looked her in the eyes.

"Because I can't do it on my own." Malina sighed and sank down uninvited on the end of his bed. "The others are weak. Cindy's a wreck, and Sherry believes that they really are going to give her the money." Her eyes narrowed. "You know that's not true."

"I know," Brad said, nodding, a look of guilt in his eyes as if he'd known all along.

The confirmation from Brad broke something inside her, and Malina looked up her lip trembling. "They fucking killed Bobbi and that cop!" She shook her head. "We either get away or we ... disappear." She stopped short of saying they would kill the girls and Brad. That was too much to bear saying, even for tough Malina.

Brad stared for a few seconds, then stood. "Alright, let's get moving. They haven't killed us yet."

Loni was dressed warmly when they entered her room. Thermal leggings, pants, wool sweater, and a parka on the bed.

"Good." She nodded at Malina and pointed to a closet. "In there. Get parkas for everyone. You'll need them."

Malina gathered the coats and handed one to Brad. "Let's get the others."

When they pushed the door open to her room, they found Cindy sitting cross-legged, face in hands, sobbing on her bed. She looked up, her eyes afraid and questioning. "What?" she simpered.

"We're leaving," Malina said.

"Really?" Cindy sat up straight. "How?"

"I'm going to take you," Loni said, resigned. She had made her choice and knew there could be no turning back now. She held out a parka. "Put this on. Do it quick."

Sore and damaged from rape and abuse by Kellin, she could barely move off the bed. Malina and Brad helped her and wrapped a parka over her shoulders. It was huge on her slight frame and dragged on the floor. "It's too big," she whined.

"It'll keep you warm," Malina said. "Or you can stay here."

Cindy pulled the bottom up so she wouldn't trip over it. "Alright, I'm ready."

They found Sherry standing at the mirror over the dresser in her room, applying makeup. "What the hell is all this?" she said, whirling to face them as they surrounded her.

"We're leaving," Malina said.

"Do what you want. I'm not going anywhere," Sherry said. "Not yet, not until I get the money they promised."

"There won't be any money," Loni said.

"Bullshit!" Sherry snapped back. "You're saying that because you want our share for yourself."

"No, I'm saying it because it's true."

"I don't believe you."

"If you don't come with us, you'll disappear," Brad said. "They won't let you go anywhere after what we saw."

He reached out and placed a hand on her arm. It was the only physical contact any of them had ever had from him. Sherry's eyes widened in surprise.

"It's true," Brad said, looking her in the eyes for once. "Think about it. They can't let you talk to anyone. You'll disappear ... or worse."

Sherry opened her mouth to speak and stopped. Brad had never said a word to her before ... never touched her. It took her a few seconds, but the fact that he did so now was more convincing than any argument. She nodded reluctantly, "Okay."

As escapes go, it was uneventful. Ted Jolly was in his kitchen, setting up the buffet and preparing the evening meal. Delbert Ottley was in the barn, napping in a dark corner on a chair where he and Arnold Cowley played cards when not running errands for Huey Cooke.

Arnold was absent. No one had seen or heard from him since yesterday. Ottley knew he'd get a royal ass-chewing when he did show up. It was pretty stupid of him to put his cushy job at risk.

As for Cooke, he'd called in and left a message with Ted Jolly and said he would be coming in late but before the hunters returned. Demeron wasn't happy about that, but he'd deal later with Cooke.

Loni led the way to a hall closet where she turned the combination dial on a lockbox, retrieved the keys to one of the lodge vans, and went out a side door. A minute later, she pulled the van to the door, and the escapees climbed in.

"Where do we go now?" Malina asked, taking a seat on the front passenger side.

"Damned if I know," Loni said. "But someplace as far away from Blanken County as we can get. Demeron has connections here. If we get spotted, someone will say something. He'd find out, and we'd be right back where we started." She looked at Malina. "Except worse off."

"Then drive," Malina said. "Fast."

Loni nodded. Things had been much simpler before she'd discovered she had a conscience. If she'd found it earlier, Mila and Riley might still be alive and not lying frozen in the grain bin.

Loni pressed down on the accelerator. The van fishtailed a little in the snow and she eased off.

"Wherever we're going," Malina said. "Let's get there alive."

FIFTY-SIX

I'm The Fucking Sheriff

Special Agent Weems was the first through the door. It was his case, so he had the honors, and although they were not executing a breach entry on a barricaded subject, he had plenty of back-up.

Five agents from the FBI field office and a tactical team from the state's Division of Criminal Investigation followed him through the front door of the Blanken County Sheriff's Department. A second tactical team, along with troopers from the South Dakota Highway Patrol, secured the front and rear of the exits.

"What the hell?" Beverly Sands said. Seated at her desk by the front window, she watched open-mouthed as the FBI pulled up in front. The cars were unmarked but recognizable as government vehicles.

When the tactical teams pulled in behind in their marked trucks, she exclaimed, "Holy shit!"

"What is it, Bev?" Captain Trundle wandered over from the coffeemaker in the break room, trailed by Sergeant Patterson.

"I don't …" She closed her mouth abruptly when the stern-faced agents came through the door and fanned out across the office area.

"Wait a minute!" Trundle sputtered. "What the hell do you think you're doing?"

Weems ignored him and held up a folded paper. "FBI. This is a search warrant for all files, communications, and equipment of the Blanken County Sheriff's Department. Everyone! Stand and move away from your workstations! Anyone who fails to comply or cooperate will be in contempt of a lawfully executed warrant and will be subject to arrest."

The few deputies and clerical workers scattered around the office stared at him in stunned confusion.

"Now!" Weems ordered

They began standing and moving to the center of the room away from their workstations.

Weems turned to Trundle. "Are you the deputy in charge?"

"I'm the day watch commander," Weems croaked. "What's this all …"

Weems held up his badge and ID for inspection, then handed a copy of the warrant to Captain Trundle. "You'll note that the judge of the United States District Court for South Dakota has duly signed this warrant and authorized our complete examination of your operation."

"But …" Trundle took the warrant and shook his head. "I don't understand."

"The warrant explains," Weems said. "You'll probably want to give the county attorney a call."

"Can they do this?" Patterson asked, looking over Trundle's shoulder at the warrant.

"How the hell do I know? They're the fucking FBI!"

"I need to let the sheriff know." Beverly Sands reached for the phone on her desk.

"No," Weems shook his head. "Move away from your desk now. Stand with the others until we sort things out."

Weems went to the door and nodded at one of the vehicles parked at the curb. Dean Weber got out and came inside.

"You!" Trundle's eyes opened wide in a mixture of surprise and anger. "Weber, what the fuck is going on?"

"You don't have to speak with him, Deputy," Weems said, then turned to Trundle. "You and the sergeant go stand with the others. Touch nothing and stay out of the way."

Trundle glared at Weber, but he backed away toward the cluster of staff now huddled in the middle of the office area. Weber glanced at them—co-workers, friends—all of them staring at him, a few angry, most confused. He felt like a traitor.

"Where is Sheriff Bedford?" Weems asked.

"Should be in his office." Weber nodded to the rear of the building. "Back there."

"Follow me." Weems led the way, trailed by Weber, another agent, and two of the tactical officers.

They were halfway to the hall in the rear that led to the sheriff's office when Bedford came charging out, red-faced and spluttering. "What's all this! What the fuck is going on?"

He looked at Trundle, standing with the others in the middle of the room. "Captain! What the fuck is all this?"

"Sheriff," Weems said, stepping in front to block him.

"Who the hell are you? Get the hell out of my building," Bedford raged.

"Willard Bedford," Weems continued. "I'm Special

Agent Weems with the FBI. We have a warrant for your arrest."

"Arrest!" Bedford shouted. "You can't arrest me! I'm the fucking sheriff!"

Weems nodded and before Bedford could react, one agent took Bedford by an arm and removed the pistol from the high ride holster at his waist. The second agent stepped behind, pulled his arms back, and handcuffed him.

Bedford sputtered, throwing out half sentences, trying to protest the injustice of it all. "This is bullshit! You can't … I'm the fucking sheriff … you have no authority to … there isn't any proof …"

"I'm afraid there is," Weems said. "Three witnesses."

"Witnesses to what?" Bedford's head twisted on his neck, looking around the room. He spotted Weber standing behind Weems. "You did this, you son of a bitch!"

"Willard Bedford," Weems said. "You are charged with conspiracy to conceal a murder. Other charges are pending the completion of our investigation."

He nodded at the two agents on either side of Bedford. They began escorting, half supporting, half dragging Bedford to the front door.

"Do something, Trundle!" Bedford shouted over his shoulder, then he was out the door, being shoved into the back seat of a car.

Trundle did something. He turned to Weems and said, "I didn't know anything about this."

"Me neither," Sergeant Patterson added quickly. "Not a thing."

"We'll see," Weems said.

In the backseat of a screened highway patrol vehicle outside, Willard Bedford sobbed, "I'm the fucking sheriff."

FIFTY-SEVEN

They Were Gone

A simultaneous raid, led by Special Agent-in-Charge Robert Grimes, took place at the Demeron Hunting Preserve. Events there were less dramatic ... at first.

Grimes and his team rolled into the nearly deserted compound at the Demeron lodge and fanned out through the snow. Several agents went to the barn and awakened a startled Delbert Ottley. Huey Cooke, returned from his visit to see the sheriff, was also in the barn, sitting in his office when the FBI and tactical units pulled into the yard.

He stepped out into the open barn area, only to be confronted by an agent wearing a tactical vest emblazoned with the letters FBI. "Hubert Loudin Cooke?"

"Uh ... yes." Cooke's eyes darted around the barn, watching the swarm of agents in similar vests searching through storage rooms and around equipment.

"You're under arrest for conspiracy to conceal a murder," The agent said.

"What?" Cooke started shaking his head as if that

would make the agents disappear. "No, no, no. You don't understand. I didn't do anything. I didn't kill anybody. Didn't have anything to do with all the girls. I swear it."

"All the girls?" The agent said. "We'll see." He Mirandized Cooke as he escorted him from the barn and walked him to the lodge.

Other agents had already surrounded the lodge residence and entered through an unlocked door to find Ted Jolly working away on dinner preparations in the kitchen. He was not arrested, but they took him into custody for questioning while they searched the residence.

Grimes led a third team to the grain bin behind the barn. Bobbi's eyes, frosted over with ice, stared blindly at them when they turned her body over. If not for the mottled, blue-hued skin and the fact that their bodies were frozen stiff, the two girls beside her on the concrete appeared to be sleeping.

Agents confined Cooke, Ottley, and Jolly in separate rooms inside the lodge while others continued to search the outbuildings and surrounding woods. Grimes paid a visit to each of the detainees, displayed copies of the search warrant for them, and started asking questions.

For the most part, Ted Jolly remained somber and silent. He answered basic questions—name, address, birthdate—but knew better than to say anything to the FBI about Demeron's activities. Activities he'd been part of and helped orchestrate.

When the questioning got to Delbert Ottley, he started talking and wouldn't stop, swearing that '*he only done what the boss said, but didn't hurt nobody.*' In a matter of a few minutes, the agents had another corroborating eyewitness.

Based on Arnold Cowley's statement, they had already secured an arrest warrant for Huey Cooke. With the addition of the information Ottley provided, they were ready to throw questions in his direction and see what might spill out.

Grimes sat in an upholstered chair across from Cooke, smiled, and began with a simple question. "Tell us about the girls, Huey."

The room had an oversized matching sofa, a liquor cabinet, and artwork on the paneled walls. It was one of several set aside for Demeron's guests to spend private time with their so-called hosts before retiring to the bedrooms.

"Don't I need a lawyer?" Cooke said. "I mean, you arrested me and all."

"Yes, you will," Grimes said, his voice calm, sympathetic, and unconcerned about the possibility of lawyers showing up. "We can get you a lawyer right now. Might take a while for one to get out here. Do you have one you want to call? I'll get him on the phone for you."

"I don't really know any lawyers," Cooke said.

"A public defender then. You are certainly entitled to have an attorney here. I can get the judge to appoint one for you. In the meantime, we'd like to ask you a few questions." Grimes smiled and added reassuringly, "Not about you, of course, but about what Mr. Demeron has been doing out here."

"About Mr. Demeron?" Cooke thought it over. "I don't know. I mean, he's the boss and all."

"I understand," Grimes said. "But the clock is running. I imagine Demeron will be back soon, and like I said it could take a while for a public defender to be appointed and get here. Any help you give us now will go a long way toward helping things work out for you in court. I'll say that to your lawyer as well." Grimes gave a sympathetic smile. "After all, you didn't kill anyone, did you?"

"No, absolutely not." Cooke shook his head. "Like I told that other agent. I never hurt anyone. Not those girls, not anyone. Mr. Demeron heads things up. I just run the hunting preserve for him."

"Exactly." Grimes nodded. "That's why the warrant on you says conspiracy to *conceal* and not murder."

"Right ... conceal it, like Demeron told me to do. That's what you're saying. I didn't do any murder. Right?"

"That's right," Grimes said. "You didn't do any murder, and it's your choice, Huey. If you want to wait for a lawyer, waste a lot of time, maybe give Demeron a chance to find a way out of things, you can. Or, you can answer a few questions and really help us out and help yourself out at the same time."

Cooke was breathing heavy now, stressed by the tension and the pressure to decide one way or the other. His eyes darted from Grimes to the other agents in the room as he mulled things over.

Demeron had treated him like a fool his entire life, made him put up with his shit. He would put the blame on Huey Cooke if he got the chance, and it wouldn't be some public defender standing up for A.C. Demeron. No, he would have the best lawyer in the state ... in the country even. The boss always had the best when he did things, and he would find a way to smile and point the finger at dumb old Huey.

Cooke made his decision and nodded. "Alright. What do I need to do to help you out, like you said?"

"Tell us about the girls," Grimes said.

"The girls?" Cooke's eyes moved to the two agents seated in chairs positioned on either side of Grimes.

"The girls," Grimes repeated, nodding. "The dead ones in the grain bin."

"Oh, those girls," Cooke said. "I didn't have anything to do with them."

"Those girls?" Grimes' brow raised slightly. According to Cowley's statement, there were others in the box truck, but the search of the lodge had not discovered them. Grimes went out on a limb and asked simply. "Where are the others?"

"Well, in their rooms, I guess," Cooke said nervously. "Didn't you find them?"

"No." Grimes shook his head, shot Cooke a hard stare, and went out on another limb. "What did you do to them?"

"Me?" Cooke's head was shaking back and forth again. "No, not me! I told you I didn't do anything to them ... never ... not once. I never touched them! I was never with them. Not any of them."

"I believe you," Grimes said and gave an understanding nod. "Who then? Who was *with* them?"

"A.C. ... Mr. Demeron, I mean ... him and those people he brings out here to hunt, and ... you know, to be with the girls. But it wasn't me ... never." Cooke looked pleadingly at Grimes, desperate to be believed.

"Alright. It wasn't you," Grimes said. "So where are the girls?"

"You're saying they aren't here?" Cooke's brow furrowed in confusion.

"They're not here." Grimes nodded.

"They must have gotten away." He looked around the room at the other agents. "Did you find Loni? She would know."

"Who?"

"Loni. She's like the foreman, the one who keeps the girls in line."

"There's no Loni here," Grimes said.

The creases in Cooke's forehead deepened. "She must have taken them ... must have taken one of the vans and drove them away. That's the only way in this cold."

"Which van? What does it look like?"

"They're all the same. White Chevy van with the Demeron Lodge logo on the side."

"Good." Grimes nodded. "How many girls would be inside?"

"Well, with Loni, that would be four." Cooke thought for a second. "Then there's the boy, young fella, about fifteen or so."

Grimes shot a sideward glance at one of the agents at his side. The agent nodded and left the room. A minute later, a bulletin was being broadcast to law enforcement agencies across South Dakota and surrounding states to be on the lookout for the van and its occupants. If found, the van and everyone with it were to be held as part of an ongoing FBI investigation.

"Now about the ones in the grain bin," Grimes said. "Tell me about those."

Huey Cooke went on for half an hour, telling Grimes about the girls who tried to escape one night, but froze to death. They'd had to put the bodies somewhere before burying them when the ground thawed, so they put them in the grain bin on A.C. Demeron's orders.

Then he explained that with the dead girls gone, and more of Demeron's guests scheduled to arrive, they needed others. That's why the truck came with replacements. He added, "Except that one was dead, killed by the men who drove the truck when she got in the way with the deputy."

"The same ones who killed the deputy, killed the girl?" Grimes said.

"Yes, yes." Cooke's head bobbed up and down. "That's it. They killed Lew Bentz and the girl."

"Where are they now?"

"I don't know. They took one of our trucks to the Rapid City airport and rented a car. I haven't seen or heard from them since."

"What happened to the box truck they drove?"

"We hid it out at Bob Shank's place." Cooke paused and added to make sure they understood, "Not me. I didn't do anything. Arnold and Delbert took it out there so Bedford could find it and blame Shank for killing Bentz." He leaned toward Grimes. "A.C. gave all the orders. He always gives all the orders."

And just like that, Arnold Cowley's statement was corroborated down to the last detail. Grimes gave an appreciative nod. "You've been very helpful, Huey. I'll make sure that the prosecutor knows. That will make things a lot easier for you in court."

"Okay." Cooke nodded and stared down at his lap for a few seconds, drained, then a smile crept across his face and he looked up at Grimes. "I'd like to see A.C.'s face when he comes back and finds you all here."

The sky was graying and night coming on before that happened. Sole watched the activity from the passenger seat of one of the tactical team trucks. Grimes was a by-the-book agent, and, ex-cop or not, there was no way he was allowing Sole into any area they had designated as part of the crime scene, which was pretty much the entire lodge compound. Demeron would have the finest attorneys in the country, at least the most expensive, defending him, and

Grimes was not about to open the door for them to question the integrity of their investigation.

The plush van carrying the hunters slowed to a stop in front of the lodge. Sole could see faces inside peering through the glass at the circle of government vehicles. Grimes watched from the front porch, waiting for someone to step out of the van, but seconds passed, and no one exited. The driver, one of the hunt assistants, shifted into gear as if about to pull away again, but that wasn't going to happen. Two FBI sedans pulled in front and behind, wedging it into place.

There was no mistaking the purposes of the vehicles ringing the compound—sedans bearing U.S. Government license plates, the well-marked tactical team vehicles—all were busy processing a crime scene.

Three pickups were parked near the grain bin with the words *County Coroner* on the sides. To avoid any conflict-of-interest issues, none of the coroners were from Blanken County.

The crime scene techs had positioned floodlights around the property, powered by gas generators. They intended to document every square inch of Demeron's hunting lodge operation.

Garish white light lit up the faces inside the van. Desperation and panic took hold among the passengers.

"What the hell is going on?" Senator Kellin shouted. "Demeron! Get us the hell out of here!"

"We can't just sit here!" Oliver Parson looked like he might try to crawl out through the rear hatch door.

"Demeron, you son of a bitch," Elizabeth Ranskill raged. "You've ruined us!"

"Oh God, no ... no," Simon Taylor simpered and put his face in his hands.

Trapped, Demeron could only bluster. "Hold tight. I'll fix this."

He slid the side door open and stepped out. "This is private property. I don't care what your business is here. I want all of you off my property now!"

Grimes stepped down from the porch, flanked by several agents. He motioned to the tactical team leader, and they surrounded the van. Simon Taylor's high-pitched wail could be heard inside.

"Check inside the van," he ordered the agents, then walked over to face Demeron.

"You'll pay for this! I'll have your job for this!" Red-faced, spittle flying from his mouth to freeze as it fell to the ground, Demeron raged. "Do you know who I am?"

"Avery Cromwell Demeron." Grimes nodded. "You are under arrest."

Sole stepped from the tactical truck to get a better view but stayed put. Grimes noticed, nodded, and said nothing.

One by one, the occupants were brought out, arguing, proclaiming their innocence, sobbing. No warrants had been issued for any of them … yet … but they were all part of the group Huey Cooke described as *being with the girls and boy*. The agents identified each. noting their names in a crime scene log. They were advised they were being detained pending further investigation, then led off to separate vehicles to be transported back to the Pierre field office.

Sole watched the expressions on their faces, stunned, fearful, and terrified. They had reason to be. At the very least, their reputations would be ruined, tied by association to the string of charges the FBI was bringing against Demeron. At the worst, they would be tried as co-conspirators.

He knew one element was missing from the FBI's case against them. The victims.

The girls and boy in the truck witnessed the murder of Lew Bentz and the girl in the truck. They were the victims of kidnapping, human trafficking, and pedophilia. Their testimony could not only put Demeron and the others away in prison, it could punch a hole in the web of human trafficking that ensnared thousands each year.

They were the FBI's best evidence, and they were gone.

FIFTY-EIGHT

Safe

"Something's not right." Loni checked the van's side mirrors and glanced at the speedometer. "What the hell are they doing?"

"Who?" Malina asked and turned in the seat to look at the right-side mirror. "Dammit."

"What is it?" Cindy asked, on the verge of tears. She'd been a basket case since the escape, terrified that some unforeseen event would send her back to another night of abuse at the hands of Senator Kellin.

"Cops," Malina said.

"We have to get away." Cindy shook her head, frantic and terrified. "Just keep driving."

Brad and Sherry squirmed around to peer through the back window.

"Were we speeding?" Brad asked.

"No." Loni shook her head. "I've been careful about that, but he's been back there a while, just following. Once he pulled up close, and I thought he might put his lights on and stop us, but then he backed off. Now he just follows."

"We could stop," Sherry suggested. "Pull over and see if he follows. At least then we'd know what he wants."

"I thought about that," Loni shook her head. "Problem is, Demeron has a long reach back in South Dakota. Trust me, I know. He owns the damned sheriff in Blanken County. That's how he gets away with everything."

"So, you think he sent the cops after us?" Malina watched the police car in the mirror keeping pace, never advancing or falling back.

"It's possible," Loni said. "It's the kind of thing he would do."

"We're a long way from there," Malina thought for a few seconds and said, "Maybe we could fake the cop out. Stop, but be ready to take off. Then we'd know if he was following us. Might be better to know what we're up against than to sit here pissing ourselves and guessing."

"And what if we're not fast enough to take off and get away? What if he wants to take us back to South Dakota?" Loni asked.

"No!" Cindy was near hysteria now. "Don't stop and let them take us back. Please don't stop!"

"Quiet!" Malina snapped over her shoulder, then looked at Loni. "We're going to have to stop somewhere sooner or later. Start looking for someplace with people … witnesses … then pull over there and see if the cop follows. They can't do anything too bad in front of witnesses." Malina turned to look at the others. "If they try, we'll make lots of noise, right?"

"It's as good an idea as any, I guess," Loni said and looked at the others in the rearview mirror. "We can't outrun them in this van."

Brad and Sherry nodded. Cindy sobbed.

With no particular destination in mind—only to get as

far from A.C. Demeron and his guests as possible—they had driven east across South Dakota and then South on I-29. Six hours into their escape, they were south of Sioux City, Iowa. As interstates go, it was a quiet stretch of highway.

Loni and Malina scanned ahead for a place to pull off ... a place with people. I-29 between Sioux City and Omaha runs through agricultural country. Exits are few and far between., and the cop car continued to follow, never approaching closer or dropping farther behind.

Several miles passed. The tension in the van increased. No one spoke. They sat frozen in their seats as if waiting for the final climactic scene in a horror movie ... waiting for the ax murderer to come bursting out of a closet, except this was their horror movie and they were the stars.

It happened suddenly. A roar of accelerating engines broke the silence in the van. Two more police vehicles sped down the highway, seemingly from nowhere, and passed the first. One soared past the van and swerved directly in front of it. The other hovered off the driver's door, close enough that they could see the face of the Iowa State Patrol trooper behind the wheel.

"Oh, God no ... noooo." Cindy had her face in her hands, her shoulders shaking violently with each sob.

The others stared straight ahead at the state patrol car in front, braking and forcing them to slow down while the one to the left closed in until the doors of the vehicles were nearly touching. Loni eased the van toward the right shoulder.

She checked the mirror. The car that had been following had closed up to their bumper, wedging them in. She had no choice but to follow the lead car off onto the shoulder.

The troopers exited their vehicles and ringed the van, hands on the butts of their sidearms. With only the scanty information they'd been provided, they were cautious.

The trooper who had driven the car behind approached the passenger door. Malina lowered the window and waited.

He said nothing at first, scanning the terrified faces in the back, then looked at Loni. "Let's see your driver's license."

She pulled it from her purse between the seats and handed it across. The trooper looked it over, nodded, looked at the others, and said, "It's them."

"What's the problem, officer?" Loni said and felt stupid for saying it, but couldn't think of anything else to slow things down so they could delay the inevitable.

"No problem," the trooper said. "Everyone out. Line up beside the van."

One by one, they climbed out, staring down at the ground. They had to help Cindy. Brad and Sherry held her arms, but as her feet touched the ground, she collapsed, fell out of their grasp, and rolled onto her side. Crying and moaning, "Please, I don't want to go back ... please don't make me go back."

One trooper knelt and put her hand on Cindy's head. "It's alright, hon. You're safe now. We'll keep you safe."

It was a well-intended, but incongruous statement since. To this point in their young lives, no one had ever made them feel safe.

Cindy looked up through teary eyes. The trooper smiled and stroked her head. "I promise, you're safe now."

Cindy threw her arms around the trooper's neck, crying now out of relief. Malina, Brad, and Sherry sank to the ground beside her. The sudden release of pent-up tension drained away in a rush like water through floodgates, leaving them limp and exhausted. Loni looked at the troopers, leaned back against the side of the van, and let the tears she'd been holding back flow down her cheeks.

Acting on the lookout broadcast by the FBI and with the descriptions provided by Huey Cooke and Arnold Cowley, the troopers soon identified the occupants as the missing victims of Demeron's pedophile ring. The first order of business was securing transportation for them back to Pierre, where the FBI wanted to interview them. The van would be towed back and impounded, along with the rest of the lodge's equipment.

Trooper Dorothy Barnes, the only female among the army of law enforcement officers who eventually showed up along the side of the interstate, rode with them on a courtesy shuttle bus that the Iowa State Patrol had requested from a rental agency in Sioux City. Cindy clung to her like a baby to its mother. The others dozed restlessly, trying to forget what had happened and not think about what awaited them.

FIFTY-NINE

Marked Men

It was a big story. A once-in-a-decade story, for some reporters, a once-in-a-lifetime chance to make it big. It was the kind of story that would dominate the news for weeks, and in a city like Sioux Falls could give a reporter national exposure and a leg up to a spot in one of the big-city markets. Detroit, Indianapolis, Atlanta ... even LA or New York weren't out of the question.

Doug Trent, a reporter for one of the local network affiliates out of Sioux Falls, was making the most of the opportunity. His lengthy exposé had all the required elements—murder, drama, innocent child victims, scandal, police corruption, and a salacious topic.

Best of all, it had a star-studded cast. A prominent and hyper-wealthy South Dakota business tycoon. Financial magnates and a lawyer whose previously obscure names would soon be the subject of more in-depth background reports, editorials, and the butt of late-night comedians' jokes. Most shocking of all, the cast included a United

States senator involved in a *pedo-ring*, as the news reports would call it.

Every major market picked it up and carried it as a lead. Trent knew what he had and milked every second of the time allotted to him, detailing the horrors uncovered by a recent FBI investigation into murder and human trafficking in rural Blanken County.

Dressed in a parka, his breath frosted and blowing away in the breeze, he stood framed on the screen in a barren, snowy landscape with the Demeron lodge and barn over his shoulder in the distance. One by one, images of the key players flashed on the screen. A reportedly gay big-name attorney, the heads of two of the largest investment funds on the globe, including one of the wealthiest women in the world, a senator who chaired the powerful banking committee, and the ringleader himself, A.C. Demeron.

The report turned to a press conference featuring Special Agent Weems and Special Agent-in-Charge Grimes. They gave predictably brief and straightforward statements. The investigation is ongoing. Further charges are pending as we produce additional evidence. We won't answer any questions that might adversely affect the case when it goes before a judge. That was it.

But you had to give Trent credit. He wasn't finished yet. The scene cut to interviews with deputies in front of the sheriff's department. It was during those interviews that he discovered something else. One deputy, Dean Weber, assisted by another man, a newcomer known as Bill Myers, helped to expose the murder cover-up and the child sex ring at the Demeron lodge.

His production team tracked the two down at a local bar in Alder, where they were sitting quietly sipping beers and trying to forget everything they had seen. Accompanied by a woman with a video camera, Trent went in and knelt by their table, thrusting a microphone in their faces.

"Deputy Weber, you and Mr. Myers have become heroes here in the community. How does that make you feel?"

Weber stared at him as if Trent had just stepped out of a UFO.

Sole shook his head and said, "We don't have anything to say. We'd just like to sit here and drink our beers if you don't mind."

"Perfectly understandable." Trent gave a solemn nod, followed by a smile to prove he understood. "But you must know that so many are indebted to you for what you did … for not giving up." He leaned in closer. "Knowing what happened, does it make you wish you could have done more … sooner?"

Sole looked up from his beer. "Leave."

"But …" the reporter began. He was cut off by other voices in the bar. He looked around to find a dozen pairs of eyes staring.

"You heard him!" Alva Langstrom led the way. "Get the hell out of here."

"That's right," Harry Langstrom added. "We don't need you here."

"Get your ass out!" a customer said.

The community's shock at the horrors uncovered at the Demeron lodge piled on top of the murder of one of their own, a murder covered up by the man many had voted for, had tensions high. More voices chimed in.

"Move on!"

"Can't you see they don't want to talk?"

"You got no right to come in here bothering these men."

Trent and the camerawoman backed away to the door but continued to record the scene inside. The final report would edit out the locals' antagonism to the intrusion and simply show the two men sitting quietly drinking a beer while Trent's somber voice played over the video. "Tensions remain high here in Blanken County but for the two heroes who were instrumental in solving the case while others did nothing, it's time for a quiet beer."

The exposé's final segment turned to the human-interest side of things, with the reporter interviewing locals for their perspectives. Most of the answers to his questions were defensive and embarrassed. Trent's questions had a common theme.

Question:
How does it make you feel to learn that a prominent member of your community was running a trafficking ring that routinely set up events for the purpose of having sex with children?

Answers:
Terrible ... I just feel terrible for those poor children.
We had no idea such a terrible thing was happening right here in our county.
Been living in Blanken County all of my life and I never suspected anything like this could happen here.
How do you think I feel? Sick to my stomach, that's how ... adults doing it with children.

Question:
How could this happen right under your nose without ever being discovered?

Answers:
I mean, how could we know? It was all out at the Demeron place ...
private property, and all. I never got invited out there.
He kept to himself, and we all do the same.
There was no way for us to know what was going on out there.
Demeron kept everything pretty much under lock and key.

Question:
Your sheriff, Willard Bedford, has been arrested as part of the murder coverup and human trafficking operation. Did you vote for Sheriff Bedford? Knowing what you know now, do you regret your vote? Would you vote for him again?

Answers:
If I knew what Bedford was up to, I definitely would not have voted for him.
You got to understand, we didn't know all that he was into. There was no way to know.
Yeah, I voted for him. Hell no, I wouldn't have if I'd known what was going on.

For the rest of the nation with their eyes glued to the story, the implications raised by Doug Trent's questions were clear. How could the residents of such a small community not have been aware of what was happening?

The residents of Blanken County were deeply offended and angry. Trent's report took liberties in framing what had happened in the most sinister way possible, casting a shadow not just over those who had committed the crimes, but over the entire community. Trent left his viewers with questions that would be the subject of pundit discussions on every network.

His face filled the screen for his concluding statement. "The question remains, should the citizens of Blanken County have known? Was it because they chose to look the other way? Were they indifferent to the plight of Demeron's victims because of his power and influence in the county? Could they have done something to end the terror for the young victims?"

He gave a somber nod while looking into the camera. "This is Doug Trent, reporting live from Blanken County, South Dakota."

Blanken County residents, never known for much of anything except living quietly with each other, became the center of the biggest scandal of the year. One late-night host even used the county's name to coin a euphemism for looking the other way when something horrendous happens. Shaking his head in disgust, he threw out to the audience a series of scenarios where people ignored horrors and misfortunes, and to each, he looked at the camera, gave the wry grin he was known for, shrugged, and said scornfully, "They *blanked* it."

"We're dead," Rick Salver muttered and stared at the television screen in a Rapid City motel room.

A minute into the evening news report on a local channel, he scrambled off the bed to answer the pounding on the door.

"Did you see?" Tom Finch rushed in.

"Watching it now," Salver said. They stood in the middle of the room, staring at the television.

"We are so fucked," Finch whispered, eyes glued to the screen.

"Yeah." Salver repeated his earlier assessment of their situation, "We're dead."

"We have to get away," Finch's voice was barely more than a whisper, the lump of fear in his throat threatening to choke him. "Go somewhere where they won't find us."

"Really?" Salver shook his head, his face twisted into a hopeless grimace. He wanted to laugh at the idea that they could run from the cartel, but his bowels were loosening and any sudden convulsion might cause him to shit his pants. "Get away to where? You really believe there is someplace we can go where they won't find us?"

"No," Finch said, the realization sinking in that his partner was right. "We're dead."

They watched Doug Trent's entire report, but the truth was they could have cared less about the feelings of the locals, or the plight of the victims. The FBI wasn't saying much, but what they said was enough. They intended to track down the human traffickers supplying Demeron's sex ring. The cartel would pick up the report, know that the worst had happened, that law enforcement was on their trail.

With resources that exceeded those of most federal agencies, the cartel would turn over every stone and shine a light into every corner to find them. They would only be satisfied by the deaths, bloody and brutal, of those whose carelessness had focused the efforts of U.S. law enforcement on their operations.

It was only a matter of time. The cartel did not forgive and forget. They were marked men.

SIXTY

Big-Balled Son of a Bitch

Detective Leonard Purdy had become a regular workaholic. Alone in his cubicle long after the rest of his squad mates were gone for the day, Purdy spent hours trying to come up with a way to pinpoint the location of the man known as Bill Myers.

He had two pieces of information. Bill Myers' name and the tag number from his pickup. That was enough.

It was tedious work, but for once, Purdy was motivated. He'd never spent so much time on any legitimate investigative case. Then again, he'd never been promised the kind of payday the cartel could promise.

So, he stayed late and used department resources when no one was watching. He also used his position as a law enforcement officer to obtain information others could not.

Knowing where Myers began, he traced out routes on the major highways leading out of the city. Then he developed a timeline, assuming an eight-hour drive time in any one day, he marked off likely locations where Myers might stop to rest. Then he identified hotels and motels within a twenty-five-mile radius of the potential rest locations.

It seemed unlikely that a man like Myers, known to the cartel, would spend his nights in five-star accommodations, so he focused first on budget motels. The next part of his plan was the equivalent of canvassing a neighborhood, old-fashioned police work knocking on doors in the search for witnesses to a crime.

He began calling motels from his office phone and, with his police authority, was able to ask if Bill Myers had checked in. Most didn't even question the call from a police department number or the unknown detective's legitimacy, and if they did, he threatened to charge them with hindering a criminal investigation. It was an empty threat, but the desk clerks at the low-budget motels weren't about to question it. Besides, they were accustomed to police inquiries about their guests, and there were no legal restrictions on releasing names and license plate numbers of guests to police officers.

He worked methodically, making call after call. It seemed a hopeless task, and a less motivated person probably would have said to hell with it, but for once, Lenny Purdy did not give up. Pleasing the cartel became his life's work.

Finally, a night clerk at a motel at an exit on I-90, two hundred miles to the west, confirmed that Bill Myers had stayed there. Purdy was elated.

He checked the map for other hotels in that direction and started again. It took fewer calls this time before he found another motel, and then another. The last was in Sioux Falls, South Dakota. The trail went dead after that.

He decided the time was right to advise the cartel. *El Gordo* answered on the first ring.

"I found him," Purdy blurted out.

"Where?" Gordo asked.

"At a motel in Sioux Falls."

"Which motel?"

Purdy named the low-rent motel on the outskirts of the city where the sign outside advertised that rooms were available by the month, week, day, or hour.

There was a pause for several seconds. Purdy thought for a moment the call had ended, then Gordo was back on and said, "You go there."

"What? Me?"

"Yes you," Gordo said. "Find him."

"What if he's checked out and moved on?"

"Find him."

"What if he's gone and I can't find him?"

"Find him," Gordo repeated. "You're a detective. Do whatever the hell it is you do, but find him."

The island home that had seemed so close began drifting away. "What do I do if ... when ... I find him?" Purdy asked, dreading what Gordo might order him to do next.

"Keep your eyes on him and call me."

"Right. I can do that." That's not so bad, he thought.

"You better." The phone went dead again. This time, Gordo had ended the call.

The next morning, Purdy didn't bother reporting to work. He called and told his captain he needed some personal time off and would use up his accrued leave days.

"Fine," Captain Mallard said simply. Leonard Purdy would not be missed.

Sioux Falls was a three-day drive away. Purdy made it in just under two and checked into the same motel Myers had stayed in. It wasn't a fleabag motel. That would have been a step up. This place was a shit-hole.

Hookers roamed the parking lot and adjacent streets in heavy coats, opening them briefly for prospective customers to inspect, then pulling them tight around them again. Shady characters with hats pulled low over their eyes came from rooms, eyeballed him, and then moved away muttering to themselves.

When he opened the door to his room, the sour smell of body odor and urine was overpowering. Bile rose in his throat, and he wrinkled his nose in disgust. He doubted anyone had changed the sheets between guests, and someone had left the toilet bowl full of piss.

He flushed it and settled in to do what Gordo had ordered … find Bill Myers. The problem was that Detective Leonard Purdy had exhausted his investigative skills in tracking Myers to the motel in Sioux Falls.

He spent the next couple of days wandering the streets, amazed that even in the middle of a South Dakota winter, hookers and drug dealers continued to ply their trades. After wandering in and out of dive bars for a couple of days, he got in his car and began going to other local motels on the possibility that Myers might have changed his name. He showed a picture of the man from the security video, stopped in his pickup at the traffic light. No one recognized him.

He needed a break. Sitting in his room, staring blankly at the television, drinking bourbon from a bottle, he wondered what Gordo was going to do to him when he reported he could not locate Myers. Then, he got his break.

There he was … just a brief image, no more than thirty seconds of him sitting in a bar somewhere, sipping a beer while a reporter talked about him and the man with him, calling them heroes. He turned the volume up to hear the reporter say that Bill Myers and the other man, a deputy, were local heroes who helped solve a murder and end a human trafficking ring that involved sex with minors.

Purdy squinted, wishing he had a remote to pause the images. Leaning toward the screen, he made out the words on a sign on the wall behind the bar—*Langstrom's*.

"Son of a bitch," he nearly shouted, then looked around quickly even though he was alone and, in a place, where no one would pay attention to shouted profanity unless it was directed at them. Lowering his voice, he muttered, "I've got you, you son of a bitch."

He grabbed his phone. When Gordo answered, he said, "I found him."

Gordo did not spend much time watching the evening news, or he could have found Myers for himself. When Purdy finished, he said, "You go there." It was an order.

"Me?" Not again, Purdy thought.

"Yes, you," Gordo said. "Contact me when you are there. You'll receive instructions."

"Okay," Purdy said doubtfully. "Are you sure ..." he began, but as usual, Gordo had already disconnected.

Purdy leaned back on the moldy bed sheets disappointed that he could not simply go home and collect his payoff. He took a sip from the bottle of bourbon resting on his chest and immediately felt better, a smile on his face. Another sip and the smile grew into a grin.

"You fucking did it, Purdy," he said to himself. "You big-balled son of a bitch ... YOU FUCKING DID IT!"

He shouted it out, but no one in the shit-hole motel paid any attention.

SIXTY-ONE

Stay of Execution

When the phone chimed, they jumped as if a gunshot had gone off in the room. Salver and Finch stared at it, lying on the table in the motel room in Mitchell, South Dakota. They began the day waiting for the GPS Tracking information from Sheriff Bedford.

Then all hell broke loose with the FBI raids, and they could only contemplate their limited future options and the distinct possibility that they would be dead very soon. Finch reacted first and reached out to press the decline button.

"No." Salver shook his head. "We should hear what they say."

"Why?" Finch stared at the phone as if a rattlesnake had coiled up on the table. "I'm already about to shit my pants. I don't need to hear."

"Any information might help us stay away from them as long as possible." Salver shrugged. "Anyway, answering the phone won't change anything. We won't be any worse off. If they just want to tell how they are going to slit us open and burn our guts in front of us, we just hang up."

"You had to say that?" Finch frowned but nodded. "Okay, let's hear what they say."

Salver nodded and answered the call on speaker. He said nothing. There wasn't any reason to.

"Do you want to live?" Luis Ibarra's calm, resonant, slightly accented voice made the question sound like he'd just asked if they wanted cream and sugar in their coffee.

Salver and Finch looked up from the phone, the same question in their eyes. Was there hope, after all?

Luis Ibarra was their primary contact with the cartel, the one who arranged and accepted their deliveries of young women and boys to be sent south of the border and sold into the sex trade around the globe.

"I know you are there, listening," Ibarra said. "I will ask this question one last time. If you choose not to answer, I promise, you will be dead within forty-eight hours." He paused, then repeated, saying each word slowly and clearly, "Do you want to live?"

"Yes," Salver managed to croak. "We want to live."

"Good." Ibarra sounded pleased. "There is someone who wants to speak with you."

A moment later, another voice came on, a woman's voice. "Do you know who I am?"

Wide-eyed, Salver and Finch exchanged a terrified look. "Yes," Salver said, and this time his voice was barely a whisper.

"Good," the woman said. "Then you know I have the power to save your lives. Will you do as I instruct?"

"Yes," both blurted out together. They looked at each other. Was there a way out of this, after all? It didn't seem possible.

"Listen carefully." Juana Elizondo gave her instructions

and then finished by asking, "Do you understand what you must do?"

"Yes," Salver and Finch said, their voices muted but tinged with hope.

"Good. Do as I have instructed, and all is forgiven."

The call ended. Salver and Finch stared at each other across the motel room table. It was a stay of execution. It came out of nowhere for reasons they could not fathom, and it didn't matter. A full pardon would only come after they did what Juana Elizondo ordered.

Fifteen minutes later, they'd packed their bags and were on the road. Elizondo was clear. There could be no delay. What had to be done must be done quickly. If they succeeded, they would have their lives back. If they didn't ... they pushed that thought away.

SIXTY-TWO

Friendly Enough Fella

Detective Leonard Purdy arrived in Alder as the sun was setting. Gray, low-hanging cloud cover held the threat of another storm and sucked up the remaining daylight in minutes. He cruised the main street slowly until he found what he was looking for and pulled into a parking spot.

When he walked through the front door at Langstrom's, Alva looked up from behind the bar and frowned. "Another strange face coming to gawk." She looked at her husband. "Tell him to get the hell out."

"Now, Alva, why would we be running business away before we even know what they're here for?" He nodded at the newcomer who stopped to look around the room and then walked toward the bar. "Let's see what he wants."

"Humph." Alva turned and stormed into the backroom.

Purdy walked up to the bar, gave a friendly nod, and smiled. "Got a beer on tap?"

"Bottles or cans ...all the usuals," Harry Langstrom said, running a bar rag over the counter in front of Purdy, waiting and eyeballing the stranger.

"Bud Light," Purdy said and turned to survey the bar and surrounding tables. He nodded when Langstrom placed the beer in front of him. "Thanks."

He tipped the bottle up, took a gulp, and noticed Langstrom was watching. "Nice place you have here. Looks pretty busy."

"Busy enough," Langstrom said. "Lot of new faces coming through … People who heard the news." He leaned his elbows on the bar. "I guess you heard the news … that's why you're here. Right?"

Purdy expected to have his presence in a backwater like Alder questioned. Small towns were full of nosy people, and after what had happened, they would be nosy and probably antagonistic to strangers.

On the drive out, he constructed a story to explain his visit. It was a lie, but lying was one thing he was good at.

He nodded. "Yeah, I heard what happened. That's why I'm here."

Langstrom stood up straight, eyes narrowed, face stern. "We've had enough curiosity seekers around here, so when you're done with your beer, you can leave."

"Oh?" Purdy put the beer on the counter. It was time to sell the lie. "Sorry. Guess I didn't explain myself too good."

"Good enough," Langstrom said. "Drink up and leave. Beer's on the house."

"If that's what you want," Purdy said. "I'll leave, but you should know I came here because I was hoping someone might be able to help me find my daughter."

"Your daughter?" The scowl on Langstrom's face faded a bit.

"Yeah," Purdy nodded and took a long swallow from the beer. "She went missing a couple of years ago. Ran away." He lowered his eyes and shook his head sadly. "Things weren't perfect around the house ... her mother and me ... we fought ... a lot. I guess she got tired of it. Then one day she left, and we never saw her again. She'd be about fifteen now." He looked up. "Things are better now and all her mom and me can think of is finding her and taking her home. I heard what happened here and drove right over, hoping to talk to someone and see if they had any news about my little girl."

"What's her name?" Alva came from the backroom where she'd been standing by the door listening to the conversation between her husband and the newcomer. She folded her arms and stared at Purdy, waiting for an answer.

He was ready. "Isabelle," he said immediately, meeting her stare with a smile. "Izzy, we call her ... Isabelle Lawton." He put a hand out to Harry Langstrom. "I'm Sam Lawton."

Harry glanced at Alva, and the tension eased. He shook Purdy's hand and smiled. "I'm Harry Langstrom and this is Alva. We own the place."

"Nice to meet you," Purdy said. "So, can you tell me anything? I saw in the news there were a couple of fellas who helped break things up for the FBI ... heroes they called them in the report. I was hoping to talk to them." He shrugged. "You never know if just one little piece of information, one little something they noticed, might help us find our little Izzy."

"That'd be Dean Weber and Bill Myers," Harry said.

"Right!" Purdy nodded. "That's the names I heard on the report. Are they around?"

"Dean's probably home with his family, taking a few days off from the sheriff's department. They might be able to put you in touch with him."

"And this other ... Myers?"

"Bill should be back here later. Went to get his pickup. He had a little mishap, and it's been in the shop getting fixed up." Harry smiled and added, "He's not from around here. Didn't know about our winters."

"Will he be coming back here today?"

"I should hope so," Alva said. "His things are in the back. He's been staying with us while Ernie Bullock works on his pickup."

"Okay. I guess I'll go find a place to stay and come back later to see if I can talk with him." Purdy nodded, finished the beer, and put the bottle on the bar, pulling out his wallet.

"Told you ... on the house," Harry shook his head.

"Thanks very much," Purdy said and started to turn away.

"Lois Tate's," Alva said.

Purdy turned back. "Pardon?"

"Lois Tate runs the boarding house at the end of the street. No hotels around here. You'd have to go back to I-90 to find any. Lois probably has a room for you. That way, you'll be close when Bill shows up."

"Thank you." Purdy smiled. "Tate's boarding house it is."

"Seemed like a friendly enough fella," Harry said. "Sad story about his daughter and all."

"Yes, sad," Alva agreed, for once not giving out a *humph* of disapproval.

Lenny Purdy walked outside and down the street to his car. Full night had come on now. A few snowflakes drifted down from the overcast. He started the engine and turned the heater on, but did not pull down the street to Lois Tate's boarding house. He leaned back low in the seat so that just his eyes were above the steering wheel and settled in to wait.

SIXTY-THREE

Plans

The dinner crowd had almost gone by the time Sole returned to Langstrom's and parked his pickup in front. Ernie Bullock's wife, Addie, didn't get much company, especially this time of year, so she wanted to talk and, as was her custom, offered Sole a cup of coffee and then another. They chatted about everything except the one topic that had everyone in Alder on the touchy side. She never brought up his role in the investigation and arrests that had rocked the county.

She was about to pour a third cup when Sole lifted a hand and smiled. "No thanks, Addie. I have to go, but yours is the best coffee I ever had." He leaned close and grinned. "Don't tell Alva Langstrom I said that."

She laughed. "I wouldn't dare."

Sole drove slowly back to Langstrom's, knowing what he had to tell them and not wanting to do it. He should have known staying on in Blanken County was a pipedream.

The cold serenity of the landscape and straightforward nature of the people were refreshing. Even Bob Shank's bullying attitude toward everyone had its own charm. Every town needs a villain and Shank fit the mold, just mean enough to talk about, but not a murderer after all.

But he couldn't stay. Too much publicity had come to Alder. After Doug Trent's exposé, others had come to do follow-up stories. It would only get worse if he stayed. Sooner or later, *Los Salvajes* would put it all together, if they hadn't already, and come to Alder looking for him. He had to be gone by then, leaving a trail that would take them away from the people who'd become his friends.

Sole walked through the door and heads turned inside. They were friendly faces, nodding at the man who was now one of them.

"How's that old pickup running?" Harry Langstrom called out from the grill.

"Better than new," Sole said and went behind the bar to start working on dishes.

"About time you got back. Things were piling up," Alva said in her brusque way, but as she passed behind him, she reached out and stopped for a moment to give him an affectionate pat on the back. Then she cleared her throat and went into the backroom.

"Well, I'll be damned," Harry said.

"What?" Sole looked up from the glasses he was washing.

"She likes you, after all."

Sole laughed. The customers at the bar laughed. Harry laughed. Alva came through the door again and their mouths shut.

"What's all this about?" she demanded.

"Nothing, dear." Harry gave her a kiss on the cheek. "Now go home and I'll be along later."

Leonard Purdy watched the gas gauge in his car and wished he'd stopped to fill up before heading into Alder. Sitting in the dark and cold without running the engine and heater was impossible.

Parked down the block, he'd been watching Langstrom's for an hour when the car drove into town. He saw the brake lights flash and the car slowed, creeping forward. It passed a small grocery store, closed for the night, but the light over the front door cast a glow that lit up the occupants inside.

It's them, he thought. It has to be them.

It was. The car came even with Purdy's and stopped for a second. Salver peered out through the window and nodded. "That's the guy they told us to meet."

"Right." Finch pulled forward to the end of the block, made a u-turn, and came up behind.

They got out and went to Purdy's car. He lowered the window. "You who I think you are?" he said.

"If you're Purdy, we are," Finch said.

"Get in." Purdy hit the power lock button, and they pulled open the rear doors.

"Fuck it's cold," Salver said. "What's the plan?"

"Really?" Purdy looked in the rearview mirror. "What's the plan? That's supposed to be your department."

"Yeah, it is," Finch said, annoyed. "Just fill us in on what's going on. Why are we sitting out here in the cold?"

"He's in there." Purdy nodded toward Langstrom's down the block. "Staying there in the back somewhere."

"He's there now?" Finch put his hand on the door handle. "Let's do this and get the fuck out of here."

"Go in and just do it in front of a room full of people? You intend to kill everybody?" Purdy shook his head in disgust. "Just sit tight. When everyone's gone, that's when you do it."

"So, there is a plan," Salver snapped.

"That's my plan." Purdy shrugged. "You got another one ... go for it, but you're an idiot if you do anything now."

"You ought to watch how you talk to us.," Finch said, trying to sound tougher than he felt.

"Or what?" Purdy turned in the seat to look at the two men in back. "I'm not some little girl you're gonna snatch off the streets."

"Alright, alright," Salver said to Finch. "Calm down."

He looked at Purdy. "We're just tense. Never done anything like this before."

"No shit," Purdy sneered.

They settled in to wait. The next few hours dragged by at an agonizing pace. Salver and Finch squirmed and fidgeted in the back seat, eager to do what Juana Elizondo wanted and terrified by it at the same time.

It was after midnight when the last customer left and the interior lights blinked off. A minute later, Harry Langstrom came through the door and headed down the street.

Finch reached for the door handle. "Let's go."

"No, wait a while," Salver said. "Let's make sure he's asleep."

"Listen to your partner," Purdy said from up front. "This guy, Myers, took on a bunch of gangbangers. Killed one of them and rode out of town calm as can be. You don't want to take him on awake and alert."

Finch slumped back in the seat, irritated but silent.

Another hour passed, and Salver looked at Purdy. "You think it's been long enough?"

"Asking my advice?" Purdy smirked, then turned in the

seat. "Yeah, probably. If he isn't asleep by now, you're just going to have to fight it out with him."

"Okay," Salver said quietly, then nodded. "Let's do it."

They pushed the rear doors to Purdy's car open and walked along the deserted sidewalk. The snow had been shoveled away, but another inch had fallen as they waited and it crunched under their feet.

When they reached Langstrom's door, they peered through the glass. The interior was lit by a beer sign illuminated over the bar. Finch reached inside the coat he wore and pulled out a tire iron they'd taken from their rental car. He was about to push it between the strike plate and door jamb to pry it open when Salver tried the handle.

It opened. They looked at each other, surprised and amused. This was going to be easier than they'd thought.

"Country people," Salver whispered, shaking his head. "Probably not a locked door in town."

"Quiet." Finch pushed the door open and listened for a few seconds, then nodded.

He moved inside with Salver on his shoulder. They crept through the room to the bar. Finch nodded at a door. "The backroom. That's where he is."

He turned the knob, slow and easy. There was just the smallest of creaks as the door opened. Both men froze, their hands on the butts of the pistols tucked in their coats. They waited, and after several seconds relaxed.

They crept into the backroom. Rows of stacked boxes and crates blocked their view of the room. They moved between the rows, searching, stepping as softly as possible, listening for some sound that would give away their target's location.

It wasn't much of a noise, just a tiny creak, but Sole's eyes popped open. He remained motionless, listening. It might be nothing, probably was nothing ... Harry or Alva returned for something, or the old building creaking in the cold.

Another sound. No creak this time, a footstep, soft and quiet as if on tip toe. Alva and Harry didn't tiptoe around their store, even when Sole was sleeping. He lifted the Colt off the box that served as his nightstand and rolled off the cot to his knees. He moved to the stack of boxes that served as his bedroom wall.

Another soft movement on the other side of the boxes, searching carefully for something or someone ... for him. Sole readied himself, controlling his breathing, waiting.

A silhouette appeared at the opening in the crates. By the size, it was a man, but not Harry Langstrom. He had something in his hand but not a gun. A knife?

Sole tensed, the Colt's heavy frame cold and hard in his hand. The man came into the space and lifted his hand, then stopped peering into the dark around the cot. The man whispered, "He's not here."

Sole swung the Colt down hard on the man's arm.

Tom Finch howled in pain. The object in his hand clattered to the floor. He called out, "Over here!"

Sole struck him hard on the side of the head with the pistol. Stunned but conscious, Finch collapsed on the cot. Sole whirled and crouched as another man came to the opening in the crates. This one had a gun in his hand.

"Drop it, or die," Sole said from the shadows.

Rick Salver nearly fell over, startled out of his wits at the sound of the voice in the dark. He stumbled backward, his arm coming up awkwardly, not seeing anything in the dark but an indistinct form on the cot. He fired off a round in that direction and scrambled back away from the opening in the crates.

The bullet thudded into the wall not six inches from Finch's head. "Son of a bitch! Watch where you're shooting!" He started to move off the cot.

"Nope," Sole said and swung the Colt's steel barrel into his face.

Teeth, cartilage, and bone crunched and snapped. Finch fell back screaming, his hands covering his mutilated nose and mouth. Despite their gleaming smiles and prowess at luring young girls and boys off the streets, he and Salver were no match against Sole.

Realizing he was up against someone far better at ambushes than he was, Salver did what his instincts screamed at him to do. He abandoned his partner and ran.

He bumped into boxes, knocking over stacks of cartons and beer cases as he plunged through the storeroom and back out into the bar area. Finch would have to take care of himself. Salver ran for the front door.

"Stop!" Two men stood in the entrance.

Salver skidded to a stop and almost fell over, then righted himself, standing up straight. Panicked, he raised his arm, the pistol pointed at the shadowy figures. This wasn't going according to plan, he thought.

It was his last thought. Four sharp cracks sent four bullets through his chest. Rick Salver crumpled to the floor.

SIXTY-FOUR

Lucky

They came out of nowhere. At least, that's how it seemed to Leonard Purdy.

The frozen streets of Alder were deserted and still. Salver and Finch disappeared inside Langstrom's. Purdy waited for confirmation that their mission was a success so that he could call *El Gordo*, who would relay it up the cartel chain to Juana Elizondo.

Except the mission was not a success. A few minutes after Salver and Finch disappeared from sight, two men approached the door to Langstrom's and went inside. That wasn't right. Nobody else was supposed to show up. Gordo had told him so personally. This was his assignment—along with the two sex-slave delivery men—but now there was someone else in Alder.

Purdy sat up straight in the seat and leaned over the wheel, watching. A moment later, gunfire erupted from inside, the muzzle flashes throwing orange bursts of light out onto the snow. He put a hand on the ignition key and started to turn it when four men in dark clothes surrounded his vehicle.

One thumped a pistol against the driver's door glass, pointing the barrel at his face. "FBI! Put your hands on the wheel!" He jerked the door open and pulled Purdy out of the car. "Leonard Purdy, you are under arrest."

"What the hell," Purdy sputtered. "I didn't do anything ... what the hell ... I'm a damned cop."

"You were." the FBI agent said, jerking Purdy around and pushing him up against the car.

"This is bullshit. I didn't do anything!"

"Really?" The agent cuffed him and spun him around so that he could see his face. "How about abuse of police powers, racketeering, corruption ..." He paused. "Want me to go on?"

Purdy stood in dumb silence, mouth agape, the images of the island paradise in his mind blasted away and replaced by prison bars.

At the roar of the gunshots inside Langstrom's, Sole jerked Finch off the cot and knelt on his back, beside the wall of crates. The injured man moaned but didn't resist.

Sole waited, pistol held at the ready, taking deep steady breaths to slow his heart rate and the adrenaline surging through his system. It was a fight-or-flight moment, but flight was not an option. Trapped in the backroom, he readied himself for whatever was about to happen.

"John Sole!" a familiar voice called out. "Where are you?"

Dean Weber was the only other Blanken County resident who knew his true name. Sole exhaled and felt the familiar post-action draining of tension. Knees up, his feet on Finch's back, he leaned back against the stacked crates, the Colt resting on his knees.

"Back here, Dean!"

"Are you injured?"

"No, I'm not injured. I have a suspect in custody!"

"Coming your way, John! There'll be two of us. Agent Weems is with me."

He heard the door into the backroom open and the lights were turned on. Weber knew where the cot was in the maze of boxes and led the way. They came to the end of a row of crates and looked around the corner to find Sole still seated on the floor, pinning Finch under his feet.

"Good to see you're in one piece," Agent Weems said as he reached down to jerk a moaning Tom Finch to his feet.

"Good to see you, period," Sole said and stood. "What the hell are you doing here? How'd you know?"

"We didn't," Weems replied as he pushed Finch ahead. "We got lucky."

"We both got lucky," Sole said.

Weber looked at Finch's bloody face and broken hand and smiled. "I don't know. Looks like you had things pretty well under control."

They started to follow Weems out when Sole grabbed Weber's arm. "Stop! Watch where you step." He knelt down and pointed at the floor. "That asshole had something in his hand when he came in. I hit him and it flew away. That must be it."

Weber knelt beside him, peering at the hypodermic syringe lying against one of the crates. "I'll be damned. What was he going to do with that?"

"Test what's inside and we'll probably know." Sole

stood. "Come on. There might be other evidence. Let's move out, and you can tell me what the hell is going on."

They made their way out into the bar area. Sole stopped in his tracks, stunned at the activity inside and outside Langstrom's.

FBI agents were already collecting evidence and processing the scene, including the dead man lying in a pool of blood on the floor. Outside, State Patrol troopers, along with some of the Blanken County deputies who'd been vetted as not being part of Sheriff Bedford's murder coverup, cordoned off the street and kept people away from the scene.

A crowd was gathering, drawn by the gunshots and the activity. A few carried rifles, ready to come to the assistance of the Langstroms, had it been necessary.

The Langstroms stood in a corner of the room watching, staring at the dead man lying in the middle of their floor. They looked up as Sole came out of the back. Alva rushed forward before an agent could hold her back.

"Bill!" She ran to Sole and threw her arms around him in a bear hug. "Bill, we were so worried about you. Are you alright?"

Sole put his arm around her and looked over her shoulder at Harry Langstrom and Dean Weber, whose stunned expressions reflected his own. No one had ever witnessed Alva Langstrom exhibit that much emotion in her entire life.

"I'm fine, Alva," he said.

"Bill, what is going on? Why are all these police here? They say they are FBI. Is that true?"

"It's true. They're FBI, and right now, I don't know any more than you." He held her at arm's length to break her grip on him. "They have work to do, Alva, so you need to stand over there with Harry."

She moved away. When she saw the look of astonishment on Harry's and Dean Weber's faces, she scowled. "What the hell are you two looking at?"

"Nothing, dear ..." Harry began. "It's just that we never saw ..."

"Oh, be quiet." She glared from one to the other, then back at her husband. "Not a word of this to anyone. Not one word or there will be hell to pay."

"Yes, dear," Harry said.

Having deposited Finch under guard in the back of an ambulance called to the scene, Special Agent Weems came back inside. Another agent followed him in, wearing a blue parka with the letters FBI on the chest and back.

It was the agent who had taken Leonard Purdy into custody. They walked over to Sole.

"This is ..." Weems began. He shot a glance at Harry and Alva Langstrom and said, "This is Bill Myers." He nodded at the newcomer. "Bill, this is Special Agent Ryder."

"Good to meet you," Ryder said.

Sole nodded. "Are you the one who's going to tell me what the hell is going on?"

Ryder smiled. "I suppose I am." He looked around the barroom. "Is there someplace private we can talk?"

Sole looked at the Langstroms. "What about it Harry?"

"Sure." Harry nodded. "The beer cooler is about the most private place we got. You're welcome to it."

"Alright." Sole led Ryder, Weems, and Weber into the backroom again, careful to stay away from the stacks of crates where the FBI crime techs were busy taking pictures and gathering evidence, including the hypodermic syringe.

When they were inside the cooler, beer cases stacked

around them, he turned to them, eyes narrowed, and said, "Was I used as some kind of bait for whatever operation you had going here?"

"Fair question," Ryder replied. "The answer is no, at least not until the last couple of hours when we were trying to put all the pieces together."

"Start explaining, Agent Ryder."

"Alright," Ryder said. "Here it is. We've been running an operation to bring down a cartel drug kingpin, Jorge Rodriguez. He goes by the street name of *El Gordo* or just Gordo. We became aware of a local cop on his payroll ... Detective Leonard Purdy ... had them both under surveillance. Trying to gather enough evidence to make a case against them."

"Then a couple of weeks ago, some stranger came into town and killed a local street thug. He and his gang were trying to jack an old couple. You might have heard about it." Ryder smiled. "Anyway, the stranger disappeared, but the next thing we know, Purdy, who never works any cases of any importance, is trying to track down the shooter. To give him credit, he did a pretty fair job, since he led us here to you."

"That's what this is about? All these resources expended to find the guy who broke up a carjacking?" Sole shook his head. "I don't think so."

"You're right," Ryder said. "There's more to it. Gordo is tied in with the *Los Salvajes* cartel." Ryder paused, reading the expression on Sole's face, the clenching of his jaw and narrowing of his eyes at the mention of the cartel. "I see you remember them."

"I remember." Sole nodded.

"You took out their operation to bring drugs in off container ships," Ryder said. "That was good work.

Anyway, you dropped out of sight after that … understandable considering what happened to …" Ryder saw the look in Sole's eyes and moved on. "Then you show up here and help Deputy Weber break up the Demeron child sex ring … your face on television, using the name Bill Myers … the pieces of the puzzle started coming together as we followed Purdy …"

"Wait," Sole said, holding up a hand. "You're telling me you followed a police detective across the country, and he never knew it?"

"Well, Purdy isn't exactly a great detective," Ryder said, grinning. "But the truth is, we had already planted a GPS tracker on his vehicle as part of our surveillance. All we did was follow the signal. By the time he got to Sioux Falls, stayed in the same motel you did, and then the news hit about the Demeron arrests, it became clear he was headed toward you. You were never part of our surveillance, and we didn't know why he was moving in your direction, but one thing became clear."

"*Los Salvajes*," Sole muttered. "They were part of the human trafficking ring supplying Demeron with children."

"Right." Ryder nodded. "I hopped a plane to get ahead of him and Special Agent Weems helped us put the operation together on the fly. When Purdy came inside the bar earlier in the evening, we staged our people around town out of sight, but with eyes on Purdy. Then the two men showed up and sat with Purdy, watching the bar while we were watching him."

"Who are they … the two who came after me?"

"Don't know that yet, but we will. On the cartel payroll, no doubt."

"Seems like a lot of damned watching going on." Sole shook his head. "And it all led you here."

Ryder chuckled. "I suppose it all sounds pretty convoluted, but that's how it went down. When the two men went inside, Deputy Weber and Special Agent Weems followed. I took a team and arrested Purdy." He shrugged. "You were inside. You know the rest better than me. We got lucky."

"That's the second time I've heard that tonight," Sole said.

SIXTY-FIVE

We Got Them

"We did it!" Hank pointed at the Jacksonville city limit sign, grinned, and turned to Riggs. "We fucking did it!"

The first part of their plan to escape the law and the cartel was successful. Hank was elated. His partner was more cautious.

"So far," Riggs said. "Calm down. We're not home free yet."

He steered the rental off an I-10 exit ramp onto I-295 toward JAXPORT, the freight cargo port. Hank settled back in the seat, but the grin remained. He scanned the skyline, looking for the Atlantic.

"Where's the ocean?" he asked.

"The port's on St. Johns River," Riggs replied. "Couple of miles from the ocean."

"Right." Hank nodded, still grinning. "How do you know all this shit?"

"I read," Riggs said, leaning forward to check a sign and then pulling onto an exit. "This ought to do."

They cruised the port area, past the lots lined with

freight containers, the tops of the cargo ships visible above them alongside the docks. It was a mostly industrial area, but a couple of turns back toward the city brought them to a district of stores and low-rent motels. Riggs pulled into one. "This should do it for now. Tomorrow, we check out getting some new identity docs and see what we have to do to get on board one of those ships."

"Sounds good." Hank got out and grabbed his bag from the back seat. "Right now, I need a shower."

"Yeah," Riggs agreed. "You do."

They checked into one room and took turns showering. Riggs came out of the bathroom last, rubbing his body down with a towel and dropping it on the floor. "What do you want to eat?" he asked, pulling on pants on and a clean t-shirt.

"Anything but Mexican," Hank said.

Riggs nodded. "No Mexican."

Neither wanted any reminder of the Mexican cartel on their heels. He pulled the door open and stepped out.

"Police!" Two uniformed Jacksonville PD officers jerked Riggs forward and slammed him face first to the pavement.

"What the fu …" Riggs began, but the impact with the concrete knocked the wind out of him and ended his protest.

Behind him, Hank reached for the pistol tucked under his t-shirt.

"Don't do it!" Another officer pushed toward the doorway, his weapon extended, the barrel centered on Hank's chest.

Two more came up from beside the door and flanked him. Hank stared into the barrels of the three pistols for several seconds, making up his mind. He wondered if South

Dakota had the death penalty. Riggs would know. Riggs read a lot.

He moved his hand away from the pistol butt and raised it over his head. "Don't shoot," he said meekly.

"On your knees!" an officer ordered. "Hands behind your head… now!"

Hank dropped to his knees. One officer came behind and reached under his shirt to remove the pistol. Then he pushed Hank forward hard enough that his face banged against the floor. The officers were not inclined to be gentle. The FBI agent directing the operation had briefed them that the two were wanted for the murder of a South Dakota deputy. They would not have minded at all if the fugitives had wanted to fight it out and go down in a blaze of gunfire, but they didn't. Riggs and Hank submitted completely.

It turned out the FBI was much more efficient than Sheriff Bedford at tracking down rental cars, and the rental agency was only too eager to assist them by providing hourly GPS updates on the car's location from the onboard mapping system. When it pulled into the motel lot in a major city with a local FBI field office nearby, it was time to gather their forces and make the arrests.

The FBI agent stood to the side, watching as the suspects were arrested and pushed into the back of separate Jacksonville PD cars. He knew the officers secretly hoped the two cop-killers would resist, but the arrests went down professionally and without injury to either.

He pulled out his phone and punched in a number. Special Agent Weems answered. "Any problems?"

"Nope, we got them," the agent said causally.

SIXTY-SIX

Thank You and Goodbye

"Well, son of a bitch." Johnny Walts looked up from his usual seat at Langstrom's bar as the door opened, letting a blast of cold air in. "Bob Shank in the flesh."

"Shut the hell up, Walts," Shank said, stomping the snow off his boots.

"And surly as ever," Walts chided, grinning and watching.

Shank pulled off the insulated canvas coat, hung it on the coatrack, and stepped up to the bar. Sole looked up from the sink full of dishes and nodded. "Good to see you, Bob."

Shank ignored him, looked at Harry, and said simply, "Beer."

Harry smiled, put the beer in front of him, and stepped away. Shank picked it up and took a long swallow, draining half of it before putting the bottle down again. He took a deep breath, swallowed, and grimaced like he had a foul taste in his mouth.

"I suppose I owe you a thank you," Shank said in Sole's direction without actually looking at him.

Sole stood up from the sink, dried his hands on a towel, and went to stand in front of Shank. "You don't owe me a thing, Bob. What's right is right. Seemed pretty clear you didn't kill anyone."

"Well, anyway, I said it," Shank growled. "So, that's that." He picked up the bottle, drained the other half, and lifted it in Harry's direction, signaling for another.

"Since you're handing out thanks today," Sole said, leaning on the bar now in front of Shank. "I hope you let Dean Weber know about your sudden onset of gratitude."

"Weber?" Shank frowned. "My taxes pay his salary. He did his job like I pay him to."

"Really?" Sole gave him a quizzical look. "Well, if that's the case, you had a helluva lot of other people on your payroll who were pretty content seeing you go to jail."

"Hah! That's for sure," Walts chuckled from the other end of the bar.

"Told you to shut up." Shank glared at him, then lifted the beer, trying to ignore the man standing in front of him.

Sole wouldn't let him. "Dean Weber risked everything … his job … his career … to uncover what happened. He's the reason you're not in jail waiting to be tried for murder."

Shank remained silent. Sole let him have both barrels.

"You know, some people are born sour. It's just in their nature … glass half empty kind of people. I get that, but being ungrateful when others put it all on the line for them …" A disgusted look on his face, Sole ended the lecture saying, "That's not a sour disposition. That takes a deliberate sort of meanness. That's you, Bob." Sole shook his head and walked away.

"I said thank you, didn't I?" Shank shouted and

slammed the bottle down on the bar, threw a ten beside it, grabbed his coat, and stomped out.

"I'll be damned." Walts turned on the bar stool to watch him leave. "I think you shamed him, Bill."

"I doubt it," Sole said.

"No." Walts shook his head. "I've known that asshole all my life, and I saw something new in his face just then." His brow furrowed, puzzling things out. "Could it be that Bob Shank has a conscience, after all?"

"Most people do," Sole said and went back to the dishes, without adding but not everybody.

It was midnight when Walts and the few lingerers went home. Sole helped Harry close up, then sat at the bar with him sipping a nightcap, scotch neat.

"So, you're leaving, aren't you?" Harry said, looking toward the front window and the blackness outside.

"I am." Sole nodded. "First thing in the morning."

"We were hoping you would stay on." Harry smiled. "Believe it or not, the place grows on you."

"It has grown on me." Sole smiled and then shrugged. "But it's time to move on."

They were quiet for a few minutes, sipping the scotch, then Harry looked up. "Bill Myers ... that's not your real name, is it? There's more to your past than we know, right?"

Sole looked down at the bar, then lifted the glass, sipped, and said nothing. There was nothing he could say. He wouldn't lie to Harry, and the truth was too complicated.

The front door opened, and Alva rushed in out of the cold. "Good! You're not already in bed."

She walked up to the bar and looked at their surprised faces. Alva never stayed past ten at night. She frowned. "Don't look so surprised. You didn't think I was not going to say goodbye, did you?"

"How'd you know?" Sole said, surprised.

"I know," Alva said. "Been watching you all day. Little things ... the way you smiled too much at someone's bad joke or listened too hard to some story about a broke down tractor or just spent your time watching everyone, like you were trying to commit everything about the place to memory." She shrugged. "Tell me I'm wrong."

He shook his head. "You're not wrong."

"We were talking about it earlier." She shot Harry a triumphant look, then turned back to Sole and stared him hard in the eyes for a few seconds. When she spoke, her voice was gravelly and hoarse, as if she had something caught in her throat. "I expect you'll be gone before I open in the morning, so, goodbye, Bill Myers ... or whoever the hell you are."

She stood on her toes and gave his cheek a quick peck, then turned and walked back out into the night.

Harry watched her, dumbfounded, his mouth half-open in shock. "I'll be damned. I think I saw a tear in her eye."

They sipped their scotch and then Harry went home to Alva. Sole washed the glasses and went to his cot. In the morning when Alva came in to open, he was gone.

SIXTY-SEVEN

The Victims

"So, what happens now?" Malina sat in one of the interview rooms at the FBI field office in Pierre. Three FBI agents, plus a technician recording the interview, sat across the table.

"First thing is to get all the facts from all of you so we can prepare a court case." Special Agent Weems sat directly in front of her, asking most of the questions.

"Right, I figured that," Malina said in her blunt way. "I mean to us ... to me. Once you have your case put together, what happens to us?"

That was a more difficult question. Normally, as juveniles, they would all be sent back to their families, but these weren't normal circumstances. The girls were all runaways who had escaped abusive family relationships. Sending them back into those relationships was not an option.

Their fate would have to be decided by the courts. That process began even as they gave their statements and prepared their testimony for the trials.

As a matter of due process, Loni was tried for her part in Demeron's child sex operation, but the judge, jury, and even the prosecutor, were sympathetic, in large part, because of testimony from Malina and Brad that without her, they could not have escaped. Loni's lawyer argued that she was another victim, taken by Demeron into a life that became all she knew.

In the end, the judge and jury agreed. She was freed and went off to live in a city back east. Eventually, she married, had two children, and divorced. A few years later she married again, and then divorced again. She remained single after that, raising her children, living a reasonably contented life, considering its beginnings, and trying never to think about the years she spent at Demeron's lodge.

Of them all, Brad's family life had been reasonably normal, if icy in their relations with him. His parents provided what many would have considered a good home as long as their son did not interfere with their lives. Insecure and reclusive since early childhood, his parents' aloofness isolated him even more. He was a solitary soul whose indifferent demeanor was a blanket, insulating and protecting him from the loneliness of life.

When he discovered as a young teen that by prostituting himself, he could make money to support himself, he left home. He felt more at home on the streets, hiding among the crowds than hiding alone in his bedroom.

After the court trials, Brad went back to his parents' home to hide in his bedroom for a while, but there was no happy ending for him. A few months later, he left again, going back to the streets and the anonymous sexual hookups that were a refuge from the insecurities that haunted him. Then one day he was found dead in an alley, robbed and beaten to death by a prospective client he'd met online.

Sherry's story is short. She stayed a month in her new foster home, then ran away again. She was never seen again.

Tearful frightened, Cindy bounced around between foster homes until she reached the age of eighteen. By nineteen, she was married and expecting a baby, much like her mother before her. She and her husband seemed happy enough for the first year.

Then one day he came home from his job as a tire changer at a garage. He told Cindy he was leaving, that he was sorry, but he couldn't handle the pressure of being a father and a husband, that he needed to get his life together. Most of all, he said, he thought he could put her past experiences at the hands of Senator Kellin behind them, but he couldn't. He said he thought about it every time they were in bed together. He apologized for that and added that they should never have married so young.

Cindy cried, threw herself sobbing on the floor, and then turned to shouting obscenities at him. He said nothing more as he gathered his clothes and personal items and tossed them in a plastic bag and left.

Cindy spent the night sobbing and holding her baby

son. The next day, she moved back in with her mother and her abusive stepfather.

Malina got lucky, or maybe her personality was just stronger than the others. She stayed in her foster home until she was old enough to leave and find a job.

She worked the night crew cleaning offices in a high-rise. Eventually, her boss made her a shift supervisor. During the daytime, she took classes at a community college until she earned a two-year degree in business administration, then a four-year degree from a state college.

After that, she found a good entry-level job at a local bank. A couple of years later, she was a loan officer at a branch and in their management development program.

She was thirty before she overcame the trust issues resulting from her experiences as one of Demeron's victims. Then one day, she met a man at a friend's wedding. Both were alone and standing off by themselves at the reception. With no pressure and no one pushing her to meet someone, they began speaking, exchanged numbers, and continued to speak. Neither was in a hurry, but when the time was right, several years later, they married.

Malina did not expect life to be perfect. She knew better than that, but the life they made together was good enough, and that made her happy.

The bodies of Mila Wray and Riley Tate were recovered from the grain bin behind the barn. It took the FBI three months to identify them from missing persons reports.

Mila's remains were sent home to her parents in Utah. Riley went to her grandmother in Missouri.

Both were runaways. Neither family had any idea that their children had been dragged into Demeron's child sex ring.

The media coverage focused on the living faces, seen coming and going from courtrooms. Mila and Riley along with the dozens of other young girls who had passed unseen through the Demeron's lodge were largely forgotten.

SIXTY-EIGHT

The Pedophiles and Traffickers

In addition to an array of charges centering around human trafficking, Martin Riggs and Henry 'Hank' Seymour would be tried for the murder of Lew Bentz and a white female eventually identified through blood and DNA samples as Martha Womble, but who used the street name of Bobbi. Womble was a known street prostitute in Seattle. She was not the sort of girl Salver and Finch usually selected, but she needed a place to stay that night and the SYPA fire looked warm so she'd come to their little camp in the park and ended up in the back of the box truck to help fill out Demeron's order for girls.

Eventually, Riggs cut a deal, testified against Hank and his surviving boss, Tom Finch, and as a reward, received a life sentence without parole. He did what he had to do to survive prison life and used his good looks to become a favorite sex toy among the inmates. They shared him around until, eventually, his good looks faded, and he looked more like a worn, lop-eared chew toy thrown in the middle of a pack of pit bulls.

His torment ended, however, when the reason for his prison sentence was mentioned by a talkative correctional officer. No one knew who actually shoved the homemade knife between his ribs as he walked down a crowded hallway to the dining room, but the chief suspect was a man serving time for armed robbery who happened to have a little sister who ran away from their abusive parents and was never seen again.

Hank Seymour was sentenced to die by lethal injection for the murder of Deputy Lew Bentz, but since South Dakota had not executed anyone since 1979, it would likely be decades before the penalty was carried out. He did manage to hurry things along in his own way.

While being moved to a new cellblock during a prison renovation, he and another inmate attempted to overpower a correctional officer and force an escape. A tactical team sniper's bullet through his brain accomplished what the state of South Dakota's appeals process had delayed.

Investigators asked a lot of questions about a young white male, Jimmy Pelt. His driver's license was recovered from the pocket of Lew Bentz's coat, but neither Riggs nor Hank admitted to knowing anything about the third member of their little delivery team. There didn't seem to be any reason to muddy things up with another murder charge.

Jimmy's body lay at the bottom of the wash somewhere in Wyoming for a month before a heavy rain sent a flash flood that carried it a mile, tumbling and turning until it smashed into a boulder and fell apart. Decomposition had already taken its toll and after the impact with the boulder, the flood scattered parts of Jimmy for several miles along the wash. His death was never discovered and his remains were never recovered.

Despite the best attempts of his high-paid team of lawyers to delay the trial, the public outrage over A.C. Demeron's crimes never diminished during the months it took to bring him to trial. The case was placed on the court's docket and Doug Trent, who gained fame as the reporter to break the story, was there to cover it all. This time, for a station out of Denver. As he'd hoped, the story had given his career a boost.

Demeron and his lawyers went back and forth on their strategy. Was it best to have a court trial by the judge, or a jury trial? There were pros and cons for each. In the end, they opted for a jury trial. In a court trial, they would have just one chance to throw doubt on the prosecution's case. The judge would decide the outcome and if he agreed with the prosecution, that would be the end of things.

A jury trial gave them twelve chances. One doubtful juror was all they needed to avoid a guilty verdict and have the judge declare a mistrial. The defense team were experts at throwing doubt into jurors' minds.

It made no difference. The trial lasted for weeks, but in less than a day of deliberation, the jury found him guilty on all counts, including human trafficking, child sex abuse, complicity in the murders of Lew Bentz, Martha 'Bobbi' Womble, and the negligent homicides of Mila Wray and Riley Jones. For his crimes, Demeron was given maximum consecutive sentences totaling more than a hundred and fifty years. He would die in prison long before he was eligible for parole.

One of the most shocking aspects of the case was the arrest and prosecution of Lorraine Demeron for her role in aiding and abetting her husband's crimes. Tessa Demeron, already devastated by the accusations against her father, was in complete shock to learn that her mother was part of it all.

She stood silently in their home the day the deputies came and arrested Lorraine. As they put her in handcuffs in the back of a deputy's car, Tessa spoke the last words she ever would to her mother.

"They were children, for God's sake," she said, tears streaming down her face. "They were younger than me." She shook her head a final time and walked back into the house as they drove her mother away.

From that moment, she had nothing further to do with her parents. She took the money from the trust established for her and moved to an undisclosed location in the South. Her only contact with them was through her attorney, who made it clear that Tessa wanted nothing to do with them—no calls, no letters, no emails, no visits in prison—they were gone from her life.

Lorraine received a hefty sentence for her part in the child-sex ring but was out of prison after serving ten years. After that, she spent most of her time drinking heavily, taking pills, and trying to find her daughter. One morning, after an especially heavy night of drinking and popping pills, she did not wake up.

There was no service for her. Her ashes were delivered

to the attorney serving as the executor of Demeron's estate, in case anyone should come to claim them. No one ever did.

During his trial, Sheriff Willard Bedford did his best to distance himself from Demeron's operation, but in the end, the evidence against him was overwhelming. Deputy Dean Weber's investigation and the physical evidence he'd gathered and sent to the forensics lab demolished any defense his lawyer tried to mount. Testimony from Arnold Cowley, and Delbert Ottley in exchange for their plea agreements, sealed the prosecution's case.

His active participation in the coverup of Lew Bentz's murder landed him in a state penitentiary with a twenty-year sentence plus another ten for his role in enabling Demeron's child sex ring to operate with impunity in Blanken County. They say he cried on the Department of Corrections bus all the way to prison.

Thomas Albert Finch was a dead man, and he knew it. He had one chance to survive. Prosecutors promised him that in exchange for his testimony and information regarding his contacts with *Los Salvajes*, he could live out the balance of his pathetic life in isolation at a federal prison. It seemed like a better alternative than the four bullets in the chest his partner, Rick Salver, had received.

Had he only been running drugs into the country, he might have been able to cut a deal for entry into WITSEC, the federal witness security program, and live a semi-normal life. Killing people with fentanyl was one thing. Human trafficking and child sex slavery were different matters. The outcry over Demeron's pedophile ring took any sort of WITSEC deal off the table.

If he didn't accept the option to testify for the prosecution and provide information on *Los Salvajes* to an assortment of federal law enforcement agencies, Finch would be tried, almost certainly convicted, and then placed in general population in a federal prison. The cartel had a long reach and its minions would eventually locate him, even in a federal prison. It would be only a matter of time before some inmate, with no hope of parole, shoved a blade between his ribs.

The alternative was to go into isolation ... and stay there permanently. Finch took that option. For eight years, he stuck it out in a small cell with only an hour a day in a tiny exercise yard outside by himself.

Then one day, morning shift prison guards found him lifeless in his cell, on his knees a sheet around his neck secured to a bed frame. They declared his death an apparent suicide. Investigators interviewed the correctional facility staff, checked surveillance video, searched his cell for contraband. There was no evidence that foul play was involved in his death other than a few bruises on his arms, that could have resulted from a struggle, but also could have come from a trip and fall.

After the investigation, prison life returned to normal. Tom Finch was dead. His aging parents were notified. They did not claim his remains, so he was buried in the prison cemetery. A few inmates with cartel connections smiled knowingly and gave hand signals to each other that the guards saw but did not understand. After a while, the prison chatter about Finch's demise faded away. He was not missed.

Senator William Kellin, Oliver Parson, and Simon Taylor all quickly and as quietly as possible, pled guilty to participating in Demeron's child sex ring. While Elizabeth Ranskill did not engage in sexual acts with a minor, she was charged as an accessory and willing participant who encouraged the abuses of minor children committed by the other defendants.

All testified against Demeron, all received reduced prison sentences, and all were out on probation within a year. The worst punishment they suffered was the damage to their reputations.

Ranskill, Parson, and Taylor lost their well-paid positions, but they were all wealthy enough not to worry about changing their lifestyles. They would never again be forces to be reckoned with in their chosen professions, and for a while, they were the butt of jokes, but the horror of the crimes they had committed against children faded with time in the public consciousness, and they were largely forgotten.

As a sitting senator, William Kellin was not subject to a recall election in his home state, despite a movement among outraged constituents to do so. The constitution makes no provision for recalling a sitting senator, but a week after his conviction, the full Senate voted unanimously to expel him. The governor in his home state appointed a replacement to serve out his term. Kellin never served in an elected office again. His well-known face made it difficult for him to move about in his home state, so he moved to another, and eventually moved out of the country. He became a recluse, living comfortably, if surreptitiously, off the profits of the insider investments he'd been able to make during his years in the senate.

With the information provided by Tom Finch and Martin Riggs, Seattle police raided the SYPA camp back at Green Park. Carlie, who'd welcomed Malina the night she was abducted, and a couple of other regulars were arrested as co-conspirators in the pedophile ring. They were waiting for Salver and Finch to return and organize another delivery to the cartel.

A dozen girls had taken refuge there the night the police raided. Most went into foster care. A few went back to their parents. They never knew how close they had come to disappearing forever into the underworld of human trafficking and sex slavery.

The trials and assorted accusations, court proceedings, and motions by attorneys dominated the news for months. Pundits became overnight experts in human trafficking and the plague of pedophilia, giving full descriptions of the victims while offering lip service to their desire to protect the identities of minors.

The defendants and their roles in the sex trafficking ring were described in detail. Charts and diagrams were displayed to explain the relationships between the major figures in the case. Reporters like Doug Trent were featured live from courthouses to give the daily wrap-up on the current trial in progress.

Then, as suddenly as it began, it all ended. Like peeping-toms looking for the next unshuttered window, the country moved on to the next scandal.

And the victims? If they weren't forgotten, they were set aside, only to be remembered when it was time for another story.

SIXTY-NINE

Jefa

"You've seen?" Reynaldo Gutierrez stood before the desk in the hacienda, hands clasped calmly behind his back.

"I've seen." Juana Elizondo looked up from her computer screen and held up a hand. "Don't say it. You were correct."

"I was not going to say anything. I am here to see how you wish to proceed."

"So loyal, you are, Reynaldo." Juana leaned back in the chair and smiled. "You escorted me ... protected me for my father when I was young. He is gone now, but you remain. Why is that?"

Reynaldo said nothing. She was toying with him. She knew full well the hidden feelings he'd had for her all those years ago, feelings that he'd kept hidden from her father and Alejandro Garza. Had they known, they would have sent him far away and he would not be here today.

"Alright, then I'll change the subject." Elizondo leaned forward, elbows on the massive desk where her father had once presided. "You were right, Reynaldo. I was wrong."

He shook his head. "There is no need …"

"Stop." She raised a hand. "There is a need. I was overanxious. I saw a chance to have him quickly, the one who killed my father and *Tio* Alejandro. It seemed logical to send the two who were so desperate to save their lives." She shook her head. "They were close. It could have been done quickly, but they had no experience in such a thing. You warned me of this … asked me to wait until you could take care of him personally. But I was impatient. For that, I apologize to you, my loyal friend."

"There is no need to apologize." Reynaldo's eyes remained fixed on hers. "I will always do what you require."

"This I know." Juana nodded. "And that is why I promise never to interfere again. I should have been more patient and trusted you." She smiled. "I trust you now to do what is necessary to deal with him."

"Yes, *Jefa*."

"Bring him to me, Reynaldo."

"I will, *Jefa*."

SEVENTY

Mutual Interest

John Sole walked through the door and looked around. The FBI field office in Pierre had become a busy place. Sorting through the evidence and victims' statements to prepare the prosecution cases for half a dozen separate trials took time and manpower.

Special Agent-in-Charge Grimes came out of an office flanked by Agents Weems and Ryder. He smiled and put out a hand. "Good to see you again, John." He paused and add, "May I call you by your real name?"

"Might as well." Sole shrugged and shook Grimes's hand. "Probably have to change it again after all this." He looked around at the bustling activity.

"We were wondering why you changed it in the first place," Grimes said, looking hard into his eyes.

"Seemed the thing to do," Sole said, sensing that there was more behind the question. Whatever he thought about the FBI, they weren't fools. People who changed their names usually had something to hide, and the look in Grimes's eyes made it clear that he wondered what Sole was hiding ... or maybe he already knew. Sole wasn't sure which.

"So why am I here?" He asked. "I've already given my statement ... told you everything I know."

"There are a few more details we wanted to go over with you," Grimes said and pointed at the door to one of the interview rooms. "And someone we want you to meet."

Grimes opened the door and led the way, taking a seat with Weems and Ryder on one side of the long table in the center of the room. Sole sat opposite them and turned toward the man seated at the head of the table.

Fiftyish, with sandy hair that was thinning on top, he wore a Grateful Dead t-shirt, cheap knock-off athletic shoes, and, despite the frigid temperatures outside, shorts with cargo pockets. He leaned back in the chair, his demeanor laid back, with an aging hippie air about him. He smiled and said, "John Sole, you do get around, don't you?"

"You know my name. How about telling me yours."

"You bet. Let's get right to it." The smile widened as if he'd just scratched off a winning lotto number. "Jason Lovell ... call me Jay."

"Little underdressed, aren't you, Jay?" Sole said.

"You mean the shorts?" Lovell shrugged and smiled. "I was busy somewhere else and didn't have time to change. I hopped a jet so I could meet with you. That's how important this is, John."

"Alright ... Jay. Why am I here?"

"Mutual interest," Lovell said. "You've heard of the *Los Salvajes* cartel, right?"

"If you know my name, you know the answer to that question," Sole shot back, his tone sharp and annoyed. "I'm not in the mood for games. Get to the point."

"Fair enough." Lovell nodded, relaxed and unruffled.

"You brought down the cartel's plan to smuggle drugs off freight container ships. That was good work, but the job's not finished. Back then, it was cocaine and meth. Now it's fentanyl and ..." Lovell paused and for the first time sat up straight in the chair and leaned forward, his elbows on the table's polished surface. "And people ... human trafficking ... slavery. Slaves to work fields, people forced to fight for warlords in third world countries, women ... girls and boys ... children sold and used as sex slaves ... a billion-dollar business for them."

Sole shook his head. "I'm not a cop anymore. I told the FBI everything I know about that case." He nodded at the three agents seated across from me. "They can fill you in if you're looking for more information."

Lovell looked at Grimes. "Tell him."

Grimes nodded. "We tested the hypodermic syringe taken from the floor where you were attacked. It contained Rohypnol, crushed and dissolved, not legal in the United States, but it is in some other countries ... Mexico for one. It's a powerful drug. If they got it into your blood, you could not have defended yourself and would have been unconscious within minutes."

"Then I guess it's a good thing you showed up." He nodded at Weems. "Thanks for that."

"Something else," Grimes continued. "Thomas Finch, the one with the syringe ... the one you subdued. He cut a deal ... confessed." Grimes leaned forward. "They weren't there to kill you. They were sent to abduct you, throw you in the trunk of their car, drive you back to Mexico, and deliver you to *Los Salvajes* ... to Juana Elizondo."

"You see," Lovell said, leaning back in the chair again, the lazy smile back on his face. "You may be done with them, but they are not done with you."

"Okay." Sole shrugged. "Thanks for the warning. I'll keep my eyes open." He put his hands on the table as if to stand. "If that's all, I'll be heading out."

"It's not all," Lovell said. "After your family ..." He stopped, looked into Sole's eyes, saw the warning there, smiled, and continued, "After what happened back in Georgia, after you disappeared, it seems the cartel fell on hard times. Their dealers in the U.S. started disappearing or turning up dead, and then the cartel boss of bosses, their *jefe de jefes* turned up dead too, along with his right-hand man, Alejandro Garza." Lovell's eyes narrowed and the smile twitched. "You might have heard about it."

Sole said nothing, waiting for Lovell to continue. It was time to hear exactly what they knew about him and his life since leaving Georgia.

"Anyway," Lovell continued in his laid-back manner. "The Mexican army came in to clean things up. The cartel had removed most of the bodies, but there was one ..." He gave an admiring shake of his head. "Hidden up in a cave overlooking the scene ... perfect sniper's position. The rifle was gone, but it was pretty clear from the blood trails that the man they found there had taken out several of the cartel people before being killed."

Sole broke his silence. "How do you know all this? Inside source with the Mexicans?"

"Oh, no." Lovell laughed. "I tagged along and saw for myself."

"You tagged along?" Sole's brow furrowed. "The FBI has some sort of mutual assistance agreement with the Mexicans?"

"The FBI has lots of arrangements internationally with local law enforcement, but I never said I was with the FBI." Lovell watched Sole's face.

"You're CIA?" Sole showed surprise for the first time.

Lovell ignored the question. "So, anyway, it took a while ... you know, identifying the body they found in the cave." He nodded at the FBI agents across the table. "But my Bureau friends have some of the best forensics capabilities in the world. It turns out the man in the cave was ..." His brow lifted and gave Sole a quizzical look. "But you know who he was, don't you, John?"

"Where is my father?" Sole said, his voice muted.

"We buried him, John. In a little cemetery in Cassit Pass, right beside your mother. Friend of yours, Bill Siever, took care of it for us."

"You involved Bill?" Sole said, his voice tinged with anger. "I didn't want him involved. I don't want anything to ... If the cartel finds out ..."

"Relax." Lovell lifted a hand to stop him. "It was all handled very discreetly." He smiled. "We're good at that ... being discreet."

"Thank you." Sole nodded. "For burying my father." He looked at Lovell. "But why am I here ... now?"

"I told you ... mutual interest." Lovell leaned forward for the first time. "They're killing our children with fentanyl ... stealing others and selling them into slavery." He shook his head. "The work you started is not finished, John. We'd like to make an arrangement with you."

"I'm listening," Sole said. He listened, and by the end of the conversation, he had a new assignment, but first, there was something he had to do.

When the meeting ended, he made his way out of snow country and headed the pickup south. The drive to Cassit Pass took three days.

He arrived at the cemetery in the middle of the night and stared at the graves, close together side by side in the plot. The moon cast enough light to read the markers—*Clara Barker Sole* and beside her *Lamont 'Monty' Sole*. He knelt between them, arms stretched out to the sides, a hand on each grave. There in the cemetery, they were together again, the three of them, for the first time since John was an infant, before his father left, running from his own demons.

After a time, he stood. He could hear their voices calling to him in the night. *Do what you must, son.*

"I will," he answered, and walked away.

Next in the Sole Justice series

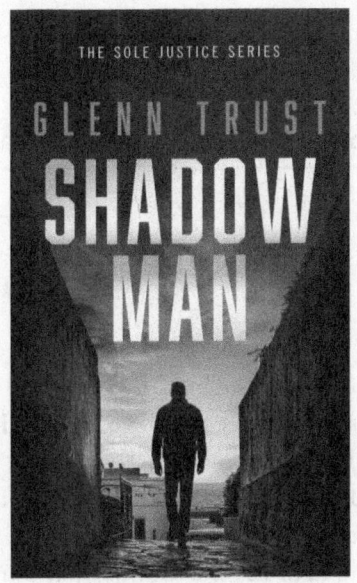

vinci-books.com/shadowman

In a covert mission to dismantle the Mexican cartels, a lone operative becomes the enemy to destroy them from within.

John Sole, recruited by NSA operative Jason Lovell, infiltrates the cartels to end their bloody reign. With the U.S. unable to intervene directly, Sole and Lovell devise a plan to turn the cartels against each other. But as he delves deeper, he realizes the price of victory may be higher than imagined.

Turn the page for a free preview…

Shadow Man: Chapter One

SAFE PASSAGE

Ignacio Pacheco was a patient man. It would be a while still before the passengers assembled and were loaded, but he didn't mind. He was in no hurry. For now, he was content to lean back in the cushioned seat and wait behind the wheel of the forty-foot bus.

Once, years ago, the bus transported tourists on excursions from resort hotels along the Baja Peninsula. It had been a very comfortable bus in its day, top of the line, but now it was old, and the air conditioning only worked intermittently. Ignacio didn't mind that either. The day was pleasant, not hot and not cold. He had the driver's window open, and a light breeze ruffled the strands of gray hair that curled out from under a battered LA Dodgers ball cap. He kept the cap's visor pulled down low as he drove to help block the sun, but now, it was pushed back on his head, and he enjoyed the breeze on his face.

He breathed deeply, relaxed, enjoying the time before he would go to work. Somewhere nearby, in one of the small shacks that lined the road, someone was cooking onions and peppers and chorizo. The aroma reminded him of his wife's cooking.

He'd left that morning without breakfast. It was early, so he let her sleep while he washed and dressed.

When he leaned over the bed and kissed her cheek, her eyes fluttered open, she yawned and kissed his stubbly chin. "You need a shave."

"When I get back." He laughed. "The passengers won't mind much as long as I get them there."

"I suppose not." His wife nodded, stretched, and sat up, swinging her legs over the side of the low bed. She flipped her long gray hair back out of her face with a shake of her head and stood. "How long will you be gone?"

"A week." He shrugged. "Always hard to say. Not more than ten days, I think."

"I wish you could stay. Felipe's birthday is on Sunday ... a special day. Father Andreas always mentions the children with birthdays during the week, and this time Felipe's will be on that very day."

"I know all of this, Lucia." Ignacio smiled and leaned forward to give her a quick peck on the forehead. "You'll have to tell *mi pequeño* his grandpa will bring him back something special."

"He would trade it to have his *abuelito* there with him on his special day," Lucia said.

"It can't be helped. We are fortunate that they hired me to drive the bus. Who knows how long all of this will last? Things change. Politics change, and there are many others who would give much to have my position." He smiled and patted her bottom. "And the dollars they pay me."

"I know." She stood on her tiptoes and gave him a quick kiss on the lips, then folded her arms. "Now go, be safe, and hurry back. The nights are cool, and I need your rump here to warm me up."

He laughed. They laughed a lot together. For thirty-two years, they'd been making each other laugh. "*Adiós*," He called over his shoulder and gave a flip of his hand as a goodbye wave.

Now, sitting in the bus on a tiny side street in Carmen Xhán, a half mile from the Guatemalan border crossing, his stomach growled. He tried to ignore it, leaning back in the seat, watching the activity in the square just ahead at the corner. Young men, the coyotes—smugglers of people across the northern border into the United States—took the money and organized groups of people for transport north through the entire length of Mexico.

Some would go in buses like the one Ignacio drove if they had money to pay the fee. Others would walk, caravans of people they were called in the media. They paid for that privilege as well, met and guided by the coyotes to the border. When they arrived there, other bands of coyotes would take them across the Rio Grande into Texas or through the deserts into New Mexico, Arizona, or California.

The coyotes were loosely affiliated and associated with the various cartels that ran the smuggling networks. Most got along with each other, but occasionally a dispute would erupt into a flash of gunfire. When this happened, some young man trying to make his fortune from the immigrants moving north would lie in a pool of blood in the streets until the local *policías* cleaned up the mess. Then it would be back to business as usual.

Today was peaceful, though. The coyotes organized their clients in the town square. There was much bustling about, new arrivals making their way through the streets, buying provisions in the shops, looking for a place to rest before moving on.

A boomtown atmosphere prevailed around the small town and in its counterpart, Gracias a Dios, less than a mile away in Guatemala. The two towns straddled the border between the two countries and had become a focal point for hundreds of thousands of migrants making their way north through South and Central America to the United States.

The border crossing itself was a simple marker along a two-lane road with a guard shack on each side. Residents of the two towns passed freely from one country to the other.

For migrants, this was where they met the coyotes who moved among them, recruiting business, making promises to get them across Mexico's northern border with the United States. Most would keep their promises as a matter of good business practice, but some would not, and the migrants who trusted them would pay a high price. Some would pay with their lives.

The prices charged by the coyotes varied. Some migrants paid as much as fifteen thousand dollars to get to the United States border, but that was the exception. The going rate was about five thousand U.S. dollars for a single person or seven thousand for an adult and a child. This was a popular option because showing up with a child greatly increased your chances of staying in the United States.

Still, Ignacio thought, seven thousand dollars was an enormous sum. He watched and wondered where they got the money to pay the coyotes. They did not seem to be rich people. Many must have sold all of their earthly possessions —jewelry, family heirlooms, cars if they owned one, their homes—to pay the prices the coyotes charged.

It seemed too much to him. He was happy in Carmen

Xhán, but if they wanted to go that badly, he was only too happy to drive them and take the dollars the cartel paid.

As he watched, a group of young men—the coyotes—herded fifty migrants down the side street toward the bus. Ignacio pulled the lever that opened the door and climbed out.

He pushed his way through the gathering crowd. "Here!" he called out, opening the baggage compartments under the coach. "Put your things in here, or there won't be room for you inside."

They looked at him skeptically, clinging to their backpacks and duffels and bundles tied up with string.

"Listen carefully," Ignacio said. "This bus only seats forty. There are fifty of you. That means we will all be packed in like sardines in a can. So, you put your belongings in these compartments underneath." He smiled and gave a reassuring nod. "I promise once we start moving, no one will be able to get into the compartments. Your things will be safe there, and you can get them when we stop." He shrugged. "But it's your choice. You can wait for another bus with more room if you like."

It was a lecture he'd given several dozen times since he started driving the bus. The coyotes with their guns tucked in their pants stood listening.

A woman put her bundle in the compartment, took a backpack from a child with her, and tossed it in. Ignacio smiled. "Good. That's the way to do it."

The woman climbed the steps onto the bus. Others followed her example.

Ignacio climbed back up to the driver's seat, pushing his way past those who were blocking the steps. Those behind him peered along the aisle and saw that the interior was quickly becoming crowded.

"Will there be room?" a man asked.

"Yes, yes. We'll get you all in." Ignacio grinned. "By the time we get you to the Rio Grande, you'll all be very close friends ... if you don't kill each other first."

There was a murmur of laughter along the line of migrants pushing their way onto the bus. The coyotes smiled. They liked the way old Ignacio handled things and kept people calm. Not all the drivers were as capable.

Outside, two coyotes with pistols tucked in their belts took up positions by the baggage compartments. The scowls on their faces warned thieves to stay away and gave the migrants more confidence that their meager belongings would be safe.

Other coyotes herded the crowd up the steps. They were a mixture of families—men, women, and children—along with younger men and a few single women traveling alone.

The loading took thirty minutes. When the last passengers squeezed aboard the overcrowded bus, two of the coyotes came up the steps and sat in the seats reserved for them directly behind Ignacio.

"Nacho!" one exclaimed and slapped Ignacio on the back. "Always a pleasant ride when you drive. Now let's go. ¡*Vamos!*"

"Why such a hurry, Rico?" Ignacio asked and pulled the lever, closing the bus door.

"I have a date in Reynosa if we can get there in two days," Rico grinned. "She's the one for me ... this week."

Ignacio laughed.

The other coyote shook his head. "Do you ever stop thinking with your balls and dick?"

"Never!" Rico laughed. "You're just jealous, Celio. Nothing waiting for you but your right hand."

The migrants in the seats closest to the front laughed. Whispered conversations sprang up.

"These coyotes aren't so bad," they whispered to each other. *"That one looks like my little brother. Even with their guns, they're just boys."*

"Yes, boys with guns that shoot bullets."

"Exactly. Bullets that will protect us on the journey."

"But can they get us all the way to the border up north?"

"We paid our money. We have to trust them. Others have and are now in America."

"But they seem so young."

"Relax. See that driver? He's older, about my father's age. He'll get us there."

Ignacio turned the ignition, and the old bus rumbled to life. The air brakes hissed as they released, and the diesel engine belched a cloud of black smoke from the exhaust. The bus rolled forward slowly, avoiding the children, who ran in front, playfully chasing and dodging it down the street.

Ignacio left the children behind and steered the bus expertly around the narrow corners and streets until they came out onto a highway leading north. Their route would take them along the coast of the Gulf of Mexico, but Ignacio avoided the main highways, which were heavily patrolled by police. Some of the local cops were honest, but some worked for the cartels and could be trouble. It was always best to avoid them if possible.

Despite Rico's wish to get there in two days, it would take at least four. In a car, driving the main highways, it might be done in three days, driving twelve hours a day, but in the bus on the back roads, that was not possible.

Ignacio settled in behind the wheel. The passengers talked in muted voices among themselves. Most did not know each other before today and were cautious about sharing their plans at first, but after a few miles, a sense of camaraderie settled over them. For now, they were all in this together.

Two hours into the journey, Ignacio spoke his first words since leaving Carmen Xhán. "Trouble."

"Where?" Celio leaned forward to peer over his shoulder. "

"*Mierda*" Shit.

Straddling the road ahead, two trucks of the *Policía Estatal* blocked their path. Five men in uniform, armed with semi-automatic rifles, stood at the sides. The leader waved an arm, palm down, directing Ignacio to stop.

Rico stirred from a nap as the brakes hissed, and the bus slowed to a stop. "What is it?" He leaned forward beside Celio to look through the windshield. "Oh."

"Probably nothing," Ignacio suggested. "Pay them a little money, and we can be on our way."

"Maybe," Celio said. "Unusual to find them on this road."

"They must have figured out that we were avoiding the main highways." Ignacio chuckled. "And missed collecting the *taxes*."

Behind him, murmurs rose up among the passengers.

"What now?"

"Policías! This can't be good."

"I knew things were going too smoothly."

"Maybe just a delay."

"But they have guns."

"Of course, they have guns. They're policías."

A woman sobbed. Ignacio turned in his seat. "Don't worry. Only a brief delay. They will want to act very official and check things out, then we pay a little money and go on our way while they wait for the next bus to come along." He grinned. "They're just hunting pigeons with those guns, and today, we're the pigeons."

"I'll check it out," Rico stood and nodded at Ignacio. "Open up."

"Be careful," Celio called after him as Rico descended the steps.

Everyone on the bus leaned forward or to the side to see what was happening out front. Rico lifted a hand in greeting. The man who seemed to be the leader of the cops said a few words. Rico nodded and returned to the bus, and stood at the bottom of the steps.

"Well?" Celio said.

"It's as we thought ... a shakedown. They want money for us to continue. We'll have to pay them a little before we move on." Rico called up into the bus. "Everybody out!"

"Why out?" Celio said, eyes narrowed. "If we pay them, why shouldn't we just drive down the road?"

"Because they're *policías*, and they have an audience." Rico shrugged and grinned. "They want to show us who's boss. Maybe make up for their tiny *pingas*." Tiny dicks.

A few passengers laughed.

"Alright then," Ignacio said and stood. "Everybody out so we can get back on the road." He waited at the bottom of the steps, helping the women and children.

When everyone had gathered in front of the bus, he went to join them. The *policías* stepped in closer, forming an arc around the group. The senior officer pointed at Ignacio. "You're the driver?"

"Yes. You must be the *comandante*." Ignacio smiled.

"Step over there, please." The officer pointed to the side of the road.

"Such games," Ignacio sighed and walked to the side of

the road, mumbling, "Play your games and let us get on our way. We have miles to …"

He turned and never finished his sentence. The senior officer raised an arm, pointed a pistol at Ignacio, and fired a single bullet through his brain.

A few passengers shrieked. Some sobbed. Celio reached for the pistol in his belt, and two *policías* sent a stream of rifle bullets through his chest, barely missing nearby passengers.

Now, all the passengers were sobbing, on their knees, and begging for their lives. The senior officer stood before them, speaking in a loud, clear voice. "Enough! We will not harm you. The money you have paid is now ours. We will provide you safe passage the rest of the way to the border. There, our people will meet you and escort you across into the United States."

He waited for the sobbing and murmurs to die down, then continued, "This is all done for you by *Los Salvajes*."

He turned to Rico, standing to the side of the group. "You understand what you are to do?"

"Yes." Rico nodded.

"Repeat it."

"I return to Carmen Xhán and pass the word that all *coyotes* are now controlled by *Los Salvajes*. No one is to drive or work for anyone else, or they will end up like him." He nodded at Ignacio's body in the dirt.

"Very good." The senior officer, Luis Ibarra, said. "Do this, and you are one of us."

"A step up," Rico said with a grin.

Three men pushed the passengers back on the bus, then boarded and drove away. Another took Rico in one of the police trucks, turning back toward Carmen Xhán.

Ibarra gave a satisfied nod. It was a good beginning.

Shadow Man: Chapter Two

MAKE FRIENDS

As commercial lobster boats go, it wasn't large, but it was typical of those working out of the Mexican village of Puerto Nuevo. At eighteen feet in length, it bobbed along on the Pacific swells like a cork.

John Sole hadn't been on board long, a couple of hours at most, enough time to sail from the transfer point into port. The brief trip was uneventful. The boat's captain and two deckhands largely ignored him. They'd been paid and told not to ask questions or engage with their passenger in any way.

With an extra month's pay in their pockets, they were happy to comply. The *norteamericano* agents paid well to simply ferry a passenger from time to time. It was a side business their captain had arranged through a local contact, a gringo he knew only as Jay, and who promised there would be others in the future and many more dollars in their pockets.

The transfer at sea from the cabin cruiser, also provided

by Jay—John Sole's NSA contact, Jason Lovell—was the most dangerous part of the journey. Timing the rise and fall of the two boats, Sole had to jump the three feet separating them. A missed step and he would fall into the Pacific waters and face the real possibility of being crushed between the two hulls.

He made the jump safely, and as soon as his feet hit the lobster boat's deck, the anonymous skipper of the cabin cruiser throttled the engine up and pulled sharply away. Sole turned to face his new shipmates.

They went about their business without looking up. He might as well have been invisible. The deckhands coiled lines and inspected lobster traps. The captain focused on the horizon and guided his boat back to Puerto Nuevo. No one spoke to him.

When the boat's bumpers rubbed against the dock, Sole stepped off. There were no goodbyes or acknowledgment that he'd ever been on board. The second his foot hit the dock, the captain reversed engines and backed away. The U.S. dollars were a bonus, but it was time to get back to work in the lobster fields.

Sole made his way through the port area. Crews and captains worked to ready their boats to go out, or, if they'd had a successful day, unloaded their catch.

He carried no bags or weapons. Jay Lovell had promised to supply everything he required after his arrival. He cautioned Sole to avoid attracting attention. A white-skinned Georgia boy with a duffel bag might catch the eye of the local *policías* and raise questions as to his immigration status. At the very least, he would have to pay off the officer who confronted him. At the worst, he might run across one who could not be bribed, not likely but possible. So, he walked through the port and down a side street, empty-handed, trying to look like he belonged.

An hour's drive south from San Diego and across the border at Tijuana brought you to the small fishing village of Puerto Nuevo, but Lovell had insisted on using the boats. He emphasized that they wanted no record of his passage over the border or his presence in Mexico.

The village itself had been in decline until it found new life as a tourist attraction, marketing lobsters the boats brought in from the Pacific. While the locals continued to live as their ancestors had for generations, well-to-do tourists paid for excursions to eat at the new high-end restaurants and sample the local lobster dishes.

Sole was not headed to the part of town that catered to wealthy tourists. He wound his way through the back streets Lovell had made him memorize. He came to an adobe-walled building in an alley and looked up. It was a two-story affair, but so low that he could almost reach up and touch the second-story window frame. He rapped three times on the door.

A minute passed. He looked up and down the alley. It was deserted, with not a person or vehicle in sight.

A black bird on the eaves of an adjacent building let out a guttural squawk and turned its head sideways to get a better look at the newcomer. A grackle, maybe, Sole wondered. Do grackles make it down to Old Mexico?

The bird stared hard at him, and Sole muttered, "I know what you're thinking. You're not from around here, are you?" He shook his head. "Pretty easy to see, I suppose."

He rapped on the door again. The bird flew away, squawking louder, annoyed that the intruder had disturbed the serenity of his alley.

He was about to retrace his steps and figure out if he'd made a wrong turn when a door opened across the alley. Jay Lovell popped his head out. "Over here."

Sole spun around, looked up and down the alley, and wrinkled his brow. "Did I get the wrong house?"

"Nope," Lovell said. "Right house."

"Then why ..."

"Just making sure you weren't followed. I was upstairs checking from the window, watching the ends of the alley."

"And?" Sole frowned and walked across the alley.

"You weren't," Lovell said. "Good job." He opened the door wider, Sole went inside, and Lovell closed the door, throwing a deadbolt lock as he did.

"What if I was?" Sole said.

"What if you were what?"

"Followed."

"Oh." Lovell smiled, ignored the question, and waved an arm around the small room. "So anyway, welcome."

Sole eyed the man who'd recruited him at the FBI field office in Pierre, South Dakota. He was dressed the same, except leather sandals replaced the athletic shoes, and instead of a Grateful Dead t-shirt, a long yellow, too large, t-shirt hung from his bony shoulders. '*Viva Zapata!*' was emblazoned across the back of the t-shirt in bright green letters, while smiling dolphins jumped through the air into blue water on the front. Sole couldn't figure out how the two concepts fit together, but he noticed that Lovell's cargo shorts appeared to be the same ones he'd worn in South Dakota almost a year earlier.

"So, this is home?" Sole asked, looking around.

"Call it home base," Lovell said. "A safe place if you need it."

"Safe from what?"

"Lots of things can go wrong down here." Lovell shrugged. "But mostly safe from the cartel."

"Which cartel?" Sole asked.

"All of them," Lovell said simply. "That's why you never come here if you suspect someone is following you."

"Alright. Don't come if someone is following." Sole nodded. "Got it. Other than that, what am I doing here? You told me you were running an operation to bring down the cartels, that you'd brief me when I got here. I'm here, so brief me. How are you … we … going to bring them down?"

"Fair enough," Lovell said and led the way into an adjacent room with a kitchen table in the middle of the floor. There were two 1960s-era vinyl and steel tubing kitchen chairs at the table and a hot plate on a shelf in the corner connected by a black hose to a propane bottle on the floor. Other than that, the room was empty.

Lovell sat in one chair and motioned Sole to the other. "Something to eat?"

Sole eyed the wrappers and bags on the table, some already open, and shook his head. "No, thanks."

"You sure?" Lovell picked up a tortilla stuffed with black beans and took a bite. "This is the real stuff, not that watered down shit you get north of the border."

"Maybe later," Sole said and sighed. It had been a long day, and his patience was wearing thin. "What am I doing here, Jay?"

"Okay, sorry. I got busy and haven't eaten since yesterday." He put the tortilla back on the table, leaned back in the flimsy chair, and said, *"Amicus meus, inimicus inimici mei."*

"I didn't take Latin in school," Sole said.

"Ancient proverb that means, my friend, the enemy of my enemy. The Arabs say it a little differently, but the meaning is the same. The enemy of my enemy is my friend." Lovell's eyes narrowed as he stared into Sole's. "You want to bring down the *Los Salvajes* cartel?"

"You know the answer to that."

"Then we are going to make friends with some dangerous people."

"The other cartels," Sole said, and he began to understand Lovell's plan.

"Right." Lovell leaned forward and put his elbows on the table, speaking earnestly, dropping the usual old-hippie indifference that was part of his cover. "Mexican authorities can't bring them down ... too much corruption in the ranks, and those who aren't corrupt have almost no power. But if ... and this is a big *if* right now ... if we can make the other cartels our allies and get them fighting *Los Salvajes* for us, we can put them out of business."

"And when the dust settles, another cartel takes the place of *Los Salvajes*." Sole shook his head, doubtful. "How does that help?"

"Because we'll be running things ... setting them up behind the scenes ... making new friends with their enemies. We repeat the cycle until the cartels are gone ... until they kill each other off. Our job is to keep them at each other's throats."

"Seems like a longshot. You really think they'll be gone?" Sole asked.

"Truthfully, never completely gone, but if we do this right, we can greatly reduce their power." Lovell shook his head. "It used to be marijuana, cocaine, meth. Hell, I smoked weed back in college, even dabbled in coke a couple of times, but it's different now. The cartels are into other markets. You saw that in South Dakota."

Sole listened without speaking.

"Fentanyl," Lovell continued. "Made here in Mexico, not imported from Colombia like cocaine. The precursor drugs come in freight containers from China to Mexican ports. Cartel labs use those drugs to synthesize fentanyl, and then they ship it across the border. Every dose from a sloppy distributor can kill. Hell, it's killing our kids every day."

Lovell paused before adding his ultimate argument. "Worst of all … human trafficking … selling people into slavery. You saw it … sex slavery, pedophilia, but there's more. Workers forced to labor for others while the cartel collects the fees, young men forced to fight and die for warlords in other countries."

Sole nodded. "I saw it."

"You know them, John. You have history with *Los Salvajes*. They are the strongest, and they want to control it all … drugs, human trafficking, things we haven't even thought of yet, but they will think of them, and then they'll send them north of the border." Lovell's hand smacked down hard on the table. "The cartel's world, the one they want to create, is dystopian … a dark, evil place without mercy or light. Our job is to get them to destroy themselves."

"By pretending to be allies of the other cartels, their friends," Sole said, thinking it over, then asked, "Why me? I'm no spy … never been involved in this sort of thing."

"Like I said, you have history with *Los Salvajes*, and this is liable to get messy … bloody." Lovell stared into his eyes. "We know what you've been up to these past few years, pieced a lot of it together at least, and we know you'll do what has to be done if it comes to that."

"You mean if someone ends up with blood on their hands, it'll be me," Sole said, with a cynical twist of his lips.

"I mean, when it comes to taking down *Los Salvajes*, you're motivated."

Sole couldn't deny it. He took a deep breath and nodded. "Alright, let's go make some new cartel friends."

Shadow Man: Chapter Three

LOVE, RESPECT, AND FEAR

"There is news, Seve."

"In a moment." Sixty-three-year-old Severiano 'Seve' Espinoza sat on the floor with his grandchildren. He smiled. "The children have almost finished."

His brother Miguel nodded and stood waiting patiently as he had for all of his fifty-five years. There were no sibling rivalries between them. No petty jealousies as sometimes happen between brothers when one is dominant, even favored by the parents. Miguel had always understood that his brother was the heir apparent to the family fortune, such as it was. Not understanding would have changed nothing. Besides, his brother made loyalty easy, protected Miguel, shared the wealth, kept no secrets, went to him for counsel, and treated him as an equal in every way. Their devotion to each other was unbreakable, forged not just through expediency and profit, but in blood.

Now, Seve sat cross-legged with three of the fifteen grandchildren his three daughters and a son had given him. Smiling and laughing with them, he handed them pieces of a jigsaw puzzle. They knelt on all fours, taking the pieces, giggling, and trying them in different positions to fit together on the floor between them. It was a child's puzzle, nothing too complicated. The picture of a cow jumping over a crescent moon was nearly completed.

A diminutive, dark-haired boy of five slapped a piece down and slid it into position. "There! Now the cow has a tail!" He grinned at his grandfather. "Did I do good, *Tata*?"

"Excellent, Juliano! You are very clever, little one."

"I'm not so little," the boy said quickly. "I'll be big one day." He looked at his great-uncle standing patiently behind his grandfather. "Big as *tio* Miguel, I think."

"Yes, I think you are right," Seve said and pushed himself up from the floor with a grunt. "And now, little ones, I must speak with *tio* Miguel."

He led the way from the playroom he'd constructed for his grandchildren. They crossed a wide tiled patio and entered a separate wing of the rambling house. This was no typical Spanish-influenced hacienda. Seve Espinoza's tastes ran to the modern. His home was reminiscent of Frank Lloyd Wright's Arizona residence, Taliesin West. Long, window-lined hallways surrounded gardens and an enormous swimming pool. Every room had a view of the manicured lawns, the countryside, or the distant mountains.

He led his younger brother into an expansive office lined with windows on three walls. Mexico's highest peak, Pico de Orizaba, rose in the distance through the glass. Seve eased himself into the leather chair behind the desk, sighed, leaned back, and asked, "What is this news, Miguel?"

"A bus is missing," Miguel said, with no explanation. None was needed.

"Where?" Seve sat up straight.

"North of Carmen Xhán."

"Do we know who did this?"

"Brother, there could only be one group who would dare," Miguel said.

"Yes," Seve said, nodding. "I had hoped this time might not come."

"It has come just the same."

"Do we know how it happened? Were our people off the main highways, as we instructed?"

"Yes." Miguel nodded. The implication was clear. This was not a chance event. To know where the bus would be could only mean one thing. There was a traitor among them … an informant feeding information to *Los Salvajes*, giving them the route the bus would follow.

Seve's eyes narrowed. "Our people … are there any survivors?"

"That is not certain. The driver and one guard are dead in a ditch by the road. Two *policías* that we pay found them and reported it."

"Only one guard and the driver?" Seve asked. "And the other guard? There should have been a second."

"There were two. The second is missing." Miguel shrugged. "Our *policías* were very nervous when they made the report. I doubt they stayed around to investigate for long. The hijackers may have taken our guard with them to torture for information or to exchange him as part of some arrangement with us." He shrugged. "Or they may have killed him, and our two *policías* have not yet found the body."

"Or, we may know who our traitor is," Seve said. "In any event, we need our own people there to sort things out,"

"Yes." Miguel nodded.

"Have the helicopter brought around from the airstrip. Take some men to investigate. I want to know for certain who made the attack ... *Los Salvajes*, yes, but who exactly and how they carried it out and where they took the bus with our cargo."

"Yes." Miguel turned and left the office.

Seve Espinoza sat gazing out the window. It was a tranquil scene—green manicured lawns, birds flitting from flower to flower or singing in the trees. His grandchildren had moved out to the pool now and were playing, laughing, and splashing the way all children do. He had worked all his life to provide a life of comfort for his family, and seeing them at play made him smile.

That the comfort they enjoyed had been purchased with the pain, blood, and suffering of others was of no concern. If the weakness of those others allowed him to profit by trafficking drugs and people, so be it. It was merely the way of the world as it had always been and, in his estimation, would always be. Who was he to change it?

Espinoza had always pictured himself as a man of refinement, a thinking man. He lived an elegant life without the showy ostentatiousness often associated with great wealth.

After obtaining a degree in architecture from the National Autonomous University in Mexico City, young Seve Espinoza returned to his family's small ranch in the state of Veracruz. He brought Elena, whom he'd met and married while at the university without his parents' permission or blessing. It seemed to them that Seve always did what he could to avoid the appearance of living a traditional life. Showing up with a new wife, without mentioning it or asking for their blessing, was just the sort of thing they expected of him.

When his aging father turned the ranch operations over to him, Seve took things in a new direction. The ranch became a sideline while Seve focused his efforts on a new business—trafficking drugs, and later people, into and out of the United States.

His university studies gave him an eye for detail. His personality made him ruthless in achieving his business goals. The family tradition was that they descended from the conquistadors who had established Veracruz as a jumping-off point to conquer the Mexican natives of the era. It seemed likely. Behind the benevolent, aristocratic, and refined façade, Seve built a cartel that ran with well-oiled efficiency and dwarfed all the others, except for one—*Los Salvajes*.

He picked up his phone and dialed two numbers. When the calls were answered, he said, "We must meet."

The voices on the other end asked no questions and simply replied, "*Sí, Don* Espinoza."

Seve Espinoza was a man of many faces. His grandchildren loved their *abuelito*. His wife of thirty-six years, Elena, loved him. His brother Miguel loved him.

As for business, his counterparts in other cartels rarely uttered a word of disagreement. If on occasion they did disagree about some issue of mutual concern, they proffered their thoughts politely and with the respect one showed to a man of his stature and abilities.

But when complications arose that might disrupt his carefully constructed plans, Seve Espinoza became brutal in eliminating the problem. For this reason, his enemies feared him.

Grab your copy...
vinci-books.com/shadowman

About the Author

Glenn Trust is the author of the bestselling *Hunters, Sole Justice, and Journey Series* of mystery/thriller/suspense novels. He has also written standalone works, including *Dying Embers, Mojave Sun, and short stories*.

There are no superheroes or knights in shining armor in his stories. According to Trust, knights are for fairy tales. His books are gritty and based in the real world, with characters who face their frailties while dealing with their roles in the story. The heroes are average people doing the best they can.

The villains, as real villains often do, look like us. Trust's monsters hide behind the smiling faces that pass us on the street. They look like us, and this makes them more frightening.

He is a Georgia native but has lived in most regions of the country at one time or another. Varied experiences, from construction worker to police officer, corporate executive to city manager, color and provide insight into the characters he creates. His stories are known for detailed plots, solid research, and realism.

Today, he writes full-time and lives quietly with his wife and two dogs, Gunner and Charlie.